Cook-Lynn, Elizabeth

Aurelia: A Crow Creek Trilogy

D1212448

Aurelia

By the same author

The Power of Horses and Other Stories
Then Badger Said This
Seek the House of Relatives
Why I Can't Read Wallace Stegner and Other Essays: A Tribal Voice
The Politics of Hallowed Ground, a Hundred Years of Struggle for
        Sovereignty (with Mario Gonzalez)
I Remember the Fallen Trees

Aurelia

A Crow Creek Trilogy

Elizabeth Cook-Lynn

University Press of Colorado

Published by the University Press of Colorado
P.O. Box 849
Niwot, Colorado 80544

The University Press of Colorado is a cooperative publishing enterprise supported, in part, by Adams State College, Colorado State University, Fort Lewis College, Mesa State College, Metropolitan State College of Denver, University of Colorado, University of Northern Colorado, University of Southern Colorado, and Western State College of Colorado.

The paper used in this publication meets the minimum requirements of the American National Standard for Information Sciences—Permanence of Paper for Printed Library Materials. ANSI Z39.48-1984

Library of Congress Cataloging-in-Publication Data
Cook-Lynn, Elizabeth.
    Aurelia : a Crow Creek trilogy / by Elizabeth Cook-Lynn.
        p. cm.
    ISBN 0-87081-539-3 (alk. paper)
        1. Crow Creek Indian Reservation (S.D.)—History—Fiction. 2. Indians of North America—South Dakota—Fiction. 3. Indian women—South Dakota—Fiction. 4. Historical fiction, American. 5. Dakota Indians—Fiction. I. Title. II. Cook-Lynn, Elizabeth. From the river's edge. III. Cook-Lynn, Elizabeth. Circle of dancers. IV. Cook-Lynn, Elizabeth. In the presence of river gods.
PS3553.O5548 A9 1999
813'.54 21—dc21
                                                                                    99-044821

08 07 06 05 04 03 02 01 00 99   10 9 8 7 6 5 4 3 2 1

From the River's Edge was published by Arcade Publishing in 1990. Parts of *Circle of Dancers* and *In the Presence of River Gods* appeared in *The New Native American Novel* (Albuquerque: University of New Mexico Press, 1986) and *Indian Artist* (Spring 1995).

Contents

Aurelia

From the River's Edge

Contents

Preface

Seeing the Missouri River country of the Sioux is like seeing where the earth first recognized humanity and where it came to possess a kind of unique internal coherence about that condition.

As you look you think you see old women leaving marked trails in the tall burnt grass as they carry firewood on their backs from the river, and you think you hear the songs they sang to grandchildren, and you feel transformed into the past. But then, winter comes. The earth freezes solid. And you wish for July and the ripe plums and the sun on your eyelids.

One August day I stood on a hill with Big Pipe and watched the flooding waters of the Missouri River Power Project unleash the river's power from banks which had held it and guided it since before any white man was seen in this country. As old Pipe grieved, the water covered the trees of a timber stand which had nourished a people for all generations, and it took twenty years for those trees to die, their skeletons still and white. It took much less time for the snakes and small animals to disappear. Today, old Pipe has a hard time finding the root which cures his toothache, and he tells everyone that it is the white man's determination to change the river which accounts for the destruction of all life's forms.

When you look east from Big Pipe's place you see Fort George; you look south and see Iron Nation, and you sense a kind of hollowness in the endless distance of the river span, at odds, somehow, with the immediacy of the steel REA towers stalking up and down prairie hills. Yet, as your fingertips touch the slick leaves of the milkweed and roll the juicy leaves together, it is easy to believe that this vast region continues to share its destiny with a people who have survived hard winters, invasions, migrations, and transformations unthought of and unpredicted. And even easier to know that the mythology and history of all times remain remote and believable.

Part One

A Trial
Issues of Law as Well as Fact

Smutty Bear

"I am an Indian, but the man then told me I would become an American. To do this, he said, my son, what you have to do is to take care of the white people, and try to raise two or three streaks of grass. I have tried to do this, and have worn all the nails off my fingers trying to do it. Ever since I have tried to raise that corn, and I am still at it, but can't raise it." (Translation)

Summer 1856

1

August 1967

The lawyer came out to Tatekeya's place along the river that day.

He said to Tatekeya: "This is not about your stolen cattle, John. It is about justice and the law, as are all cases brought before the United States bar."

"But what's the chances of gettin' my cattle back?" asked John.

"Well, we don't think in terms of getting your cows back or getting paid for them, necessarily. We think in terms of what is *fair*."

Very quietly and with mixed emotions, John answered that he thought the two things, i.e., the return of his stolen cattle and *fairness*, were one and the same.

"Not necessarily," he was told.

2

He stood in the cluttered, stuffy little kitchen, looking out of the narrow window, stirring the bean soup boiling in a pot on the gas stove, and absently watched the wild turkeys mince toward the brittle weeds along the dirt road, their small heads jerking up and down as they pecked at fallen seeds, their beady eyes alert for any quick movement. A suspicious kind of bird. They stepped prettily into the trees, disappearing quietly as John's thoughts rambled.

He was glad his wife, Rose, had moved to town with their married daughter, giving him the opportunity to live by himself for the first time since their marriage thirty years ago. His was now a solitary, thoughtful life, as he had, perhaps, always wanted it to be.

A tall man in his early sixties, a man who had been nurtured on the prairielands of the Dakotas but one who showed little evidence of that hard life, John Tatekeya had black hair imperceptibly streaked with gray, his face was unwrinkled, the delicate, fine bones of his profile were strangely sharp, unburdened by the passage of time.

On this day, the kind which began with a morning so cool and bright as to seem extraordinarily bountiful, he lost himself in private thought, absorbed in the precious moments like this that he shared with no one, secretly and selfishly savoring his own feeling of insularity.

It was an important morning, but soon the heat from the stove in the small three-room house would become unbearable, he knew, and the sun would climb into the sky, and his clothes would get so damp they would hang limply about him, and he would be sucked empty of energy and vitality by the muggy, shimmering air. And he would cease to move about with such spirit. Only those born into the hot, dry Dakota winds of August ever got to know how to really thrive in it. The others simply tolerated it.

The tall man at the stove seemed untouchable and remote at this moment, as he meticulously spooned the thick soup into a bowl, turned off the gas heat, and seated himself at the bare table. He ate silently, methodically, taking great care in breaking the salty crackers and dipping them slowly in the mild liquid. When he was nearly finished, he sugared his coffee generously and sat stirring with quick, short strokes, holding the spoon palm-up. He looked through the gauze curtains at the hayshed, a recently moved and converted trailerhouse, corrupted by the dispassionate sun and relentless prairie wind long before it was moved to John's place.

Tacky.

Makeshift.

Cluttered and distracting.

He lifted his eyes toward the hills which spread out and away from the river, like earthen monuments of the past, forever, ophidian, resolute. John did not give much thought to himself as a man of the north prairies. But he was as much that as are the men of the other prairielands known to the world—the men of the pampas of Argentina, the llanos of the South, the steppes of Eurasia, the highlands of Africa, and the tundra of the Arctic. Like them, John Tatekeya of the Dakota prairielands and his people had forever possessed great confidence in their collective presence in their homelands. More than he thought about it, John felt it and simply held it in his heart.

As his eyes scanned the windswept hills he knew this: It is here that the spirit himself can *wokeya. Wo-ki-ca-hni-ga-to?* Didn't Benno say these things when he talked to them in the sweatlodge? His crying sometimes helps human beings, Benno said. But not always. What can I do now? men have eternally asked, and John Tatekeya was no different. What can I do now, he asked also.

The wind bent the tall grass to its will, brushed weeds haphazardly across the roads. Even the birds seemed frail in its grip as they lifted their wings and dropped across the sky.

Minutes passed, and John sat at the little round table in the bright stillness, mixing, cooling, stirring his coffee with quick, short strokes. Finally, he lifted the bowl to his lips and quietly drained it. He stood up and reached for his hat just as he heard heavy footsteps on the front porch.

He stepped outside, slamming the door shut quickly.

"*Hau,*" he said, smoothing his hair down with one hand and fitting his Stetson on with the other. He shook hands with the young man from the Federal Bureau of Investigation and pretended a graciousness he did not feel.

"You ready, John?" asked the young man, whose red hair almost matched his flaming cheeks so recently burnt by the August wind which never ceased to blow across these prairies and hills at this time of the year.

"Yeah."

U.S. government agents, or "FBI men," or "*wasichus,*" as Tatekeya now thought of them, were nothing new to this Indian reservation in recent years. Nor were they absent from the other Sioux Indian homelands in South and North Dakota. The joke used to be that in every Indian home, there is the mother, father, children, grandparents, and the anthropologist. In the sixties, that joke changed to include the "G-man." Figures of almost unrestricted federal law enforcement activities had a long history on Indian reservations, beginning even before the passage of such legislation as the Major Crimes Act and other "congressional violations of Indian Nationhood," as John described the white man's law of the nineteenth century.

The theft of John Tatekeya's cattle occurred just about the time when groups of young American Indian men began to patrol the streets of urban America. Streets like Franklin Avenue in Minneapolis–St. Paul, where men in red berets would resist police violence toward "relocated" Indians and participate in a variety of activities which were soon to become the substance of a full-fledged political movement called "Red Power" and "AIM," claiming national and international attention.

Before John's case would go to trial, the American Indian Movement would be full-blown, and people all over the world would know the meaning of "justice" in Indian country. And because of the controversial nature of the activities in urban America during this period, the rural, reservation, so-called trust lands were also under FBI surveillance in ways that they had not been since the late 1800s. It was then, John's older relatives had told him, that the Department of War/Interior police force was placed on most of the reserved lands in the country, a colonial law-and-order force which changed Sioux justice for all time. Though he thought of himself as essentially a law-abiding man, these facts of history indicated to John the presence of some kind of alien force on Indian land that was at one and the same time coercive, obligatory, discordant.

The federal agent with the flaming cheeks who appeared at Tatekeya's door this day seemed innocent and somehow frail. John walked beside him to the government rig, which had THE DEPARTMENT OF THE INTERIOR, U.S. GOVERNMENT stamped on both its doors. John peered into the slats of the shiny blue and silver trailer, checking on the saddle horses, which were nervous and stamping and blowing dust from their nostrils.

John, who had been, "just for the hell of it," a rodeo saddle-bronc rider in his earlier days and even now considered himself an expert horseman in the tradition of the great Sioux centaurians of the past, looked with quiet suspicion at the mares which had been brought to his place from the Agency pastures.

"You think these old gov'ment nags are gonna make it?"

"Just a minute, John," said the young man, laughing. "They're pretty fair examples of fi-i-ine horseflesh!" But he, too, peered into the trailer, as though to either confirm or deny John's assessment.

John shrugged and got into the rig.

Together the men and the horses would conduct a futile search of the long-grassed hills of South Dakota and Nebraska for forty-two head of John Tatekeya's cattle, stolen months before, all of them carrying the ID (Indian Department) brand.

3

As they pulled away from John's place, they looked sideways at the large tipi at the rear and the small house in front, both set apart from a recently planted grove of elms and oaks to the west, the large corral standing in the tall grass, and a couple of outbuildings blazing in the morning light. Red Hair, unaccustomed to the rough, rutted reservation road, drove carefully and slowly. The house, looking like someone's bad joke, was set up on blocks, the front screen door was hanging ajar, and the front steps were detached from the stilted porch. There was no foundation under the house, but electrical lines had recently been connected and John had begun to have hope.

The pickup pulling the horse trailer moved laboriously from the scene.

Along the road, wind had blown clumps of weeds into the barbed-wire fences, which held them there. And more were piling up. By late fall the fences would be so clogged with thistles a jackrabbit couldn't get through. It became a metaphor in John's imagination for his own struggle, and he silently watched a small whirlwind sweep dried leaves and weeds in its path.

The wind knows how to do things to interfere in the lives of men, thought John, and Dakotahs have explained to themselves the significance of its power through various means. His mother had resisted it all, having been persuaded finally by the simplicity of Christian beliefs to give up the complicated and difficult worship of the Four Winds, and he himself, because he had been her favorite son, was also dissuaded to some extent from practicing the old ways.

"Si-i-i-lent ni-i-i-ght, ho-o-o-ly ni-i-ght" rose incongruously in John's memory as he watched the thistles being swept before the wind. He remembered himself as a child of seven standing first on one foot in the bitter, sweeping snow, and then on the other, then entering the church singing Christmas carols and holding candles, which acolytes set ablaze as each communicant entered. He had looked over at his mother for approval and she had smiled at him, and her smile would forever haunt him. This Christian way was less time-consuming and easier on the physical self than any of the Indian religious practices John had come to know, and it had been a comfort for both of them and an assurance that everything was all right. He had believed that until his mother's death when he turned nine years old. It was only at her graveside that he was faced with the fact that he knew none of the important songs which would assist her journey into the next world.

He thought of the ease with which they had been persuaded to believe in the white man's religion, and as the pickup truck driven by Red Hair made its way down the graveled road and out of the bend in the river, John put the memory of his mother out of his mind, pulled his hat down over his eyes, and pretended to sleep. Now at sixty years of age, he knew that the white man's law was no more powerful than his religion but just as pervasive, and he decided that he would try to pretend that this trip with Red Hair was something more than a futile gesture. It was, after all, the best they could do at this time, and it might lead, eventually, to the truth about who the men were who had committed this crime against him. He had to find the truth and get his cattle back.

The horses in the trailer grimly held their positions as the government rig pressed southward, Red Hair talking and chewing gum with equal vigor and John silently musing about his own culpability concerning the theft, which had cut his herd nearly in half.

"I betcha some one of your neighbors done it, John," said Red Hair. "Who do you know who doesn't like you? Who needs money?"

That's just about everybody, thought John, though he didn't raise his head nor did he answer. He really didn't want to enter into this discussion; he considered it small talk, that chatter designed just to fill up the empty spaces which he had begun to realize were intolerable to the white men that he knew. Though they taught in their Sunday school classes that silence is golden, none of them that he had become acquainted with could stand silence. This young man, he decided, was a real talker. Liked to hear his own voice.

Sorrowfully he turned his thoughts to his own recent behavior. He had been drunk and absent from his place for nearly two weeks and was told later that he had been seen in Presho, Chamberlain, Pierre, even as far as Sturgis and Rapid City.

"They've been sold piecemeal, John," Red Hair went on, totally oblivious to John's unresponsiveness and now warming up to his subject enthusiastically. "And we're gonna have to get on these horses and ride some of those ranches down there and see if we can identify any of your stuff.

"You know, selling them piecemeal is what a cattle thief will do because it makes them harder to trace that way," continued the younger man with his one-way conversation.

Yeah, thought John, and if the government and me don't find my cows we're probably gonna come to the end of our bargain, ennit, Red Hair?

As the Department of Interior rig pressed on through the grasslands of western South Dakota and emerged into the endless Nebraska fields of cornstalks, dry and brittle from the August winds, John began to wonder about the issues at hand and thought that they might not be as simple as they seemed to be at first glance.

John had been one of the few men in the district to qualify for the government "payback" cattle scheme. The U.S. government provided you with fifty head of cattle, for example, and you paid them back with your calf crop for the next thirty years. He still had his own allotment, he had over the years purchased the allotments of his brothers and sisters, and so he was considered an Indian landholder who could be assisted to financial security through a federally funded cattle ranch project. John had always run a few cattle. It was the way he and his father and his brothers had always lived in the contemporary world. But in the middle of a booming postwar economy it was thought that Indians ought to become big cattle ranchers. Run cattle for profit. Enter into the free-market economy of the greatest democracy in the world. John was one of the first to be contacted by the agent to apply for the funds.

He'd been at it now for three years along the Missouri River, in the midst of a time of great confusion and upheaval during the harnessing of the river for hydropower, the building of several huge dams (one of them near Pierre the largest rolled-earth dam in the world), and the subsequent flooding of thousands of acres of Indian land.

Some of John's own land was now under water, as were the lands of his neighbors. In the middle of this confusion, John had to ask himself, What kind of man is out to ruin me? Who among my neighbors would do this thing and why? I know them all and have known them all of my life; I've worked and boozed around with them, prayed and grieved with them in times of sorrow; shared their joys and triumphs. And now I am getting to be an old man. And this, now. Just at this time. Who?

No, he thought, it must have been outsiders, men who are unknown to me, strangers who have crept in to steal a man's livelihood without compassion, men I don't know, men to whom I am not related, and, therefore, men without conscience.

This was John's hope, but the depth of sadness in his heart acknowledged that his hopes might not be upheld. He might never know the answers to the troubling questions he now posed, and even if he did find the answers, they might not be the ones he would want to hear. He might never see his cattle returned, which not only would be a loss of great magnitude, financially speaking, but would also serve as a reinforcement of his secretly held notion that the world in which he now lived, the modern life which he tried to be a part of, unconnected as it was to his past, was cruel and without honor.

We Dakotahs used to know how to live, he thought. But they told us to settle down, and become like them. This is not the world in which we can steal the horses of the Pawnee, and they ours.

Ah, well. . . . The four wires of his fence had been stretched and held to the ground, he knew now, and a couple of large trucks had driven into his pasture, up to the corral and loading chute, and more than forty head of John's one hundred and seven horned Herefords had been loaded out. John had one of the best and largest herds on the reservation, the envy and pride of everyone around. His relatives could come to him now and expect that he would feed them. He gave meat for the feast at every summer dance, and he was known throughout the country for his generosity.

It had probably taken three or four men to do the job on a moonlit night, and silent and unnoticed, they had probably driven down this same isolated road, John mused.

Regretfully, John recalled the agony of his own recalcitrant behavior, and he could think of no excuses. He had driven into the barren yard nearly two weeks after the theft, looked around for reassurance though he knew that Rose would not be home, and petted his big hound dog as it emerged from under the front porch. John had felt nauseous.

He was red-eyed and aching from too much liquor and too many nights laid out in the bed of his pickup or slumped behind the wheel.

He'd gone into the house and sunk tiredly into the overstuffed chair for a few minutes before he headed for the bedroom. He slept for a couple of days, thinking that if he stayed in bed the dizziness in his head would stop, but it only seemed to get worse and it caused skips in his heartbeat every time he stood up. He couldn't eat. Before he could get better, he shuffled outside and went around to the back of the house. Shaking and weak, he had started the fire to heat the stones for the sweat he knew he needed.

Later, he had gone from pasture to pasture, at first driving his rig because he felt so weak; the next day, he'd saddled the old buckskin gelding and ridden slowly through the bottomlands near the river looking for any telltale tracks. He did this for days, not knowing what else to do.

One late afternoon, after such a search, he sat in the saddle smoking a cigarette, and when he looked up into the sky he noticed perched in a nearby cottonwood a silent, handsome owl keeping watch over his activities. As he moved along the subirrigated eighty acres, he felt on his neck the old carnivore's gaze.

"That old man," he said under his breath. *"A i sta wa hna ke sni"* (why does he not take his eyes off me?). He turned in the saddle and hollered irritably, "Get the hell outta here!"

John found himself wondering about this owl, sitting there in a kind of ineffable quietness that was disturbing, turning its head toward him since its eyes, set immovably in their sockets, could not change their positions, purposefully keeping track of his movements. He felt it to be less innocent than many of the species known to him, and he wondered what it knew.

Some owls hunt night quarry only, John thought. Those were the kind with eyes on each side of the head so that they seem not to be looking in the same direction at the same time. And since it was getting late in the afternoon, John at the first thought this owl keeping watch on him might be one of those.

But it was not. On the contrary, this owl, which had become John's attendant, however briefly, in this matter, seemed to be one of those splendid companions of prairie dogs known in this country to exist for the purpose of maintaining the balance of nature in other than obvious ways. Yet it was too large to be one of those burrowing owls, those tiny creatures who run about prairie dog towns on long, spindly legs. It was huge. Magnificent. And John rode on, thinking, and listening, and holding the reins taut, the old gelding's prancing gait forcing him to stand crouching in the stirrups.

Uninterested in violence, disconnected from the natural urge to strike out, this owl seemed ageless, and John began to imagine that it might even be one of those said to have accompanied the people on their migration into this world. Was it not, though, a hunter? What was it hunting? It seemed not to be trying to frighten those who inadvertently came upon it. John was, if not frightened, at least startled by its persistence.

Even as his horse swung gracefully into the tall grass along the river's edge, and as he bent over the saddle to look for signs of the movement of his cattle, John had the feeling that there was nothing here worth searching out, nothing that would answer the question of the whereabouts of his cattle. And the presence of the handsome bird seemed to affirm that feeling.

Looking over his shoulder, John watched the great bird's silent flight to another tree, where it perched higher, with its toes placed so that there were two in front and two in back. It detached itself a second time, and then another, its hush wings lifting it toward the highest tip of a huge cottonwood. From that vantage point this bird of prey stared into the fading light, and John kicked his horse in the flank and they plunged on and went away.

When he reached the road which wound its way into the bend of the river, John again put the spurs to the buckskin and rode hard and fast back to his own corral. He would have to seek answers elsewhere.

4

"Ti ma hed hiyu," said Clarissa graciously. Harvey Big Pipe's elder daughter greeted her father's old friend John Tatekeya at the door, and she gestured for him to come in.

The rooms smelled of meat and onions; a clutter of tinted photographs of children and young men and women, some of them in military uniform, hung on the walls. A large curtainless window overlooked a backyard filled with old cars, "junkers" everyone called them, except when they were in need of something, anything from bolts and brackets to carburetors and drive shafts. Then they were called valuable resources for auto parts and taken seriously. A black-and-white charcoal sketch, carefully hand-framed in black plastic, of the infamous Santee chieftain, Little Crow, was propped up behind the radio on a makeshift shelf, and a long braid of sweet grass, burnt at both ends, was carelessly draped over it. Caked white paint peeled from the windowsills and doorways, and the scrubbed linoleum covering the floor glittered in the afternoon light.

"Are you looking for my father?"

"Yes."

"He's not feeling too good," she said softly as she offered John a chair.

John sat down, and when Harvey came slowly from his bedroom, John asked about his health and was told that he was feeling better. The conversation consisted mostly of complainings about old men's ailments, starting out as a discussion of a serious nature; and it went on and on, one man's story told to best the other, one story getting more obscene than the next, until all the family members who had begun to gather in the room, even Clarissa, who usually feigned shock and embarrassment at hearing these kinds of stories, were laughing good-naturedly about the willfulness of old age, the instability of a body hesitating, wavering, hemming and hawing, no longer possessing the strength to do what was asked of it. Then John was asked to stay for supper.

After the meal and as the two old friends smoked, John began to talk seriously of his ordeal, saying what everybody knew, that he had forty-two head of cattle missing.

"I walked that subirrigated eighty acres along the river but saw no signs," John told his old friend. "I even saddled up the old buckskin for another look but I didn't see no signs.

"Just then," he continued, "I decided that I would come over and see if you had heard anything."

"No. Nothing," he was assured.

John went into great detail about the recent signs inside the narrow pathways of his pasture corrals and around the loading chute and the tire tracks which had been nearly obliterated by the hooves of the remaining cattle.

"I finally had to admit to myself," John told Harvey, "that cattle thieves was on my place, and then I went to the Agency and I filed papers. Me and that FBI man, you know, that one with the red hair, we've been all over looking for them," he said, gesturing widely.

"We even went to Ainsworth. All in all we found three with ID and my brand on 'em. And there's another one that I know is mine but the brand is gone.

"But, I've still been looking," he continued, "because over forty head is missing.

"I just don't know where else to look," he concluded.

Big Pipe said nothing, merely shaking his head and offering his condolences.

When John left the house and walked to his pickup truck, darkness had fallen. He saw one of Harvey's sons, who had been chopping wood, walk slowly toward the barn and tack shed carrying a lighted flashlight. The light, yellow and gloomy, swayed about the foreboding outlines of the buildings and abruptly disappeared. John felt a strange uneasiness as he drove slowly home.

5

It was in the last days of September that John parked his International pickup truck at the curb and walked across the immaculate lawn, still green in spite of the fall chill, surrounding what was called the Federal Building in Pierre, South Dakota, where the trial was to be held. He looked at the cars parked along the curved street and hoped that he wouldn't see Aurelia's old Dodge among them. She didn't say she was coming and he hadn't asked her not to, but he hoped that she would not.

John's experience with the law was considerable. He had been hauled in by the police many times. The tribal police, municipal cops, the state patrol. Driving under the influence, speeding, resisting arrest, illegal parking, no license tabs, assault. You name it. One time when he was too drunk to get his pants zipped up after he took a leak outside the Silver Spur in Fort Pierre they even booked him on indecent exposure charges.

"Hey, listen to me, officer. This is a big mistake. I'm not . . ."

"Shut up, chief. We gotcha."

So he had a sheet on him as long as his arm, and it didn't look good and he wasn't proud of it. He'd gone to court many times. Always "guilty as charged."

Though facing up to it was nothing particularly new for John, this time the tables were turned. He was the guy bringing the charges. He and the Feds, that is. And he didn't know exactly how he felt about it—a bit apprehensive, if the truth were known. On the one hand, he needed to get his cattle back or get paid for them; on the other, he had no real assurance that any of this would turn out all right. He alone faced the white lawyers, the white defense attorney, white prosecutor, white jury, and white judge. The FBI said it was on his side in this matter, but he knew enough about the FBI to make them seem more unreliable than they owned up to.

Inside, he went up the white marble stairs to a desk where a tall, large-boned, graceful, and dignified white man sat, checking in the participants for this awkward meeting, Indians and whites coming together to testify for or against, telling the truth or making up lies for the "jury of peers" to see who is more believable than the next, like pawns in a chess game of legal mumbo-jumbo where John's rules for survival no longer applied. A game, for Indians at least, which had its origins in the not-so-distant past, it was an ongoing and consistent fraud, set up to make all of those concerned believe that justice in Indian Country was real. But such games seemed totally oblivious to the presence of historical duplicity in any particular case. The white man has always stolen from the Sioux, he thought as he climbed the stairs. First it is our land, then our way of life, our children, and finally even the laws of our ancestors. And now this white man, the son of my white neighbors, has stolen my goddamn cows.

John approached the desk. The white man's chin was covered with the hairs of a short beard which hung straight down in vertical streaks of black and gray, and his dark mustache was clipped short. His forehead was smooth and white and it sloped back into a receding hairline of limp, brown hair combed thinly to one side. His blue eyes seemed kindly, his mouth soft, uneven, expressing a shyness next to obsequiousness.

John looked him over and unaccountably tried to imagine who he was. He saw a man with probable Czech peasantry in his lineage, one of those often derisively referred to as "bohunks" out here in the West where there was a corrupted myth that ancestry hardly mattered; a scion of those peasants who had determinedly and valiantly resisted fascists in Middle Europe for generations then became fascists themselves in the new country. They now found themselves living supposedly quiet and nonviolent lives, yet undeniably, in John's view at least, lives of imagined conquerors with fully implemented laws of their own making, transplanted into the midst of a relentless and unfathomable indigenousness virtually unknown to them and therefore unacknowledged.

The bearded man looked solid, somehow official in his casual, expensive plaid shirt, his fingers and thumb making circles of airless discontent as he went about his paperwork. Those who knew him thought him to be the kind of man who was fond of talking about people with "lots of dough," for to have great wealth was a major objective which he held out for himself, and he took note, usually, of those who might serve as examples of these values he held.

Certainly, as he tentatively faced John Tatekeya, the Dakotah whose cattle, it was alleged, had been stolen by one of his white neighbors, he dismissed John as anyone who could measure up to his private dreams of success. He faced a man who was from the Indian reservation, which, for the bearded man, was light-years away from his own life, and the Indian exhibited none of the criteria necessary for consideration. The bearded man might have been among those in the community who had already made up their minds about this case.

Disdainfully, the bearded man asked John to spell his last name. T-a-t-e-k-e-y-a, John said slowly. Then he pronounced it. Tah-TAY-kee-yah. When the bearded man did not respond, John pronounced it a second time. John knew he was supposed to feel unworthy in the man's grand presence, like a miscreant of some vile order as the man wrote the name down and shuffled papers on his desk. But he didn't. It only made a tacit hostility rise in his heart, and he silently watched the circles of the man's left fingers and thumb turn to broad stroking, like the dusting strokes of a cleaning woman on the smooth varnish of the table. On his left hand the dignified man wore a heavy, square ring of glittering, ornate Black Hills gold. He wrote with his right hand carefully and quickly, an air of efficiency and pretentiousness pervading the room.

Unexpectedly, the man yawned and his teeth were very white.

"Sally went over there several times," said a woman's sharp voice from the rear of the room, the shrillness dissolving into a murmur of muffled sounds resounding oddly into the huge ceiling, an empty, hollow sound.

John Tatekeya watched the nameless blond woman and the efficient, graceful white man writing his name in a book and yawning. There was nothing here to bring cheer to John's thoughts as he began to feel that his case, the business of trying to get his cows back, only cluttered up a system preoccupied with much more important matters. His worries were made insignificant by a world which had long since dismissed him as merely troublesome and his way of life as unworthy. He began to understand that the theft of his cattle was neither life nor death to anyone here but himself.

He sat on a wooden bench in the hallway to await the arrival of his lawyer, the District Attorney who wore cowboy boots and tried Indian cases for the federal government now and then, a man who prided himself on being an amateur historian on the life and times of General George Armstrong Custer.

Born in New Haven, Connecticut, to Quaker parentage, the lawyer now, after twenty years in the Northern Plains, took on the attitude and historical perspective of a place which had been only in the imagination or fantasy of his childhood, and John recognized immediately that the two of them had little in common. The DA was a man who, much like his neighbors, acted on these private fantasies.

"Most of what we know about the Custer battle at the Little Big Horn," he began eagerly when he met John that morning to decide on the details of the trial, "is based largely on the work of General E. S. Godfrey.

"You know," he went on enthusiastically, "Godfrey wrote quite a bit on this as early as 1892." He was blissfully unaware that John was not even remotely interested in this kind of information. Godfrey's account about Custer, as far as he was concerned, was the white man's history. Not his.

What's shaping up here, thought John as he waited in the courthouse, leaning his arms on his knees, is a big waste of time. Half of my herd is gone and I am probably not going to get them back.

He and the redhaired FBI man had ridden their horses for a week through the pastures where it was thought the cattle might have been taken after the illegal sales. They found three head with his brand and the ID brand on them, one at Irene, another at Highmore, and one at Ainsworth, Nebraska. There was another steer that John knew was his but it could not be officially identified. That's what's left of my forty-two head, he thought sadly.

"Shit," he said into the empty hallway.

Waiting.

The waiting seemed interminable.

Often, when he was a kid, he had sat with Benno in the blind, waiting. And together they had waited for the Canada geese to settle on the glaring ice and eventually waddle ashore where two or three of the honkers could be picked off with Benno's old 12-gauge. John remembered this now as he sat on the wooden bench in the courthouse, and he thought of it in retrospect as the kind of childhood activity in which there was no such thing as failure or guilt.

The solutions to life's problems often seemed clearer under these kinds of circumstances, John knew, and so they had become activities which he had carried over into his adulthood. Now, John clasped his hands together in a nervous gesture of desperation.

"Old Hunka of the People," he thought to himself:

> *your scarred breast*
> *grows soft and translucent*
> *in blue-gray photos*
> *on the wall in oval frames*
> *hidden under dust*
> *a man to be remembered*
> *your ancient tongue*
> *warms men of fewer years and lesser view*
> *you tell of those who came*
> *too busy fingering lives with paper*
> *to know what they can't know*
> *they liked the oratory*
> *but thought the case was hopeless:*
> *go home, old Benno,*
> *it loses something in translation*
> *drink the wind and darken scraps*

of meat and bone
stars won't rise in dreams again
heads bent
*   to clay-packed earth*
we smoke Bull Durham
*   for bark of cedar*
but know
*   in council, talk's not cheap*
nor careless in its passing
*   the feast begins with your aftervision*
we speak of you
*   in pre-poetic ritual.*

His wish at this moment was that he could go back to those days when Benno was showing him how to survive and that such survival was possible. He remembered that they would quickly pluck the soft feathers from the underbelly of the goose and from between the legs, and then they would stuff the plumes into the buckskin bag, paying no attention to the blood and the limp neck and the latent death twitches which often took place as the plumes were gathered.

The aging Benno, breathing hard from the exertion, would drop a smooth black stone into this buckskin bag, say his prayers, and walk slowly through the heavy snow the three miles to his house, which was situated on a hillside away from the river and the wind. John would follow along, bearing the dead goose in anticipation of the family feast. Benno would carefully place the bag in an old brown mahogany dresser with his clothing and other articles he used in ceremony.

John tried to make sense of why this "aftervision" of Benno was so much on his mind lately. He could not say why that was so, and even after the trial was over and for the rest of his life he continued to carry with him the ever-present memory of the old man. Perhaps it signaled some kind of change as he grew older, a reconsideration brought about by age. Perhaps it was because the old man in every gesture, in every word, in every action had restored the ethical nature of how a man might live in this changing world, and John could not let go of that.

Whatever the reason, John knew, now, sitting in this white man's courthouse, despairing over the loss of his cattle, that this kind of ethical influence was reserved for certain others like Benno, not for himself. But when he thought about how he was going to make it out of this life, he began to wonder, facetiously at first, if he was going to have to become celibate as Benno had in later life, giving up women and booze and the "good times." He continued to regret that the events of the past months did not make him look like a man of honor. He was, after all, responsible to those who depended upon him to be good and upstanding, And his recalcitrant behavior was inexcusable. Not knowing what message for the future was possible, he accepted the fact that his lands were flooded and his cattle were missing. More significantly, he accepted the sorrow of the loss of Benno, of the old man's companionship that had, in retrospect, meant everything to him. Thus, the memory of the old man continued to be everywhere around him, indelible, profound.

Even though John did not speak his name and had not heard it on the lips of those around him for a long time, he knew that he was not alone in the belief that the old singer was one who, like Smutty Bear and Little Crow and Gray Plume and the others, had seen the shadows moving near and had warned them. He had been among those, John thought now, who had been moved by the power of the gods, toward wisdom and freedom. Too late, perhaps. Too late.

6

Testimony: Day One
October 1967

District Attorney Walter Cunningham: "Well, now, Mr. Tatekeya, do you know whether or not you sold any cattle from the first of that year, 1966, up until the time that this count was made by the officials?"

A: Yes. I sold some cattle last year.

Q: Last year?

A: Yes.

Q: Was it before or after this count was done by the Credit Association?

A: It was after.

Q: I see. Well, did you sell any cattle before the count was taken?

A: It was after.

Q: I see. Well, did you sell any cattle before the count was taken? In other words, from January 1, 1966, to this April date when you made the count?

Mr. Joseph Nelson III, attorney for the young white man accused of stealing Mr. Tatekeya's cattle, at this point in the trial stood up slowly, and as though the whole process had already become loathsome and tedious to him, he said, "Again, your honor, I'm going to object to these leading questions. Now . . ."

The judge, Mr. Niklos, turning toward the younger attorney in an attitude of apology, said, "Well, now, let's remember, first of all, this witness is, as he says, an Indian. He is halting. I'm not entirely sure how readily he understands the English language. I'm not placing him as a reluctant or a hostile witness, but I think we do have to consider his education, his background; and I am going to rule out questions that suggest the answer, but I am going to permit the United States Attorney to ask questions that may be somewhat leading for the reasons I've just given you.

"Overruled.

"Now," turning to the clerk seated a few feet away from him, he said, "would you read the question again, please."

Clerk: Did you sell any cattle before the count was taken? In other words, from January 1 of 1966 to this April date when you made the count?

A: Yes. I sold cattle before the count was taken.

DA: When was that?

A: Well, that was sometime during the fall; later part of the summer or early fall.

Q: Well, what year would that have been?

A: That would be last year.

Q: The latter part of the summer or early fall of last year. Is that right?

A: Yes.

Q: Well, Mr. Tatekeya. Maybe you don't understand quite what I am getting at. Now, last year was 1966. Is that right?

A: Well, last year is when I sold them cattle.

Q: OK. And you say that was in the summer or fall?

A: That was in the fall, I'd say.

Q: In the fall. Well, now, what I'm getting at, you said that you sold cattle in the fall of 1964. Is that right?

A: That's right.

Q: And that's the only bunch of cattle you sold in 1964. Is that correct?

A: That's right.

Q: And you said, I believe, that you didn't sell any cattle during 1965.

A: That's right.

Q: Now then, did you sell any cattle from the time that you had these missing cattle—that's in the fall of *1965*—up to the time that you made the count in April of last year?

Before John could answer, the young defense attorney got to his feet. Indignant now and anxious to show the jury how he and his client were being wronged, he shouted, "Just a minute, Mr. Tatekeya!" and he waved his hand menacingly toward John on the stand.

Turning toward the judge, the attorney for the accused, his face beginning to redden in resentment, said plaintively, "Your honor! Sir! I would like to make a standing objection here. . . . This can't be allowed. . . . This cannot go—"

"You may have a standing objection," answered the judge quickly. Then, looking down at the papers on his desk, he continued:

"I call your attention to a United States case of *Antelope vs. The United States,* an Eighth-Circuit case, in which you have an Indian whose testimony is somewhat halting, who was a little hesitant and had difficulty in understanding all of these legal matters, and where it appears necessary to ask leading questions to get the material facts involved. Now, I'm not going to let the U.S. Attorney testify or put words in this man's mouth, but I think that he is somewhat confused on dates, and because of the fact that he is Indian, I am going to permit leading questions."

"Well," said Mr. Nelson III grudgingly, "just so it is understood that—"

"You may have a standing objection to all such questions," interrupted the judge. "Now, the minute it reaches the point where the District Attorney is doing the testifying instead of the witness, you call my attention to it and I'll sustain your objection, probably, because I'm not going to permit leading questions."

"Well, I believe that to be the case right now, your honor. That's why I made the objection."

"I don't believe so," said the judge. "We have to get the material facts out here." He looked at the lawyers, scanned the courtroom. His head down, eyes peering over the rim of his glasses. The wise old man. Fair. Judicial.

To the clerk, he said, "Let's hear the question again."

John, during this exchange, sat with a controlled, sullen look on his face, his elbows on the armrests of the great wooden witness chair, his large hands hanging loosely. He knew he had only a limited capacity for what he considered to be phony, self-serving behavior, and anyone who looked at his face knew that his tolerance for it was being strained.

It doesn't take too much brains to know what is happening here, John thought. The defense attorney's legal maneuvers are being used simply to distract people's attention (especially the jury's attention) from the accused, and I, myself, am now the focus of suspicion. What about the wheels of justice, white man? Are they turning forward or backward? What in the hell . . . ? He was not confused, now he was angry.

Before, when they tried me for being drunk or driving without a license I deserved to be treated like crap. Not this time, *wasichu.* Not this time. In the white man's court, though, there is no difference between the guilty and the innocent. All the same. That's what they call equality, ennit?

A faint smile touched John's lips as he looked up and saw the bearded, yawning sentinel, the man from the outer hallway, carefully opening the heavy, polished door to the courtroom. That guy, thought John. He just can't quit.

The doorkeeper came inside and tapped a woman seated in the third row on the shoulder. He motioned for her to follow him and she did so. The door swung silently shut and John turned his attention back to the business at hand.

John looked at the cowboy lawyer and wondered at his naïveté. He really believes in this, he thought. He really thinks he is winning the case. But that should be no surprise. In all cultures and in all times, people have made laws in which they have found faith and in which they have found self-affirmation. People have always found processes of thought and modes of reconciling conflicting considerations. Certainly, the Dakotahs have done this for longer than is known.

John's thoughts got more specific. It does not matter to this "good" white man, John said to himself, it doesn't matter to this cowboy from Connecticut that everyone here is casting doubt upon me in the process of the trial. It doesn't matter that he has to make me look like a fool in public as he "defends" me. He sees no contradiction.

It's kind of like those book-writing men who come out here to the reservation, John mused, and they ask the people all kinds of questions, write everything down, and eventually go away to write their books in which they tell lies about us. There was one scholar who came here to Fort Thompson and Crow Creek, John remembered, and he passed out cigarettes to everybody and we all stood around smoking and visiting with him, being polite and entertaining as is our custom these days to a stranger, a visitor who didn't seem to know much about us. And then, just recently, just a few months ago, my youngest daughter brought that book home with her from college and in it this white man wrote that we had no toilets, sometimes didn't even bother to go into the trees to urinate, and that we really didn't care what kind of meat we ate. *Tado,* he said, was our only word for meat and we didn't make any great distinctions about it.

I should know better by now. Indians like myself should probably avoid participating in such white man's doings. And we should avoid trials and courtrooms. I should know by now that the white man's notions about these things are almost always in direct conflict with what my people know to be ethical.

Only rarely have I known the Dakotahs, John thought, to seek truth by victimizing the aggrieved one. And when they have done it, everybody has known that it was not a part of the institutionalized process of legal reasoning and ethical base of our cultural survival; that it was behavior unsanctioned by our elders and therefore unprincipled. Dakotahs have always had confidence in their own lives.

I, too, must have confidence in such things, and, of course, I still do. Some people who have lost faith in the old ways have begun to think of Old Benno, our teacher, when they think about him at all, as just an old windbag.

But I do not. It is widely believed among us, John thought as he sat waiting for the questions to be asked that everyone knew the answers to, that we must not dehumanize our opponents in the process of seeking the truth. Else, the truth becomes meaningless. To legitimize such a thing would allow anyone to accuse anyone else of the most outrageous crimes and to be forever after in doubt. And here I am. By implication, accused. Of an outrageous crime. Stealing from myself and my own family. Everyone who knows me knows that, since I have become an old man, my pride in myself would not allow me to do such a terrible thing.

The court dialogue resumed.

"Now, then," read the court clerk in an expressionless voice. "Did you sell any cattle from the time that you had these missing cattle—that's in the fall of 1965—up to the time that you made the count in April of last year?"

A: Uh . . .
DA: Now, take your time, John. . . .
A: *(long pause)* I, uh, sold some cattle.

Looking about the courtroom, he felt everyone's eyes on him, and he began to feel the burden of rising paranoia. How careful need he be here? What were they accusing him of? No. No. He wanted to protest. I am not the accused. Why . . . ?

John wanted a cigarette. Was there no end to this tedium? As he looked around he saw two of the Big Pipe brothers, Jason and Sheridan, seated in the courtroom in the spectators' section. His own wife, Rose, was sitting just behind the railing, and he worried again, for just a moment, that Aurelia might show up and it would be embarrassing for everyone concerned. Perhaps he should have cautioned her.

The little courtroom seemed unusually packed and stuffy at the beginning of this little trial, the first day of the official proceedings. People were even standing in the back of the room, arms folded, shifting the weight of their bodies from one foot to the other, shuffling, whispering. John's apprehension momentarily diminishing, his thoughts gave way to his own curiosity. He cocked his head and lifted his eyebrows and wondered, almost contemptuously, of what interest this foolish little trial could be to most of these spectators. Didn't they have anything better to do?

Only as a last resort was this whole thing something that John had considered appropriate. He had always held to the traditional belief that Dakotahs living on their own lands should handle their own affairs in their own way and that the federal government's intrusion into these matters was not only foolish, it was clearly illegal.

And now, endlessly answering these tiresome, repetitious, dangerous questions, he worried that his decision to join the United States government in this legal matter against a white cattle thief on Indian reservation, "trust" lands might not have been a wise one.

What had the United States government ever done for him? John had asked himself before entering into this agreement. Did it ever protect the lands of my grandfathers? Did it ever come to the aid of those who wished to practice our religions and teach our children in the old ways? No. On the contrary, he answered himself silently, it was an accomplice in all of the thefts historically suffered by my people. John felt certain that it would be again the white man's way which would turn against him, an Indian.

That was the way of history. Why, then, did John participate in what he viewed as a corrupt system of justice? Many years later, when John was very old, blind, and nearly deaf, he would still pose that question, and oddly, he would continue to answer it in a way which one could only see as an effort to explain the ambiguities of his existence to those who still loved him and surrounded him in a protective and familial circle.

Private solutions and individual decisions about matters of this kind, John would concede, were not always possible, regrettably, nor were they definitive. This explanation did not, of course, exonerate him, but at the same time, neither did it condemn him.

So he would tell a story or two:

Story #1

"To be an allottee and a citizen of the United States," the agent told Benno, who stood before him holding a form letter addressed to him from the Bureau of Indian Affairs, Washington, D.C., "you must do what it tells you in that letter."

"No."

"You must choose your allotment."

Benno took out a huge handkerchief, wiped his face, and paused.

"No, thanks."

"You must choose your allotment."

"No. Sir."

They stood staring into one another's eyes.

Later, the agent chose the allotment for Benno and registered it in his name.

"It is way up the Crow Creek, somewhere on past that little white man store up there. Way on up there," the protesting Benno told everyone, his arm flung out in a wide gesture.

"Taskar and them live up there, but me and my family have never lived there. We don't want to live there. There's too much trees there along the ridge and it gets too dark in the winter."

He got another letter in the mail telling him he was an allottee:

Each and every allottee shall have the benefit and be subject to the laws, both civil and criminal, of the State or Territory in which they reside.

Benno had said no again, and for the last time. He never again spoke a civil word to the agent. And he sent the letter back by his eldest daughter, who lived at the Agency. He continued to live along the *sma sma* creek where he had always lived. And when the agent and his secretary came to "talk some sense" into the potential but recalcitrant allottee and citizen, Benno took a few warning shots at them with an old .30-.30 he kept by the front door. He shouted at them in Indian to go away.

"Han sni! Hanta wo!"

Benno was declared "incompetent" by the Department of the Interior at the request of the agent very shortly after this hair-raising event. The agent, after all, was an ex-schoolteacher from Sioux City, Iowa, who had taken up government service because there was more money in it, and he was not, he would tell you in no uncertain terms, accustomed to taking gunfire from crazy Indians.

The allotment which bore Benno's name, then, was put up for sale eventually by the agent who was acting "in his behalf," and a white man from Pukwana who raised pigs and turkeys purchased it.

Story #2

Eddie Big Pipe, Harvey's younger brother, rode over to the "squaw man's" place and shot fifteen head of prime, fat hogs. He did it because the white man, married to a tribal woman and living on her land, would not keep them away from Ed's watering place along the creek.

Big Pipe had paid dearly for the individual action he had taken upon himself. There had been no further dealings between the two antagonists, and the Bureau of Indian Affairs officials at the Agency ever after that looked upon Ed as a troublemaker, one who was unreliable and dangerous.

In defense of this admittedly astonishing behavior, Eddie Big Pipe had later made a joke of it.

"Well," he would say in mock seriousness, "I could have shot *him!*" and everybody always roared with laughter.

Some others in the community, however, the "squaw man," his wife and her relatives, and, especially, the Bureau of Indian Affairs officials, were not amused. Seeing no humor in the situation, they avoided Big Pipe, and when they could not avoid him, they glared at him from a distance.

Tatekeya used this story to discuss the ideas of justice as they applied to Indians, and he always gave the impression that shooting the "squaw man" might not have been such a bad idea.

7

Except for wise men and the colonized, almost no one pays attention to the fact that history repeats itself. Though John Tatekeya may have considered himself neither wise nor colonized, he was, nonetheless, a man who knew his own history. He saw the ironies inherent in the historical relationship which his people had long since established with the invading whites; sometimes he was entertained by it, oftentimes dumbfounded, and always appalled and uneasy.

Just across the river from where he sat in the witness chair in the federal building, in this crowded courtroom testifying in a legal process which seemed to be directed toward the improbable notion that he had himself stolen his own cattle and was now falsely accusing a young white man of the crime, one of his grandfathers, Gray Plume, had once attended a great Council meeting where nine tribes of the Sioux Nation had met with the white man soldier William S. Harney. Even at the time that it occurred, in 1856, all of the people had recognized that they had been ordered there to defend themselves from the accusation that they were thieves by the very people who were stealing the Sioux homelands.

True to his grandfather's memory, John now sat in quiet contemplation of those events of a century past and, in his own silent admission, concluded that what had happened at the Harney Council was known to have happened over and over again and was happening at that moment.

Sometimes, John thought, it takes only a small event in the life of an ordinary man to illuminate the ambiguities of an entire century. I know now, at last, finally, John reasoned, that the council which Harney directed all those many years ago must have been very much like this one, that it is the white man's thievery which is legalized and the Indian's behavior which is made criminal in either case. It is always a part of the strategy that the white man's whim must be satisfied and that he must be made to look fair and decent. Reasonable. Compassionate.

John Tatekeya was beginning to understand why he was a cynical man.

"The Council lasted many days," the grandfather Gray Plume had told everyone, "and Rencountre, the half-breed Frenchman who was the Sioux language/English interpreter, worked very hard to make sure that there were no misunderstandings.

"It was very clear what General Harney wanted," said Gray Plume afterward. "He wanted all Indians removed and he wanted Indians to obey his law. He wanted all Indians who were said to have committed murders to be delivered to the nearest military post so that the white man, not Indians, could decide upon their fate; and, more important, perhaps, he wanted all Indians to stay away from the roads traveled by whites.

"In our own land," said Gray Plume, "we would forever after that be told where we could go and where we couldn't, who among us must be punished and how we must punish them. Hang them. By the neck with a rope. This, we think, is barbaric. And the Sioux have never administered justice in such a manner."

Gray Plume had listened carefully, and he had heard many things which influenced his thinking from that time on. He had heard Zephier Rencountre interpret endlessly for the officials:

Indians must not obstruct or lurk in the vicinity of roads traveled by the whites [and] certainly Indians must not molest any travelers through their country.

In response to it all, Gray Plume, a man who had a good understanding of the meaning of reciprocity, had wanted to ask, "And what is the obligation of those visitors and travelers to our land? Are they blameless? Right? Guilty? Innocent? Poor? Rich? Who are the thieves here?"

Well, thought Gray Plume. We are accused, often, by the white man who knows a thing or two about thievery.

What are they doing here? Who are they? Tourists? Sightseers? Explorers? God's men or the devil's? Gold seekers? Do they not possess their own homelands? Will they let us go into their homelands and settle there as we please?

He had wanted to ask all of these questions, but, of course, he did not. In the retelling of the event it was clear that he had not then, nor in the rest of his long life, received an acceptable answer to these tacit inquiries.

The observation is still made by those who examine history, and it was certainly made by the grandfather Gray Plume, who had witnessed these particular events, that great forces had clashed on this continent and the old order for each was changed forever. It was clear to John that Gray Plume had understood what had happened, thus he never questioned the old man's interpretation: that from the very beginning there must have occurred a vast release of energy, unequaled in the experience of North America, and it manifested itself in a compelling behavior pattern of interaction which would forever plague Oyate, the people. It was clear to John, as it had been to his grandfather, that the thousands of years of life force and occupancy by the Sioux upon this land would be from that time on at grave risk.

Whenever Gray Plume spoke of these historical matters, he made it clear that it had seemed to him the zeal with which the white man soldier Harney, the Christian missionaries who preceded him, and the justices who followed pursued their own goals was surely unique. To be sure, Gray Plume had given little thought to the apostolic age which had inspired such behavior in the so-called new world, and so it was left to him to ponder alone the conception of justice which the Council articulated, just as it was now left to the grandson John Tatekeya to wonder about his lawyer's purpose, the motives of those in the courtroom.

Though John was now past sixty and was just in these late years beginning to understand the consequences of former times, the grandfather Gray Plume had been only twenty-six years old when he attended this Council and learned these things. Very early in his life, then, Gray Plume had become a man to whom the people listened, and his influence, surely, continued throughout his life.

Whenever the grandfather told and retold his remembrances of the Council's deliberations, he philosophically speculated that if the Dakotapi were to survive the modern world, they would have to recognize that the religious views that brought about what he regarded as the eminently unfair system of justice for Indians in America promulgate in their followers the notion that a righteous good father may be displaced by identification with Jesus Christ. And that displacement, Gray Plume reasoned, was what allowed men to become gods themselves.

"It is a dangerous way," he would say.

This became Gray Plume's view, and he had many, many relatives.

Gray Plume, like an Ancient Mariner of the North Plains doing penance, went about repeating word for word the Harney oration delivered to the nine tribes, which was forever in his memory:

Now, listen to what the Great Father says: first, that all Indians who have committed murders, or other outrages upon white persons, shall be delivered up for trial to the commander of the nearest post; second, that all stolen property of every description in the hands of any Indians shall be restored to its rightful owner, for which purpose the chiefs must be responsible that it is taken in without delay to the nearest military post; third, that Indians must not obstruct or lurk in the vicinity of roads traveled by the whites, nor in any way molest a traveler through their country.

Gray Plume warned that Harney was a powerful and vicious enemy of the people and that their lands and ways were under severe attack.

The grandson John Tatekeya, now in a modern court of law participating in a way of justice condemned by the ancients of his people, looked into the eyes of those in the courtroom and knew genuine hostility. What is the meaning of a man's history here? he raged silently.

Since the days of Gray Plume's attendance at that Council, moralists have argued that the sanctity of international ethics was clearly under fire during those proceedings, but on this day Tatekeya himself was momentarily at a loss for words. Was he the only one who saw that it was useless for him to have to come here and defend himself and his honor? Was he the only one who knew of Gray Plume and remembered his warning?

Tatekeya could not shake from his mind the drama which had been witnessed by his grandfather. He could not rid himself of the image of the old man doing penance for his mere presence at the Council and for his very participation in such historical events. The old man's final and oblique interpretation of it all which rang in his ears now had made him forever sad:

"In the previous year to this Council, my relatives," Gray Plume had said, "Harney himself had massacred the Sichangu at the Blue Water in Nebraska."

The old man had always feared that he would not die before the theft from the people of the sacred Black Hills would be, finally, legitimized by the white man's corrupt law; that the white man would say to his people, you can get along without your life, because I have mine; that an unjust world would make it impossible for his grandchildren to live just lives.

Nonetheless, he made his annual pilgrimages to the significant mountain in those hills that would forever bear the enemy's name, not only because he was a holy man, but because in his dreams he was welcomed by the winter scent of the pine trees, the soft rumble of thunder in the summer rain, and the reverberating flashes of orange and blue lightning upon the darkness of the land.

Finally, sometime after the turn of the century and just before the first great war in Europe, Gray Plume had gone into the next world, his irreconcilable fears unappeased.

8

Testimony: Day One (continued)
October 1967

Q: Let me repeat the question, Mr. Tatekeya; when did you sell these cattle?

A: *(pause)* Well, unh, I sold some cattle last fall, and then this fella come out this spring to check my herd.

Q: Well, Mr. Tatekeya, last year was 1966. Is that a fact or isn't it a fact?

A: Yes. That is a fact.

Q: Now, is it correct that you say you sold cattle in the summer or the fall of last year, 1966. Is that right?

A: Yes, that's right.

Q: Now, these here missing cattle that you testified to earlier. That was in the fall of what year?

A: 1965.

Q: All right. Now, from the fall of 1965, then go on through the winter months of 1966, the first part of 1966, January, on up to April of 1966. Did you sell any cattle during that time?

A: No.

The District Attorney, with considerable relief showing in his face, looked toward the judge as if to say, "You see? We did get to the right answer, didn't we? Between the fall months of that year and the spring, when the cattle were missing, he didn't sell any cattle!"

The lawyer's face expressed both pain and triumph.

John looked at the lawyer and thought, But there was never any evidence that I sold cattle during that time. There were never any receipts, no checks. Nothing was ever presented as evidence for the accusation that I sold my own stuff.

Nonetheless, the lawyer seemed jubilant that John had at last uttered the appropriate words, that he had not sold his own cattle, that he seemed, now, to be an honest man whose cattle were indeed missing and that he had nothing to do with it.

"Fine," the lawyer said to no one in particular.

Everyone in the courtroom seemed to understand, too, that a milestone had been passed and that John had finally given the right answer, and there was the sound of feet shuffling and the clearing of throats following this long and confusing exchange.

John looked into the faces of the members of the jury, the spectators. Did they really think that I stole my own cattle? Do they still think this? Do they believe that I would accuse a man falsely? I wonder if their doubt will still linger long after this trial has ended and that, when this is all over, people will still think I'm a liar.

The young white woman who was married to Sheridan Big Pipe got up from her seat during this brief pause, sidled up the aisle, and started toward the door, tiptoeing so that she would not disturb the proceedings. John watched the backs of her heavy, white legs, mottled with the blue-gray shades of varicose veins, propel her toward the exit. Her purse flapped noisily against the side rails of the spectators' seats, and Sheridan glared at her retreating figure. Her conspicuous behavior called attention to Sheridan's presence, and John again was puzzled by his interest in this theft and trial.

What is he doing here? John wondered. This does not concern him. And his family has already declared to me that they know nothing about the theft or the whereabouts of my cattle.

He turned again to his lawyer, who was smiling brightly at him.

"Fine," he repeated.

"Now," said the lawyer, drawing in a breath, "now, Mr. Tatekeya, when you noticed your missing cattle during the fall of 1965, do you know what kind of cattle you were missing?"

"Sure."

"What were they?"

"Herefords."

"Well, now," said the lawyer uncertainly, "well . . . I mean . . . what were they? Steers? Heifers? What?"

"There was eight cows and eight calves, eight yearling steers, and eighteen yearling and two-year-old heifers."

The judge raised his hand and said, "Just a minute, just a minute. I'm sorry. I didn't get all of that."

The clerk, also taking notes, said, "I didn't get it all either. Let's hear that over again."

The judge turned to Tatekeya. "Would you say that again, please?"

John said very slowly: "Eight cows." (Pause) "Eight calves." (Pause) "Eight yearling steers." (Pause) "And eighteen yearling and two-year-old heifers."

He glanced over at the court officials meticulously recording the information as though this was the first that they'd heard of it.

More in sorrow than in impatience or anger, John looked down at his feet. His Tony Lamas needed polishing. He should have polished them before coming to the courthouse this morning. Oftentimes, Aurelia sat on the edge of the bed and polished them for him. Chatting comfortably. Her round shoulders glistening and soft. He wanted to apologize. He wanted desperately to see her.

9

The commitment John now had to Aurelia had started simply enough, perhaps. A diversion, he sometimes alibied privately and in retrospect: at first, an embarrassed admission that the physical nature of a twenty-year-old marriage might not be enough for his sexual appetite. He even went so far as to suggest to himself that the striking young woman's love for him eased the pain of his middle-aged life, made him feel less agony because of the upheaval of the last ten years. When he had been forced to move his cattle, his home, and his outbuildings out of the way of the backwaters of the hydropower dam called Oahe, one of several such federally funded dams forced upon the Missouri River, he felt great despair.

He saw his mother's allotment, those of all her brothers and sisters, the Poor Chicken land, the Walker and Howe and Shields allotments, and many, many more disappear under the great body of water; thousands of acres of homelands all up and down the river which had nourished the people, now gone. Cemeteries and Christian churches were moved out of the way of the flood at the last minute, and cottonwoods, elms, and ash trees which had stood for hundreds of years along the banks of the river turned white with decay as their roots were swamped. Nothing survived the onslaught. The medicine roots and plants, the rich berry and plum bushes, the small animals and reptiles, were swept away, trivial sacrificial victims of modern progress.

And the world was again changed forever.

"What is happening, John?" his wife asked one day when she returned from hunting the *ti(n)psina*. "It has moved and now

I can find it nowhere. Do you think that it has disappeared for good?"

John didn't know how to answer her.

That spring, which seemed to signal the dam's completion, when the disaster had somehow come to a point of no return, when most of the people had moved out of the way of the incoming water, Tatekeya's small house had also been moved, across the small rise in the land to the draw about four miles away from the river. There was no time to move anything else. And for years after that he had none of the promised electricity, no fences to hold in his cattle and horses, no water except the ever-seeping backwaters, no barns for storage, and no haystacks to feed his stock for the coming winters. It was a time when his wife nearly gave up, a time of great stress, waste, and confusion.

One day, he had taken Rose to town for a brief visit with their grandchildren, and upon his return home he attended the peyote church meeting which had been hastily arranged as a grieving ceremony for the death of one of Aurelia's young cousins. The people of the community wept together and prayed for the restoration of health to everyone. They ate the sacred food. And when the meeting was over, John had walked to his car with Aurelia. He had taken her into his arms as though he were a penitent. Humble and touched.

From that time on, self-conscious and bitter, he had loved her.

When they entered the large room, they saw an array of narrow beds, and all of them were filled with the skinniest, most wraithlike bodies that John had ever seen. It looked like something from the war, like the pictures that you saw in the newsreels.

The air in the room was nauseating; it reeked of the human odor which was the aftermath of bodily functions performed in a limited space. The smell hung like death in the windowless rooms and remained trapped in the high ceilings and closets. John was sickened. He felt inept, clumsy, and useless. He had never been good in sickrooms. In fact, when his wife, Rose, underwent a gallbladder operation at the government hospital years ago, he had not been able to bring himself to visit her there. He had instead sent his sister in his place and later suffered pangs of guilt for seeming to be uncaring.

Everywhere he looked, there was an array of rumpled bedclothes and frail, skin-and-bones men whose lives had brought them to this imperfect place to mend or to await release, whichever came first. John had been instantly thankful that Benno had avoided this long and relentless kind of decay which can precede a man's exit from this world. Benno had simply gone to sleep one night and never awakened. On this day, as he surveyed the scene of human misery, John didn't know whether to laugh or weep.

He felt Aurelia move toward the nearest bed, and as she approached her beloved grandfather, John knew that he needn't have worried about how he could help her. She simply knew, instinctively, how to love and comfort the old man to whom she had been devoted since infancy.

"Grampa is going to get better," she had told John as they were driving to the rest home. And now that she was here, she behaved as though that were a certainty.

"*Tunkashina,*" she shouted into the bony, hollow face of the old man, whose deafness was becoming more profound with every passing day.

John could tell, almost instantly, that the old man did not recognize her.

"It's me, Grampa." She took his bony hand in hers.

"It's Aurelia."

Startled and afraid, the old man, lying with his mouth open, lifted his head a few inches from the pillow and stared. "How are you?" she asked in a loud voice, ignoring what John thought was fairly obvious, that the old man was, to use a phrase from his catechism days, right on Jordan's banks.

There was no answer from the old man.

"Are you OK, Grampa?" She was nearly hollering now.

Still the old man did not speak. She waited. Then she leaned closer, and suddenly lowering her voice, she moved in and leaned toward the old man's ear. "*Toniktuka he?*" she asked softly.

She waited for him to look directly at her.

Hoarsely, the old man repeated the question: *"Toniktuka he?"*

Bewildered, he looked at her searchingly, trying to remember who she was, his dark eyes clouded, the pupils empty. John, standing beside her with his arm at her waist, thought for a moment that she was close to tears.

"... relia ... *wicincina*," the old man whispered pitifully, recognition finally breaking through his mental confusion.

His withered hands began to feel around the bed for his cane, moving the bedsheets this way and that, until Aurelia grasped his wrist and held his arm. With just a little pressure she got him to lie back down, and then she started to talk to him as though everything were all right.

"You don't need your cane, Grampa. You can't get up right now. OK?

"Look, Grampa," she said. "Look. I dug some wild turnips. ... They're really hard to find. ... I dug them a while ago with that stick you made for me. Do you remember? Look. They're really good. See? I hung them over the stove to dry. These are some of the smallest ones. Here."

She lifted up his head and put a huge pillow under his thin neck, and he was pushed into a forward position like an old, wrinkled turkey thrusting out its skinny beak.

Aurelia took no notice of his awkwardness.

"Here's one, Grampa." She handed him a small turnip.

"They're pretty dry, ennit?" she shouted. "Just suck on it, hunh?" Then she put one in her own mouth and chomped hard on it.

She smiled into the clouded eyes.

As the old man tried to get enough saliva in his dry mouth to suck on the tiny turnip, John nearly burst out laughing. The gracelessness of old age and the innocence with which Aurelia confronted it seemed suddenly outrageous and sad. Obscene, yet humorous.

Oblivious to the hilarious spectacle of the toothless old man's effort to comply with her wishes, Aurelia began talking about the old times. She told him conspiratorially, "It got dark and the coyotes had to leave me on my own," sharing with him an old story they both knew.

Tucking in a blanket at the edge of his narrow cot, she asked, "Do you remember that, NaNa?" calling him by the childish nickname she had given him when she was just an infant and barely able to talk, trying to share with him now the old story which held some of the secrets of the irretrievable past they both had known and he, for the moment at least, no longer remembered.

An old man from the next bed, startled out of his daze by all of this activity in this ordinarily silent room, rose from his pillows like a graying Lazarus and shouted to no one in particular, "I'm fine! I'm fine! *Oh-ha(n)* . . . yes!! I'm doing OK," and then lay down again as though in slow motion.

A tragicomic scene, thought John, touched by the pitiful nature of these final days, still half-amused at this disconsolate drama of unblest senility. He sat in the big, orange, leatherlike chair beside the old man's bed that day, and even though he knew that the old man would have been angry at his presence, he had stayed: compelled, somehow, to be with Aurelia as she made her duty-visit to the old grandfather now living out his latest illness in the new tribal rest home.

John, like the old grandfather, had become an appreciative listener of Aurelia's. And even when she was drunk and behaving contentiously, as she sometimes was, he was always reassured by just the mere sound of her voice. He noticed that she had the ability to adapt the rhythm of one language to change the sound of another. And so, when she talked in English she often used the sounds of Dakota, the cadence and tone of Dakota speech. This day, he sat and listened to the cadence of her voice, and in his own heart he knew that what it amounted to was a kind of purity of speech, an attempt on her part to retain some of the sense of Dakota aesthetic in everyday life. And it always seduced him in ways that he could not completely explain.

He sat and listened to her work her spell on the old grandfather, and he wondered how long it would be before she would do these things for him, no longer a lover, merely a nurse easing the life of an old man, caressing his dry forehead, speaking to him as though to a child. The thought filled John with dread.

The difference in their ages had only lately begun to be an issue between them. The last time they had made love he had covered her breast with his hand, put his lips to her neck, and whispered, "You will find someone else one of these days, Aurelia. Some young man. And you won't be able to catch your breath. What will I do then?"

She had only smiled. And her touch was cold.

10

There had been rumors about Aurelia since anyone could remember. That was because men had always wanted her. Even when she was twelve, still long-legged and sallow from a sick childhood filled with hardships, men were drawn to her beauty. Some of her growing years, when she was not attending a boarding school or living at her grandmother's place, she spent in a three-room house abandoned by the U.S. Bureau of Indian Affairs employees who no longer wanted to live forty miles from the Agency, a house which had been built across the road from a Catholic church and a cemetery at a time when the services and religions of white colonizers were brought in to create the center of a little community adapting to an enforced relocation and agrarian lifeway.

Because of her beauty, Aurelia was watched constantly. Her grandmother, in particular, took it upon herself to open her eyes to the realities of the kind of life she thought Aurelia could count on if she were not relentlessly compelled to duty. This was the child who had been given to her in infancy, the child who would have the responsibility from birth to be the companion of her grandmother. Such a child, it might have been said by others who had greater insight, should not have been given also the responsibility of great beauty, for the contradictions of living in such a way are often overwhelming.

Such girl children who are meant to accompany the aged are ordinarily plain and docile, and because Aurelia was neither, her grandmother's suspicion became the very attitude which nurtured intolerance and accusation. It was her grandmother who first noticed that men wanted to put their hands on this youthful beauty, and she reported it to the sisters of the child's mother. From then on, every action of Aurelia's was noticed and commented upon, and her natural tendency toward vibrancy and joy was taken to be the sign of recalcitrance and mischief.

The home in which she spent some of her years prior to womanhood had three rooms, one for cooking, the second for eating, and the third for sleeping and loving. As a consequence of these circumstances, Aurelia was never innocent. She had never been one of those protected children forced into speculating about the mysteries of sex. She had never had to wonder nor fantasize about what was done between men and women in the night, for she grew up listening to the words and sounds of passion. She grew up knowing that for her parents, grandparents, uncles and aunts, married sisters and brothers, cousins, and all who slept in that long, narrow room making love, quarreling and relenting, weeping and laughing, this momentary and transitory offering of human passion was the best that could be expected. The family members who functioned as her role models were, in her view at least, frail and needful. Early on, then, she "played around" as a kind of quiet resistance to all this, and she began to indulge the men who sought her. Early, then, the gossip had started.

By the time she was almost a teenager, she seemed already mature, already an adult. And when the grown men returned in 1945 from Germany and Japan and the Pacific wars, her family, because there were many daughters of marriageable age, received special invitations to the "honor dances" for returning warriors. It was expected that she too would put on her finest clothes and dance and, sooner or later, make the choices that her sisters had made in finding suitable husbands.

But she did not. She had become contemptuous of those young men who wanted to bring her things, and she became the kind of young woman who, for reasons known only to herself, drove away those who might have comforted her, even frightening them so that they began to watch her from the corners of their eyes.

She continued to accompany her grandmother. Some of the time they lived along the Crow Creek and sometimes in the breaks of the Missouri River country where her father ran cattle. From her grandmother's little house along the creek they could take a footpath to the flat prairie above and worship in the Christian way at the gray Presbyterian church, which faced east in a clearing surrounded by tall prairie grass and wildflowers. Grace Mission, an Episcopal church which stood as evidence that the missionaries of these various Christian faiths understood the jealous spirit in which they competed for the souls of the natives, was not far away. It was to the Presbyterian church, however, where Christian hymns were sung in Dakotah language every Sunday, that Aurelia took her grandmother and sat beside her to share in the warmth of the wood-burning stove in winter and in the oppressive heat in summer. A winding road led to the Agency, past a small hill, past a dry creek which also, at one time, fed into the Missouri River.

One Sunday evening, Aurelia and her grandmother left the potluck dinner being served at the Presbyterian church to join their relatives gathering in the Indian way to console one another on the loss of a young man of the community who was a cousin to Aurelia. An army corporal, he had been shot by unidentified persons in Korea on the eve of his departure for the States, and the grief that this unexpected death bore into the community was profound.

The old lady and Aurelia walked in the sunset to the gateway and entered the house of the young warrior's parents, shaking hands with those seated on the floor along the walls.

The singer began, his voice deep in his throat. Later, near the edge of sobs unuttered, deep agony in every hard breath he took, he sang of the story which told of his gift and how he must share it with the people. Aurelia sat, unmoved, and it was only when her grandmother unexpectedly began to talk that she straightened her shoulders and tried to listen: slumped near the wall, the old woman told of petting the she-buffalo when she was an infant, and how it had followed her, and when she turned around, her infant tracks were blue.

"You must guard the scaled doors of the room," Aurelia heard someone say. "Don't let his power out."

The men lifted the singer off his feet and held him.

Much later, a drummer started to sing as the morning light dawned, and the others joined in:

wana anpa'o u we yo
wana anpa'o u we yo
wana anpa'o u we yo
wana anpa'o u we yo heyana he de do we

Exhausted and spent, the singer sat on the mattress on the floor in his room and changed his clothes.

His new wife put pans of food out for the worshippers and mourners, and Aurelia began to carry the bowls into the outer room. She sat next to John Tatekeya and ate heartily, and it wasn't until she opened the door to the silent fall air that she decided to walk to the car with him. She was seventeen years old at the time but not too young to make a deliberate and important alliance—an alliance which she knew would be denounced by her relatives, and which would be filled with both pain and joy for the rest of their lives.

11

Testimony: Day Two
October 1967

The second day of testimony opened as the chilly fall weather began in earnest. October. The earth was losing its summer warmth, and John's worries deepened. It wasn't just the cattle now. It was something else. It was a failure of values, a failure of community, a failure of esteem and respect among men, those ever-important considerations for Dakotahs.

This was the day that Jason Big Pipe began his testimony against John, and his appearance cut to the core of what was deepest and best in the view of the world that they both had learned throughout their lives. Many witnesses were subpoenaed, thus forced or manipulated into taking sides, but this one, John was told by his lawyer, volunteered. As it turned out, his testimony against his father's old friend initiated the public, familial, and tribal humiliation in the white man's court of law that John would forever afterward recall with a deep sense of loss.

Jason was now a man, no longer the infant that John had held on his knee, no longer the boy who had fished with him at the river's edge. Few people at the trial grasped the moral dimensions which now became the foremost considerations in the trial for John.

He does not believe that I have stolen my own cattle, thought John as he listened to the leading questions now being asked by the defense attorney, so that cannot be his motivation for slandering me. He doesn't, either, believe that I am incompetent, for he has worked side-by-side with me since he was old enough to saddle a horse. He rode with me as a youth, fixed fence, and put a brand on my cattle. This is a hostile act against me, and I know of no explanation for this young man's actions.

Justinian, the Roman lawyer and politician, who codified law in the context of Christianity, wrote in the sixth century that neither God nor human law could forbid all evil deeds, and if John Tatekeya had been a scholar of European history and religion, which he knew concentrated on the nature of evil, he might have agreed. But what he did know as a Dakotah was that the ethical aspect of "natural law," that to which a man is inclined naturally, the kind of law that the Dakotapi had always believed they specialized in, fails only when it is encouraged by reason and practicality and fate. There was no doubt that John considered this action of Jason's outside of the category of natural inclinations, and he would have to wait and see what explanations might emerge.

Joseph Nelson III began the questioning:

Q: Now, Jason Big Pipe, you are a young man of the tribe and you are knowledgeable about farming and ranching operations, would you say so?

A: Yeah.

Q: And you and your parents are neighbors of Mr. Tatekeya, is that so?

A: Yeah.

Q: Now, Mr. Big Pipe, you have identified the place which is Tatekeya's home place here on this map. *(pointing)* Will you show the jury where you say you saw his cattle out of his pasture? Where would they be?

A: This is the home place right here. *(indicating on a map)*

Q: Yes, now where would the cattle be out?

A: And this would be the highway. *(indicating again)*

Q: Yes?

A: It's got to be right in here *(indicating)*, right through here. There's a fence line on this side of it. He should have put up better fences to hold them in.

Q: Now, this is all his pasture here. *(indicating)*
A: Yes. This is his whole unit here. *(indicating)*
Q: And where would they be, on the roads?
A: Yeah.
Q: How many would there be?
A: At that time about forty to fifty head. Maybe the whole bunch.
Q: Who would get those cattle back?
A: Well, he'd take a pickup out there and run them back in.
Q: Did he have any saddle horses on the place?
A: Yes, but he never used them.
Q: He didn't use them. Now, are you personally acquainted with Mr. Tatekeya's operation?
A: *(pause)* No.
Q: Well, what I mean is, you would see them, wouldn't you?
A: Yeah.
Q: What kind of a ranch manager was he?
A: Well, he ain't much of a manager. A lot of things he should have done better than what he's doing now.
Q: Has it improved recently?
A: No.
Q: Still as bad as ever?
A: Yeah.
Q: Now, do you know whether Mr. Tatekeya was ever absent, gone from his place?
A: Oh, yeah.
Q: Do you know how long a time he would be gone?
A: Yeah. There was a time there I think he was gone for a whole week.
Q: And when was that?
A: That year I don't remember. Well, let's see. That's in '64.
Q: '64. And how about in 1965?
A: Yeah, in '65, too.
Q: Was he there or gone in '65?
A: He was gone for about three, four days, or three days, maybe.
Q: When was that? Do you remember the time of year?
A: Well, in the summer some time.

Q: Now, did you ever run into Mr. Tatekeya anyplace off the ranch in 1965?

A: What was that?

Q: Did you ever find or see Mr. Tatekeya anyplace besides the ranch in 1965?

A: The place he'd go is to town, up north there.

Q: Were you there in Chamberlain in the fall of 1965?

A: Yes.

Q: Did you see Mr. Tatekeya?

A: Yeah. In the bar there.

Q: Do you know how long he was in Chamberlain?

A: Well, about a week; seven days or so.

Q: And where did you see him?

A: I seen him in the little Indian bar there in Chamberlain. They call it Buck's, I think.

Q: What was he doing when you saw him?

A: Well, he was under intoxication. He was drunk. I think he was still at it when I seen him; he was getting worse.

Q: How many occasions did you see him in that bar, how many times?

A: About four times. At least.

Q: And would those be on the same or separate days?

A: Separate days.

Q: I see. And on each of those occasions what was he doing?

A: Well, he was driving around in his pickup.

Q: And did you see him in the bar there, too?

A: Well, in the afternoon I seen him in the bar and towards evening he was in his pickup but he wasn't driving.

Q: Oh. He had somebody else driving?

A: Yes.

Q: Who was driving?

A: Some woman in there. I don't know.

Q: But, it was his pickup?

A: Oh, yeah . . . sure.

Q: Now, Mr. Big Pipe . . . you are . . .

12

John could feel the presence of his wife and daughter in the back of the room as Jason's words *Some woman in there. I don't know* reverberated and receded in the stuffy courtroom. The unspeakable had been uttered and now it was out in the open and nothing would be the same. John looked out of the corner of his eye at the cowboy District Attorney who was making a big pretense of taking notes, his boots planted squarely in front of him. He stroked his eyebrow with his left thumb and forefinger, noncommittal, refusing to acknowledge John's tentative glance.

Just that morning, John's daughter had picked out the shirt he should wear to court.

"Wear this one, Ate," she had said with enthusiasm, handing him a maroon and gray western-cut shirt she had helped him select in the store months ago. At breakfast with the family the eldest grandson had said, jokingly, "Lookin' go-o-oo-d, Grampa," fingering the sleeve of John's shirt and finally giving in to his emotions by flinging his arms about his grandfather and giving him a tremendous hug.

No, thought John now, sitting at the narrow table fearing the worst about what else Jason was going to say. But anything more could not hurt as much as this. Grampa doesn't look too good, *mitakoja*.

He was overcome momentarily by a sense of despair and deep sorrow for the shame these public proceedings would inflict upon his children, his wife, the young children who held him in high regard; upon Aurelia, whose only flaw was that she loved him; upon Benno and his father and all those who held on to the idea that what distinguished the Dakotapi from all others in this world was the powerful and compelling individual sense of obligation toward one's relatives.

Jason Big Pipe, the young man whose testimony was being used to discredit John Tatekeya, was the grandson of Red Shield, the old, respected leader of the Kaposia band of the Isianti, a contemporary of Benno's, a man who lived from crisis to crisis but one who provided for others' stability and faith in a world of swift and unpredictable transition.

When John was just a boy this old man had brought to the Tatekeya home the striped quills and the tobacco and requested that John's father take part in the important ceremony which would make them relatives, thus forever obliged to one another. John's father had participated in the ceremony because it was unheard of to refuse the invitation from a person of honor, even though his Christian wife had said that he must not do so.

"Be careful," she admonished him, "they will say that you are a heathen."

John's father had gone against his wife's wishes because he knew that the refusal to "makerelatives" in the traditional way was to ultimately take part in the attempted destruction of the nationhood so relentlessly defended for hundreds of years by the people even before the invasion of their lands by Europeans.

John's father had been purified in the sweatlodge, and then he sat on the ground for the pipe ceremony. Benno had prepared the ground, brushing the leaves away from a small space and making four little holes filled with red and white plumes as the beginning of important vows.

Sitting before these, John's father had taken the sacred pipe and held the pipestem to the ground saying, *"Uncheda, smoke this pipe and give me this day something to eat."*

The people in various groups had approached and entered the medicine lodge, and members of each group were made relatives to the other. To smoke ceremonially was to *wacekiya*, and what this meant, John's father had told him, was that these ancient rituals at Old Agency, done in secrecy because of the many levels of resistance and opposition by those in the community, these acts between the fathers and grandfathers renewed relationships and respect between them. These acts caused these relatives "to have trust in one another," he was told. *This is a sacred day. This is a sacred day. This is a sacred day. This is a sacred day.*

John looked at Jason's handsome face, his guileless eyes, and wondered what had prompted this young man's incriminating testimony against him. Why would this young man do this thing?

He knew no answer. And he began to believe that perhaps he deserved this kind of humiliation. He was himself, after all, culpable.

John looked out across the courtroom and saw Jason's older brother, Sheridan, sitting beside the huge, pale woman who was his wife. He looked like he was about to go to sleep, bored and sullen.

John glanced over at his own wife, her smooth face bland and expressionless. She was sitting beside their daughter in one of the back rows of the courtroom. Neither of them looked up at him.

After that public reference to "some woman in there" driving John's pickup, these two women so important in his life would cease attending the trial, and John knew he would not go to his daughter's home as the weekend recess loomed ahead. John also knew that they would not come again to the courthouse in support of him, and from that time he felt alone in the same way that he had felt alone since the death of Benno, and he wished for the whole insufferable, abusive ordeal to end. There will be no winners here, he thought.

13

Testimony: Day Two (continued)

Q: Now, Mr. Smith, where do you live?

A: Out in East Pierre.

Q: Are you a member of the tribe?

A: No sir. But I've always lived amongst 'em. Some of my best friends are them Indian boys out there.

Q: Now, during 1965, the months of January, first of all, we'll take it January to June of '65. Where were you living?

A: Now, let's see. I think I was living out on the reservation then. Yes, I was sort of camping out in an old house there that used to be the old Standing place. Just renting it, you know, for little or nothin' because I do some custom work out there now and then.

Q: Where is that from the home of Aurelia Blue?

A: Just across an eighty acres there.

Q: Across a pasture? Or a field?

A: Yes. I lived on the south side and she lived on the north side of that eighty.

Q: Did you know Mrs. Blue?

A: Yes. I know the young woman. And the old lady, too.

Q: Did you know Mr. Tatekeya's vehicle, what kind of a vehicle did he have then?

A: Yeah. He had an International pickup. I rode with him a few times.

Q: Did you ever see Mr. Tatekeya down there during that period of time?

A: Oh, yes! He was down there a lot. Well, I think he was down there practically ever' week. Sometimes . . . I don't know whether he was there, but when I'd go to bed his pickup was there, and when I'd get up in the morning it was there, and sometimes *(laughing)* it would be there 'til Wednesday, and sometimes Monday it would disappear. And, you know *(laughing)*, you drawed your own conclusions. *(more seriously)* Generally, on Saturday is when it would show up, Saturday afternoon. *(nodding his head to show agreement with his own statement)*

Q: Have you ever been with Mr. Tatekeya in his home?

A: Yes. I was in that house twice just for a few minutes.

Q: When was that?

A: Oh, that was in . . . must have been the summer of '65.

Q: I see. On that occasion, did Mr. Tatekeya have occasion to tell his wife where he was going?

A: Yeah, well, he'd tell her that him and me was going to fix fences.

Q: Then where would he go?

A: Well, he'd generally wind up out to the Blue place. Sometimes I'd go with him, too.

Just as Mr. Smith began to warm to his subject, the judge intervened, saying, "Well, I think that all that's relevant here is the absence of Mr. Tatekeya from his place. I don't think we need to go into anything further, either the Aurelia Blue matter or anyplace else."

Looking at the District Attorney with just a trace of impatience, he said, "Sir. Mr. States Attorney. Mr. Cunningham. Do you have any objection?"

"Objection," Mr. Cunningham said, raising his voice finally. "Yes. I think that this is irrelevant."

"Well, now, your honor," said Mr. Nelson III, "may I go into the drinking patterns of Mr. Tatekeya, your honor?"

"You already have," said the judge. "You've certainly gone

into that," he said, shaking his head. And then, "I have no objection. Certainly."

The questioning resumed:

Q: During this period, would you observe whether or not he was drinking?

A: Well, yes, we was both drinking a little. I drank a little myself at that time. I don't deny that. I haven't drank now for a year and a half, but at that time, I'll admit, I was drinking a little.

Q: And how much would Mr. Tatekeya drink?

A: Well, I don't know. It's hard to say. All he could get aholt of, I guess. *(laughing)* He done a fair job of drinking and a pretty fair job of holding it.

Q: Okay. That's all I have.

The District Attorney stood up and walked carefully to the middle ground. He cradled a pencil in the palm of his hand.

Q: Now, Mr. Smith. Are you a convicted felon?

A: What's . . . that?

Q: Are you a convicted felon?

"Objection, your honor," began the defense.

"Overruled," said the judge. "Answer the question, sir."

Q: Are you a convicted felon, Mr. Smith?

A: Well, but . . . that was . . .

Q: Answer the question, please.

A: Well, yes . . .

Q: No further questions.

14

That night, John and Aurelia lay quietly beside one another, unable to put aside thoughts of the intimidating testimony of the past days.

"John," she said into the darkness. And, talking Indian, she mused, "When the grass dance was disclaimed by my mother and the people of her tribe, uh, well, you know . . ."

He said nothing.

The silence between them was taken over by their own private thoughts, which were filled with the flawless memories of a prophetic history they shared and both feared would end badly. Only now were they beginning to understand that events would move relentlessly forward, that there was little they could do.

When they had both nearly forgotten her half-finished sentence, John answered, "Yes. I know." And he covered his eyes with his arm, pretending to be unmoved by this intimate feeling that Aurelia was trying to express.

She continued, then.

"They said, I mean, the Christians said and therefore some of the people said, too, that to take off their clothes and paint themselves was evil and they should not dance to those precious songs."

He listened in silence to this story of hers, not really attentive to the subject matter because he had heard her tell it many times, and he knew that his mother, too, had been a part of this startling, shameless truth of history, and so the story itself was nothing new.

Aurelia went on.

"They said to pray to the east, west, north, and south"—in the darkness he could feel her motioning with her hands—"was to pray to the winds, and it was, therefore, evil."

With her slim fingers she lifted her heavy, black hair from her neck and smoothed it behind her ear, and he felt her move toward him.

"And my mother came to believe that." She drew herself up as though feeling suddenly cold.

"M-m-m."

He turned toward her and touched the warmth between her bare thighs, and in the darkness, he could feel her look at him as if from far away, smiling.

"A-aye-e-e," she scoffed quietly, pushing his hand away. "You're always *doing* that."

But she turned to him quickly, stretched full-length beside him, and her body was warm and soft, and the story she was telling him, as she had told it before, was forgotten. For the moment. John felt the tension in his body diminish as she held him.

Aurelia fell asleep in his arms, and as she slept, he struggled with his thoughts. Jason's testimony. How the testimony of the old drunk, Smitty, made him look like a fool, and, ultimately, what the woman beside him thought of her own intimate participation in such a debacle. Even more puzzling, what was it that the woman beside him wanted from him as she tried to fathom the impact of the aggressive religion and law of white men upon the people and their lives?

He could not help her. There will be no reprieve, he thought. No means of escape. At that moment, in the darkness, John instinctively knew and, regretfully, accepted the fact that it was over. The solemn and extraordinary liaison that he and Aurelia treasured would, finally, be done. Forever changed. His desire reconciled. And her urgency turned to indifference.

How Aurelia felt about her mother's response to new religious thought and practice had begun to take on a kind of desperate importance for her, and John feared that it would, sooner or later, be clear to her that she, too, like her mother, and his, had played with marked cards, played her hand against her will. The game would have to be taken into account. By all of us, thought John.

Because he was the only one who knew of her fragmented but continuous attempts at understanding her mother's rejection of tradition, John began to wonder in recent months, and especially since the trial began, if she was going to be able to reconcile herself to the consequence of this trial, their separation.

He again felt the anxiety about the outcome of the trial. Not whether he would win or lose. Not whether he would get paid for his missing cattle or have them returned to him. Not even whether the thief would be punished or go free. Rather, his fear that an honorable life for his people was no longer possible rose in his throat. There were so many things that he had not paid attention to, and he knew now what terrible risk there was in such inattentiveness.

It was true that the young man who had stolen his cattle, a young white man who had grown up on his parents' ranch bordering the reservation, the spoiled son of well-to-do white cattlemen and -women, was no bargain as far as the white community which surrounded John's place was concerned, and it might be true, too, that Smitty's damaging testimony gave people a bad impression of John. But it was only when he heard it aloud, spoken in the courtroom, it was only then, when he looked into the eyes of the people who loved him, that John acknowledged in his heart the uncompromising pride and courage inherent in the Dakotah way of life, and the loss of it, momentarily at least, in the behavior of everyone connected with this miserable trial. Now, at this trial, humiliated in front of his loved ones, he knew that the claims the Dakotahs had always made concerning their ideals would never again be seen as invincible. Not by him. Not by those who were present at this gathering. That was the price of the entrenchment of white civilization in his life and the lives of others.

Jason Big Pipe's testimony rang in his cars, and he knew that for some the old, familial bonds of respect for one another, those significant communal codes of behavior as old as the tribes themselves, were no longer held as intrinsically valuable. It began long ago, he now believed. But because of the recent flooding of the homelands, the constant moving about and resettlement, and the repeated destruction of the places where the people were born and buried for century upon century, one generation upon the next generation, it was now a crucial matter.

He sat up, naked and shivering.

Who would his children be?

Where would his children live? His grandchildren?

In the darkness, he buried his head in his hands. It was these kinds of questions that kept John awake at Aurelia's side that night. For his deep-seated suspicion would not go away: the attempt to find justice in the white man's law would unwittingly reveal the fraudulent nature of all their lives and the lives of those who were to come after him.

15

Testimony: Day Three
October 1967

Nothing could have prepared those at the trial for the subtle meaning of the events of the third day of testimony, and indeed, for many of them, the testimony held little significance beyond the rather generalized setting forth of the so-called material facts in the case. For John Tatekeya, however, the time had come to put his suspicions to the test. As he took the witness stand again, he had determined in some forlorn yet angry way, deciding on the spur of the moment in just the few minutes that it took him to walk from his vehicle into the courthouse, that he would sift purpose from this otherwise empty and insignificant ritual in whatever way he could.

He lingered briefly on the steps of the gray, imposing building and pulled the smoke heavily from his cigarette, inhaling deeply. Such a day as this, he thought, held no promise at all, unless one forced out the existent decay which it held with whatever distasteful and foul means were at hand. Goddamn! Son-of-a-bitch!

With his third finger and thumb, he flicked his cigarette butt viciously toward the gutter and entered the building through the heavy glass doors, passing the dignified, bearded sentinel without a glance.

Q: Now, Mr. Tatekeya, since the fall of 1965, have you seen any of those missing cattle since then?

A: Yes. I seen several of them.

Q: You have?

A: Yes.

Q: Where did you see them?

A: Well, I seen one of them over there north of Highmore. I seen one of them up east of Yankton, by Irene.

Q: And did you see one down there, near Ainsworth, Nebraska?

A: I seen *a couple of them* down there.

At this answer, unexpected but hoped for by the young white man's defense attorney, John looked squarely into the cowboy's disbelieving and astonished eyes, then at Mr. Joseph Nelson III, who saw his chance and leapt to his feet shouting triumphantly, "Just a moment! Your honor!"

Waving his arm at the judge, he called, "I have a motion. I have a motion."

Because of a technicality, the second critter at Ainsworth which John identified in testimony was not mentioned in the indictment, and those closely connected with the trial knew that his seemingly offhand mention of "a couple of them" was a blow to his case. Three critters were named in the indictment. Not four. A cause for mistrial, surely.

"May we approach the bench?" asked the District Attorney, agitated, fearful.

"You may," answered the judge.

As the three lawyers conferred quietly but earnestly, John looked over at Sheridan's heavy, round face. He was no longer lounging carelessly in his seat. The young man's eyes were suddenly alert, attentive, and he leaned over to whisper something to his wife, who looked merely frightened. He grabbed his brother Jason's knee and then hit it with his fist lightly, triumphantly.

John stared into Sheridan's face and knew, at that moment, that he had put together some of the pieces of the puzzle. The missing information. He knew now why Harvey had been so noncommittal when he had gone to his place to ask for help in finding his cattle. He knew now why the Big Pipe brothers had attended this trial so fastidiously and why Sheridan lounged in the spectators' seats so casually every day, though he was neither witness nor participant. And he knew now why Jason Big Pipe, the relative of his grandfather Red Shield and the middle son of his own brother, had testified falsely against him.

The sons of Harvey Big Pipe, John decided at that moment, had been engaged in the theft more fully than they had let on, quite possibly as participants in the actual crime. Gravely, seriously, John took in these thoughts and began to realize that if he never knew anything further concerning the theft, and even if he lost the trial, which was quite possible now, he would not again feel pain with such temporal clarity. He sat still, astounded. Humbled. His face felt feverish. The blood throbbed in his temples.

Judge Niklos excused the jury, and the twelve men who were sitting in judgment on this strange little drama began to file out of the courtroom into their small chambers. Some of them, who had seen nothing significant in the testimony and had perhaps not heard the Tatekeya statement, looked around the room, confused and perplexed.

"I will see the defendant and his lawyer in my office," the judge said, looking at John.

"But first, Mr. Nelson, what do you have to say?"

"Comes, now, the defendant and moves for a mistrial," said Mr. Nelson III with enthusiasm, "upon the grounds and for the reason that shortly before the commencement of this trial, a motion was made for a continuance on the grounds that a fourth cow had not been disclosed to the defendant and his attorney, in accordance with the pretrial order of the court and the discovery proceedings, at this time the United States Attorney agreed that no mention would be made of the fourth critter. No pictures were introduced. And that he would caution his witnesses not to mention the fourth animal in Nebraska."

He drew in his breath and read on from notes obviously prepared beforehand for just such an eventuality as this. The defense, it seemed, had been lying in wait for such an answer and could not contain its glee.

He read on:

"That the court indicated that in light of that ruling or that announcement by the United States Attorney, the motion for continuance would be denied.

"That the fourth animal has now been mentioned by the complaining witness before this jury. The jury heard the testimony and, by necessity, it was brought home more to them because of this motion.

"That this is prejudicial; it violates the rights of the defendant in this matter, in that the continuance was not granted.

"That the fact that it was unintentional, if such is the fact, does not any the less remove the prejudice of the defendant's rights. The jury now knows of a fourth cow."

In his chambers, the judge turned to the District Attorney.

"What do you have to say, Mr. Cunningham?"

Visibly shaken, the cowboy lawyer looked over at his client.

"Mr. Tatekeya," he began uncertainly and slowly. "Do you remember my talking to you in my rooms about not mentioning that steer calf down there in Ainsworth?"

"Yes."

"I take it that it was . . ." He groped for words and started again.

Clearing his throat, "I take it that it was . . . just an accident? Had you forgotten about that when you mentioned that you found two of them down there?"

"It could be. I'm not an expert in this courtroom . . . so . . ." John, spreading his hands on his knees, refused to look at his lawyer.

"Well, your honor," the District Attorney said, turning to the judge, "I'm sure that the witness did it unintentionally. The court and counsel is well aware of the fact that the witness is not one of a very high education."

John still did not look up.

The lawyer went on, "He's been, you know, a rather difficult witness to handle as far as the questioning is concerned, and I'm certain that whatever he did or said, it was not intentional.

"Furthermore," he said, gathering his composure, "I'm certain that no prejudice was created by any such comment by the witness before the jury; in fact, I . . . uh . . . I think that the statement was probably not even heard by many of the jurors. It wasn't said very loudly. And I certainly didn't intend to have the witness disclose two head of cattle down there at Ainsworth, even though we took pictures of both for evidence and, I think, it's obvious from the way I asked the question. I think of any question I asked, that was certainly a leading question."

The conference in the judge's chambers became more composed as the District Attorney talked in a reasonable tone and the judge attempted to regain the protocol expected of this proceeding.

"Sir," the judge said, addressing Mr. Cunningham, "I assume from the question that you asked Mr. Tatekeya, you did assure him that he was to strictly limit his testimony to three cows, or three animals at least, and not to mention the fourth."

"That's correct, your honor," the District Attorney responded. "But, after all, he is missing forty-two head, and he doesn't like the idea that we're going to trial on only three. And that this technicality should . . ."

"Now, now . . ." admonished the judge, in a tone something like that of an all-knowing adult addressing a recalcitrant child. "You know as well as I do that is immaterial to this particular indictment. This indictment, let me remind you, is for three animals and three animals only. You surely know the law, and the only question now is, does your client know the law?"

With that, he turned to John.

"Now, Mr. Tatekeya, how much education have you had?"

John said nothing.

Mr. Niklos began again, enunciating carefully, thinking that John did not understand the question.

"How far did you go in school?"

"Oh, about far enough . . . " John said tiredly.

Sternly, the judge said, "Just a minute now, Mr. Tatekeya. You must answer my question. How much education have you had?"

"I passed the sixth grade at Rapid City Indian School," John answered, paused, and then volunteered, "and then I went into the army. It was 1916."

He thought it best not to mention that he had lied about his age to get into the U.S. Army, that he was not even a citizen of the United States at the time, that he had run away from that boarding school like an escapee from a jail, and that his educational experience had been limited, mostly, to learning to speak English, play the clarinet, and milk cows.

"Well," said the judge rather vacantly, not realizing that this educational and military experience was probably on a par with or even superior to most of the educational experience of the white farmers and ranchers in the area, and therefore not evidence that John was in any way incapacitated.

'Very well." Absently.

"I'll tell you. I'm tempted," he said to the room at large. "I'd just as soon go home, actually. I'd like to grant the motion for a mistrial."

Do it, thought John.

"Your honor," began Mr. Nelson III, trying to take advantage of this seeming pause and hesitation on the part of the judge. "I would like to say this: the fact that the U.S. Attorney might have cautioned him does not remove the prejudice and the error."

"Well, Mr. Nelson. I'm going to tell you this: I am not certain that the jury heard the remark, either. It was said in a rather low manner. I know the court reporter heard it. And I heard it."

"And I heard it, your honor," said Nelson.

"And you heard it," repeated the judge, smiling. "And you were looking for it, weren't you? I don't think there is any question about that! And I'm not sure whether the jury heard it or not."

The room fell silent momentarily, and the only sound John could hear was the ticking of the huge clock which stood at the end of the room. The prospect of finishing the trial filled John with despair, for it seemed obvious to him now that this judge and these lawyers could do nothing for him. He listened with little interest as they resolved the dilemma his testimony had presented.

"Now," the judge told Mr. Nelson, "if you want me to, I will caution the jury and tell them, right now, when I have them come back in, that they are to consider only three cows, that there are only three cows in question in this indictment; that he's testified here already that he missed a lot of other calves and yearlings but that they are to consider the testimony only as it relates to three critters and that all the other cows are not to be considered. Nor are they to draw any possible inference that this defendant had anything to do . . . and that he's not even charged with any more than three cows."

The judge dabbed at his face with a white monogrammed handkerchief and sat cleaning his glasses.

"Now, if you want me to so instruct the jury, I'll do it at this time."

He paused and put his glasses on, looking up at the defense attorney, and folded his handkerchief carefully, lifting up the folds of his black gown and putting the handkerchief in his shirt pocket.

"Now, if you prefer I not so instruct the jury, I won't. But I'm leaving it up to you."

"I feel, your honor," said Joseph Nelson III, a young man whose father and grandfather had both, in the not-so-distant past, tried cases before this same judge, and who saw himself as therefore having a family reputation which he thought would get him a more favorable ruling, "I feel, your honor, that such an instruction would work to the prejudice of my client, the defendant."

"Very well, then," said Judge Niklos. "I will not so instruct the jury."

"But," protested young Nelson, "that my client, in light of this, is entitled to a mistrial."

"Well," said the judge, "I'm going to deny your motion for a mistrial."

As he got up from his desk, he said cheerily to all, "Now, do you want a little recess?"

16

Inexplicably, a three-day recess in the trial was called by the judge, a move which was seen by John as just another delay and an unreasonable way to prolong his own personal agony. He was looking for any excuse now to quit this matter.

As John and the District Attorney walked back into the courtroom to collect their belongings and leave the building, the lawyer said tightly, "That was a close one, John. "This thing could have gone into a mistrial over that mistake, John," he said, "and we can't afford another one like that! But, I think we're okay. Remember, John, you can't . . ."

As the lawyer paused, trying to find the right words to chastise his client, John said quietly, "I have a good memory, cowboy."

"Uh . . ."

They looked at each other warily.

Instead of leaving the building, they both sat down suddenly at one of the tables and started to talk and listen to one another for the first time since the case had come to trial.

"I cannot begin to explain what happened as I answered your questions, lawman," said John, "because it is of no concern to you and it is too complicated. But one thing you must understand from me is that all of us who were born in this country naked have been taught something other than your ways. What you talk about and what you care about has very little to do with my life. Do you understand that?"

"No, of course I don't," said the lawyer.

"And besides," he went on indignantly, "I just don't believe it. The law is important to everyone's life, John, even an Indian's. Maybe *especially* an Indian's."

"Mr. Cunningham, we have been taught from the time we are infants that with all of the people around us we should live happy and friendly with them and then we will have everything turn out all right," John said. "Everything in our way of life points to the idea of doing the right things with our relatives. Your history books say that all the Dakotahs and Lakotahs do is fight and murder all the time. That is not true about us, you know. We know how to live with our relatives."

This was the longest speech that John had engaged in since the attorney had met him, and the white man tried to make sense of what he was saying.

John knew that he was not getting across what was most significant on his mind, and he ruefully thought about Jason and Sheridan, the sons of his own brother who had somehow and for some reason violated the ways that the people had worked out for thousands of years as survival tactics in a hostile and dangerous world. John did not know how to explain the significance of this finding to his lawyer.

He got up and walked across the room. He pulled a pack of cigarettes from his shirt pocket and offered one to his lawyer, who shook his head and said only, "Those things are bad for you, John."

John carefully lit one for himself, drawing the smoke deep into his lungs.

"You know, lawman, this circus here"—he waved his arm to indicate the courtroom still being cleared for the recess—"it is all being done to shame me, to make me look bad."

"Well, John . . ." began the District Attorney, who then lapsed into silence, sensing that his lecture on unbounded pride might not be useful at this moment.

Quietly, John continued: "I do not agree to this foolishness! And I do not want to go on with it."

He looked deeply into the lawyer's eyes, trying to convince him that terrible damage had been done as the result of this trial and it would be forever seen as a threat to the faith and humanity of his relatives. But he said only, "This young white man who stole forty-two head of my cattle, he can sit there and lie and pretend his innocence and he does not even have to testify. He will not come to the stand as I have done."

He paused.

"The lawyers ask me questions about things that are none of their business and suggest that I stole my own cattle. How do you account for such a stupid way of getting to the truth of things? What is this?" he asked indignantly.

"I do not agree to this foolishness," he repeated with more vigor this time, jamming his cigarette into the ashtray.

Instantly, the lawyer knew that he must prevent John from walking away from this.

"But you will agree, John," he argued, "if you expect this man to be convicted on this indictment and if you expect to get justice. You did agree essentially when you came to this trial."

"Do not misunderstand me, lawyer," John said tersely, angry now and thinking seriously about walking out of the courtroom, out of the building, and driving back to his place on the reservation.

"I am an Indian, just like that judge said," explained John. "And what that means these days is that I've got myself to look after. I don't have anything invested in your law, and it has never defended me or my people. I don't have my forty-two head of cattle. I don't have any reason to believe that I will be paid for them even if we win this case. The most I could get is payment for three head."

John sat at the edge of his chair with his head down, his elbows resting on his knees. "I am a poor man, you know, and I am mad as hell that I have been made even poorer now," he said.

He could talk about these things that made him angry during this unexpected moment of intimacy between himself and the attorney for the United States of America, but what he would not talk about was the thing which brought him the greatest sorrow: the unaccountable behavior of two young men, the Big Pipe brothers for whom he had been supportive as they had grown to adulthood, two young men whose parents had accepted eagle plumes from John after each birth.

Aloud he said, "I don't have my reputation. You can see here that many people have testified against me. Yet I am not the thief! Even my wife refuses to come and listen to this with my eldest daughter. I don't have the goodwill and respect of anyone here. Not even you, lawman, if you were to be honest."

He had seen the shame in the lawyer's manner when Jason Big Pipe had talked of the woman driving his rig, intimating that John might be involved in what the lawyer would surely term adulterous behavior.

The lawyer said nothing.

"I have only the pity of some people. They're saying 'that poor goddamned son-of-a-bitch.' And the hatred of others."

The sullen face of Sheridan Big Pipe flashed before him, and the testimony of Jason echoed in the marble halls of the courthouse. What has happened here? John tried to understand the hatred of these young men toward him. The extent to which present behavior may be accounted for in terms of historical expectations troubled John, and he fell to thinking about the issues of this kind raised in his recent conversations with Aurelia. What happens to the people when new ways are forced upon us? Do we begin to hate one another? If so, why? When my mother became a Christian, did she set in motion my uncertainty? As my land is inundated by the white man's deliberate flood, is my spirit also weeping for its lost strength? Is Benno looking for me? What can I do now?

Such questions were profoundly disturbing.

"Listen, John," said the lawyer, suddenly drawing John's attention back to the stuffy courtroom. "You can feel sorry for yourself if you want to, but I'm not going to let you give up. I'm going to win this case for you because it is right and fair for us to win. No one hates you here, John," he said as he picked up his briefcase.

John stood with his back to his lawyer, gazing out of the window at the street below. Noon traffic clogged the fourway stop, and people straggled from the Federal Building into the restaurants and shops across the street. An old man with a cane made his way slowly down a side street, away from the people and the traffic, and John found himself wondering where the old man was headed. And as he stood in deep thought, he knew more than ever now that winning or losing the trial did not matter.

Silence hung in the warm, close air.

The lawyer tried again. "John, you can't afford to have all this pride. Don't worry about your reputation. So what if some things have come out that make you look bad? What we need to do is . . ." And then he changed his thoughts: "John, have you heard that to have too much pride is to . . ."

"Yes. I have heard that," said John, interrupting. "Christians say pride goeth before a fall. I am not totally without knowledge, you see," John said as he turned and smiled for the first time since the conversation began.

"It comes from the Bible, yes? A story about Adam and Eve, first man and first woman, something like the *Tokahe,* I suppose. They were told to leave the Garden because they disobeyed God, is that so?"

"Yes."

"So, what do you think it means?" asked John.

"What it means," said the lawyer with certainty, "is that arrogance in the face of justice and the law and God is no virtue, John. Do you know what I am getting at?"

John lapsed into silence.

"Do you know what arrogance really means, John?" asked the cowboy lawyer tentatively.

In near despair now, John looked at his lawyer and forced a smile. You and I will never understand each other, he thought. How can you chastise me, a Dakotah, about arrogance when it has been your people who have forced your religion on everyone throughout the world, your people who changed the rivers that we live by and flooded our lands and brought to us the kind of world that Gray Plume and Benno and the others feared?

John picked up his jacket and turned with seriousness to his lawyer. As he shook hands with him, he said, "I am grateful to you for your efforts here in this courtroom. I know that you are a sincere man."

He walked out the door.

The lawyer looked after him wondering if he had insulted him. He worried that his client might not show up for the Tuesday morning session.

John had said nothing to the lawyer about what he had finally begun to accept concerning the significance of this trial, for it had precious little to do with arrogance and justice and God. It was the understanding which came to him while he watched Sheridan's face during the testimony that morning. I put the case up for grabs, so to speak, thought John, and when I did so Sheridan behaved in such a way that I knew he had more than just a passing interest in its outcome. While this issue may have seemed to the District Attorney, had he known about it, parochial and trivial, it consumed the thoughts of Tatekeya.

It is not only that I now know Harvey Big Pipe's sons to be implicated in the theft, he mused. I know too that their father, the man with whom I am expected to behave as a brother, the man with whom I share important responsibilities, this man and I share the risk of losing our lives as brothers for the first time in nearly half a century.

Frail and sick, unable to work and take active part in community affairs, Harvey would now be faced with loss of the sacred meaning of trust in his brother, a relationship which signified for them both the moral quality of the social world in which their kinship duties were strictly ordered.

As he drove toward his daughter's house located out on Airport Road, John suddenly made a left turn at the stoplight and headed east toward the reservation. Traces of snow fell on his windshield, the merest flecks of icy moisture which melted as quickly as they touched the glass.

Part Two

Summation
A Recapitulation

The Man That Is Struck by the Ree

"I am not going to beg for my life; I believe I am a man, and I am not going to beg you for my life. I see you here, and your manners and situation are enough to scare any of us; but if I was afraid I would squat down, but I don't." (Translation)

Summer 1856

17

At home, alone, John stood at the door peering into the dusk at the sparse snowflakes drifting down, minute light flakes which probably wouldn't last long, the kind recognized by those who live on the Dakota prairie as fleeting signs, brief warnings of the beginning of winter, harbingers of those freezing, blinding blizzard winds which often accompany the relentless cold.

The wet flakes melted listlessly away. To John they seemed gentle, almost benign, though he knew better. With a fork, he speared chunks of the boiled beef from the cold broth left setting out in a bowl on the kitchen table, careful to remember not to use any salt. He ate them hungrily, gulped down the rest of his coffee, and pulled on his leather gloves.

It would be dark in a couple of hours, he thought. Even now, the sky, the dull glare of the river, and the whitened, cold earth merged into a bluish-white grayness that chilled him to the bone. This would be only the first of several brief cold snaps that would precede the relentless winter, and he looked forward to the inevitable letup which invariably followed these first signs, thinking about tomorrow when it would probably turn warm, and the sun would shine, and he could fix fence in his shirtsleeves.

He dreaded the two-mile walk to the church and he was tempted to drive, but he decided to follow Benno's wishes again this time.

"You should always walk," Benno used to tell him. "Because then you have time to think and prepare yourself, and whatever is around you can tell you what you need to know.

"It is a good time, then," Benno said, "to get yourself ready."

But now he was in a hurry and he was late. He had to open up the building and get his own things ready. The little water drum, the hide, along with the seven stones, were kept in his bedroom, and he had to make sure that he delivered them to his nephew, who tied the drum, in time to ready it for the ritual singing and drumming.

This would probably be the last service to be held in the little church before the bad winter weather set in, after which they would meet in the members' homes. Ordinarily, John would be perspiring in his preparations, and he would have to take off the extra sweater he wore, but this time, for some inexplicable reason, he felt a chill.

People would probably bring blankets to cover their legs or shoulders throughout the night, he thought. And then, selfishly, he wondered how much they knew about his trial. News travels fast in this community, he thought, and one might say that bad news travels especially fast. He smiled and decided that it didn't matter.

When he walked into the barren churchyard, several cars were already there, motors running. But he paid no attention to the fact that he was late again. He noticed Harvey's daughter Clarissa sitting in her car, waiting, with her two boys and her mother. Harvey wasn't with them.

John hurried into the building, opening the unlocked door, and hauled some wood and kindling into the back room. He lighted a small fire in the black, oblong heating stove. Harvey's grandson Philip helped him, dashing in and out with armsful of wood and offering a match when John searched futilely in his pockets. Outside near the sweatlodge, which was almost hidden in the brush, the fire man already stirred the glowing embers in preparation for the sacred fire which would be placed in a crucible in the middle of the room, to be replenished and reshaped throughout the night.

"Is your grampa sick?"

"Yeah."

"Why didn't he come? Gray Iron will be here, and maybe he could help him."

"I don't know."

People began drifting in and seating themselves around the room wherever they could be comfortable. Some of the older women brought pillows and blankets with them; the younger people with children brought sacks of extra clothes, bedding for infants, were settling the children and spreading blankets.

John felt helpless as he watched the young man beside him, for he was reminded of himself so many years ago. He had been content to work as an assistant to Benno, to learn the songs, a helper to his father and others for whom the philosophical speculation concerning the meaning of life was a serious matter. And he could see that this young man was also one with great potential such as he had possessed at one time. He knew that it had been widely expected that he would, sooner or later, enter into these religious matters as a significant figure, but, of course, he had not done so. He was a devotee and a believer in the medicine. He knew all the songs. And he continued to help in whatever way he could. But nothing more was possible for him.

Often he served as instructor to the young children who gathered at these festivities, especially those meetings held in the summer.

"Your own tipi will have four sacred poles," he would tell the younger relatives.

"You must have the three main poles"—and he would cross the forefinger of his right hand over two fingers of his left hand—"and, then, one which is the doorpost."

He would turn his right hand over and then lay two fingers diagonally across the others.

He repeated his grandmother's story, that these poles "represented the land tortoise because of all the animals, that land tortoise had the strongest paws, and as a consequence, it was adapted to hold up the lodge."

"Besides," she told him, "he is the mythological creature who makes the apposition between the water and the land a bridge and not an abyss."

John returned to the stove and stood there with Philip, warming his hands and waiting for the singers to compose themselves. He wanted to speak to the young man, tell him all the stories he knew about the preparations for such religious ceremonies.

"I haven't told those stories in a very long time," he said aloud to the young man and then said nothing more, leaving Philip puzzled and quiet. The thought occurred to John that he was very likely no longer worthy for such tellings, for when the fathers and Benno had approached the medicine lodge and sent out invitations over and over again, they sorrowed silently that John was never among the real initiates.

It was a sad thing for Benno, who had many expectations of his children, and it was with regret that John recognized that he had been, indeed, a disappointment to others. The way he lived his life and conducted himself certainly lacked propriety, and no one was more aware of it than John himself.

He looked at the young man standing in front of him. And he said nothing.

Later, as the drum chief knelt beside him, he sang: "*Heciya ya yo wiconi ye ye do. Heciya ya yo wiconi ye ye do. Heciya ya yo wiconi ye ye do. Cekiya ya yo wiconi ye ye do heyana he de do we.*" He began to feel warm. Soon he would have to remove his coat and sweater. And the spirits would surely come.

18

He was more tired than he cared to own up to, but he consoled himself as he walked home the next morning by remembering that Benno would have found such a day as this one calming, soothing, and he would make the most of it. The sun rose higher in the sky, the leaves were golden and withered, and the air was sharp and sweet. The glare of the river blinded him and he turned away. It's that time of year, he thought, when you just want to fold your arms and sit in the warm sun.

Instead, when he reached his place he swung the tailgate of his rig open and carefully placed spools of barbed wire, sacks of nails and a hammer, his posthole auger, and a wire stretcher in the long narrow bed. He motioned for the dog to jump in and sit.

He drove down the graveled road about two miles, pulled off into the ditch, then up to the fence lines, and parked. He began the tedious task of stretching the fifth barbed wire on that half-mile hillside next to the watering trough where the cattle always seemed to sense the weakness of only four wires.

With the sun climbing into the sky behind him warming his back, he thought about his dilemma and wondered what his mother, that lady of propriety and manners and modesty, the daughter of a respected Isianti Presbyterian churchman from Old Agency, would think of this impeachment which had suddenly become a part of his life, though he had neither sought it nor given it purpose. He held each end of the short rod and walked backward, laying down the wire on the ground diagonally to the posts. Absorbed, he began tacking the wire to the fence posts.

He didn't hear his younger brother drive up and was startled by his voice.

"Hey, they got you workin', huh?" Dan hollered from the window of his red Pontiac four-door.

John looked up and smiled.

"Where the hell you been?" he asked.

He walked over to the passenger's side, opened the door, and sat down beside his brother.

They shook hands and John repeated his question.

"It's not where I been," said Dan, laughing. "It's where I'm going."

He reached under the seat, took out a bottle of Early Times, unscrewed the cap, and took a long drink.

Smiling, he handed the bottle to John, who shook his head.

"All right," John said, trying to enter into the good mood, "where you going?"

And they both laughed.

Relaxed now, they sat together and looked out over the brown hills. John lit up a cigarette, cupping the match with his hands. The wind was gusting a bit now, and the dried leaves and grasses rolled gently. Stark white clouds hung against the brilliant blue of the sky, and a small cluster of birds swung toward the river.

Neither of them mentioned the trial.

"I'm headed to Bismarck for the celebration," said Dan, breaking the brief silence between them. "You want to come along?" His words drifted into the insistent wind.

"I'm broke," said John.

"Hell, what else is new?" scoffed his brother. "You won't have no coins tomorrow either, will you? Or the next day? Or next week?"

He pulled out his wallet and showed John several hundred-dollar bills and gave him one.

"Hey," he said enthusiastically, "I sold that Appie mare that Steven has been wanting and I made him pay for her. Look at that," and he slapped his hand against the wallet.

"You coming?"

"Yeah," said John. "Just a minute."

He walked back to the fence, cut the wire at the last post, placed the spool of wire in the cab of his pickup along with the rest of his tools, locked both doors to the rig, and left it parked alongside the fence.

"Let's go," he said as he got in Dan's car and slammed the door.

The dog, accustomed to such inconsistencies, turned down the opposite way and headed for home, trotting amiably, listing to one side, tongue lapping.

John and his youngest brother had not seen each other in several months, and as they settled in for the long drive to Bismarck they began to catch up on their lives. Dan put the bottle of whiskey under the seat and began to reminisce.

"You remember that time we sold them chickens, John?" he said, laughing.

"Jeez," he went on, "that was a long time ago, ennit?"

John's three little girls had come running toward Dan as he entered the house.

He picked them all up, tussled one onto his back and held the other two, one in each arm.

"What did you bring us, Uncle Dan?"

"Say, I didn't bring you nothin' this time," he said seriously as he bent over and put them all down on the floor. "I forgot."

He could see by their faces that they didn't believe him, so he pulled three Tootsie Rolls from his pocket and gravely handed them out, one for each little girl, the youngest getting hers first, then the middle child, then the eldest. They shook hands with him politely.

"Ina is in the hospital," they told him. "We don't know when she will come back."

Dan went into the kitchen and spoke to the woman he called his mother, the sister of his deceased blood mother, the woman who had raised him since childhood.

"He's out in the barn," she told him and then turned her back when she smelled the liquor on his breath, indicating that she was not interested in any further conversation with him.

John was putting the horse tack away when Dan approached him and asked if he wanted to go to Bismarck.

The dialogue was strangely precursory:

"I got no coins, younger brother, my wife's in the hospital at the Fort, and things are pretty tough around here."

"Yeah," Dan said, lurching just a little as he put one foot up on a railing. "But I got this," as he pulled a bottle from under his jacket.

"We sat there for nearly an hour," John remembered. "We got damn drunk, you know it? And that's when we got the idea."

Liberated by the booze to begin what he then considered to be a creative idea, John had said, "Listen, when the chickens go to roost, let's catch a bunch of them and stuff them in these empty grain bags. We can take them over to old Rasmussen. He'll buy them from us."

"Good idea," Dan had agreed.

The sun was just beginning to dip behind the hills when John and Dan got out some long wires from the hay barn, bent them into deep hooks at one end, and crept toward the chicken house "like a couple of wet dogs looking for a place to shake," they'd said later. They waited. Then they opened the door stealthily and stood in the darkness listening attentively to the muffled clucking of one or two of the more suspicious old birds.

The first two catches were executed brilliantly, and it wasn't until the chickens began squawking as they were stuffed into the grain bags that the whole operation went awry.

Alerted by their more unfortunate sisters, the roosting hens began to step agilely out of the way of the wire hooks. Some began to screech loudly and flap their wings, flying blindly like untargeted missiles toward the brothers' heads. John's hat was knocked off and he felt it crunch under his boot as he lurched forward, off-balance, then caught himself. Like a player in some kind of relentless farce, Dan fell toward the roosts, breaking one long pole from its moorings and whacking John across the nose with it as it swung toward the door.

The air was filled with chicken feathers. The loud squawking stirred the dogs from their sleeping places under the porch and brought them yelping toward the little chicken house. They scratched on the closed door and barked frantically. They started digging in the dirt at the door.

"I pressed myself against the wall and just stood there," John remembered. He had touched his nose carefully with one gloved hand and poked gently at the soft tissue under his eye, knowing full well that he'd have to explain his black eye to everybody for the next several days.

"You were cussin'!" he said, laughing.

As if by some prearranged signal, they had both tried to stand quietly, scarcely breathing. John heard Dan thrashing around and swearing softly in the midst of the feathers. He knew that the woman who was his mother must be standing at the door of the house listening to all this, but he also knew that she wouldn't interfere. At last, though, all got quiet for a minute and the hens went back to their roosting places. The dogs returned to their beds under the porch.

"Hey," John whispered loudly. "You OK?"

"Yeah."

"You want to quit?"

"Hell, no. I'm not quittin'. I just . . . got . . . to be . . . a little more careful."

Dan then pulled himself up from a crouching position. He decided that he would crawl under the tiered roosts and quietly pick off the hens from behind with his bare hands. John heard him crawling slowly under the roosts.

They both waited, again, for the hens to settle down.

John hooked a bird neatly, this time quickly grabbing her wings so that she couldn't flap them, and he stuffed her into the bag.

In the quiet he heard Dan swear hoarsely, "Jee-e-e-sus Christ!"

"*Taku? Taku?*"

"That goddamned chicken shit went down my neck!"

John guffawed.

And, later, "Jee-e-e-sus Christ!" Dan repeated. "The stink on these goddamned chickens . . . whoo-o-o-e-e-e-e-e."

But he, too, was hurriedly stuffing the birds in his sack, oblivious to the ludicrous spectacle of two grown men crouching in this smelly, cramped chicken coop making off with some of the most unattractive of God's creatures.

"Shit!" Dan muttered redundantly. "I never did like chickens." And then, "Jee-sus, they smell, ennit?"

"I'll never eat a piece of chicken again!"

And, in contradiction, "I used to like fried chicken, you know it?"

And, finally, "I can't believe I'm doing this!"

The two brothers worked quickly, then, sweating and swearing until they had looted the better share of the flock. What else were these useless, smelly creatures good for?

Dan backed the car up to the narrow door of the little shed, and they loaded the heavy sacks of chickens into the trunk, amidst loud and ongoing squawks and cries for help from the frantic birds that rang into the night.

"Hey, don't shut the lid," Dan admonished as though he knew the protocol of chicken stealing better than his brother. "They might smother."

They went to the now-darkened house to change their clothing and wash, then, after a quick visit to the startled and puzzled Rasmussen, whom they roused from a warm bed to buy their chickens, they slipped on through the night roads. They were on their way to the Bismarck celebration, the last of the late-summer meetings of the tribes and the largest gathering of Plains dancers and singers in the north country.

In the mnemonic retelling of that long-ago event, the brothers reconciled the reverential and historical with the comic and absurd. They kept right on telling the stories as they stopped for Claude and Hosie and picked up the drum at Eagle Butte.

"Where are the chickens?" Rose Tatekeya had inquired when she returned from the hospital and the strength had come back to her body and she walked innocently around the yard. Her husband pretended that he hadn't heard, saddled up his horse, and rode over the hill.

Later, at the evening meal, however, she wouldn't be put off.

"Where are the chickens?" she insisted.

When John left the table and she had the old lady by herself, she asked again, and the old gramma finally admitted that John had sold them.

"Sold them?" Rose asked in disbelief. "But why? Who did he sell them to?"

They sat at the table in silence, each of them a little hesitant to push this inquiry any further. But Rose, being a woman of forthrightness and action, refused to accept the nonanswers she had been getting.

"What did he sell the chickens for, Gramma?"

"He went to Bismarck," the old lady finally blurted. "With Dan."

Furious, Rose stormed out the door and confronted John.

"While I'm in the hospital you sell off my chickens just so that you can run around with that no-good brother of yours? What am I going to do now?"

Crying loudly and despairingly, she retreated to the house, and John walked disconsolately to the corral. Later, he accused the old lady who was a mother to him of being a troublemaker, and she packed her extra clothing in a black shawl and set out walking to her own house a mile and a half away, down on the creek. The little girls ran after her, calling, *"Unchi, Unchi."*

They cried for her to come back, but she wouldn't listen to them this time, refusing their pleas.

On the north road to Bismarck, Dan recalled, "The old woman was eventually forced into telling the truth of it, wasn't she?"

"Yeah," said John, chuckling.

"Oh, shit!" He went on, "When Rosie got home, man, was she mad!" He shook his head as though in wonder that he'd lived to tell of it all.

"Those were the bad old days, ennit, brother?" said Dan,

looking over at John, and they both, regretfully, and in hindsight, knew in their hearts that their behavior had been childish and irresponsible.

"But we were much younger then, ennit?" Smiling.

In unison, they started singing an old cowboy song: "From this valley they say we are going . . . do not hasten to bid us adieu . . ."

Claude and Hosie joined in.

19

It was Monday, the day before the beginning of the Bismarck *wacipi,* and the men who had driven through the night arrived in the city not long before the morning stars began disappearing. They drove along the outskirts to the powwow grounds, cut the engine of their vehicle, dimmed the lights, and, slumping into cramped sleeping positions in the car, dozed fitfully until the morning light.

Stars were barely visible as they slept, for the sky was becoming increasingly overcast on these near-winter days and nights. Some of the forms of life on the prairie had already started to acknowledge that they would not survive the time when the white storms would blanket the land, bearers of a cold so vicious it could crack the limbs of trees. The tree sparrows, those constant companions in such cyclical events, those survivors that nest year-round in the Northern Plains, slept in the trees hovering over the still vehicle and the men, intermittently and restlessly flitting nearby, adjusting themselves to the warmth of the flock, safe in the midst of their species. With no sense of dread such as must be felt by those birds which had already begun to gather for their long and difficult flight to warmer climates, these drab little sparrows were the only creatures to hover near the automobile where the singers slept.

It was said that there had been, in the old days, a great Sioux trading camp near this place. In order to exchange goods at the new settlement, Indians lighted their fires near this spot when the white man first came into their country. Their children, mounted on quick ponies, played a game much like the white man's polo. And the men and women of the tribe were sometimes forced to place their dead on high scaffolds in this vicinity.

Their songs, in times of grief as well as in the time of celebration, filled the air in those days, it was said, and it may have been the spirit of that history which now held watch, as did the tree sparrows, over the men in the semidarkness, as they slept under the nearly starless sky.

Several hundred Sioux traders lived near this spot in those previous days nearly a century before, and Tatekeya's relatives had kept those days in their memories. His great-grandmother had been among this regular nucleus of Sioux traders. She had been a young married woman at that time, just beginning her adulthood.

When the U.S. Cavalry thought that Little Thunder, the principal chief of the Platte Brules, found refuge among these people at this distant settlement following the Harney attack at Ash Hollow on the Blue Water (an unfounded rumor which was later abandoned), the soldiers burned their possessions and Tatekeya's great-grandmother's arm was ripped off at the elbow by the bullet of a soldier who had been, at one time, one of Harney's sharpshooters. After that, the woman bore seven children. She lived to a ripe old age and became unforgettable as a historian of the tribe and the possessor of a remarkable memory.

If anyone had asked, Tatekeya might have confided that the story of his great-grandmother's life here might have been one of the significant reasons for his continued annual participation in this far-north celebration; that, indeed, his own need to remember the songs that she might have sung to give strength to the people, his own wish to create new songs for the future lives of his children and grandchildren, brought him here. He placed great faith in the old songs, and he and his younger brother, Dan, knew them all.

After the traders moved from this place, it became a bivouac area for U.S. Army troops. Even later, the yellow-haired George A. Custer, the adversary of the powerful Sioux, and hero to

Cunningham, Tatekeya's hapless defender-in-law, had led his unfortunate troops from this area to their deaths hundreds of miles away.

Perhaps it was some kind of perverse sense of irony which brought the modern Sioux here for the annual ceremonial, for Custer was supposed to have said, after a particularly successful prior engagement with them, "Yes. I hated to see those savage redskins killed, but it had to be done." The tellers of that tale smiled secretly. Whatever the reason, the ceremonial had the reputation of being the largest single gathering of the year for the nations of the Northern Plains. It was now like challenging an enemy, a matter of tradition, not only for the Sioux but for the Cheyennes, Crees, Chippewas, Gros Ventres, and countless other peoples. These plains Indians hosted tribes from all over the country and taught every visiting Indian singer their victory songs.

As the Tatekeya singers slept late, the silent, dark night ended with the start of a deep violet hue in the east which lasted only a few minutes, a brief breaking of the dawn which was usually witnessed by only a few of the earliest risers, a couple of old men perhaps, whose habit it was to make prayers to the sacred re-creation of the world.

The hardy sparrows began to chat as the dawn appeared, and the travelers stretched out their stiffness in the morning light, resisting the temptation to close their eyes again.

The sun rose into the sky, and they began their preparations for the dance, washing at the communal faucet, combing, brushing, and, finally, preparing the drum.

There was never a time when John Tatekeya had come to sing at the last, fall intertribal dance of the year that the bald eagles hadn't appeared, and this time was no different. First one eagle came and circled over the dance arbor as the singing started. Then another. And another. Finally, four eagles had kept watch on the singers and dancers that first afternoon. Everyone commented on the presence of the great birds, and the four men who had driven through the night welcomed the sign.

Under the arbor, the Tatekeya brothers and those who traditionally sat with them at the drum sang the song of nationhood that reminded the people of who they were and who they had always been. Old men of the tribes carrying flags, traditional female dancers, youthful fancy and shawl dancers, grass dancers—they all emerged from the entrance and formed the spectacular circles which everyone recognized as symbols of survival. The witnesses in the arbor rose up, men removed their caps, and women covered their shoulders with painted shawls. "Sh-h-h," they whispered to children.

The Tatekeya drum and the drums of all their relatives were heard all day and far into the night.

20

November 1967

The courtroom was full, and he could see the tension fade from his lawyer's face as he spied John across the crowded room. What a puzzling phenomenon, thought John, trying not to be drawn into the attorney's enthusiasm for what could be the final day of the trial. Who cares about this strange ordeal?

Perhaps, as people of the city will flock to the most talked about movie or theater presentation, he reasoned, so do residents of a small, rural community gather for even the slightest acting-out of a resolution of conflict.

Let's get on with it, he thought, for it had all now become anticlimactic for him, and he cared little about its outcome.

John and the young Big Pipe brothers were not the only Indians present on this day, and as he looked around, John recognized others from the community: the fellow from Lower Brule who had stolen his car a couple of years ago, the act of a drunken spree that had not been so quickly forgotten; the white rancher who lived next to him and was recently reelected County Commissioner; his crippled son; several Indian women who sewed quilts at the church with Aurelia's grandmother; Clarissa; and her youngest daughter. Even Red Hair, who had now become a spectator rather than an investigator or a witness. And many others.

John took his seat at the broad, shiny table with the District Attorney directly in front of the judge and to the center of the view of the jury. The Big Pipe brothers sat together in one of the middle rows of spectators.

The accused cattle thief sat with his counsel, Joseph Nelson III, just across the aisle, expectant, puerile. His gray-haired mother sat directly behind him.

The District Attorney began a long review of his findings and then faced the jury.

"You know," he said, "when you get right down to it, this is a case of do you believe Mr. Tatekeya was missing the cattle that he claimed he was missing at the time he claimed they were missing. Now, stop and think of that," he said carefully, summing up the case which John Tatekeya and the federal government had brought against the young white man.

"Was he missing these cattle?" he persisted.

He walked over and put his hands on the railing.

"Now, the defense of this young man here"—gesturing toward the table where the accused sat with his eyes glued to the jury box—"they claim that Mr. Tatekeya sold them himself, or he probably let them run off; that he didn't keep them fenced in and they might have just run off into the backwaters of the dam, the river, and drowned. Or they just, somehow, disappeared. Now. Stop to think of that."

The amateur historian of George Armstrong Custer paused and put his head down as though thinking about it himself for the first time.

"Now, here is a situation . . . where"—he paused—"sure, they've made him out as a heavy drinker, and apparently he likes to visit the Aurelia Blue home. And he probably wasn't there every day to watch his cattle. And he doesn't have any horses to use and he's too lazy to ride them, anyway."

He looked into the faces of the members of the jury and fell momentarily silent. He knew that, unfortunately, they were apt to share the view presented by the accused's lawyer. All men. White men. Hard workers. They lived around Indians all their lives and did not have a good opinion of them, thinking that they were parasites on the federal government, that the BIA "took care of them." They were earnest men who slept with somber women, wives with large hips and rough complexions who turned away from them in the night. They worried about paying the bills and the price of commodities. They grieved that their children left for the cities when they grew up. And, more than most people, they believed that someone who didn't stay home and pay attention to his range work probably deserved to have his cattle stolen.

"I wonder," mused the lawyer as if to himself as he kept his eyes on the jury. He had to believe that they were fair-minded, that they could rise above their own prejudices.

"Who is on trial here? The question. Who is on trial? Who is missing these cattle? And do you think he is telling the truth? Do you believe him?"

Gesturing toward John: "There's a fellow that"—another pause—"well, he just didn't like the white man's court. It was pretty difficult for him to get up there and testify. The question is, was he telling the truth, members of the jury? Is it possible that he is telling the truth and this young man here did steal his cattle?"

The District Attorney didn't look at the short, blond young man who sat at the defense table.

"Here's a fellow, gentlemen, here's my client, Mr. Tatekeya, that was a pigeon, gentlemen of the jury. He was a sitting pigeon for this fellow here." The lawyer's arm swept toward the defendant but he still did not look at him. He kept his eyes fastened on the jury.

"This defendant knew him! Knew his operation! Knew that his place was flooded out by the dam and that he had to move his operation and that he didn't have adequate fences! Knew that he was gone sometimes! Maybe even knew *when* he was gone."

He paused for a long time.

"Knew," he said softly, "that this was a place where he could pick up cattle from an Indian who might not—"

At this point, Joseph Nelson III jumped to his feet dramatically.

"Just a moment, your honor!" he said indignantly. "I hate to object during argument, but I don't believe there's been any evidence to this effect whatsoever! It is an insult to my client."

The accused blinked toward his mother, whose stricken face turned ashen.

The judge, calm and deliberate, ruled: "Well, I think it's an inference that he may be able to use by way of argument, simply for the fact that there is testimony as to the map as to how close they live to each other. They know each other and the testimony suggests that this may be inferred. The objection is overruled. It's argument."

John looked around the courtroom. He saw the tension in the faces of the young Big Pipe brothers. He longed to see Rose's face among the spectators, some evidence of the imperturbable certitude she often shared with him and that over the years he had come to depend on. Her absence left him with a deep sense of loneliness.

He turned back to the presentation of argument.

"Just look at the kinds of things they brought into this case," the District Attorney was saying. "This is the stuff of a guilty man, to come in here and say that a man drinks too much or he is seeing a woman who is not his wife. This is absurd, and you know it and I know it. What else can a guilty man bring up but that which casts doubt on another?"

Jason Big Pipe, the young man who had testified to John's culpable behavior, got up and walked out of the courtroom. He was stopped at the door, told by the sergeant at arms that he shouldn't leave in the middle of the lawyer's presentation of argument, but he shoved his shoulder in the man's face and left.

"If they had a good defense they would come in here with a good defense," the lawyer continued, "not just, why doesn't he do this, why doesn't he do that, he should have stayed home, he should have done better.

"Gentlemen of the jury, I've seen this done many times and so have you. Especially in cattle-rustling cases. They are the toughest because you don't have a moving picture out there of people loading a truck up in a corral and trucking cattle off. This is done in the stealth of the night."

He paused to allow this imagery to be realized in the minds of the jurors.

"What kinds of witnesses were brought in? Were they reliable? Do you believe them? Or do you believe Mr. Tatekeya?

"We submit, gentlemen of the jury, that you will find that my client is telling the truth, that this young man here, sitting at this defense table, stole Mr. Tatekeya's cattle. And you should find him guilty.

"Thank you."

Part Three

A Verdict
Something Said Truly

William S. Harney

"Long Mandan said that he did not want the soldiers to go further up the river. But the soldiers will go wherever they please. The Great Father owns all the country, his soldiers go where they please and take what they please, but they will always be just to his red children."

A Report to the Proceedings, Council at Fort Pierre
March 3, 1856

21

The Last Dance Before Snow Falls
1967

The deliberations of the jury would take little more than a couple of days. At the moment of the judge's formal instructions to the jury, Aurelia was at home putting clean clothes on her grandmother following the old lady's bath. And just then, Jason Big Pipe appeared at her front door.

She looked at him, trying not to show her surprise.

"Uh . . . a . . . *'el naka' huwo,"* he said, at first. (Are you home?) Almost fearfully.

She said nothing.

Then, in English, as though he had changed his mind, "Uh . . . is your grandmother home?" he asked. Confident now.

Aurelia moved away and he stepped inside.

His eyes were on Grandmother Blue as she waddled across the room, huge and grandiose in her ankle-length black dress, so fat she required Aurelia's help to get from the bedroom to the living room couch, and as soon as she was seated, Jason went over and shook hands with her. In some kind of supplicatory way that made Aurelia turn away to conceal her scorn, he asked about the old lady's health, using the old language which he knew to be her preference.

Young men often directed what the old lady regarded as superfluous conversation and phony politeness toward her because she was the grandmother of the lovely Aurelia. Such gestures usually went unacknowledged, but this day there seemed to be a faint truce in the air, and Aurelia wondered what it all meant. The old lady smiled, uncharacteristically, but ended up simply grunting in his direction and gesturing toward her damp, tangled hair. Aurelia immediately fell to combing the long, steel-gray strands.

Jason stood awkwardly at the door until the grandmother poked Aurelia and whispered *"wakadyapi"* under her breath.

"Oh, yes. There's some coffee on the stove if you want to help yourself," Aurelia said in English as though by some vague signal she wanted him to know that she was hardly neutral or indifferent to his recent behavior.

"Thanks," he said, paying no attention to her aloof tone, glad for the chance to be in the presence of this lovely woman and show that he might be attentive.

He poured himself a cup of coffee and sat across from the grandmother, trying to ignore her unblinking stare.

"You gettin' ready to go to Fort to the dance?" he asked softly.

"Yes," said Aurelia.

"You don't need a ride, huh?"

"No, thanks."

While they carried on this harmless and stilted dialogue the old grandmother reluctantly closed her eyes and listened to the drone of their voices. Aurelia separated each strand of hair and lifted it carefully, braiding and smoothing and patting, pressing with her thumbs the limp threads of flimsy tapers, then wrapping the ends with strips of soft buckskin. She took the scarf from her grandmother's corpulent fingers, folded it, and placed it low over the old woman's forehead and tied it at the nape of her neck.

When she was finished, she poured a cup of coffee for her grandmother, who continued to doze intermittently, and one for herself and sat down, making casual conversation. No one mentioned the Tatekeya trial. Finally, when their talk dwindled to awkwardness, Jason said, "Well, maybe I'll see you at the dance," and he stepped toward the door.

Aurelia said as he left, "Maybe."

Jason noticed that the old lady's eyes were wide open, suspicious and cold.

He walked carefully down the faded wooden steps, avoiding the pail half-filled with ashes from the stove, the dog's old beef bones, the clutter. Before he left, he went over to the woodpile, picked up some chunks, and spent the next few minutes hauling stovewood up to the door, a gesture at once intimate yet generous and neighborly. He stacked it meticulously in the large wooden box at the head of the steps. Aurelia watched him from the window without expression.

As he walked to his rig, he was painfully aware that he had been treated with extreme politeness but had not been given even the slightest hint that Aurelia would be looking forward to seeing him again. She had not taken the opportunity of his visit to talk with him about his damaging testimony against John Tatekeya. And he felt that was a promising sign.

When he talked to his cousin, later, about his visit to Aurelia, and about going to the dance, his cousin said, laughing, "Hey, she's a little old for you, ennit? What? She gonna rob the cradle?"

"(K)unshi," said Aurelia, "Auntie Mart will bring NaNa, and Cecil said we could borrow his car. He should be here any minute, so hurry up." Her grandmother didn't open her eyes.

Aurelia could not remember when her grandparents had lived together. The old man, NaNa, had gone to stay with his youngest daughter, Martha, when he was only about sixty years of age. That was some time before her grandmother had taken her to raise, but Aurelia felt then, and even now in retrospect, that the two events were quite unrelated. It was not in Aurelia's memory, either, that there was any animosity between the grandmother and grandfather. The whole family adjusted easily to these changes and preferences of old age.

As she got herself ready for the dance and as her grandmother snoozed in the living room, Aurelia, in warm remembrance, thought of the time that she and John Tatekeya had gone to visit NaNa at the rest home, the time she had taken the old man some new turnips and he had sucked on them, toothlessly, while she talked to him about times past.

In response to her storytelling that day, he had begun to talk in his high, thin voice. He told her about the time he had, alone, driven twenty head of cattle from Greenwood to his parents' place along the Crow Creek at the time of his uncle's marriage and how it had rained and the leaves were golden brown. He remembered with astonishing clarity the places where he had camped and how the trees looked and which turns in the ravines were to be crossed, which to be followed. The cattle drive had taken him four days, and he hadn't eaten anything except dried meat the whole time. Packs of dried meat. *Wa co ni ca ka sa ka.*

He told her how the stars had looked and mentioned the brightest ones, saying, "Women, you know, have always been related to the stars in ways that are better than the ways of men, yes? Nevertheless, I watched them at night and knew that I would find a woman. Sometime.

"I didn't get married for a long time after those events," he mused, his tongue lisping against his sunken cheeks.

"I guess I was just not very interested in being a married man," and he laughed dryly.

"My sisters, you know," he had told Aurelia that day, "they were originally from Cheyenne River, you know. And they treated my wife very bad. And she had to put up with their insults.

"All of this was probably my fault," he went on, "because my father, who died when I was four years old, was really a more important man than their father, who had married my widowed mother. We went to live with them up at Thunder Butte. But we didn't like it there, and so we forced them all to return to our homelands at Crow Creek after the two sisters were a little older."

The whole matter, he had told her laboriously, had caused great enmity between his mother, her second husband, and his half-sisters, Corrine and Sylvia. They often claimed precedence and insisted upon making him insignificant even though his own father had been an important figure in the tribe, one who had been known for his youthful bravery during the Ghost Dance time, and one who was sent immediately to the Carlisle Indian School in the east, even before the fighting had stopped.

The visiting day, now seemingly so long ago, that she had spent with the grandfather was in her thoughts as she finished her preparations for the dance, and she was looking forward with great enthusiasm to seeing him again, listening to his songs, his stories, his prayers. The desultory tellings of stories by the old people with whom she lived informed her daily life and gave meaning to the world she knew. Such familial experience almost made Aurelia a tribal historian, though she would lay no deliberate claim to such a role. She could, however, trace with great attentiveness the important relationships, the genealogies, and the events, both historical and personal, of all those around her. And this ability was thought to be one of her special virtues, as it was always thought to be a quality of excellence in anyone who claimed to be a Dakotah.

John had sat with Aurelia and her grandfather that day far into the evening. And now, she cherished the memory of it. He has always known me, she thought. John has always known me. As much as anyone has ever known me. What will I do without him?

Assembling the family for social occasions was hard work for everyone. Clothes had to be cleaned and repaired. Children, infants, and the aged required the help of those who were mature and in good health, and so, naturally, Aurelia found herself faced with unusual responsibilities during these times.

After she had bathed, changed her clothes, and combed her hair, she awakened her grandmother, packed provisions in the car, and drove with the old lady to join the family at the Agency.

Making a right turn off the highway, Aurelia pulled the car into the grassy parking area, assisted her grandmother to the arbor to find a place to sit, and then returned to the car to get herself dressed for the dance. The grounds were filled with cars, people, a few horses, and kids of all ages everywhere. Since she was not one of the campers, she began the tedious task of pulling suitcases from the trunk and arranging her dance regalia on the front seat of the car.

As always when she prepared to dance with her relatives, she began by burning some sage and saying her prayers for making the historical past and the contemporary present significant and meaningful. This time, as she meticulously donned each article of clothing and jewelry, tied the quilled medicine wheel in her hair, put on her breastplate and adjusted it, she was aware of a feeling of anxiety she could not explain.

She walked across the grounds to her aunt Martha's old station wagon, where NaNa sat all bundled up, drinking coffee from a thermos and enjoying the crisp smell of the fall air. NaNa took the sage from Aurelia's hands, struck a match to it, and, cradling it in his hands on the small, cupped stone he carried in his pocket, helped her continue her prayers for the dancers and singers who gathered here in the old way.

Aunt Martha, not given to prayerful illumination of the deeds in one's past, nor even in one's present, rudely grabbed some folding chairs and ushered several youngsters toward the dance area, saying, to no one in particular, "I hope he doesn't burn up the car with that," and then, "Help him over here, Aurelia."

When the old man's prayers were finished, Aurelia gave him his walking stick, and together, each thankful for the other's presence, they walked slowly, in step with one another, across the grounds and found places in the family circle to seat themselves.

They looked around to see who was present, what drums were here representing their tribes and communities, and they felt reassured that the world was right with itself. After a few moments, one of the old man's nephews came over and asked him to join the Old Agency Singers at the drum. As he did so, Aurelia and her aunt drifted toward the arbor's opening so that they could be a part of the ritualized entry from the west of the colorful procession of hundreds of dancers, filling the dance grounds as the flag songs began. At the beginning of every dance, everyone was aware that these were occasions of great importance, and they behaved with dignity and composure.

It was later, when the evening turned cold and the wind began to rise, during the hoop-dance demonstration by her aunt Martha's grandson, when she strolled casually to the car to get her grandmother's blanket to cover the old lady's knees, that she encountered Jason Big Pipe again.

"Oh, you decided to come." She pretended to be surprised, though she suddenly knew that this meeting was not a chance one. It was, in fact, what she had anticipated throughout the evening.

"Yeah," he said, smiling. "I decided that I would come for you."

Though she had heard such declarations many times before in different circumstances, she stood away from him for only a moment, and then, with the air of a woman who knew what she was doing, she put out her cigarette, twisting it carefully under her foot.

She turned to him, her face serious, luminous, and beautiful in the night shadows, and handed him her grandmother's blanket. They walked together to the dance area, but neither of them had any idea at the time how frail such moments were, nor how irrevocable.

Jason, however, who imagined himself during that moment of acquiescence better than anyone around could see him, knew that his dark eyes were filled with unaccustomed tenderness, and he felt his every step and gesture filled with confidence and faith. He gave the old grandmother a brilliant smile as he handed her the blanket to cover her lap in the evening's brittle air. He turned, then, and took Aurelia's hands in his own for a Rabbit Dance.

They are all watching, the song warned, *Pretend you don't care.* It was a lover's song, and because it was, Aurelia shaded her eyes, avoiding Jason's direct gaze as they stepped together, in time together, her arm resting lightly at his waist, in perfect cadence with the drum and the sounds of the Old Agency Singers. Their dance was full of grace, as though they had always held each other close to the heart.

Aurelia, in all the years of her youth, had never danced with John Tatekeya, for he had given it up long before he knew her. She had forgotten the playfulness, the fun of such activity, and her smile came easily as she moved in the circle with the young man who had just a few days before testified falsely against the man she had loved for so many years; the young man who had given false testimony against an important fellow tribesman in the white man's court of law; a traitor; a collaborator. There are always those among us, she thought. And we are taught to know them.

She despised his lies.

She felt his strong arms around her. Her face softened in the dimness of the night circle. Though she had always believed individual transgressions to be inexcusable and the responsibility for them unavoidable, she, at the time, listened only to the song, *pretend you don't know me.* Her face was turned away from him and she thought, He is smiling and wondering about me, just as I am wondering about him.

"You really gonna come home with me?" he asked, half in jest. Teasing, yet urgent.

She said nothing aloud but she knew, even then, that she would go with him this night. She looked over and met her grandfather's uneasy glance for just a moment. He was singing, his mouth wide open and his body shaking as his right arm came down again and again, rhythmically and surely. That song. Do I know that song?

She turned toward the place where her grandmother and all of her relatives sat beneath the arbor, and as she moved away from them in the dancers' wide circle, she wondered what they would think.

Well, they have never approved of me, she thought defiantly. Never in the past. Why should they now?

Jason caught her eye.

"I mean," he went on hesitantly, "what about . . . about . . . John Tatekeya?"

He was serious now. No longer smiling.

"You . . . ah . . . you been with him . . . a . . . long time."

The night air was turning frigid. The wind continued to rise, a signal that this last dance before winter was a prelude to the deep, heavy snowfall of a long season. Expected. Inevitable.

Yes. I have loved John Tatekeya for a long time, she remembered. All of my important years have been shared with him. I have watched with my own eyes the changes of our lives, the land. The river. And now, another betrayal. And I, too, have become a part of it.

Let me think. Don't listen to the song. Yes, it was last year at the beginning of winter that John and I began to realize we would not be exempt, that even those things that are as old as the earth itself—like honor, and virtue, and love—they are not eternal. That everything must change.

We began to know it for sure that one night. When was it? Last year? *0-hanh* . . . last year . . . about this time. We were walking the streets of Rapid City with his brother Ted, talking with him about going back for treatment to the Indian hospital: the Sioux San. That place built by the U.S. government on a hill overlooking the Rapid Creek, its long, brick driveway the path for the coming and going of its native patients as tuberculosis attacked the cell system. Silently. Surreptitiously. And it wasn't until the cough started that you even suspected its presence.

The hospital was a dreaded place which both Ted and John saw as a place from which no one escaped. It seemed not unlike the places where the fish in the northwest rivers go to spawn. Where you go to breathe your last breath, or perform your last helpless act. The saddest place on earth.

Ted and John saw it as a place from which no one escaped. A place of death; for their youngest sister had come here in 1939 and left only when they finally put her in a wooden box. Her lungs were attacked viciously by the rod-shaped bacterium which caused the weakness and the waste in her body. But her response to the cure, her apathy and acute depression, they thought, had been as devastating as the disease itself. Their grandmother told them, ever after that, "It's where they take you to die."

Ted made several Peyote songs to sing for her recovery. Yet Sister gave up her life in this world, saying only, "You must try to remember me." She was, at the time of her death, thirty-two years old, and her babies, without her, were forever quiet and forlorn.

Instead of returning to the hospital, Ted drank steadily, his bottle of Ten High in the pocket of his heavy sheepskin coat, which, unzipped, flapped into the bitter wind. His clumsy movements made him seem to lunge, again and again, into the wind as we paced the streets, as though:

The world he lived in
was like some vast museum with rock walls
but lifeless as artifact,
cellophaned, preserved. He put
great faith in the holy men who sang
to hailstones because, he said, there
are four posts holding up the Earth,
and four beavers busily gnawing
at each.

He lived in the museum of rock walls,
paleolithic and alone, habitually ascetic,
questioning the reliability
of messages from curators
only recently revealed. Fraudulent.
Capricious. Their imaginary
lives and deaths encompassed his misery.

Eventually, he became the man who walked
into the day, following a ditch
along a country road so luminous
be couldn't find his way home. Heat from
the glossy rocks on this isolated country road
marred his forehead and cheek, and when the others
found him, he was too weak to breathe,
supine, and covered with dust.

Because we were nearly broke, I went into a coffee shop across from Duhamels' to see if there might be somebody who would buy some of my beaded jewelry. Just a few doors down, there was a hock shop, but I didn't know that until later when it really didn't matter anymore. I sat down and stared at myself in the mirror across the counter. My eyes, narrow and black, like solitary, distant crescents in a brilliant mask, shaded my misery. And I looked, I thought, like I was all right.

"What'll you have?"

I pulled out a sparkling, beaded hairpiece from my purse and held it idly.

"You wanna buy this?"

"Chrissakes! What would I do with that?"

I looked up and, for the first time, focused upon the woman's weary sallowness. It was the face of a person whose passion for life was all undone, after years and years of solemn, unhappy survival.

"Oh, well . . . yes," I said uncertainly.

I put the brilliant hairpiece back in my purse and moved toward the door.

"Well, what do you want? Don't you wanna order nothin'?"

The woman threw her order pad on the counter in disgust, and I escaped through the heavy doors.

John turned his back to me as we slept that night in a seedy motel, lights flickering and wheels grinding, as trucks met the stoplights just a few feet from the motel courtyard. Ted sat in a chair, coughing up spittle throughout the night, and by morning was running a mortal fever.

We had no heater in our car but drove back to the Agency anyway, over two hundred miles, with Ted asleep in the backseat, burning up with a deathly high temperature, his lips parched and swollen. When we got there, they told us that we should take him to Chamberlain, to the white man's hospital about twenty miles away, a place where Indian patients are sometimes treated in emergency cases.

Ted died that night, during the first snowfall of the season, just before his son arrived from Fargo.

As we walked out of the waiting rooms, John said to me in Indian, "Ah, the grandfather has come," and for just a brief moment, I had no idea what he meant. Then he held out his hand to catch the falling snow, and for the first time in days, he seemed to relax and give in to the whims and absurdities and inevitabilities of our lives.

As I think of it all now, as I look back on it, I know that we both sensed that it was, as John said, "all going to hell."

The song ended and Jason and Aurelia walked out of the arbor to the foodstands which rimmed the dance area. They walked the circle several times to make sure that they were seen by everyone who mattered; then they sat down to a serious conversation at one of the picnic tables. He brought her a steaming cup of coffee and she began:

"John Tatekeya is a man of the past." She smiled wistfully. "A man who has taught me everything."

"He could not predict the theft," she said defensively. "Nor the betrayal. But when it happened he knew that it was the changing of the river that accounted for his dilemma. Even though it started long ago."

Jason sat without looking at her, his fingers curled around the warm cup.

"It was the river. . . ." Her voice trailed off and was lost, momentarily, in the wind.

Jason said nothing.

"He used to listen to me talk about my mother's ways, her new ways"—she paused—"and he used to tell me it was all going to hell. The flooding of his place. It made everything for him distorted. Strange.

"Finally," she said in a low voice, "he became very angry about the trial. The stupid trial. And he doesn't quite know what to do."

It was the first time that she mentioned the trial, and Jason held his breath.

"He doesn't know, really, what to do," she repeated.

"And neither do you," Jason said, his voice rising as if he had asked a question.

The cold wind began to whip around her legs and she covered them with her shawl. She looked up at him and shrugged.

He waited for her to speak.

At last she said, "And you?"

People were beginning to head for their cars to get their coats and blankets. Even a few of the dancers, carrying feather-bustles and suitcases, strolled through the circle taking a final look at the display of wares as the evening's activities seemed to be drawing to an untimely close while the weather worsened. Dust, brittle leaves, empty paper cups, and other trash from the foodstands swirled about the grounds.

Reluctant to leave this last dance of the year, people stood around in small clusters, talking quietly. Waiting for the inevitable wind to turn to sleeting rain. They pulled their wraps closer.

"He always told me, you see, Jason"—she sounded like a mother talking to a recalcitrant child—"that you don't accomplish anything in life for personal and individual reasons alone."

"But, yeah," Jason interrupted. "Sure. I believe that, too."

"That all accomplishments and events and doings"—she swung her arm widely—"must contribute in a good way to the communal life given to us by our ancestors."

"Yeah," said Jason, nodding his head.

As though she hadn't heard his agreement, she mused, "And the river was always a part of . . . a part of . . . and the land . . .

"But, now, you see . . ." Her words again drifted away in the wind.

She left unsaid what they both knew: that her own relationship with Tatekeya as well as the ugly testimony given by Jason at the trial had successfully shifted the guilt of the white man's theft to the people, *Oyate,* to themselves and each other and all who clung tenaciously to the notion that, even amidst devastating change, the Dakotahs were people who were obliged to be responsible to one another.

This has always been true, she thought. Always. Until . . .

As the two talked into the darkness, mindless of the rising night wind, they began to feel better. What can we do, they asked one another. They held each other's hands and they began to understand. Nothing lives long, and it is only the tribes and the land that continue.

At last, Jason stood up and said gently, "Come on. Let's go. We must take your grandmother home."

To Aurelia he seemed very tall, and she no longer thought of him as a boy. He stuffed one hand in the pocket of his jeans, put the other around her shoulders, and they walked silently away from the lighted dance area into the darkness.

Jason felt Aurelia's small hand at his waist, and he listened to the long strands of beads echoing in perfect rhythm against the bone of the breastplate she wore. The fringes of her shawl swung up and down as they walked together, and Jason knew that there would be no moments so sweet as this. They had danced together this night, and it was the first time that he had touched her, and he was dazzled.

"We, the Jury,

Find the defendant guilty of the crime of stealing personal property of a value exceeding $100 on the Crow Creek Indian Reservation from Mr. John Tatekeya, an Indian, as charged in the indictment."

Late fall, 1967

22

In the aftermath of the trial no one knew quite what to expect, and they mostly went about their private ways.

While the lawyers went on to other cases in their continuing pursuit of justice, the litigants and spectators took up their lives, and the trial's end and the days after the verdict were much like any other endings and all days for many of them. For Tatekeya, however, the world was changed forever.

In his own first thoughts concerning the events of the past several months, he felt: *be mac 'ena* (I am still the same). But, of course, he was not. And in his heart he knew better. His life was changed irrevocably just as the river had been changed for all eternity.

He drove to the Joe Creek at the West End of the reservation immediately after the verdict was read and the court dismissed, then followed the gravel road around the bend in the river. He stopped and parked his vehicle at the small U.S. government-installed boat dock without speaking to anyone, arriving there just before sundown.

He sat for a long time with the pickup door open and the chilly wind whipping at his legs. There were great ponderous waves on the gray water. They seemed to come from its depths, and, looking at the phenomenon with great interest, John remembered the stories about the remarkable *unktechies* who, at the beginning of time, ripped off first one arm and then the other and flung them into the water. One was a female figure and the other a male. They taught the Indians what they needed to know about religion, and, it was said, they subsequently went deep into the earth themselves. *"They are still there,"* the old people would say. *"Waiting and listening for the prayers of Indians. They are listening to hear the drums of Indians."*

That's what Benno used to tell me, thought John as he looked without emotion into the rough, wind-driven waves. He remembered, too, how he had walked to his mailbox in water up to his knees when the water seeped in, higher and higher every day, when part of his lands were flooded. One day, the road was still there and the mail carrier drove his vehicle on his appointed rounds, and the next day, the road was under water. It was just before the men came up from the Agency and moved his little house out of the way of the vast destruction. His youngest daughter had been with him and he had consoled her panic, though he had felt it, too, as they and others from the community watched from the hills.

At last, sitting slumped in his pickup, he knew that he would not be among those who were driven from this land by such violence. He knew that he would stay here. Die here. Because of the *unktechies.* Because of Benno. This thoughtful assurance brought him some measure of peace.

And he knew he was not alone. He remembered with pride the efforts of John One Child, that old Santee who was more than ninety years old now, and how he came to the Council chambers last September with a small request; a request which was, in John's mind at least, emblematic of the tenacity with which Dakotahs faced such brutality. Yes. It was just about the time that the trial started. And One Child asked that the lake which had been formed at the bend in the river be named Dakotah Lake. For the people. Rather than Lake Marcus in honor of the old lawyer and politician named M. Q. Marcus, a white man who had participated in the litigation by the federal government and "sold out" the tribe for four hundred dollars per capita.

It was One Child's second request for the name change, but nothing could be done, he was told. The Agency, you see, he was told, had already celebrated its one-hundredth birthday. Its centennial. Back in 1963. And so, you see, he was told, there would be no occasion for changing the name at this time. John's mouth turned down in a sardonic smile.

Tatekeya turned in his seat and looked out across the road at the land which he and his people had called their own even before the Indian Reorganization Era forced them into individual ownership. It was Dakotah land which he and the others had defended all their lives in ways that ordinary people could not imagine, against theft and fraud and exploitation of every sort. Sometimes they were successful. Sometimes not. He remembered the gardens they used to plant along the river there. Every summer. The good sweet corn and the squash.

Back at the time of his birth, just prior to the turn of the century, the beef cattle industry had become a major economic force after white men found out what the Plains Indians had probably known all along, that beef cattle would not only survive the hard winters of the north along this river, but actually thrive on the northern prairie grasses.

And soon after, as the white man continued to bargain for the land from indigenous peoples, who resisted in their desire to save their own lifeways, the exploitive and brutal policy of colonialism, a deeply felt impulse of the European newcomers, became a powerful force, at once legalized in the courts and yet denied in history.

In a few brief, hurried decades, John thought, we made unbelievable adjustments. We knew, better than most, perhaps, that new nations rise out of the blood of other nations. And we therefore changed our lives over and over again so that we would not die. Even as we dealt with the Americans, though, we never expected that we would become beggars. We never expected, as Europeans continued to leave their native countries for this land, as they made contracts with us in order to satisfy their needs, that it was their desire to manifest total authority over the vast rich lands of our fathers. My Sioux relatives, John thought, had always had confidence that no one who faced the providential spirits of the land could be so arrogant.

Finally, we have come to understand the force that we are up against, he thought with a sigh.

John returned his gaze to the water and watched its energy wane as the sun fell behind the purple hills and the wind ebbed. He watched it without thought, without emotion, without despair or panic. As darkness fell, he slumped in the front seat of his pickup and slept.

At sunrise the wind had blown itself out, and Tatekeya drove back to town to his daughter's house. His wife, Rose, met him in the yard, and she put her arm around his waist and hooked her fingers in his belt and walked slowly with him into the house. They stood inside the door, the strong sunlight slanting in the windows, and held on to one another; and he knew that while he stood accused of many things by others, of adultery, foolishness, of malice, and deceit, and theft, this woman would say that none of it carried as much weight as the years they had given to each other.

One time, when they were just children together, probably no more than nine or ten, Rose had told him a secret. She said that the cottonwood tree, the sacred tree that is used at the Sun Dance, holds inside of it the perfect five-point star.

"How do you know that?" he challenged.

The next time her older brother and the others cut down a tree for the secret ceremony and put a crosswise cut in one of the upper limbs, the two children crept in beside it, and when they looked at it, awed and hushed, they saw the whitened star, a direct link to the time when the Sioux were the Star People.

She hadn't been able to resist. "I told you so," she had said gleefully.

He had chased her home that day, angry and jealous of the secrets she knew.

Now, at the kitchen table, Rose poured hot coffee into two cups and placed one in front of John, taking the other for herself, and they began to speak, unaccountably, of the distant past. And they began to laugh together, and they laughed until tears came into their eyes and neither of them could say anything more.

John looked into the anguish in this woman's face, the furrows deep across her brow, and he knew that her laughter was a spontaneous release of tension and anxiety brought about by the events of the last days. His marriage to Rose had been one of the last arranged unions in the old *tiospaye* tradition, the last in both of their families to be given cultural sanction, and he knew that neither of them would let go of it.

He could still recall the approbation and endorsement of family members toward them. The gift giving and the feasting. The praise and flattery that had given way over the years to a devotedness and cordiality that was often taken for granted.

After a few minutes they regained their composure, and John said to Rose, "I have no cattle returned to me."

"Yes." She nodded. "I know. That is the white man's law."

They sat in silence.

"There was that old *tōka'* woman," Rose began. "Do you remember her? She was very tall and always wore long, black dresses. And the kids used to be afraid of her. Do you remember her? No one knew where she came from, but her brother lived there on the Crow Creek. They used to think that maybe she was Oglala."

John said nothing.

"I remember how she used to tell us that there is nothing we can count on, nothing in this world we can depend upon. Don't you remember how she used to talk about how it is that the Dakotahs turn around and around and see nothing on the horizon? We can turn around and around, she told us, and look in all directions, and never even see a tree. In some places, you know. We, then, see nothing on the horizon."

"H-un-m."

"That it is . . . as though, after all, only the wind is the source of thought and behavior. The wind moves. And it is a determinant, yes?"

She wanted him to respond.

"The white man doesn't know these things, and so he always believes that his solution is significant," she went on. It was as if she had to explain to John that it was nothing new to them that the white man's law was ineffectual.

"I don't know why they sometimes called her Saul woman. She was not a Christian, I think."

When he said nothing, she said at last, "If we expect something else I think that we will be disappointed."

Instead of joining in on this focus of the discussion, John said quietly, "People know me here. They know that I have never tried to be something other than what I am."

As he sat watching her pack into laundry baskets the clothes and food that she would need so that she could drive out to the reservation with him, he began to dread the aftermath of this trial. For while Rose spoke of the failure of the white man's law, she said nothing about what they knew to be of paramount importance, the failure of reciprocity among the relatives.

What Aurelia had meant to her husband would never be asked about nor commented upon by this woman who had the ability to know secrets, the ability to distinguish between matters which are merely profoundly serious and those which are tragic. The sons of Harvey Big Pipe had directed hostile acts toward this good relative, John Tatekeya, with apparent deliberation and reason. And what this meant to all of them was that such a transformation of Dakotah values might progress, unfortunately, to somewhere outside of history. To the end of time.

"Are you ready to go?" he asked.

"Yes."

They both felt uneasy and uncertain as they drove home. Afterwards, whenever they spoke of this uneasiness they could never be sure of its cause. Had it been something between them or had it been something else, a premonition perhaps?

As they drove around the last curve within sight of the river, they saw the smoke rising and at first thought it was coming from that old, abandoned Standing place, but as they drew closer, their worst fears were realized. The makeshift trailerhouse on their place that was filled with hay was ablaze, and both of them knew that the fire would spread in a few minutes to the dozen or so haystacks set close together in the feedlot.

They raced to the scene and John stopped the pickup, leapt out, and shouted to Rose to drive quickly to the Community Center where she could use the telephone to call everyone in the neighborhood to come and help.

As she pulled out of the yard, she saw Guy LaPlant's pickup careening up to the gate.

"I seen the smoke," he hollered. "Where's John?"

She gestured toward the shed where John was already pulling around the tractor and disk, getting ready to shove dirt between the trailerhouse and the haystacks.

"Kennie's coming with his backhoe," said Guy.

Rose pulled out of the yard, scattering dirt and gravel with the wheels of the pickup.

Waves of heat swept into the dismal sky, and the yellow-gray smoke filled the lungs of the men who fought the blaze, which left behind only the outlines of charred posts and barbed wire and a large scorched circle on the earth for a quarter-mile radius. Faces blackened, their clothes torn and filthy, John and the small gathering of his neighbors sat or stood in clusters, too exhausted to speak, their lungs seared, their throats too charred and dry to breathe. Only after it was all done did the fire truck from the Agency arrive, and then two young men numbly hosed the embers with water.

To the west the grove of elm and oak which John planted two years prior to the flooding of the banks of the Missouri stood as weary sentinels, reluctant witnesses untouched by the conflagration, their leaves swept away in the wind. The house, untidy and remote, a few yards beyond the stand of trees, was undamaged by the fire.

As their energies returned, the firefighters began to drift toward the porch to commiserate with Rose and members of the family, who stood solemnly, dry-eyed.

"That didn't take long, did it, John?" said Guy, echoing his despair against the wretchedness felt by everyone.

"No. Twelve stacks and a shed full of hay . . . it don't take long to burn when there's a little wind."

They found places to sit on the wide southern porch. Some went to the pump and hauled pails and basins of water and, unmindful of the cold, began washing their faces and arms. Pretty soon they were drinking coffee, and Rose was making fry-bread. The sun went behind the hills and the exhausted little group sat in the cold shadows.

"Guy," said John softly, "tell me what you think started all this."

He was speaking philosophically about the flooding of his lands, the disappearance of life forms along the river, the trial and subsequent fire, the historical thefts of land from his people, and the agony of existence without the support of Benno. In his thoughts were the words of Gray Plume and all of the grandfathers who had said that life in accordance with the white man's ways was indecent:

> I am an Indian but the man then told me I would become an American. . . . Now, listen to what the Great Father says. . . . Harney himself had massacred the Sicangu. . . . I am not going to beg for my life . . . the soldiers go where they please. . . .

Guy, being a literal and fundamental sort, replied, "That's one thing I'm sure about . . . but we'll never prove it."

"What do you mean?"

"I'll tell you what he means." Jason Big Pipe spoke from the darkness of the porch. John hadn't seen him come during the excitement of the fire but looked at him at that moment, his long hair streaked with mud, eyes reddened by the smoke. And with great relief he acknowledged that Jason had been there with them to fight the fire.

"That son-of-a-bitch was out on bail before you got out of the courthouse, John."

"Yeah? But . . . how?"

"His mother and his uncle showed up and paid the bail, and they've started an appeal already."

"But . . . would he do this?" John gestured toward the ruins of the trailerhouse.

"Why not? He stole your cattle," Jason said bitterly.

No one spoke in the silence that followed this angry remark, and John felt the hollow inside his chest start to burn as if from some terrible wound.

Finally John asked tiredly, "If you knew this, Jason, what the hell were you doing testifying against me?"

"He paid Sheridan to help him load that night, and I was coming home from town late and saw them. When I confronted Sheridan he said that he'd beat the shit out of me if I didn't lie for them."

Through clenched teeth and fighting back tears, he finished the story. "And, hell, I couldn't let my brother go to the pen, could I?"

Suddenly, the hollow in John's chest seemed to cave in and he couldn't breathe. He gasped and coughed. He coughed until he thought he would vomit, and he stood up and walked out to the gate. His body shook and he took great gulps of air. At last the spasm left him and he went into the house and took a long drink of cool water. He sat down in an easy chair in the living room and let the tensions loosen from his body. He felt his thoughts drift. My children were born here, right here in this room, he thought. Is that why I had the house moved to this place when my land was flooded? Where is the horse, Red Hand Warrior, that Chunskay broke to ride?

He saw Aurelia and she was crying. He repeated the words that she had told him: *"They said that to pray to the east, south, west, north"*—and he saw her motioning—*"was to pray to the winds. And it was therefore evil."* I have nothing, he thought. Nothing is mine. And there is nothing that I can take with me when I see Benno again.

The firefighters and neighbors sitting on the porch soon began to leave, one by one, to return to their homes. Jason stayed and Rose gave him another cup of coffee, but even he, after a while, left.

When Rose went into the house she found John sitting quietly. She touched his arm. He put his hand on her hair and awkwardly smoothed it.

"I have no memory of ever wanting to hurt you," he told her.

Weeping quietly, she said. "I believe you."

"We are the children of Gray Plume," he said slowly, his head resting on the back of the chair, his eyes closed. He said it in confidence. Not in defeat or sorrow, but matter-of-factly.

23

Aurelia heard about the fire almost before the last ember had grown cold. Though she and her grandmother saw the smoke from their place, they paid scant attention until one of the white women from the church stopped by to leave a sack of old clothes from which Mrs. Blue usually cut the bright squares and triangles for her quilts.

"Tatekeya's barn was leveled by fire," the woman rasped. "But I guess they've got it out by now."

Neither Aurelia nor her grandmother responded, but Aurelia felt the slow pangs of desolation in her heart when she heard the news, and she thought immediately that this destruction would be the last of the undeserved events that John would endure. She knew that from this time on, his discontent would be equal to hers, and he would never again ask for her love.

"They are saying," the church woman went on, "that there might be something suspicious about it."

There are some people in this world who are born old, NaNa used to tell her. And Aurelia knew that she was one of those. Perhaps it was that quality which accounted for her long-standing feelings for Tatekeya, the love she had felt for him the first time he'd touched her shoulder as they'd left the church meeting together that day so long ago.

Now that the trial was over amidst the gossip that a deliberate arson might have occurred within hours of the verdict, Aurelia was forced to reach some conclusions about the situation. She reasoned that John's natural reclusiveness would become more profound, that his habitual tendency toward isolation would be intensified. He would now become a man less broadly involved in the sphere of human concerns. She knew that, now, his admiration for her would become a part of his past and his manner toward her stilted and unnatural.

She would therefore have to live her life without him for the first time in years. Her loneliness for him would be unimaginable, she feared. But she would be able to accept his absence, sooner or later, as all people are able to sustain grief and loss.

These were Aurelia's thoughts as she contemplated the very recent happenings, but she shared them with no one. From now on, she thought, she would have to pretend that she was unafraid. The trial and the fire, events which seemed to be, in her mind, as inevitable as any of the events that she had ever witnessed, rendered the questions which she and John had posed together irrelevant. She determined that she would cling no longer to the notion that the lofty ideals of her ancestors could confirm and encourage her spirit.

Because the questions no longer mattered, Aurelia felt calm and poised. As she leaned forward into the bathroom door mirror she could see herself in the dimness . . . a pretty girl, thin, not very tall, looking years younger than her thirty-odd years, her silky hair falling to the middle of her back. Her eyes, though, her eyes . . . she leaned closer . . . black, liquid . . . eyes that barely revealed her lifelong melancholy, her new fears, her present pain, all the result of her recognition that the life which she now re-created in quick, blurry scenes of the last decade or so was to change forever. *I had to grow up and I do not regret anything.* As she turned, she seemed not to care that the deceptiveness of her youth had been dangerous and destructive, and she grabbed a sweater from the closet.

The significance of the traditional past, she knew now, was only a personal and individual matter, not consanguineous as she had supposed. Thus her mother's abandonment of tradition was her own business, and the effect such an action might have on family and tribe was worth examining only if it could make a difference. With this cynical and pragmatic recognition suddenly and profoundly thrust upon her, she knew, finally, what it meant to be alone. Even Jason, whose smile had tempted her that night, whose laughter and passion haunted her even now, could make no difference.

Aurelia stood in the darkened hallway and listened to the church woman drone endlessly as she took each piece of used clothing from the sack and remarked upon its virtues and possibilities. Her grandmother's occasional murmur did nothing to assuage the tremendous ache in her heart. From now on, now that she could no longer depend upon anyone to accept the way she was, and the way she wanted to be, and the way she had always been with Tatekeya, she would have to pretend that she was vital and that she loved life. In her future relationships with men she would have to think of ways that she might tempt them and keep them from looking at other women. She would have to force herself to seem loving and happy. And the artless beauty she had possessed so impudently all those years might now become useful as it has always been useful to women of contemporary worlds.

When the church woman drove away, and her grandmother began to talk about the cutting of quilt designs, the young grief-stricken woman turned and left the house. She felt tears fill her eyes, and as her grandmother watched from the window, she leisurely saddled her horse and rode toward the river. She looked upon the dead and dying whitened trees along the banks and knew that in spite of the river's grotesque new image and what it meant to the uncharted future, she would constantly have to remind herself of her disavowal of its avuncular nature. It would take great discipline. For here, in this place which represented the cyclical dramas of her people's past, it seemed certain that the wretchedness inflicted upon human beings by other human beings was inseparable from the violation of the earth. And only here, only now, at this time, did she take comfort in the knowledge that she was no longer completely isolated from the secret that human beings are capable of violent and destructive malice, and she was pleased in the knowledge that she would no longer ask futile questions.

She knew now that the flooding of the homelands had to be taken into account in any explanation of her devotion to Tatekeya, and his to her; that chance would have played only a slight role in such an important matter. As she looked at the waste along the edge of the endless gray water, she saw the outlines of many tipis, a village which had once stood on these inundated grounds. In the haze, horses bearing youthful riders, horses pulling travois, children and mothers carrying colorful shawls, walked slowly toward her. A slow-motion montage of all things past and eternal, unassuming and habitual, came toward her and passed over her in an indistinct white fog. It was an abstraction which moved toward the purple hills, a fleeting moment of thought to make nothing of, for it was a materialization, she knew, rising out of her grief.

John would be gone from her now, and the questions of what their lives had meant to each other as great changes occurred would not need further speculation. There would be no one else to understand that the love of her parents and grandparents, and the love of those for whom she cared deeply, and even the unalterable devotion of a lover or husband, would not make her happy. Nor would it give her peace, seize her soul, satisfy her intellect. No one but John had discovered this about her nature.

It had taken a long time, but finally she had become convinced that the reality of her mother's abandonment and the questions concerning it were futile, meant only to make her forever sad. Worst of all, she now began to accept as fact what she had always suspected, that the stories of the pipe stone quarries of her people were apocryphal. Like the sacred grounds of Palestine, they could no longer symbolize the final restoration in the modern world.

She felt herself at the edge of sobs, deep and terrible. Headed north, a sudden wind hurting her nostrils, she stood up in the stirrups and held the reins high, taut. She drove her horse up a stony hill and when she got to the top, the wind, unaccountably, stilled . . . *ma tuki* . . . the horses in the adjoining pasture looked at her and the stallion flattened his ears.

As Aurelia moved on, the sky in the west turned crimson and gray as though a storm were trying hard to get started. In the dark of this night, the first of the winter snows would blanket the earth, confirming their own inevitability. The hills above the

Missouri River would become white and unfathomable, secret in their private subterfuge, preoccupied and selfish in their knowledge.

An ageless gray owl turned its head toward her as she moved effortlessly along the river's edge.

Epilogue

The Afterpart

As the hide was placed over the opening, Tatekeya let his head drop to his chest in the darkness and he gripped his arms tightly around himself. Sweat poured from his body and his agony seemed interminable.

He moaned and silently wept.

As he began to sing, he lifted his head and thrust it back against the curve of the lodge. His eyes, wide open in the total darkness, looked upon the antiquities of the universe and his mind adjusted itself, by degrees, to his own triviality.

He turned toward young Philip, who put the sage carefully into the trembling hands of his venerable grandfather, Harvey Big Pipe.

Circle of Dancers

Contents

Part One

Myth and Memory

Out of the traditions of the Dakotapi there are myths that still matter. They direct the lives and spirits of the ones who care, women and men who seek the circle. Daughters, brothers, wives, fathers, mothers all search for a direct link to the origin tales of the people.

Any journey of Oyate matters, then, and particularly those journeys that require the people to cross the river, face the east, and call to the Corn Woman. The magic and the whirlwind will then consent to accompany them.

A long time ago, they say, the reluctant brothers left their father's lodge to travel to the four directions on an essential journey toward being. Three moons they traveled to the Fourth Place which is colored with yellow edges.

If the brothers' journey was to be considered successful, they would have to learn that in all ways, large and small, they share their lives with the Corn Woman.

1

A Yellow Dress

In the summer of 1941, when she was just eight years old, just a few months before the war started, a thing happened that made Aurelia forever vulnerable. Different yet ordinary. A contradiction. It might have seemed to others, had they paid any attention, such a little thing. Nothing visionary. Just a little something to make a picture in the mind's eye.

It was the first time Aurelia had seen her cousin, Corrine, since Corrine's marriage to Stanley, and Corrine was wearing the yellow dress. It looked like taffeta. Aurelia was reminded of it again four or five years later when she had to wear her own yellow dress to her eighth-grade graduation from Stephan Mission Catholic School, K through 12. In fact, the memory of the yellow dress never left Aurelia's mind and, like many other unaccountable events of her childhood, it was simply an inexplicable moment which may have shaped her view of an ever more disconcerting moral world.

If there was anything Aurelia was noted for throughout her long life, it was her exemplary memory and her self-possession concerning its function. She did not always tell the stories of remembrance. But when she did she did not tell what happened as it really happened or even as she remembered it happening; rather, she told stories as she desired them to be. Because of this passionate selfishness, and because those who loved her recognized a melancholia about the stories, and mostly because they could not help but believe the stories as she told them, her inconsistency was rarely challenged.

Corrine's yellow dress, she remembered, had a popular, sophisticated A-line look, but her own was all gathers and frills with a wide half-sash that started at the sides and was tied in an enormous bow at the back. Its exaggerated puffed sleeves made her thin arms look extraordinarily long and emaciated. Dangling like leafless limbs.

The eighth-grade graduation ceremony was anything but a happy occasion as far as Aurelia was concerned. Stiffly, she had let her mother, Myrna Two Heart Blue, sober and strangely parental for this day of celebration, on one of her rare visits to the daughter who had been given to her paternal grandmother in infancy, push the dress over her head. As this happened, the memory of Corrine's yellow dress had flashed before Aurelia's eyes.

It had been raining that night when eight-year-old Aurelia had seen her cousin, clearly and by mere chance. One side of the bright yellow dress was pushed up over a generous hip, the other side ripped loose from the waist and hanging almost to the ground. Aurelia saw Corrine's white panties, her bra just under her armpit. Corrine was pinned, wriggling, to the side of the wooden building by Stanley's huge shoulder, his right hand shaking her head this way and that as he pulled at her long, loose hair.

Corrine, Aurelia thought in retrospect, had had her eyes closed as if bracing herself for the next wrenching shove, but she wasn't giving up the struggle. She was drunk and she was furious and, even though she could hardly stand, her flailing arms were delivering stunning blows to Stanley's contorted face and weaving head, and one of her big feet, clad in a huge-looking white pump, was kicking him in the shins, trying for his crotch.

Later, as an adult, Aurelia thought the characters in the little drama had looked very awkward and ridiculous, hidden in shadows from the view of the well-lighted entrance to the country dance hall not far from Grace Mission. At the time, though, what had impressed her the most was the fact that the pair struggled in a pool of muddy water, their faces wet and shining, neither of them aware of the heavy, chilling rain drenching them in some kind of boundless, divine curse.

Aurelia and her Auntie Mart, hand-in-hand, heading for the outdoor toilet, nearly fell over one another on the slick path as they turned to gawk at the soundless struggle taking place in the shadows. It was like something out of a silent movie, a frightening scene of both revelry and debauchery, turning the world upside down or backward. Indelibly, Aurelia's vision of the grim event placed itself in her consciousness, but she did not know then that it would stay there forever, a clinging abomination that would feed unreasonable fears for years and years. She did not know then that her future relationships with others would bear the knowledge of this silent image. *"I-nah-hee-nee-ya,"* she heard Auntie's warning voice say and felt the adult woman, tugging at her hand, attempt to shield her from the disgraceful sight before them by putting her free hand over Aurelia's staring eyes.

In spite of Auntie's efforts, Aurelia caught a long and indelible glimpse of the struggle and for months afterward she had roaring nightmares filled with gushing torrents of dark rain and tangled streamers of long, black, shining hair. Later, the silence of hours upon hours of wracking insomnia magnified her emerging consciousness about what she had witnessed: as she grew into adolescence, she understood that the engaging, obdurate, but oftentimes failed struggle that went on between women and men, in spite of their desire for order, shape, and beauty, more often than not ended up in angry, chaotic violence. Like young girls throughout history, she casually resolved that she would like to be an old maid, unmarried and alone, free and isolated, unsurrendered to passion. In her adult years, after a mutinous ten-year affair with a married man old enough to be her father, and, later, during her marriage to Jason, the recurring image of that rainy-night struggle made it forever clear to her that a child's mind, in some rarified and inexplicable instances, does not—perhaps cannot—surrender its unwanted images to time; that memory is indeed burdensome, vivid, portentous; that its knowledge is preserved and thrives in its own force forever.

Aurelia grew up with many such memories of a changing world, as a rather isolated member of a large and cumbersome Dakotah family, individually noted as one who remembered things "far back," things that could sometimes be called the simple minutiae of uneventful lives, oftentimes events that were recognized as outside of the traditional Dakotah story, better forgotten, ignored, or hidden. During the better times, she could recall the things that were of the most historical and profound interest to her people. Because the ability to remember seemed to her to be innate, she took little responsibility for it and was, more than most, aware that a remarkable memory could be as unpredictable as a dry spring or as falsely wise as a crazy man.

Most of the time, she simply accepted the idea that human and tribal understandings of how memory works are fragile and have always been so. Thus, the bits and pieces of life seemed to her simply to gather, to collect slowly, eventually to begin the dance of an interior spiritual life and occasionally, in the best of times, to finish off in a kind of rare and unforgettable sound and motion that only a true storyteller praises. For her, bits and pieces of the past would come to a point of deafening roar, when she could think of nothing else, when sleep would not come, when lovers turned away. It was then that she would say to herself that the ability to remember things "far back" became as burdensome and unwelcome as a divine gift to a provoked sinner. An old sense of her failed relationship to the traditional storyteller of the Dakotah past would seize her momentarily and she would spend unhappy hours trying to recognize the source of her inner incompleteness, her melancholy.

Annoyed, vainly clinging to the belief that the keeping of stories would furnish useful knowledge about the changing world and her own frivolous life, she endured her role as transient witness but did not know for the longest time how essential it was to look beyond the past. Whenever she tried to talk about these matters and listen to her grandmother, she could make no sense of the old woman's musings.

Teeth missing, lisping loosely, Grandmother Blue would say: "The woman with the yellow dress, you know, talked the people into come here to the Big Bend in the Missouri River. And she give them corn seeds."

"What woman was that, Gramma?"

"Oh, you know. That one."

"But . . . "

Taking out a blue handkerchief and wiping her broad face, the old grandmother would end up by giving unfathomable advice: "You cannot hide beneath your dress, you know. You have to do your part."

It has been said that any story begins in the memory of its cause. In Aurelia's case, and, perhaps, in the case of all the stories the Dakotahs tell, the cause may have been a desperate fear of *nominis umbra, the fear that when one cannot know one's name and place, there is only outrage.*

Aurelia was born in modern times—1933, to be exact—a time of abeyance in American Indian life, a time of near oblivion, hollow, shadowless days. But if memory really plays an essential part in life, as some contend, then maybe her story begins long before she was born, even before her parents' or her grandparents' time.

Perhaps this story began when the people of Aurelia's Indian Nation, called the Sioux, were first driven from their lands by the white farmers and politicians whose origins were European. Almost anyone who tells Indian stories eventually gets to that place. For the Sioux, or the Dakotapi as they called themselves, it was then that they went to war in earnest. They fought terrible wars, wars that were no longer sacred. Different from anything they had ever known. Wars that went on for decades. Wars that made them seem cruel and heartless and hate-filled and desperate. Wars that took away their children and their hope and brought death to their communities in numbers that they had never experienced before. Contrary to what most people think and what has been written in a one-sided history, this warfare really ended in a military standoff for the Sioux. The Americans wanted peace with the Indians, they said. The Indians wanted to keep their homelands. And for the most part those goals were met. In the beginning.

They say the Sioux won more battles than they lost because their warriors were honorable and their wives faithful and by being so they made memory synonymous with geography and event and they became phenomenal in the universe of tribal nations. After battle, they composed victory songs saying *"mitakuye ob wani ktelo! epelo!"* and they taught the songs to everyone, even their enemies. Because of this, those of Aurelia's generation, whether they were singers or not, whether they were dancers or not, clung to the emotions and prayers that had arisen from those tribal experiences. For some of the people of the tribes, the impetus for all creative and artistic expression was the recognition of their own histories, that such recognition filled their lives and made all human endeavors worthwhile and unique.

Because the Dakotahs were neither savages nor primitives, they clung to the idea that memory was not only an individual matter; that it operated, as always, for the sake of a kind of unconscious collective no matter how fragmented a people, no matter their oppression. They knew that no story, no matter its inception, was prehistoric if the people remembered it.

"When my aunties talked about me," Aurelia told one of her husbands, some years later, "I hated them. But that was because I didn't understand then that all of the stories must be kept by someone. Even those that we want to keep hidden. It took me years to understand that when the storyteller becomes part of the story, it somehow makes sacred the whole, and it is a good thing."

After the aunties told her story publicly, then, and everyone knew of it, Aurelia made up her own. This is what she eventually told about herself:

> In a tribal camp, they said . . . Oyate t aka wic o ti, keyapi, a *perplexing and uncertain love affair ended. It happened as the winter came, and it was the love between Aurelia Two Heart Blue and an old man named John Tatekeya, a Santee, and it came to a certain end. It was, that is, the love and the loss of it, an inevitable calamity. Out of her longing, then, and, some said, selfishness, the woman went to the bed of another man who had many brothers. A man younger than she by ten years. A man who would give her a child. And then her life and the life of Oyate were renewed. Women, however, must never be*

*still. They must never be content even if they are the mothers
of the hero's son, even if they know they will live in the Big
Bend of the Mni Sosa (Missouri River).*

Aurelia didn't tell this story until she was an old woman
with grandchildren at her knee. Many years had to pass before
she could make sense of it. "It is only in retrospect," she told her
takojas, "that you can really know anything about life. Maybe
some would say that my life was a mere love story. Yet love is
never separate from war and death and grief, just as life is never
separate from history. And nothing is ever isolated from the
obedience to the memory of all of the people.

"It is believed, therefore, my grandsons, that such a story as
mine is not unconnected to the other kinds of stories told by
the old people who say how history treated us, that we, in spite
of our prowess as warriors and lovers, were to become just like
the nations of the world before ours, signing peace treaties with
our aggressors that would redefine us, remaking our ancient
homelands in ways that changed the universe. They put down
their weapons, the old people always told me, just like I am
telling you now, and relinquished their war ponies and set
about making new lives in a reconstructed, yet familiar world."
Her talk often sounded very formal when she used Dakotah
speech.

Some of the people who listened to the old woman, especially
the young children, could not know that since the Oyate had
never been in the business of making wars of conquest, the old
grandmother was talking about morality, not surrender. They
could not know of that time in history when the Oyate faced an
enemy who believed not only in conquest but also in genocide,
annihilation. They could not understand that the ancestors were
helpless to do anything but grasp their own lives with an
absoluteness that seemed utterly beyond words.

Even Aurelia herself had not known these things in her
youth.

❧

"You remember that yellow dress?" she asked Auntie Mart
out of the blue.

"Hunh?"

Aurelia was sitting on the couch, one hand over her still-flat stomach in a gesture both protective and surreptitious.

"You know, that yellow dress of Corrine's?"

"Corrine's?" You could hear the shock in Mart's voice. No one had mentioned nor even thought of Corrine in years.

"Yeah."

After a moment of silence, Mart said dismissively, "No. I can't say that I do remember it."

Martha, her broad behind hiked up in the air momentarily, bent to unplug the broken television set while at the same time wiping the dust from the top of it with an elbow and wrapping the cord around her hand.

"I had one, too."

"What?"

"A yellow dress." Musing.

Martha said nothing.

"Don't you remember?"

Instead of answering, Martha started to puff and grunt as she pulled the TV away from the wall.

Oh well, thought Aurelia. Probably nobody else remembers it either. Nobody but me. All the external associations with the yellow dress seemed to come back in a rush. Aurelia sat staring out of the window as her aunt got down on her knees and started picking up the papers and lint that had collected behind the TV set.

Whenever Aurelia thought of the yellow taffeta dress, which she did surprisingly often over the years, she wondered whatever became of Corrine's. Did the young bride, the morning after, carefully wash and repair the dress, shamefully putting out of her mind the episode of awful violence? Or did she, in a gesture of hateful recrimination, confront her new husband with it, perhaps throwing it out in the trash as he watched? Just as she wondered about Corrine's, she was puzzled about whatever had happened to her own yellow dress. She had never worn it again after the graduation ceremony and could not recall ever seeing it after that night. It was as though it had disappeared materially, though it continued to exist in dim childhood thoughts, a symbol of deeper significance in the face of the oppressiveness of conventional growing-up expectations and rituals.

She remembered peering into the looking glass at her fourteen-year-old self. By then five feet seven inches tall, a head taller than every girl in the class, taller than many of the boys and even taller than the little nun who taught the eighth grade, she knew she would look ridiculous in the puffy, yellow taffeta dress. Towering over her mother, who had snatched it from the used clothing rack at the Stephan Mission's Oblate Sisters Spring Rummage Sale and was holding it under her chin, she had shouted, "No! Please. Don't make me wear that. It's ugly."

When her ordinarily absent mother decided to do such rare and motherly things as getting Aurelia ready for a special occasion, however, there was no stopping her. For a mere quarter it was theirs and Aurelia wore it, looking, she thought, like a yellow grasshopper, arched legs and arms dangling crookedly into the tiered yellowness of the stiff, shining skirt, her braids passing the huge yellow bow at the back like long black antennae in a glaring sea of misery.

Her grandmother, who ordinarily didn't agree with her mother about anything (the two women hadn't spoken a civil word to each other in years) shuffled beyond the mirror saying, "You look very nice, 'relia. You will do your part good." Puzzled and angry, Aurelia had gone with her family to the fateful ceremony of passage and they put on a collective false face of benign agreeableness so well known to flawed families filled with distress and acrimony.

Thinking back on it, Aurelia could see that her childish ordeal with the yellow taffeta dress couldn't have been as devastating as Corrine's. Hers, after all, was a simple dilemma of childhood agitation. Corrine's, in contrast, representing a commitment to her marriage with Stanley of less than a month when Aurelia saw her that rainy night, became a public matter. Here was a woman cousin, a daughter, a sister of all those present. In her yellow dress, filled with the promises of a new marriage, a young bride at a community gathering, drunk and fighting as though there were no promises to keep. She had become disgraceful and would be the subject of community gossip. Later, Aurelia knew that it was a terrible thing for a woman to be slapped around by a wild man who claimed her love but, of course, being a child at the time, she knew little then of the tribulations of young lovers in a changing world.

Her grandmother's explanations were always quite simple ones and, in many cases, undeniable and self-evident: "Those white-man dances," she would say scornfully. "There is an 'anything goes' attitude! Indi'ns forget who they are!"

Indeed, from what Aurelia could tell, those dances were often occasions for outrageous behavior by the people in the community. Her father, Albert Blue, who, along with many classmates had learned to play musical instruments in his youth spent at the federal boarding school in Rapid City, oftentimes proved Grandmother's point. When he got together with Cecil Crow on drums, Auntie Mart at the piano, and Elgie Creek and others playing guitars and whatever to furnish the music for these kinds of "white-man dances," there was, to use the old woman's phrase, "drinkin' goin' on."

The communal dances of those reservation times in the thirties and forties were, by definition, gathering places for the entire family; grandparents and children of every age accompanied parents and young marrieds as well as unmarried relatives looking for all the right people in all the right places. They travelled there in wagons, on horseback, and some, the lucky ones, even drove there in automobiles. These were boisterous and cheerful occasions but could just as easily turn menacing and threatening. Aurelia's grandmother, more thoughtful than most, would listen to the merrymaking and buffoonery with simple forbearance. "Green eyes, those cool and limpid green eyes," "The red, red robin goes bob-bob-bobbin' along," and later, "Bongo bongo bongo, I don't wanna leave the Congo," as well as "The Red River Valley" and "Shenandoah," were the tunes of the day. There was laughter and joking and no one had trouble finding a bootlegger for whiskey.

"You remember the time when you and Uncle were sitting in the back seat of the car waiting around for everyone to get packed up to go home?"

"Um-humh."

"Remember? He was drunk and he shoot a hole in the ceiling of that old Ford." Her voice rose. "He missed you ear by that much." She held her thumb and forefinger three inches apart.

"You were just a baby then."

"Well . . . not really." She hated to disagree with the old woman. "I was about four or five."

"Well, that's a baby. You remember that?"

"Yes, Grandmother. I remember."

As always, she felt her grandmother's outrage.

Claiming no destinies, only responsibilities, this grandmother was an important figure to Aurelia in the management of her life as well as the stories. Together, having lived all their lives with one another since Aurelia's infancy, these two women, though they seldom spoke of it, were a comfort to each other. Like women everywhere, they simply knew of the burdens of life and told each other they had to "take care of business." They knew that Cousin Corrine had died in childbirth a year after the night of the yellow taffeta dress and they watched Stanley very soon marry again. Later, he divorced and married again. All within three or four years. Every time Aurelia saw him over the years she imagined him jerking Corrine, his bride, by her long, beautiful black hair, and it made her regard with great suspicion all men and most women and, surely, marriage and conjugal love. Grandmother simply said, "A woman has a hard life," and Aurelia did not argue the point.

Forever after, in her memory, whenever something reminded her of that time, she thought of the yellow dress and was never sure whether it was Corrine's trauma or her own that she was recalling. Often, when she realized she would never be free of it, she felt saddened, mournful, almost as if she were grieving over the birth of something terrible in the universe, something to be feared since humans knew little of its origins. Her grief did not keep her, however, from steadfastness as a silent witness to the events from which the stories arose. Like all the dancers and story-tellers she had ever known, she continued to seek the sacred place.

Ma-tuki. In spite of her own need to keep the stories for herself, she doubted their future. She worried about living in a world where no one cared to know the old stories, yet she continued to ask the questions about who was really listening now for what the past could tell them. She became suspicious of the ancient tribal belief that if you listen for the stories for the sake of the people you will play a crucial role in a good life.

Like the story of Corrine's yellow dress, her humiliation, her death from giving birth, most of the stories Aurelia came to know throughout her life were unfathomable, useless. Still, they took possession of her dispersed life, and people said of her that she was the kind of storyteller the Sioux people had always known, secretive and worthy, yet the one least likely to be revered except by those who held close to the heart the unwritten silence of the fragile ancestral presence.

In the silence of her life with her grandmother, then, which was moving toward wrenching change, she was unpossessed of the joy and vibrance of the famous tellers of the world's stories. She was not, after all, the stunning singer and dancer from the East, Sheherezade. Nor was she one who went to Delphi. She was just an American Indian woman who carried the fear in her heart that the stories of her land and her people, the Dakotahs, were invisible and unrecoverable in an alien world.

The real change for Aurelia, as for many people in America, had begun in the 1960s. It was not only because she was getting ready to bear the child of Jason Big Pipe, an unplanned circumstance that changed everything; it was because of the nature of the times. Mid-century change. Modernity. Besides, she would soon have to move on from her filial relationship with a grandmother with whom she'd lived all her life. She would have to search for a life of her own. Her ties with the old woman, though some observers may have thought they were mere convenience, were profound and binding. Aurelia dreaded what was to come.

"You just gonna sit there?"

Auntie Mart, now in her middle age a community health worker, often showed up at the home Aurelia shared with her grandmother to interfere in their lives because, at last, she had some authority to do so; she often sounded angry, tired. Today, she was merely frustrated because no one was taking her seriously.

Aurelia sat up abruptly.

"Wha . . . ?"

"You get Jason next time he come over, to take this old thing to the community center." She placed her hand on the smooth surface of the television set.

"Oh, okay." The yellow dress was forgotten.

She noticed Martha's greying hair plastered across her sweaty forehead.

"They said they could fix it and bring it back over here."

"Oh. Okay."

Aurelia really didn't give a damn about the television set. Such trivialities filled the lives of the women around her and she hated them for it. Besides, at the moment, she had decisions to make that far outweighed the stupid television repair. She was pregnant. And she had told no one. Her own life had recently become more complicated and the realities of the unseen and unknown seemed to haunt her every thinking moment.

Because she was a woman of limited emotional experience, Aurelia thought that she might get away with ignoring her personal pains and regrets. Yet, single emotional states being unsafe, and contradictory emotional states being even more risky, she wavered, and became incapable of making any decisions. At the mention of Jason's name by her Auntie Mart, contradictions flooded her thoughts like streams of light and she felt her face get hot. How could she have given herself over to such passion? How could this have happened? She recalled Jason's elegant hands, his hard kisses. Was he at this moment remembering her? Was anyone at this moment or at any moment remembering her life?

Aurelia stood at the door and opened her eyes to the sunlight. Her eyes stung and she closed them quickly and watched bright streaks like the yellow of old embossed taffeta gather on her eyelids. When she opened her eyes again she saw the old Dodge station wagon sag to one side as her Aunt Martha struggled into the driver's seat. Aurelia smiled and waved as the car made its way laboriously onto the gravel highway.

2

1968

The deadening quiet of fall had hung on that year weeks after Labor Day and it would not let up nor would it move on. A season when everything stops, withers, chokes, and dies of thirst. In the cities and towns of America there was still air conditioning in the musty porno shops where unshaven, unkempt men, some just home from the Asian war, huddled toward photos of naked women; where overloaded electrical circuits made light bulbs dimly flare into the oppressive stench around them. On the Crow Creek Indian Reservation of the Dakotahs where Aurelia lived, the same kind of grim deadness surrounded those in Indian villages and ranches who witnessed the changes they had nothing to do with settle into their lives.

The people watched dust rise from the wheels of slow-moving dump trucks moving away from the ruined river; huge orange trucks still moving rocks and earth and history and god's rare future as they might have done had they been in Greece at the building of the Acropolis. Miles and miles of treaty-protected Indian reservation land, like the stricken people who watched, seemed docile and expressionless. Everything was muted. Life and land and estate changed beyond tribal fears and extinction.

Aurelia had been among the watchers. The brothers and sisters she encountered every now and again, those who had stayed with their parents or went off on their own when she was taken to be raised by her grandmother, had been among the watchers, too. The separation of the family and the destruction of the river, long a lifeline to the history of the people, accounted for the isolation felt not only by Aurelia but by all of them. Though they lived within a few miles of one another, they lived as unnamed and undefined tribal relatives, polite and formal with each other.

For many years this deep silence among her relatives had mystified Aurelia. But now, being forced into giving herself over to the idea of motherhood and the next generation, she felt marooned, overwhelmed by her own surrender to that silence, and knew that sooner or later she would have to move toward some kind of kindred design that would make sense of her present dilemma. She looked toward it with dread.

Now past thirty, she recalled a time when she, isolated from her siblings and committed to taking care of her grandmother, had told old Tatekeya that she loved him; the time when, refusing to want anything for herself, she would become the old man's companion, a mistress to the grieving of a passing era they both wanted to share. She had never confronted that period of time when she had refused to care for her life, refused to want anything for herself. Her bitter will had kept her in that distance for most of a decade.

Now she could no longer remain indifferent and, in fact, there were moments now when she felt great joy, a brilliance breaking through the surface tones of detachment. Perhaps, she thought bemusedly, childbearing is, after all, that essential event. She found herself smiling but unconvinced.

It was eleven o'clock in the morning and Aurelia stood at the window, her breakfastless stomach making strange noises. After Jason loaded the broken TV set into his rig, he lingered. Now he sat alone at the cleanly wiped table fiddling with the radio. The silence between them seemed comfortable and unthreatening. As usual, there was very little talk as they concentrated on their private thoughts.

There was a certain elegance about her, he thought, even in jeans and an oversized black t-shirt big enough to cover her slightly expanded waistline, the shirt with an emblem of a long-haired Indian outlined in white standing next to an autumn-yellow hoop streaked with darker splashes of orange. It was a shirt he'd never seen her wear before and only after he looked at it closely did he recognize it as one of his own and he thought she looked perfect, her eyes slanting and arrogant and shining. No silk gowns for this one, he thought. No yellow taffeta, as he remembered her story. No cashmere sweaters or whatever the current fad might be. Just plain clothes, jeans and cowboy boots, her hair long and straight.

In a moment of tenderness he reached over and pulled her toward him, putting his hand on her stomach. "You have been a foolish one, hunh?"

She looked at him over her shoulder and lifted her eyebrows. He grinned up at her, feeling himself a little foolish, yet he always liked to talk like this as though he had her trapped . . . as though he had tempted her with his irresistableness which they both knew was, in some indefinable way, of course, the truth, yet at the same time ridiculous. They both knew no one trapped Aurelia unless she wanted to be trapped.

"Who's foolish?" she demanded.

"You."

"Me??" She pretended astonishment.

"Yeah. You . . . " he puckered his lips playfully.

Ignoring the gesture, "Why am I foolish? Hunh?"

"Cuz! Look at you." He rubbed her stomach. "Look at you now," he teased. "A fine mess you got yourself into."

He tried to hold her but she moved away from him and pulled back the curtain and stared out the window. "I'm okay," she said defensively.

After a moment he got up from the chair and stood behind her saying nothing, his hand gentle on her shoulder.

"You?" she asked, still staring unseeing toward the hills just outside.

"Uh-hunh. I'm okay." His lips touched her hair, uncertainly.

Jason wondered if this was the time to say that he would be better than okay if they were to get married, if she would just forget about the difference in their ages, if she would just forget the past with that old man, if she would just say that she loved him.

They stood still at the window, afraid to break the closeness of the moment, absently watching two little birds that flitted across the dry grass behind the house, noticing how they seemed to have white armbands when they stretched their wings. White armbands, like messengers of charity and hope.

The weeds were tall and so was the grass as far as the eye could see.

As in many of the sacred places of the Dakotah, the prairie grasses along the river in the beginning were astonishingly collaborative in the new ways of the reservation people, providing healthy stands of hay to assist in the development of the beef cattle industry of the nineteenth century. Aurelia felt herself thinking about the grass now so often in so many places overgrazed, the birds gathering in for scant food. She felt herself moving away from her personal dilemma, moving away from Jason's urgency.

"Jeez, what's the matter with you now?" asked Jason, puzzled and disgusted as he sensed her changing mood.

I don't have to answer him, she thought, even if I could. It's like you must feel when you're both happy and afraid and you don't know the difference. Like when you go swimming in the hot summertime and you want to just jump into the water, clothes and all. Experience the exhilaration of the splash you make, but you're afraid. You don't know how cold the water is or how deep.

Aurelia, unsmiling, watched the masses of dark gray clouds barely moving in the sky and thought, momentarily horrified, well, I've done that all right. Just jumped in, I guess, clothes and all. Ah! Sometimes you set things in motion without even thinking about it. Even when you're old enough to know better.

Here I am, way past thirty years. And pregnant. And if there is anything I don't want, it's marriage. I don't want a child. I don't want a husband. No. No. No. She felt tense and angry. Not at Jason, only herself. She turned and put her arms around him and stood there for just a moment, her heart against his suddenly filled with sorrow and compassion for both of them.

Before Jason could speak, she turned and looked again in the distance. She saw the white farmer who rented her grandmother's land driving his white pickup along the road, slowly, as though searching for something on the ground.

"What the hell's he looking for?" she asked no one in particular, not expecting an answer, glad to change the emotionally charged moment to something outside of themselves since neither she nor Jason had the courage at the moment to confront one another with their unspoken needs.

The white farmer's grandparents had been among the homeless and wandering whites who moved westward back in the 1800s and were encouraged by politicians to seek riches and power in the "wide open" west, which most of the time meant stealing treaty-protected Indian lands if they felt like doing so. When they didn't steal it they simply leased it for pennies from the Bureau of Indian Affairs. It was a fact that the white farmer had never spoken more than a greeting to Aurelia, nor to her grandmother, whose land he used as if it were his own.

Jason watched her staring at the pickup truck. "I'm supposed to be over there, to his place early next week," he said. "I guess he's gonna do some fencing and he's gonna work on that well again. Try to get that pump out that fell into it."

She said nothing.

"Before it gets too cold, you know. Me and Sheridan are supposed to be there early as we can get there Monday."

She felt him turn away and knew that he was put off by her silent and seemingly inexplicable anger, her aloofness. As she saw him reach for the radio dial and furrow his brow, seeking just the right country music station, she noticed the darkening of the sky as shadows fell in the room. She looked over at Jason and knew that she could not expect that he would notice the change, as he seldom noticed the simplest things. Without emotion, she thought of the coming cold days.

She turned to him quickly and said, "Maybe you should go now. That church lady will be bringing Gramma home soon."

"And?" He switched off the radio and looked up. Serious now.

"And, well . . . I just don't want you here when Grandmother gets here."

"Why not?"

She looked at him and anger flashed in her eyes.

"Just because, Jason."

"She knows! Who do you think you're kidding?"

Again, she said nothing.

"What's the point, 'relia?" Jason was angry now too.

She hesitated.

"Well, shit, 'relia! What's the point?"

In spite of his protest at being told to leave, he got up and reached for his cigarettes.

"You know . . . you gotta make up your goddamn mind, 'relia . . . "

She looked at him and shrugged.

"I'm part of this, too, you know."

"I know."

When she said nothing more he said, "Shit, 'relia," and stood as though struggling for words, waiting for her response.

Aurelia turned away from him, put one hand in her back pocket and slouched against the window sash as if to give him the impression that the conversation was finished.

No longer present nor yet lost in time, the memory of the man old enough to be her father, her lover for ten years before she had taken up with Jason, was in an instant entangled in her thoughts. Part of her recognizable past, Tatekeya's face emerged from the flat grasslands in the distance. He was smiling, wholeheartedly and somehow complete, and his smile took such possession of her that she completely forgot about Jason standing expectantly across the room. When she had been just a young girl she had decided that she would love the old man and, years later, when the land was flooded and the river changed, it was over, her love turned to sorrow, his passion spent. Neither on this day when she was standing in simple stillness at the window, nor in any of the subsequent long years of her life, had she any idea why she'd loved the old man nor why she had stopped.

Still standing at the window, she heard Jason's rig start up. The decision about whether he stayed or left seemed trivial as she looked out on the landscape. It was not just then a matter of significance. For just a moment, as she watched the bare tree branches sway in the gentle wind, she wondered why she could never find the words to tell him the things that were on her mind. Though she had often talked to the old man Tatekeya about her fears and the changes in the world, she had never once been able to share them with Jason.

Without words shared between us, she thought, who are we? What is the meaning of anything? After the white people killed off the buffalo, she mused, and made places nameless, they even killed the sacred meaning of the mythical river that for many generations had helped humans to understand themselves. Tatekeya knew of this. And so did her grandmother. So many others did not.

Long before the river was dammed up and changed forever, there was a story her grandmother told her and it remained important to the people. Looking at the glitter of the river in the distance, she said out loud, "Fish and wild rice have always been food for the people." No longer true, she thought. Her eyes glittered. "*Yuk'a' Hoga'-Wak'a' ki heya'ke,*" her grandmother's voice rang in her ears, "there exists a Fish-God and he became a helper of the people when they first came to know that they were Dakotahs. And it is because of Inyan that such river gods and the earth could be caused into being and it is because of Hoga-Waka that *the people will never be homeless* nor poor, and that they will always know who they are."

She shook her head. Why do I continue to care about these stories? The whites have never known of these gods, she thought, and neither do many of our own people, like Jason. So some people have no words for things that others know and that's the reality of it. You cannot find the words for the people you love and then the spirits of providence are truly in control of your being, so that's okay, too.

I'm a contradictory woman, she admitted to herself, and I've never honestly subscribed to the enchanting idea that Jason and I are made for each other. Yet, his words "you have to make up your goddamn mind, 'relia," echoed in the room and she felt compelled to answer them. These were the only words that Jason could utter these days and her defiant response was, "maybe I don't have to make up my goddamn mind." Her lips tightened for a moment. But, of course, she knew better and she knew that decisions would have to be made.

At the time of the river's flooding, Aurelia had no intention of marrying anyone, least of all Jason Big Pipe. Somehow, though, she seemed to be living proof that not all women escape their own coming of age. A woman's childbearing and marriage were serious, serious business to the Dakotahs. She knew now that it was sacred business from which only a few escaped.

As she stood at the window, she wondered what it was that she truly wanted and whether it mattered. What did Jason want? Why should he want to marry her or she him? Why should he be in love with a woman who couldn't make up her goddamn mind? Painfully, she saw the yellow taffeta dress again. It seemed as though someone, though she couldn't see anyone's face, was putting it over her head. It seemed for a moment that she was both eccentric and mad. The mythic, always a part of Aurelia's oblique remembrances, overtook her completely at times when she least expected it.

As Jason drove out of the yard, she hardly noticed his going. Instead, this is what came to her mind:

Le wo yakapi ki li la eha ni keyapi. She listened. And, in her imagination, she could envision the exact places where her grandmother had often taken her as a child, to eat and rest and to tell her things. *This story, they say, comes from very far back in the history of the people.* In a well-timbered place, a place of reverence, an island in the middle of the Missouri River that has a great number of red cedar on it, an old man comes. He comes with his two wives to accompany him, sits in a cross-legged manner and makes tobaccos and ties them in bunches to put in a leather pouch. He does this to make this place and himself necessary for the tribe's survival, a place and a man and a ritual that the tribe cannot do without. The Missouri River tribes always knew that he was a sacred man and this a sacred place. Yet they knew, too, that some people said he was not a Dakotah Wicasta at all, that he was Ree or Cheyenne or maybe even Ponca.

With the muted sounds of Grandmother's story and Jason's angry demands mingling in her thoughts, Aurelia went into the kitchen to prepare a lunch of sandwiches and soup for her grandmother.

3

Flaws of Old Men and Old Women

As she fell asleep that night she heard the whispers of the sparrows crowding themselves into tight little groups on the bare limbs outside her window. Several times during the night she woke to the crying of the grandfathers out in the hills and she heard the shriek of her grandmother's snores in the next room. She tried not to think of Jason, who seemed sometimes like a little boy, too romantic and self-centered to be taken seriously.

"I love you, 'relia," he had said that first time.

"No," she had said, smiling at his untroubled passion.

"Yes. I love you . . . "

"Um . . . well . . . " she had tried to think of ways to talk to him about the difference between physical passion and love, but failed because of her own uncertainty. And, anyway, a man who had been to war, as Jason had, was not about to listen to some sentimental female chit-chat about sex.

I'll have to come to some conclusions, she thought as she drifted off. The time to make up my goddamn mind might be fast approaching. Still hoping to make her getaway, she tossed and turned, a profound sense of dread permeating her dark dreams.

The river lay in the distance, darkly lapping at the barren shore. Withered, whitened cottonwoods sank into the cold sandy shoreline and coyotes were the only silent prowlers on the land.

Aurelia kept her eyes closed but troubled thoughts and images of the past kept her from an unconsciousness sleep.

Jason Big Pipe's people and Aurelia Blue's were among the Indians of America who were witness to the startling phenomenon of the making of a great modern nation, and because of what they had seen they began to comprehend slowly but surely that their lands would be taken and their lives would be forever different. They knew, too, that the war between their people and the newcomers would never cease. They slowly came upon the answers to questions posed by all people whose native lands were envied:

> *would he return*
> *the dead who lay about the plain as the sword*
> *had strewn them, and allow their burial in*
> *proper graves? Nobody may sustain a*
> *quarrel with the dead and lost-to-light.*
> *Let him show mercy to his one-time hosts . . .*

For some, like the old grandmother and the old lover who had had so much influence upon Aurelia, it became clear that the answers were unsatisfactory ones. With the images of the ancients stamped indelibly on her mind, Aurelia herself witnessed the going-out of the old ways and the coming of the new with such incredible swiftness that for her everything was made unforgettable.

She had forebears who were people who would not forgive nor rationalize the historical dilemma that brought about discomfort, annoyance, hunger, squalor, filth, disease, death, and poverty. She had forebears who were inspired by the contempt they felt for the new ways, people who believed that they had found a profound way of handling the gift of their continued existence, and that way was simply to watch the invaders, understand their motives, hear their stories, and make up their own tales about them and, as a result, they would find alternative intentions.

It would not be easy, they said, and they shook their heads in disbelief as white men and their families moved across the

173

lands like locusts taking possession of everything, plowing up thousands and thousands of miles of fragile topsoil as far as anyone could see, settling everywhere as though the people, Oyate, were invisible, unseen, and unknown.

As usually happens when one race bears the rage of another, when long and bitter wars are ended, a separate peace ensued. The new colonizers saying, in the tradition of the heroic Aeneas, who was ordained by Jupiter to promulgate a new, ersatz race of people: "I would never have come here had not *destiny* allotted me this land to be my home." The natives, sick of one of the bloodiest wars known to mankind, put down their arms and said, in the tradition of their own ancestors: "Our lands are sacred. The Earth is our Mother. And we shall live." It was a separate peace that stopped time and the future.

When peace was made, it was not known whether the natives or their adversaries believed that the preordained and inevitable course of heroic acts on either side would be forever in opposition, but as the history of the new nation unfolded, the Sioux became more certain of it. It took years for them to articulate the new stories, even to themselves.

"They were like the leaves on the trees," said the Santees who were first to encounter the invaders. "As some wither, more bud forth."

Gold seekers, German farmers, laborers and Swedish ranchers. Norwegian, Dutch financiers. People from all over Europe became the new Americans and renamed themselves in acceptable historical terms "pioneers," "trailblazers," using words of definition that convinced them of their own reality, "those who venture into unknown or unclaimed or unoccupied territory to settle."

"It was like watching giant red ants," the old people said, "scurrying back and forth, carrying objects twice their size, heads bent to the tedious tasks of their own making. Building. Building. And, every now and then, they fell upon one another striking death blows to their own fellows, biting them until they were stilled. Remorselessly dragging the carcasses away into the mass of pebbles and stones. And it was like we were invisible to them."

"Then," they continued, "when they looked up and saw us they struck out at us, too, in whatever way suited them, began calling us lazy and obstinate. This kind of thing went on for a long time."

Even at the turn of the century, when it was thought by whites that the Indians would soon "vanish," the Sioux had their own vanishing wishes. They wanted to rid themselves of these strange people now called *wasichus*, who had by then become their white overseers: the military first, then the field missionaries, and finally the religious and governmental bureaucrats.

How to survive the invasion became the subject of great controversy and conflict among the people, and there were many differences of opinion. Some were aware that collectively, they frightened the wits out of many of the whites who lived next to them and they feared the knee-jerk response to that fear, which was to call in the soldiers. They had seen it. At Wounded Knee. And they had no desire for that to be repeated.

They reasoned, then, that individually Indians didn't seem quite so threatening to their white neighbors. For this and for other reasons as well, many of the Sioux accepted the rise of individual Indian leadership, even though they knew it to be largely unconnected to the cultural ideologies and *tiospayes* of the past, even though they knew that federal Indian policy of the time was still based on theft and the intent of breaking up of Indian lands still held in common.

Aurelia's maternal grandfather, Amos Chante Numpa Two Heart (he had an important name, one that was old and well known among the people), was quick to play the white man's game. His father had gone to Carlisle; thus, he too went to the local boarding schools where he was set upon becoming literate and cunning and smart in the white man's ways.

This was a man who was very different from the old grandmother and the old lover who told Aurelia the stories. He was a man they spoke of often and not in admiring terms.

"I think he got the ideas for his political life from the reading that he did," said the old woman in response to Aurelia's youthful questioning. "After he came home from that school in the East, you know, he read everything he could get his hands on. And he decided to just become an important man. He wanted to be important and rich, you know," her voice heavy with sarcasm, her smile a sneer, "like a white man." There was no mistaking her contempt for upward mobility and the American Dream.

Quite by accident, Two Heart had discovered some papers of the Indian reformer Lewis Meriam, the white scholar of American federal policy toward Indians who at that time was laying the groundwork for what was called the "Indian Reorganization Act." This legislation had at its heart the democratic one-man, one-vote ideal based on the concept of majority rule, something that rarely made sense to tribal people who labored toward the ideal of communal consensus. Meriam had during these years brought to the attention of the public the facts that so-called modern Indians were on the whole making less than $100 per year (only 2 percent, he said, making $500); and that their children were dying at an unconscionable rate. This was happening in modern America, he raged, and this meant that the very physical survival of the American Indian was at risk in what he called the "greatest democracy on the face of the earth." As Amos Two Heart read these papers, he decided that he would lead his people to a better life; that he, because he was educated and smart, was destined to make decisions.

"Amos knew many things," said Aurelia's grandmother, "and he really believed that Indians should come out of the blanket."

"Yes," agreed Aurelia, though she was not sure what "out of the blanket" really meant and she knew better than to ask. It was a white-man idea, after all, one that the old woman would probably dismiss without discussion.

Such ideas about Indian life were seldom a part of the communal discussion concerning itself, yet it was a public matter in the white world. During those spring days in 1932 when Amos found himself waiting for his married daughter, Myrna, to finish up her chores as cleaning lady at the St. Anne's Episcopal Church, he began to cogitate about these matters.

Myrna, at the time pregnant with her second child, who would be named Aurelia and given to her father's mother to raise, paid little or no attention to the files kept by the Christian fathers, but Amos found them fascinating. Thus, he started reading these newly distributed reports surreptitiously and made it a practice to come earlier and earlier to pick up his daughter.

"Public Health work and administration and relief work is inadequate," Amos read. "Living conditions are appalling." He looked across the road and saw rundown houses, tarpaper shacks, tents, and tipis just like those in the glossy black-and-white photos enclosed in the reports. He knew he was on to something and he began to talk to his fellow tribesmen about their situation.

"There wasn't very many of us in those days who could speak and read English, you know," said Grandmother as a way of explaining the leadership role of Amos Two Heart. "Everybody thought Amos was real smart because he could read and even write in English."

Amos, of course, did not discourage them. Every week for several months he looked forward to the three-mile trip to St. Anne's, where he sat in the minister's rooms unbeknownst to and undiscovered by the churchmen, reading the papers that were first acquired and then often kept secret by the religious bureaucrats who had a hand in running the missions.

Some time later, before Aurelia was out of her cradleboard and when the U.S. Congress had set in motion the appropriate legislative apparatuses for individual Indian leadership to emerge, Two Heart filed his petitions with the Bureau of Indian Affairs to run for election to a "district" councilman position in the new government, the first such elected official in the history of the tribe.

"He won the election not because he was any smarter than any of the rest of us, but because his name was well known among the people and he had many powerful relatives," Aurelia's grandmother told her as they analyzed the event. "You know. In the old way." She didn't mention that he had other attributes as well. He could, for example, speak excellent English and was fluent in all three dialects of the tribal language. The old woman didn't mention that he was often asked to serve as translator in court cases involving tribal members, and as a consultant to the bureaucrats on other professional matters. All she said was, "He was a man who knew how to make himself useful to the system of making Indian/white relations appear to be just."

Most important of all, though, according to observers, was the fact that he had the good luck to have married a woman from Sisseton with a large inheritance of "allotted lands," lands he began selling off, piece by piece, to any white man who had the money, so that he could travel and purchase the things he needed to promote his political career. He enjoyed being "classy," everyone said, he wanted to be "somebody." If Two Heart saw the contradiction in rising to a leadership position in the tribe by taking land out of tribal, communal trust and thereby diminishing the people's land base, he gave no indication.

"He's just a sell-out," some of the people said, "a collaborator."

Others believed he held a position of great status and importance.

"He went to Washington, D.C., many times." Grandmother laughed an ugly laugh as she told of his behavior. "He even wore an eagle-feather headdress that had once belonged to the revered Grey Plume, had his picture taken with dignitaries, presidents, senators, and congressmen."

People who knew Two Heart saw him carry on like this for more than twenty years, enjoying the fame. He continued to read everything he could get his hands on and he developed into a great orator.

"Eventually," said Grandmother as a way of summing up, "on one of his trips to Washington, D.C., he signed the documents permitting the flooding of hundreds of thousands of acres of tribal lands for the federal government's hydropower development of the Missouri River."

"The Mni Sosa was no more." The old woman waved her hands in the air as though dismissing the entire story along with her anger.

The signing of the papers was very nearly Two Heart's last official act and it heralded in the essential mid-century events which, again, robbed the people of independent economic well-being. The old grandmother was not the only critic of this historical event. Everyone, after a few years, said that the destruction of the mythic river simply brought on more "relocations," more "terminations," more so-called anti-poverty schemes.

Bitterly, Aurelia's grandmother, though she had never cared for Amos's wife and failed to behave as a good in-law toward her, assessed what she considered the final obscenity: "It was in 1952, Aurelia, that his old woman died. You remember, don't you? Didn't you go to her funeral?"

"Yes."

"We heard that she was alone in her little one-room 'gov'ment' house on the day of her death. At the last minute, you know, they saw him ride into the yard on his bay stallion. You remember that one with the white blaze? He was just returning from a meeting of the tribes at the Agency."

"Yeah. I remember," Aurelia said. "It was when the Corps of Engineers announced that everyone, each and every tribal member, was going to get a $400 per capita payment for the lands that were flooded."

"Um-hunh. Well, the story that was told is that when he went to her bedside she tried to say something to him. He put his ear down to her mouth but she could not speak. And so she died unknown and unexplained."

"I wonder what she was trying to say."

Her grandmother smiled wickedly. "She probably wanted to say, 'Go to Hell, old man.' "

4

An Attempt at Escape

Roused by her own muffled sounds of anguish, Aurelia startled
herself into wakefulness. It was one of those grey-dawned days,
when the early winter cold permeated the morning blackness to
cast ominous shadows on the inner walls of the old frame house.
She held her hands briefly to her stomach and lay still for only a
moment, contemplating the secret knowledge that women have
contemplated for all generations. Then she rose and dressed
slowly and with great care. She picked up the leather case that
held her artwork and crafts, her beaded jewelry and fine pieces,
and stood in the darkened living room for just a moment listening
to her grandmother snoring, unsuspecting and alone, in the back
bedroom.

The place was deathly quiet except for a clock on the wall
ticking away the minutes. Silently pulling the door closed after
her, she looked briefly into the darkness of the sky and then
straight ahead. The pole fence encompassing the spacious yard
came into view. It seemed like a symbol. A barrier. Beyond it
there were limitless possibilities and she was ready to seek them
out.

She drove away in her grandmother's old car, which usually
sat in the yard almost abandoned, rusty and unreliable from
disuse. The low growl of the engine made her worry that it might
be too loud, but then she remembered that the old lady slept
like the dead and nothing short of a tornado could waken her.

The car crept past the gate and creaked on down the dirt road like a badger sniffing a trail and Aurelia held her breath.

It was a spur-of-the-moment act. No planning. It just seemed to Aurelia on that grey morning that an escape was possible. A last chance, perhaps, an act of desperation and rebellion and denial. She didn't switch on the headlights until she turned onto the gravelled road and she felt uneasy until she had fled the nearby tribal housing compound and raced toward town on the paved highway.

She drove nonstop, nearly two hundred miles, through the sleeping capital city, past the sparse little one-horse villages, DeGrey, Rousseau, Philip, Wasta. She met few cars and passed none until she reached the freeway at Wall. She kept an anxious eye on the rear-view mirror as though someone might be following her. She reached Rapid City just as the stores and shops began opening their doors.

As she pulled into a city parking lot she saw what looked like the same old picnic tables on the grounds of the Sioux Museum, a place established by the federal government for the keeping of tribal antiquities on the very grounds which the Sioux believed had been stolen from them, a place run by white bureaucrats which was seen by some as an overtly paternal, yet supposedly benign symbol of the paradoxical attitude whites held toward the Sioux, a sort of kindness mixed with contempt and aversion.

A skiff of sparkling snow covered the outdoor tables. Withered leaves still clung determinedly to the trees. This was a familiar place to Aurelia: her father used to like to come here, especially in the summer, and sit on the grounds where he would usually be joined by some of his relatives whom he hadn't seen in a long time. Often someone would have a bottle of whiskey which he or she would share with the others. It seemed to Aurelia to be an off-reservation meeting place for the people, like those isolated summer swimming places out in the hills where the Dakotahs could gather in convivial family circles whenever the heat of the town drove them out.

Sometimes, if her father was on good terms with her grandmother, he would bring them both here and afterward they would go around and visit relatives. A cousin. Or an aunt. They especially liked to visit an uncle who came to the Black Hills back in the "dirty-thirties" to work in the sawmills. Though the man's wife had left him to return to the reservation, he had stayed on. No one in the family could really understand his motives, but he had a large circle of friends in town and many women.

Aurelia's grandmother, who never liked to leave home for faraway places, objected strenuously to what she called Albert's "running around the country," but it was part of her father's way and Aurelia found it interesting, exciting.

∿

"Okay to park here?" Aurelia asked the man in uniform. He nodded. She took off her wrap and pushed down the sleeves of her shirt, buttoning them carefully. The air smelled of the coldness of the pine, a characteristic of the South Dakota/ Wyoming Black Hills, and she saw her breath white and chalky.

Now on this cold wintry day she walked toward the familiar museum, wearing jeans and cowboy boots and carrying the little case that held her quillwork and jewelry, her beaded medallions and earrings, which she hoped to consign for sale with the museum keepers. Or, maybe, she thought, they would buy it immediately. This selling of arts and crafts was something her grandmother had done for many years. The door of the stone building opened easily.

A family of tourists, adults with several children at their sides, walked silently about the rooms admiring the wall hangings, the tables holding cases of artwork. Bright lights shimmering against glass fell on a stunning hide painting that looked very ancient and precious.

The museum seemed to Aurelia to be less formal than she remembered, possessing now an air of familiarity and warmth. She felt encouraged and found herself thinking that this was an important step she was taking. For the first time on her own. Her thoughts strayed beyond the material objects before her. Maybe there was a world of art and culture out there beyond the menial jobs she had been holding down, intermittently, as her mother had before her: cleaning the church houses on the reservation, cooking and serving cafeteria food at the schools.

Maybe there was a place where she could work, a place where she could bring her grandmother. This was a time, after all, when people were moving away from the homelands in great numbers because of the flooding, because of the "relocation," as they called it. The Shields family left and "relocated" in Minneapolis. The Joneses and Ashleys and St. Johns and Red Eagles all had moved away just in the last few months. Thinking of this, Aurelia looked upon this journey as an experiment, a little test, as, she thought, all things must change.

Indians weren't the only ones in America who didn't know quite what to do in these times of modern progress. The war in Vietnam was still raging despite the groundswell of protest. Thousands of Americans across the country, believing themselves to be facing terrible hostility, unnamable and confusing, were in the streets marching, demonstrating, and protesting against the continuation of a war they felt was becoming less and less defensible as a noble American ideal. So-called movements of liberation were afoot in the land: the generation gap forced young people away from the hopes and desires of their parents; drug use became a way of life.

Many Indians, however, whose lands were flooded, many tribes who no longer had a land base, found "relocation" to Chicago, L.A., Seattle, the only way out. Many stories have been told about what happened to the people when they went to the cities, gathered at the friendship houses, and became urbans.

It is certain that the Indians who stayed on the reservations have told different stories. Only half the lands of the Big Pipe family were under water, and while the brothers Sheridan, Jason, Virgil, and Antony served in the armed forces, their father, Harvey, continued to live on the homelands. Uneasily, he watched his livelihood as a cattleman undergo destructive modifications. He became ill when his sons were sent off to the baffling American/Asian war and with caution he simply waited for their return.

He saw the subsistence farms and ranches of his relatives, friends, and neighbors disappear in the flooding backwaters of the hydropower dams, saw the cattle moving ahead of the incoming water, and saw them become scattered and lost. The livestock of his neighbor John Tatekeya was stolen and never recovered.

The Midwest was illuminated by electricity and white power brokers made their deals. Irrigation was at long last possible in semi-arid regions. Eventually, overall farm income in the white communities of the region would rise to unprecedented heights. Federal agencies profited from water sales throughout the West, while Indian income fell to an all-time low.

"They're gonna starve us out," said the old men like Harvey Big Pipe. "Gettin' us off our lands, one way or another," was the way he talked about the new government policies. He refused to cash his government check for $400, letting it lie on the table amongst papers and discarded mail until it somehow disappeared. Yet, for what was left of the homelands of people like Big Pipe, "programs" were devised. A newly organized Farm and Ranch program administered by the white bureaucrats employed in the Bureau of Indian Affairs was started during this period, with the purpose of renewing and revitalizing the subsistence ranching done by Indians since the late 1800s.

What was envisioned was this: If the government bureaucrats could find an Indian who still possessed land of his own—that is to say, someone who still had some allotted land—and if they could find an Indian who had not gone to war or had not been relocated—that is, sent off to the cities to learn a useful trade like welding or barbering—or if they could find a tribe that still possessed its trust lands, they would immediately make these Indians and tribes "eligible" to develop themselves as beef and pork producers for "greater America."

Without much fanfare and even less enthusiasm, and on the basis of how much land they had available to them, Indians who qualified signed up for the plan and were provided with x numbers of cattle purchased and distributed by the federal government. An Indian (or Interior) Department brand (ID) was burned into these critters so there would be no confusion about who really owned them, much as the federal government had always held title to Indian lands. Credit systems would be run out of Washington, D.C., where massive regulations and procedures were promulgated. As the cattle multiplied, Indians would pay back with the expected calf crop.

This plan, the politicians told everyone, would cost the American taxpayer nothing, since the thousands of acres of flooded Indian lands, the miles and miles of destroyed timberlands and riverbottoms had already paid the sacrificial price for such "progress." They seldom publicized the fact that Indian-held lands had been reduced by five hundred and fifty square miles nor that each Indian had received a $400 check for his loss.

"You will increase your net worth over a period of years," the Indians were told. "And you will become as white men." Though no one knew exactly what it all meant, many of the Sioux leaders and certainly Harvey Big Pipe lived in dread that they might, indeed, become as white men.

In this time of great chaos in America, Aurelia, the Dakotah Sioux woman from the reservation homelands of the Crow Creek, strolled the aisles of the museum. She was not immune to the events of the world. She too was seeking assurance, community, purpose in a world of seemingly hodgepodge, inexplicable events. She hugged her arms against herself and felt the warmth of the well-ordered museum.

For a few serene moments she walked quietly about the silent Indian Museum, a return to a place with which she was acquainted, absorbing momentarily the presence of the past glory of the Dakotahs. Old pictures of tribal chieftains, all of them now deceased, hung on every wall. Behind glass, mannequins stood in full regalia, the male models dressed in war shirts, the females dressed in yellowed buckskin or the shell dresses that had become popular after trade cloth became available out on the Plains. An Indian saddle adorned with brightly beaded accoutrements caught Aurelia's eye. She touched the long strands of horse hair tied at the corners. No one had these saddles in their possession any more. They were given up, one supposed, when the U.S. Government confiscated the huge herds of Indian horses at the turn of the century, just about the time of the Wounded Knee Massacre.

In the parades and celebrations at home which used to take place when she was a child, she had watched her grandmother's sister ride in such a saddle showing off her finery. The people had stood along the road and smiled and waved to show their pride in such a woman. Blankets covered the rump of the bay mare she rode and there was a drum group on a flatbed truck following and their songs filled the warm air. Aurelia felt, suddenly, like her breath was coming hard, and she gripped the little leather bag she carried.

Her eyes fell upon a drum placed just inside the doorway to the book section of the museum and she thought it looked very much like the one Harvey Big Pipe kept in a room just off the living room where the family and visitors often gathered. Aurelia thought of Jason sitting beside his father at the drum when visitors and family came to sing. He was probably at home right at this very moment, Aurelia said to herself, getting ready to eat with his father, his brothers. And here I am, she thought. What am I doing here? How could I have left Grandmother alone without any explanation, deserted Jason as if he were a mere whim?

Within minutes of entering the museum, Aurelia knew with a calamitous suddenness that coming here had been a mistake. The silence and the warmth, so soothing at first, turned morgue-like, threatening. She began to feel great panic. For some reason, her own violations and sins and errors seemed all at once to resound in the chilly rooms, intensifying the presence of the objects collected there. Her small deceptions, her carelessness, her denial, and finally, her appalling violation of all the rules women have been taught to live by and the dishonesty of her role during the years she spent with Tatekeya, the old man who was married to someone else.

The moccasins with beaded soles and the wax figurines with false, stiff hair; the ancient redstone pipes and the hoary peyote rattles covered with dust behind the glass, opalescent in death and disuse; medicine-wheel hair ties of every color and size, gaudy earrings and silver bracelets overflowing the cabinets and counters—they all seemed only to mourn her demise, her failure, both past and present. Suddenly she could not bear to be in their presence any longer.

Just then she heard a pleasant voice say her name. "Aurelia," said the woman behind the counter, smiling and coming toward her. "What on earth are you doing here? We weren't expecting you!"

When Aurelia did not answer the woman asked, "Did you bring some more of your things for sale?" She came closer. ". . . and did you bring your grandmother's . . . ?" The pleasant-sounding woman reached for the square case, but Aurelia quickly turned away from her.

She recognized the woman as someone who often purchased things for the museum from Indian craftsmen and women, and she was the person Aurelia had come to see. Yet a rising paranoia, unexplained and indistinct, moved her like a sleepwalker toward the door. Suddenly, she turned and quickly left the building, fully aware that her actions seemed rude and strange.

She ran to the car where she had left her canvas wrap and struggled into it. Chilled and afraid, she sat with her hands deep in her pockets.

Afraid of what? The women who worked at the museum were not strangers to her and they had always been kind and helpful. They had always acknowledged her Grandmother Blue as an important Sioux woman artisan, had asked often to market to the public, especially to the tourist buyers, the beaded and quilled things they both made. Her fear was unexplained. She backed the car out of the parking lot and, trembling, drove downtown and parked on St. Joe street in the icy sunlight.

She watched herself, real, material, in the reflection of the plate-glass windows as she walked past the Alex Johnson Hotel. She went to the end of the block, crossed the street, and kept going. Then, starting the whole circuit again, she carefully avoided the same windows so that people inside the stores wouldn't get the impression if they noticed her that she was walking the streets indecisively. They always think the worst about Indians, anyway, in this town, she thought. Educated and enlightened as I am, smiling, little good it does me here in a place like this. And if the waitresses and others were to see me walking aimlessly they would think I'm a whore looking for work. That's what they really think about Indian women, anyway. Pulling the wrap around her legs, she thought, winter is here already. What can I do?

Her random thoughts stirred in her a terrible melancholy. She began to recall the times she had come here with Tatekeya. Many times. Many times. With great arrogance they drank whiskey and laughed and made love and then became saddened because of the failed promises, the unwillingness of either of them to recognize that what had drawn them together was loss and grief. And then they took another drink. And laughed again. It had gone on for many years and now it was over. She looked into the windows of the hock shops filled with the abandoned treasures from lives in transition or lives of despair. Used quilts and clothing. Knives and guns. Old desks and typewriters. Children's toys. A child's bicycle. Blue. Trimmed in white. Did he outgrow it? Did he weep at its loss? Thoughts of a child's abandoned playthings, precious and imbued with sacred powers for the memory, washed over her like the pain of her own childhood memories.

Wa-cin-i-bo-sa-ka. That was the way Grandpa Blue used to explain his own feelings about his own discouragement, and standing near the window, near tears, she treasured momentarily the times he shared with her. He told her *wa cin i bo sa ka* was one of those words that has great emotional tension, one not heard or used very often: it really means to lose one's heart, to no longer have the heart to go on. Though Grandpa Blue's life seemed to Aurelia to be unflawed, he nonetheless had confided to her that there was a brief time when he was seventy years old and in grave ill health that he had been filled with hopelessness, grief. Aurelia had been surprised at this confidence by the old man, because she had always thought of him as the great survivor, the one with the capacity to overcome his own doubts and she wanted to be like that, to put aside trivial concerns, to rise above any stubborn and troublesome and parochial conviction about private wishes and personal need. Truth was, now she too was on the verge of losing her heart to go on.

What of our secret, she mused, Jason's and mine?

What of the awesome secret of a new life growing inside me, only a tacit and guarded luminescence of the spirit at this point?

As she stood looking at the abandoned objects of lives unknown, she felt a strange dizziness. Just then her secret knowledge seemed overwhelming, like a moment of religious entrancement, like being deafened by the swelling sound of the drums which sometimes happens as you are caught up in ritual, at first the sound is small and flat, yet flowing into long and narrow echoes. When it stops there is a withering silence and you hold your secret both in joy and in terror. Confused and near tears, Aurelia turned away from the window not knowing whether to regard herself as the greatest fool or as a woman blessed.

Unseeing, Aurelia walked into the Bar and Grill on St. Joe Street and sat down. When the bartender came over, she pulled some change from her jeans pocket and ordered a beer. The bartender, wearing a soiled half apron and sporting a huge beard, put down a doily before carefully placing a mug of foamed brew in front of her.

On the doily, she saw the words *"Days of '76"* printed in a semicircle around the picture of a pack mule train and a wizened old miner holding up a gem. She cupped her chin in her left hand and with her right twisted the glass in its own watery rings. Strains of a bass guitar pulsating from the record player and the moan of a Cajun song of despair accompanied her own feelings of failure. *A song like that sounds good,* Tatekeya used to tell her, *when things is goin' to hell.* She swiveled in her seat and looked at the flickering lights beneath the tinted plastic of the record player and a faint smile touched her lips. She was lost in a private reverie.

"Say . . . ain't you one of them LaRouche girls?"

Startled, she looked into the exhausted, red-streaked eyes of a man of indeterminate age, his black shiny shirt open at the neck revealing a ruffle of red chest hair. She had never seen such naked pain in anyone's eyes before, and it frightened her. She turned back to her beer without answering.

She squinted into the mirror across the bar as the man, lurching and clumsy, sat down one stool away from her.

"I ain't in no condition . . . ," he began, wiping some imagined spill of liquid from his shirt.

He breathed heavily. "You know, I been here . . . " he looked down with suddenly empty eyes at the glossy counter and stared, unseeing. In moments, he wet his loose lips and swallowed the gathering saliva and began again:

"Ah . . . I been here," he took a long, deep breath, "ah . . . a long . . . time," and smiled what she supposed was calculated to be an engaging grin, apologetic and boyish.

When she said nothing, he took this as an invitation to go on. "They call me . . . Diab . . . " he hiccupped, " . . . Diablo," he said.

She started to button her wrap but he hardly noticed.

Smiling still, he said, " . . . and they don't call me that . . . for . . . for . . . nuthin', ya know whatta mean?"

He leered and moved to the empty stool between them.

There was almost an hypnotic effect to the whole scene as Aurelia's mother's face, at first shining and formal, then suddenly pale and haggard, flashed before her. Disgusted, Aurelia thought about her mother's drunken ravings: "Ya know whatta mean, baby?" was one of her mother's favorite sayings when she was tying one on and, for Aurelia, there was nothing more disgusting than a slobbering drunk's gibberish. She pushed her beer away and fled.

Hurrying from the bar, her footsteps echoed emptily on the sidewalk, hollow as sounds from the canyons surrounding this tacky tourist town of mid-America, a place that was, before the whites came here, the heart of activity for the Pte people, the Buffalo People, the Sioux.

The leering man did not follow her, perhaps because he could not, and she was thankful for that. She got into her car and sat quietly, listening to the distress in her own breathing.

When she drove out of town, up the ramp entering I-90 and headed east toward home, she had the feeling that the beat-up old car wasn't going to make it. The engine labored, grinding its dry gears. At the Badlands Exit the transmission started to slip again, and the rig had no power. She pulled the shifting gear into low, but the engine only raced and she had to turn off the road and roll the car to a stop at the side of the interstate.

She got out, lifted up the hood of the car, and looked blankly at the engine. She checked the oil dipstick, then checked it again, but couldn't see the mark without a flashlight. She held the stick to the headlight but still couldn't make out the mark. Weeds at the side of the road were blowing recklessly in the wind and the chill of the night was all around. Feeling panicky, she slammed the hood down and got back in the car.

After a moment she tried the engine again and, miraculously, it started. Tentatively, she put the car in reverse. She was startled when she felt the old car move laboriously backward. With one foot on the clutch and pressing hard on the accelerator, she felt a surge of power and then, carefully, she shifted to "drive" and waited. As soon as she felt the shifting mechanism fall into place, she pulled cautiously out into the right lane. She drove slowly down the empty road off toward Wall, Philip, Hayes, expecting any moment that the car would lose power. Her eyes stung as she looked into the night illuminated by her headlights. Her body was rigid, shoulders hunched forward.

She made it nearly to Hayes before the transmission went out completely. Then, no matter how she manipulated the gas pedal, the engine simply roared and the car remained motionless.

Exhausted, she managed to shove the car to the side of the road. Then she covered herself with an old sheepskin blanket. She fell asleep lying curled on the side of the front seat and though she slept soundly she remembered an old story even in her dreams:

There was a woman who got jealous of her husband's second wife and left him, and she started walking back . . . to the camp of her parents. She walked and walked for a long time and then, when she got tired, she had to find a hole in the earth where she could lie down and sleep, hidden from her enemies. The grandfathers came . . . to help her . . . and, later they made a fire for her. And . . . they told her where to find the ti(n)psina. She cooked the meat they had provided . . . and the roots . . . and . . .

The coyotes kept watch over the sleeping woman but she did not hear their cries. Neither did she see, as dawn appeared, the hardy sparrows flitting about. Like the cottonwoods along the roadside shaking off their last withered leaves into the rising wind, Aurelia stretched her stiff body in the morning light and watched without emotion the start of the deep, violet hue in the east signalling the sudden blaze of the sun. In the next few moments of awakening, she wondered how this beautiful scene could turn to pure menace, but she was certain that it could and she felt apprehensive.

She was chilled, her hair matted, but the sun seemed to hold some promise for the day. She sat up and tried to start the car again, but when she couldn't, she wasn't surprised. She began walking, carrying with her the small brown suitcase that contained her beaded things and quillwork. She walked doggedly for nearly eight miles before an old farmer in a green Dodge truck stopped and asked if she wanted a ride.

"Sure is a hell of a day for walking," the old farmer said, smiling cheerfully as she reached for the open door with aching fingers. He spit some tobacco out of the side window before he shifted gears. "The goddamned wind is startin' up again and it's enough to make a fella want to move clean out of the goddamned country."

Her lips stiff with cold, Aurelia nodded.

"You live around here?" the old man asked. "I ain't seen you around here before."

"No. I live out past Pierre," gesturing.

"Well, I ain't goin' that far. I can take you as far as East Corner, though. And then I turn off there . . . oh . . . about . . . I'd say . . . about four miles southeast of Hayes is where I'm headed."

Aurelia nodded again.

Her feet and knees ached as they began to warm up in the truck. Thankful for even this little bit of help and good humor, shielded from the cold wind, she smiled foolishly as she listened to the old man talk.

"I'm lookin' at some Registered Hereford bulls over there," the old gentleman said conversationally. "I'm prob'ly not gonna buy 'til spring, but I'm a-lookin'."

He paused.

"You know, when you get to be my age . . . a lotta folks think you're too goddamned old to be runnin' cattle, but I don't give a shit what they say. I'm not quittin' 'til I'm six foot under."

They passed a roadsign that read: *"Lost Enjun? Make a Reservation at Sioux Motel, Murdo, South Dakota."* The old farmer kept driving and talking, oblivious to the tasteless pun, and Aurelia stared straight ahead.

At Hayes she thanked him for the ride, and he waved cheerily as he drove south to look for breeding stock for his herd.

Aurelia had two dollars left and with it she went into the store and bought a bag of potato chips and a cola. She stood uncertainly in front of the man at the cash register, then, in a moment of optimism, she put her leather case on the counter, opened it, and held up a beautifully beaded hairpiece.

"Ah, say, uh . . . you wouldn't want to buy this, would you?"

The man laughed a short dismissive laugh. "What the hell would I do with that?"

"Oh." She felt embarrassed, like a beggar. She closed the case and escaped quickly through the swinging doors.

Now I'm really broke, she thought as she resumed her homeward journey munching her chips, the can of cola in her back pocket. I guess this is what they call "flat broke," and she shook her head in disgust with herself. She had felt certain that the people at the Sioux Museum in Rapid City would have bought her crafts, as they often traded with and bought from Indians in the area. Because she had been taught by her grandmother, she was considered an excellent and respected craftswoman. Together, she and her grandmother were known for their quill and beadwork, knowledgeable of the traditional designs and techniques, famous as quiltmakers, too. Not, however, she thought with a grudging smile, by that guy behind the cash register at the Hayes store. If only she hadn't left the museum so quickly.

It had caught her by surprise. That presence of the spirits in the museum. And her fear. That, too, surprised her. She gave in to an exasperated smile as she remembered. She stretched her arms, yawned, and felt glad to have made her escape from that place. Suddenly, the vastness all about her was quickening. In the summertime these hills were always like green velvet. Now, only brown and brittle grasses covered them and the constant chilling wind, inevitable precursor of the first blizzard of the season, made its own sounds of discontent.

Listening to her footsteps crunch rhythmically on the gravel at the shoulder of the road, she felt defenseless against the wind and, as an occasional car swept past, she was pushed forward in its wake. The canvas serape she wore whipped about her jeans and for the second time as night fell, she grew more apprehensive.

In the dark the sounds of her own footsteps echoed and she kept turning around to see who was following. She didn't know whether to worry about the occasional oncoming automobile lights or what to do about Jason and her pregnancy. She withdrew from all of it into private thoughts about her beloved grandmother. Who was taking care of her? They would all be angry at her that she'd gone off and left the old woman unattended. It was the first time in all their lives that the old woman would prepare for bed not knowing the whereabouts of her granddaughter. She must be sick with worry.

Across the ditch and beyond the barbed wire fence she saw in the moonlight the dark streak in the land that she recognized as Dry Willow Creek. Once, a long time ago, when she was here hunting rabbits with her father and his father, they had shown her this place where it was said the great chieftain Sitting Bull of the Hunkpati was born. Way out here on Willow Creek. They said his birth was a happy interruption of his parents' trip to the Oglala country. Aurelia's grandfather, because of his familiarity with the places between the prairie and the pine-covered Black Hills, often talked about the various landmarks as sources of interest in the universe. It was a habit that many people of that time shared.

In an attempt to rid herself of her rising fears of the darkened road and those traveling it, she next tried to put herself into the old man's frame of reference concerning this place, which turns unaccountably red and rich as it approaches the sacred places in the west, the precious lands stolen from Oyate by men from a different world. "I can't blame any man for wanting to live here, in this place," said the grandfather who had had so much influence on Aurelia, and in his telling of history his grand-daughter understood that he no longer even blamed the thieves for their lack of honor, their greediness. What he continued to believe, however, was that they were enemies of the land.

He had continued to tell Aurelia that the mythology of those invaders was a creation of the mind, not the heart, and when he spoke to her intimately, he always told her that he found them to be forever remote and incapable of introspection. "Don't ever marry a white man," he told her, though the idea had never crossed her mind. She supposed that his cautioning words had more to do with her mother's example than anything else. "Don't ever bring a white man into our family."

Finally, the darkness was all around and Aurelia, near exhaustion, left the road to find a place to sleep. She tried several places, but when her strength gave out she simply lay down out of the bitter wind at the foot of some haystacks near cottonwoods by a small ravine. Damp leaves covered the cold ground and she rested her head on the hard, brown suitcase filled with her valuables. Fearful and alone, she wept for herself and her grandmother and the new life she was carrying, and, in the dark, she came to the reluctant conclusion that in reality all of her many worries were now reduced to one: Jason. She had not yet made him a man of legend, but she knew that any man who is the father of a child is more than mere impulse; that, sooner or later, he becomes the central figure of any narrative, an imposing protagonist about whom stories will be told. If this fateful little journey to Rapid City told her nothing else, it told her that. She squeezed the tears from her eyes as she held them tightly closed.

The night was miserably cold and ominous sounds came from all around her. In the morning, she walked on though her ankles and feet were swollen with the cold and her legs trembled. She wondered if her fingers were frostbitten, as they felt numb.

A faded Chevy van bearing a South Dakota license plate starting with the number nine slowed to a crawl beside her and two shiny-faced men smiled from the windows.

"You wanna ride, ma'am?" She thought they sounded polite yet phony, and she was in a moment alert and on her guard. She looked at them warily, instantly calculating, her thoughts racing. First the drunk in the bar in the city, now this. She felt for her pocketknife, but her numb fingers could hardly grasp it.

"Uh . . . no . . . thanks."

When they continued to drive slowly beside her and grin, she said, "I'm just going over there." She pointed by lifting her chin toward a rundown farmhouse in the distance. She shifted her little carrying case to the other hand and knew that if they had any sense at all, they would not believe her lie. The wretched little farmhouse, it was quite obvious even from this distance, had not had any occupants for at least fifty years. She put her hand in her pocket and felt the knife again and managed to close her fingers around it.

"You sure you don't wanna ride, Pocahontas?" one of the men persisted, his questioning now close and threatening.

She said nothing.

She walked faster. The van picked up speed.

"Hey, little Injun gal. You're a swe-e-e-et looker." His voice turned soft now. "Hey, we could have a good time . . . a good time. C'mon."

The van stopped and one of the men got out and grabbed Aurelia's arm.

She shook off his grasp just as a grey car drove past slowly and stopped about a hundred feet ahead. Aurelia ran and got in. A middle-aged man with two blonde teenaged daughters smiled at her apprehensively.

"You . . . you . . . in trouble?" the man asked, peering at her anxiously.

"Yeah. I'm . . . they . . . they . . . "

She was breathing hard and she had a frightened look in her eyes as she put the small knife back in her jeans pocket.

"It's a good thing you stopped," she gasped. And then she repeated, "Thank god you stopped!" feeling panicky and foolish at the same time. "I don't know what would have . . . "

She left the sentence unfinished as she tried to catch her breath. She had never been so frightened.

"My car . . . it stalled . . . way back there. And I've been walking for a couple of days."

They murmured their consternation.

They all looked out of the rear window and saw the men standing beside the van laughing.

Aurelia put the carrying case on her knees, put her head against the cushions, and closed her eyes.

"I really appreciate your stopping . . . " she said. Her rescuers didn't know exactly what to think, fearing for her predicament, yet awkward and silent. They drove several miles in silence.

"Yeah, that was scary," said one of the blonde daughters. "Maybe we ought to report them."

"Too bad we didn't get their license plate numbers," said the second daughter.

Within the hour they let her off at the downtown post office building in Pierre.

As she waved and smiled and thanked them profusely, gathering up her wrap and jewelry case, she assured them, "I'll be fine," but they regarded her with skepticism, smiling halfheartedly. Because she looked younger than her thirty-five years, it was often difficult for her to convince others that she was a woman of some competence, the arranger of her own destiny. Even she, though, after this journey into the presence of misfortune when she had put herself in harm's way through her own miscalculation, her own foolishness, even she was unsure of her own glib prediction.

"I wasn't sure you would come," he'd said a few days after her return from the disastrous journey to the museum, his pickup parked behind the low trees, windows open to the heavy air. He handed her the bottle of wine in celebration of her homecoming.

"Just had to wait until after dark."

She saw his look of love, his youthful face, bemused yet unafraid, coming close and bending over her as if in a hurry. There was little talk of love but she felt his warmth, suffocating and unbearable. All of a sudden she couldn't breathe.

"Whatsa matter?" He drew away from her.

"What?"

"Are you nervous?"

"So?"

She took another drink.

"No need to get hostile," he said, momentarily put off. "I just don't want to . . . to . . . make you nervous." His eyes showed confusion, tenderness, his face flushed.

She turned toward him and said softly, "Yeah. I know."

"I want to impress you, you know, so you will want me."

"Well, I'm . . . I'm here."

"Does that mean you want me?"

She found it hard to admit, " . . . um . . . I had to come, didn't I?"

She began to realize that all he wanted was the complete experience of being loved, with no need for defining what it meant, no need to fix on every embrace, every conversation some question of intention. Love and passion had never been enough for her and the manner in which the two of them had gotten together in the first place, by chance, surreptitious and furtive, created barriers for her every time they saw each other.

He was whispering in her ear, "Why are you like this?" Even as he asked, he was excited by her reluctance.

She put her hand to his smooth face and looked at him.

"I don't know, Jay."

He looked down and started unbuttoning her shirt, slowly. He looked into her eyes and smiled.

Smiling back, she said again, "I don't know."

"It's gonna be okay," he told her as his mouth found her breast.

She felt his breath on her. She was in way over her head, like the way she imagined it felt when you overdosed on something. It was, literally, like Tatekeya had told her, "you'll not be able to catch your breath."

She felt Jason brush her hair from her forehead, and then he asked, "It's gonna be okay, isn't it, Aurelia?"

"It's never gonna be all right again, Jason, and I . . . " Her voice trailed off.

"Never, huh?" he was preoccupied, his tongue in her ear, no longer thinking nor listening. "Whaddya mean 'never'?"

She did not answer.

" 'relia? What do you mean?"

"Oh, nothing. I don't mean nothing."

His lips were on hers and she put her arms around him, helplessly.

She felt the length of his body on hers. Under the low thick grey sky bursting with dampness, the wind seemed wavery, strangely empty.

That's the way it was. Awkward, sometimes furious. They hid about, refusing to commit themselves one way or another. Sometimes they would drive someplace together, then separate when they got there. She would sit with her relatives, her grandmother and sisters, her aunties Pearl and Mart, her many nephews and nieces. Jason would hang around with his brothers, his cousins. Watchful.

It went on that way and the lovers confided in no one, not even each other. Weeks and months passed.

When Aurelia's pregnancy began to show, people became uneasy with both her and Jason. Some, on the one hand, were saying that Aurelia, now thirtyish, should have known better and they would begin to wonder if she had taken advantage of Jason's youth. He was, they would remind one another, a lot younger than she. They seldom took into account that he had been in Vietnam for more than two years and, surely, was a man of some experience himself.

On the other hand, they pondered, as though it was any of their concern, what kind of a man was he to take up with her when he knew her to be the long-time mistress of a man old enough to be her father? Or, they would say, perhaps Aurelia was just becoming desperate. An old maid, you know. Over the hill, so to speak.

There was plenty of gossip. But that was nothing new to Aurelia.

In a community like hers, which revered its "young warriors" and believed them to be in charge of the future of the people, she was sure to get most of the blame for having behaved outside of the rules. And, after all, wasn't she known for carelessness about the rules? What about the thing with Tatekeya? Didn't she always break the rules? Why, when she was younger, she had had a chance to marry just like her sisters did. She could have given herself over to the safety of marriage and family.

As far as Aurelia was concerned none of it mattered. The gossip. What people thought. That had never mattered. Always having believed that the rules by which men and women lived their lives were made for the benefit of the future, the struggle to know of her place in it was unrelenting. When Tatekeya had said, "Things is goin' to hell," she hadn't ever asked what she should do about it.

Sometimes she thought she couldn't bear the uncertainty of her life. And now, Jason. She could not account for Jason's interest in her. He was ten years younger and seemed, in many ways, immature. As for her own feelings, she was drawn to him by a physical attraction that astounded her. She didn't want him or anyone else to have any claims on her but now, there seemed to be no escape from her dilemma. She didn't want him to have any claims on the baby either. She certainly didn't want to marry anyone, least of all a young man so eager. She wished she could hide from him but he was everpresent. His desire for her sometimes overwhelmed her, which made it easy to just go along with things, thoughtlessly.

5

Six Months Later—Spring *Wacipi*

It was three in the afternoon before they were all ready to go. Bags, suitcases, shawls, bustles, grass-dance outfits carefully placed on hangers. It was April and the first spring dance, a welcome relief from a long and tedious winter. Aurelia and her grandmother loved to go to *wacipi*, and they often were the first ones to arrive, driving themselves separately, not waiting for the others. "I want to hear the songs and the drum," Grandmother would say in anticipation. This time, with Grandmother's car still beside the road miles away, they borrowed Auntie Mart's old pickup and headed to the dance early.

The old lady was too fat, too decrepit, and her feet were always giving her too much trouble to do anything but her own version of the traditional Dakotah/Lakota Wiyan Dance, the stand-in-one-place kind of a woman's dance that was as old as the tribes themselves. Nonetheless, she was an enthusiastic participant and, no matter how her bones ached, she would not be left at home.

Aurelia, while she also danced the traditional way, was a dancer of great versatility. From the time she was four years old she was a show-off dancer, fancy shawl; later, even that jingle-dress dance of the Ojibway; and in her maturity she was greatly admired for her talent.

On this day as they sat amongst the others and as the spectacle began, the bleachers were full. The rows and rows of folding chairs, where Aurelia and her grandmother sat, were tightly arranged. Crowded. A singer began and his was followed by other voices. Grass dancers started with intricate steps, shoulders turning in perfect rhythm. *Warm-up time! Warm up!*

Several white spectators pushed forward to take pictures. This was the late sixties, or early seventies, after all, that period when blond people from around the country, wearing headbands and long hair, often braids, visited Indian reservations in great numbers, a time when white hippies were everywhere.

Aurelia, the dancers she knew, and most of the people of the community who had danced all their lives without much enthusiasm being shown toward them by outsiders, decided when the phenomenon first began to just ignore the intrusion of these unknown people. If for a hundred years the people could put up with the BIA officials who did all they could to disparage the faithful, to insult and ridicule those who kept up the traditions, they could just as surely ignore these new interlopers. Unlike the BIA, they seemed harmless enough.

Even though the people in the Indian community probably didn't think of themselves as analysts of social phenomena, they figured that this sudden interest in their lives was a denial of some sort by the children of middle America, a mass rejection, perhaps, of American imperialism, colonialism, materialism, a way for young Americans to cleanse themselves of their own histories which had become loathsome to them all during the Vietnam War.

Whatever the reason, they never failed to show up at every gathering. Others did, too. The nuns, self-conscious in their newly adopted civilian dress, those altruistic people who worked for charity who were known well by Aurelia and her grandmother, even the so-called "VISTA types." It was not unheard of for these searching souls to join in as dancers and when they did they were often called "wannabees," sometimes derisively, other times in kindness.

The long and bloody wars fought by the Sioux to retain their ways, their customs, their songs, was unknown to these white people who came, uninvited, to join them, trying hard to become a part of what they viewed as freedom in what they wanted to call the New Age. But what had been paid for in human misery and death was always in the minds of the Indian dancers themselves, and of the singers who began every ceremonial with a flag song in memory to that history. Thus, the white spectators and photographers at this dance and all the others illustrated, for those who cared to think about it, an ironical sense of history.

Their presence was deeply resented by many in the community. "Ever'body wants to be Ind'in," said an old man to his grandchild as they stood in the midst of the crowd. "I can remember the time when nobody, not even the Ind'ins, wanted to be Ind'in." He took the child by the hand and went away, shaking his head.

Aurelia watched as one tall man with camera in hand, his nose large and imposing, a fixed smile beneath his faded blue eyes, began to creep forward into the crowd, stepping between the seated spectators, in between the close-set chairs, bending, crouching, working the camera's buttons, sneaking quietly like a hunter taking a bead on his prey, stalking as though in the middle of a flock of unsuspecting mallards or ducks in a wet marsh. Clicking. Clicking.

Printed on his t-shirt in black cursive writing was a logo: *East African Ornithological Safaris, Ltd.* He adjusted the lens of his camera, pushed forward to within six inches of an old woman's wrinkled cheek, catching a perfect shot of the red-orange medicine wheel tied in her hair. The elderly woman leaned away from him but said nothing. Swiftly, the cameraman bent to the next dancer's moccasins, then to the heavy braids laced with buckskin. Clicking. Clicking. Turning suddenly, but with the grace of a large disciplined dog, he rushed to the side of the arbor, walking next to the dancers, his lens posed toward the faces of first one dancer, then the next.

Aurelia tried to look away but the awkwardness of it struck her as hilarious, absurd. Trying not to watch, but drawn like a magnet to the comic intensity of the man's actions, his long, hairy spider legs beneath baggy tan shorts, she slipped down into the chair and drew her shawl up to her chin, smothering laughter. The dancers seemed not to want to look at the man with the camera either, as though their refusal to acknowledge his rude presence would make him go away. With the exception of a couple of young fancy dancers, who took the whole thing like it was some kind of friendly joke, and thus distracted were posing and laughing, the other dancers seemed to concentrate on the song, the sound of the drum. It was obvious that they, in their distance, were unaffected, fluent, as though they had been born to such sacred and meaningful business as the dance.

The announcer, his voice becoming harsh and loud, almost shouted into the microphone: "No cameras. That's enough cameras!"

When the lithe, blond photographer ignored him, he repeated, "Wait a minute! You camera people. Get out of the way!"

As he turned away and covered the mike with his hand, he said out of the corner of his mouth to no one in particular, "Who the hell are these people, anyway?" The question, though it was not meant to be and no one thought of it at the time, was historical. Profound.

"Jeez! Don't they know . . . nuthing?"

The bird-watcher with the light blue eyes did not hear this commentary and was, in any case, unfazed, unaware, enthralled by the color, the movement, the spectacle. Finally, when he did not respond to the announcer, a tall Indian with red-wrapped braids and wearing a cowboy hat strode over to his side, talked to him quietly, then walked with him to the outside of the arbor where one seemed to be explaining to the others his actions. The camera man was smiling and nodding, acquiescent and agreeable.

Again, the speaker made the announcement: "Photographers. Please! Remove yourselves from the dance arena."

The Indian and the camera man disappeared from view.

Aurelia and her grandmother looked at each other and rolled their eyes. Soon the bird-watching incident was forgotten. They chatted amiably about inconsequential things, neither of them bringing up Aurelia's strange flight to Rapid City and her return. They listened to the songs, smiling. Aurelia knew that Jason stood outside of the arena lost in the crowd and that he would be watching, too. She spread her hands across her stomach and imagined she felt some faint movement of the child she was carrying. She closed her fists and rubbed her knuckles together and worried for just a moment about the fact that Jason would fearlessly want to claim this child, especially if it were a male child. He would never leave them alone, she thought, and now I'm trapped. Her life would never again be her own.

Neither of them had mentioned it, but both of them believed that she had conceived during the very first night they had spent together, that fall night after the dance when she had not resisted him. They had looked at each other in the dim light, listened to the wind outside, and, as they had held each other close, they both seemed to know that a miracle had happened. When he had asked if she would love him, she had not answered and he had wiped the tears from her eyes.

Reflective now, and sitting with the shawl held up to her chin, still vaguely amused by the funny bird-watching camera man, she started thinking about a story the Dakotahs are fond of telling about women: *A woman who became the second wife of a man and had a son. She became angry with the other wife and so she took her son and left.* These things happen, you see, her grandmother always said as she recounted the story, though they are unfortunate. *The husband followed her, of course, and tried to get his son but each time he almost got his son, the second wife took the child and moved on again. The second wife did this over and over again as a way to plague her husband who had failed to defend her in the face of the other wife's disagreeableness.*

Aurelia believed in the worth of such stories. To her, then, this meant that if her child was a boy she would have to behave very carefully, for, like the father in the story, Jason would come after his son. She knew that the family of Jason Big Pipe and Jason himself would no longer let her go her own way. They would try to get the boy away from her because, after the first few years of infancy, she could only be a mother to him when everyone knew he would need so much more than that as he grew to manhood.

She looked across at the singers and heard their rich rendition of a song that, like the narrative tales she knew, was as old as the hills. They were absorbed in a long version of an exceptional story of the people's desire to be together, and she wondered for a moment about how distracted the listeners like herself and even the dancers, talking amongst themselves, seemed. She would want her son to know the narratives that are told, and the songs that the Dakotahs sing, the stories and songs that no one claims for themselves.

Her eyes suddenly dark and serious, she frowned. She couldn't remember how that story about the woman and her son ended. That was the trouble with Grandmother's stories. The endings were not really endings. Too often they just drifted off into uncertainty. Seemed like, though, she mused, wasn't there something about the husband in the end tricking the wife into coming toward him? Oh. *O-hanh,* she remembered now: *He oils her hair and braids it very carefully and treats her with great care. And when she isn't wary anymore, he goes outside and whistles. The wolves, who are going away . . . they stop . . . and they look back . . . and then . . . then . . .*

Serious now, she gazed almost absentmindedly at the dancers . . . *i'wahtelasni,* she said under her breath. (This is an expression which means that she can be disgusted with someone on account of some specific reason, but she can like him otherwise.) It was the story of her life since she had taken up with Jason. She looked out into the crowd across the arbor and caught sight of him. He was standing with his cousins, Sherman and Vic Eagle. He had a cigarette in his mouth and was watching her. She looked away quickly.

"What are you going to do?" her grandmother asked suddenly, as though she was reading Aurelia's mind.

"About what?" Innocently.

"You know about what!"

"No. I don't know."

"About your baby. About Jason."

It was the first time that either of them had mentioned this tenuous subject.

Aurelia said nothing.

After a few moments she stood up, adjusted her shawl, and said, *"Hwo, Kunchida. Wacipo. Wacipo, he is saying."* (Come, my grandmother, let us dance together.)

She reached for her grandmother's arm and helped her out of the chair. Solicitously, she leaned toward the old woman and smiled as if to reassure her.

This is a woman, after all, thought Aurelia, who had lived through it all, for ninety-some-odd years. This grandmother who had raised her since infancy had been a child herself during the so-called years of peace, those years of 1880 and 1890 when the peace treaties had been signed yet the enemy continued to kill the people and steal the land.

This old lady remembered when Sitting Bull was murdered, when everyone was sent to reservations and the Allotment Act was forced on the people, when the children were captured and sent to white-man's schools and the people starved. This was a woman who had had a hard time, a long marriage and many children, a woman who had seen the sacred lands of her people stolen and occupied by others.

Surely, she shouldn't have to worry now about my pitiful life. Suddenly, Aurelia was filled with an overwhelming love and sense of gratitude toward her grandmother, and her eyes stung with brief, quick tears.

Together, they walked toward the circle of dancers. Slow and deliberate.

Anyway, *wacipi* was a time for pleasure, not for facing up to things.

Wait until next week, Grandmother, Aurelia thought as she fell into the dance steps and the rhythm of the drum. Maybe next week. I'll worry about it then. Not now. Not just now, when this day is so fine.

The fringes of her shawl began to swing back and forth and she lifted her head and, in her habitual pretense that everything was all right, she smiled with pleasure as she and her grandmother began the dance. She looked over at Aunt Mart and her nephews. They were laughing and they acknowledged her briefly. This is the way for each good day to be, when a woman may dance with her relatives in the sun. When the old songs are sung. And new ones made. She would be happy this day.

❧

The next morning:

The sun was shining. She stretched full length, untangling the sheets by throwing them off with a well-placed kick of her legs. She opened her eyes, then closed them momentarily, still putting off any real decision making. Just as suddenly she sat up and, in a hurry now, got dressed for work.

She left her grandmother sleeping quietly in the next room. The sun felt good. I ought to see Grampa at the rest home, she thought, as the old rig rumbled through the dampness of the dirt road, almost sloshing in the April thaw.

Grampa Blue had been too ill to go to the spring celebration, the first one he'd missed in a long time. Aurelia had never thought it odd that her grandparents had chosen to live separately, though now, as they were getting closer to the end, she felt sad about it. Of course, they told her, they hadn't always lived apart. When they were young, she was told, they'd lived as a family up at Big Bend and they'd stayed together raising their children.

"It was a one-room gov'ment house," her grandmother told her, "on a piece of dry land. No trees. Away from the river and its tributary, the Crow Creek. I had never lived away from the water before. A jackrabbit couldn't hardly live there, but we did. And we raised our children. We had to haul water and it was a very hard life."

It was only after they had gotten a little past middle age that Grandfather went to live with a daughter, Martha, and Grandmother lived in her own little house down on the creek with the infant, Aurelia, who had been given to her in the old way as a companion to the aged.

The old man was now back in the "tribal rest home" called Minneluzaha and, though he'd been hospitalized many times before and in ill health for years, this time it looked like he wasn't going to make it. Maybe his time is up, thought Aurelia, as she slowed down on the slick road, tediously avoiding the deep, soft ruts. The last time she had seen him he had told her in his humorous way, "I'm not long for this world, my girl."

Only a few days ago she had received a very depressing letter from the director of the Home:

Dear Aurelia Blue:

I am writing to tell you that Mr. Blue, your grandparent, is not at all well. As you know, he has lost considerable weight and, unless you come and feed him, he refuses to eat. His bed sores are getting worse even though we shift his body every hour.

The letter was addressed to her at the Catholic boarding school called Immaculate Conception Junior and Senior High School where she was a cook-helper, preparing food daily in the school cafeteria for nearly four hundred students.

The letter had been on her mind all morning:

It takes three of us to get him bathed and dressed in the morning even though he is frail. He no longer helps himself and this has happened just in the last week since you were here Wednesday. He asked me to tell you that he needs some cigarettes and Bull Durham next time you come.

It was noon. She kept the letter in her apron pocket, her dark eyes worried in her strained face. She began carrying the huge aluminum bins in to the serving tables. Bread. Salad. Chocolate cake cut into neat, thin squares. Even without frosting it looked good, she thought. Cartons of milk were arranged in tiers on trays.

She felt the baby move in her abdomen and thought, God, I shouldn't be lifting these big things. The baby was not due until August and she hardly showed, yet he had been moving a lot lately. It's not as though I'm so young, she said under her breath. Having your first baby at thirty-plus is probably not the best idea, nor is it the safest thing to do.

Her thoughts returned to Grandpa. He told me a couple of weeks ago that he needed tobacco, she thought, and here it is Monday and I haven't taken it to him yet. There was no excuse for her neglect.

All of a sudden, students appeared at the locked door and she let them in. They were impatient, talking in loud voices, shuffling feet, hurrying to be the first in line. As they went about grabbing trays and pointing their orders, Aurelia fingered in her pocket the letter with its troubling message and she wondered if the old man might drift away at any moment, perhaps even now as she and the others served goulash and corn onto the fast-moving trays.

Aurelia was distracted. How could she just stand here at this table, spooning out macaroni when her grandfather, barely a half-hour's drive away, might be at death's door? Maybe even drawing his last breath. She felt the hair stiffen on the back of her neck and knew that something was going on though she didn't know what it might be.

She looked up into the faces of the handsome children. Some of them were smiling, flirting, laughing. Others, more solemn, seemed to have the cares of the world on their shoulders. Dark-eyed, afraid, weary. Those who were her relatives chatted amiably. Others, who came to this boarding school from hundreds of miles away, Crows and Cheyennes from Montana, even Arapahoes from Wyoming, and some Ojibways from Minnesota, were often silent, lonesome in their distant thoughts. They often forgot, being youngsters, that they had their whole lives ahead of them, that simply because they were young, they should have had great exuberance.

"Let's go have a cigarette," said Etta, her kitchen-mate, interrupting her thoughts about the old man and the youthful students. "Let them serve themselves, hunh?"

"Uh . . ."

"What's the matter with you? Don't you feel good?"

"Huh-uh," said Aurelia, uncertainly. Then suddenly, "I've gotta go."

She pulled at her apron and almost ran from the room, snatching her wrap and purse from the hallway as she headed out the door, across the gravel driveway to her car.

She barely noticed the muddy spots in the driveway, which was an indication of the fear and apprehension Aurelia felt at the moment. The great piles of snow of the past few months were gone and what was left was what the locals called "gumbo," a sticky kind of mud that perhaps takes its name either from the word *gum*, or from the hash made in New Orleans that gives novices indigestion. Looks like, thought Aurelia, we've seen the last of the snow but, Jesus, the mud! Just then the wind came up, and it nearly blew her across the parking lot. She struggled against the force of the gale to open the car door and when she got in she thought, I don't know which is worse, the mud or the wind.

When she got to the rest home and hurried to the old man's room, she was too late, just as she had feared.

She listened in perfect stillness to the nurse's words: "He just went to sleep, honey. Just like he was soo-o-o peaceful. Just now! Minutes ago. Right after the noon trays. We tried to get him to eat, but he wouldn't."

Aurelia stared into the drawn, shrivelled face of the old grandfather and her emotions kept her silent for only a moment. She took no notice of the cluttered, unswept, untidy room but heard the insistent wind whistling at the window. "I knew I should have come sooner," she said finally in a choked, strained voice.

"Don't, dear," said the white-uniformed nurse, putting a consoling hand on Aurelia's arm. "There was nothing, nothing you could have done."

She wished that was true. Yet she hadn't said goodbye and she had let him go alone and she hadn't brought him his Bull Durham. And when he couldn't wait any longer, he just left. Alone. Alone. She looked at the ashtray and saw bits of dried sage. Prepared. Waiting. She put a match to it and was comforted.

"Yes," Aurelia agreed quietly. "People don't just leave this world, when it is the perfect, 'right' time, do they?"

She stood in thoughtful remembrance: it doesn't happen just when everything is in order, lessons of life all taught and learned, questions posed and answers probed, unequivocal lines traced from thought to deed. That's not the way of it, is it?

She looked at the nurse who nodded, patted her arm again and left the room. Yes. In the same way, neither are they born whenever it may be said to be the best time, when everything is in order. She stared at the old man's face, thinking about the new life she was about to bear and she was, for just a moment, aware, perhaps for the first time, the human pain and sacrifice necessary to re-enact the renewal of life on earth.

She stayed a while longer, wandering about the tiny, cluttered room, touching the curtains, the bed covers. Then she walked over and carefully closed the door. Unexpectedly, she began to sing quietly and for the first time a long and probative song of life and death, a song she had heard the women sing during the old peyote meetings which were a part of her childhood . . . *wa . . . na . . . anpao u we heyana he de do we* . . . the dawn, it is coming now.

She was surprised that she knew the song and the words. There's no one now to look after me, to give me the real songs. And I hardly know them though I have heard them many times.

Why didn't I tell him about my baby, she thought regretfully. In August. Just a few months. Maybe he would have waited to see my baby.

She was filled with a longing for what Grampa called "the old days," even though, of course, she knew them only by his memory.

6

Endings and Beginnings

Aurelia kept her secrets. The next day she sat on the open whitened porch in the cold wind picking lint and prairie stickers from her heavy blue socks, curling her toes to keep them warm and feeling the nearness of her grandfather, his face turned toward her as if during their last conversation. Without thinking, she started to sing again, this time an old Christian song she knew only because the old people she lived with knew it, *mahpiya kin taokiye . . . Iyuhpa hin . . . idowan . . . po. Wicayuhapi tonaka . . . ni . . . yuhapi . . .* her breath came so hard, her lips drawn in pain . . . *datanpi nun . . .*

Her voice changed to an octave higher, the high whine of grief . . . *anpetu wi . . .* and then her voice trailed off only to start again . . . *han yetyu wi. Wakantanka idowan po; Iyoyanpa wicanhpi kin Icah niyanpi yatan po.* It was obvious she didn't know how to deal with her feelings. She bent her head and saw her grandfather's face, again, and her gaze met his and she thought she could not bear the pain.

She felt slightly nauseated and her song, filled with pause and breathlessness, went on. It was a confused mixture of resentment and sorrow, and even though she didn't know it at the time, she may have been poking fun at what she always felt were the old stupid songs of the Christians. Those songs taught to them when they were captive children had, somehow, become part of what the people sang at significant moments in their lives.

What Aurelia felt now, an ache in the heart that would not go away, had nothing to do with all that, she thought, but she sang the songs anyway as if in defiance.

Aurelia supposed it was a little like an expression of Grandpa Blue's ambiguity when he would describe his own enforced Christian religiosity for the amusement of the family. He used to say, tongue in cheek, "Yes. I am a Christian. But it doesn't interfere with my religion." Then he would laugh his soft laugh. It didn't seem so funny now.

Aurelia held her sobs in check when Grandmother Blue came out, put her hand on Aurelia's shoulder and said, "Those are good songs . . . "

She did not look up.

"Oh, Gramma, they're terrible songs. Terrible."

It was necessary to express sorrow but it was also necessary for her to be angry. For all of the mistakes she'd made lately, she needed to be angry. For all the events of her past life, for the uncontrollable resentments brought about by the past, it was all right to be angry.

Aurelia stood up as if to go into the house and then sat down again.

"Come in, now . . . " her grandmother urged.

"Yeah. I will, soon." She pulled on her socks and slipped into her boots.

She turned away and walked out the gate, silence now pounding against her ears. Without haste she walked on. Coatless. Mindless of the sharp wind. It was dark and damp before she returned to say goodnight to her grandmother and prepare for bed. The phantoms of nightfall accompanied her and sleep would not come as she lay motionless during the long night.

Aurelia was thirty-six years old when Grampa Blue died, her first child had not yet been born. It was late April, that time of year when on any one day it can be warm with the leaves beginning to bud, then suddenly, swiftly, the wind rises and a foot or two of snow falls overnight just to remind the people of their tenuousness.

Sometimes, though not often, thought Aurelia during the following grim days as she made preparations for the old man's funeral, the death of a family elder occurs and it seems oddly unexceptional. Sad, perhaps, sorrowful or dismaying or regrettable in some unaccountable way, sometimes it is even a relief. Yet it usually remains even after all is finished and its finality recognized as one of those events that will not change the world.

That was not the case, it seemed, in Grampa Blue's death, for even as the preparations went on she realized that it was one of those events that alters the world of the living. Even before the family had conducted any retrospective ceremonial, his death seemed to function to help Aurelia bring into focus her own chronology. As Grampa dies, I bring a new life into the world, she mused, surprised at such a realization. To what effect beyond mystery, though, she could not say.

It turned out to be the kind of passing that enabled his granddaughter to seek meaning in her present condition for, perhaps, the very first time. Aurelia wondered about such philosophical matters in her loneliness but she shared them with no one.

Not her Grandmother Blue who, during the communal singing, laid an eagle feather on the old man's cold chest and, later, sang one of those wailing songs of widowhood now known only to those of her generation.

Not even Jason, who came to the funeral with his brothers and stood silently in the back of the church; nor did she glance up at her onetime lover, John Tatekeya, who came to this, the ultimate ceremony, with his old wife and eldest daughter and sat in agony, his soft face wet with tears.

Long afterward and yet well before she came face to face with her own death as an old woman, Aurelia wished that she could stop the agony of wondering about the distinctions concerning death, why this happens or that happens, what the relationship between chance and design signifies. On that day, however, the day she had looked into the pale, still face of the old relative for the last time, she knew that nothing mattered except that he had made their lives together a season of ethical and worthy pathfinding.

If Grandpa Blue's death meant anything, it meant that Aurelia would now have to rise to the occasion of her own life.

It had to happen and it had to help her toward maturity. When she was taken as an infant by her father's relatives, the Blues, to live with her grandmother, she was carried away from a shabby, graceless, vulgar life of robbing and stealing and poverty and sniffing glue for comfort and drinking booze to escape. Now in her sorrow, she knew that she had been very lucky. Had she been left with her mother, her path would have been far different.

"The other side of the family," as the Blues often distastefully referred to this matter of genealogy, was thought by them to be a family of renegades who threw away custom as well as children and there were dire consequences felt by everyone close to them. After Myrna Two Heart, Aurelia's mother, left Albert and abandoned the children, there was much speculation about the Two Heart "side" of Aurelia's family, how the old patriarch Amos, in developing his political life, had abandoned tradition, how Isabelle did nothing to prevent her daughters from becoming sluts to white men.

Dire consequences seem always to be connected to religion, no matter how much one denies it. And so, when Aurelia had started questioning the meaning of endings and beginnings, she had come to feel early on that the "other side" of the family, the Two Heart side of the family, was proof of the darkness of the human soul.

When she was only twenty, she had found herself sitting in the church pew attending a very different sort of funeral from the one commemorating old Blue's death. It was that of Isabelle, the unfortunate wife of Amos Two Heart. That death and funeral was probably as much responsible for Aurelia's lifelong isolation and uncertainty as any one event in her life, but she had made no sense of it at the time.

I almost refused to attend the old lady's funeral but, then, at the last minute, I went. It was because old Isabelle had never stood up to Amos. It was because she did not demand from her children their respect. And it was because he treated her any old way. Even now, I hate the thought of that old woman. Death and life and history and religion and ethics are ideas which are inseparable from each other but . . . thinking about old Isabelle . . . it was 1950-something . . . I have refused to admit my blood ties to the Two Hearts.

I was used as some kind of pawn that is unfathomable to me. When my mother rejected my father as a suitable husband, she rejected me. When she rejected Dakotah belief and history, she made the family future shameful.

I was what they call a "throw-away" child but no one blamed me. Yes. I was blameless. Maybe that's the reason that even my anger, years of turmoil and avoidance and regret and sadness didn't matter. I went to the burial of the old lady. It was because to acknowledge the immemorial function of death in the Santee tradition is a binding thing. Even . . . no, . . . especially, if you are a child who is abandoned.

If you are abandoned but blameless, you can face the enemy.

Aurelia could not get the memory of that other funeral out of her mind even as she held her hands close over her growing stomach. She was so young then, she thought, and everything mattered. Though youthful witnesses are seldom given to consulting the holy ones, and Aurelia more than most resisted prayers that asked the ultimate questions, yet, looking into the face of Grampa Blue on the day of his death, she almost relented. She felt if only for a moment that even though the holy ones rarely spoke to anyone she knew, they never purposefully concealed their knowledge from the people who were deserving. Maybe, she thought, there was still hope for her.

Now calm, she remembered with great clarity her apprehensiveness at Isabelle's funeral. Everything was changing in some kind of drastic and dangerous way then. As she had driven down the gravelled road that awful day through the dismal morning fog along the Crow Creek she feared that life would never be as it was supposed to be: predictable, satisfying, full of grace, plain and honorable.

Passing homesites filled with dilapidated cars and tall weeds, she speculated about how it is that a name, a person, a family disappears into history with barely a trace. It can never be wholly known, she supposed, but, she admitted, such disappearances sometimes happen. It is not because of poverty, she thought, as she glanced at the passing reservation rural scene. Unpainted buildings, tipi poles leaning into the arms of cottonwood trees, vehicles without wheels propped up on blocks, children racing toward one other in the wind, laughing and stretching.

These disappearances occur in good times and bad, in written histories as well as oral ones, she thought, and, perhaps, for many of the same reasons: neglect, error, greed, hate, murder, selfishness, circumstances and events of all kinds. She knew that most of her relatives would say that despoiling inheritances and embracing corruptive alien ways are what account for the disappearance of Indian families into meaninglessness. Aurelia's obsession about matters of family had seized her. Without family, she thought even then, without that vision of what it means to be a daughter, a husband, a loved one, history and human life could only fall into chaos. In spite of what she knew in her heart, her fear of it had all too often inhabited her daily life.

The Two Heart family, the maternal side of the family, at the time of the so-called Federal Reorganization Policy toward Indians, way back in what has been called in history "the dirty thirties" left its scars on everyone. Aurelia witnessed it through her mother, Myrna, but everyone knew that it originated in the lives of Myrna's parents Amos and Isabelle as they moved from tribal traditions and took up modern ways. Transitional lives like these are often lives of disillusionment, for they take in uncritically the dealings of the whites and bring about political careers like that of Amos Chante Numpa Two Heart, which are corrupt and tragic.

The teenager Myrna, marrying a fellow tribesman, Albert Blue, felt that because she was a daughter of Two Heart the politician, she had married beneath her, and therefore she treated her husband with great contempt. Reluctantly, she had borne several children. For much of her adult life, she worked as a cleaning woman for the church, the more prosperous whites in the area, and the people who ran the boarding schools.

Myrna was an attractive woman whose flawless skin never seemed to age and whose black hair did not whiten as the years passed. She was a hard worker. She wore sensible, flat working shoes which she bought at J.C. Penney's and, always, winter and summer, a man's long-sleeved blue denim shirt over a full skirt.

She was a woman who went through her life trying not to "be Indian" which meant, at least to her, that she spoke only

English, didn't take part in tribal ceremonials, and ignored the so-called tribal ways and her relatives as much as she could.

Myrna divorced Albert, an act that was not unheard of in the community and one that might have been acceptable. But then she married a white man, gave away her children to her husband's people, and never again spoke a civil word to the paternal relatives of the children, nor they to her. Later on, Myrna divorced the white man and married another. She got caught up in the alcohol life of the white cowboys, ranchers, and drifters who hung around Indian reservations.

Even as Myrna gave her infant Aurelia to her father's people, she did so with little thought of how it is to be condemned by an unloving mother. She did so for selfish reasons, because she wanted more than anything to leave Crow Creek. Even if it was only to move to the scrubby little cow and turkey towns nearby, which were filled with white people whose ancestors had always hated Indians. The Two Hearts wanted to live in those towns, never to come back to tribal lands, to become like whites. Americans. To pursue the American Dream. To be the generation of American Indians who would begin the new tradition of assimilation. As time went by, Myrna and her brothers and sisters had their dreams come true. They moved to the little towns, away from the reservation. They sold their allotment lands and it was rumored back home that Myrna, like every single one of her siblings, became ashamed of her name.

Aurelia had no idea how to explain it fully. Maybe it had something to do with religion and the eternal conflict between whites and Indians concerning the nature of the universe. Something about the spirit of man, she supposed. It was up to tribal people, she had always been told, to be responsible to the land, the primal species, the environment, and, most important of all, to each other. This idea about tribalism was embedded in all of the prayers and had been held as matters of the spirit. Until recent times, at least.

In 1950-something, when the unfortunate wife of Amos Two Heart died, such spiritual ideals were being abandoned as part of the thinking of the people. Many were unable to live their lives as they had been taught. Perhaps it was that Isabelle and her daughter, Myrna, and her husband, Amos, had simply given up. Perhaps it was a despair of some kind that overcame the people.

Whatever it might have been, Aurelia did not want to share her maternal grandmother's fate, that of a woman largely lost in time. She did not want to share her mother's fate, that of a woman who rejected her people. Yet at that time she hardly knew how to avoid either destiny.

When I visited the Two Hearts, I hid behind the bed in the back room as the drunken parties went on, and on, sometimes for days. Eventually, I would get thirsty and would have to come out. Slowly. Carefully. I would creep carefully around the kitchen table to avoid the rough, grasping hands of the man at the table, boozing with my mother. One time, I did not escape the fat, freckled hands. It was then I found out that prayers are not answered. Even today, I carry a pocket knife that opens into a sharp stabbing point. Even today. I have come to see myself as "the one who cannot pray." I have told no one of this event. Not anyone. It is a terrible secret that I have kept.

Always, it has been in my heart.

At the time of the old Two Heart woman's funeral so many years ago, then, it must be said that Aurelia had been a young woman with many secrets. Secrets that made her an orphan. Wayward. The yumni *child, going around in circles. She had been suspicious of everyone and everything for so long it had become part of her nature. Even though she did not feel the weight of a continuing disapproval from community members for the way she lived her youthful life as the lover of old Tatekeya, she felt enormously guilty about other unrelated matters like her unspoken hatred, her ruthlessness toward people like Amos and Isabelle.*

Self-reproachful, sheepish, she knew little then of the importance of forgiveness, compassion. As she grew older and as she prepared to have her own child she knew that all of this personal history had now made it impossible for her to approach a new life with Jason in innocence.

Guilt had always been a part of it.

There was that night before Grampa Blue died. In the evening light, Aurelia had sat with Jason and had come face to face with her own fear and though she ever after that remembered the alarm she felt of the moment she had little notion of why or how.

They were sitting at a small, cluttered kitchen table in Grandmother Blue's home, an ordinarily tranquil place unused to family quarrels, stuffy and defensive conversations. It was an agreeable room with shining linoleum on the floor and washable throw rugs in front of the gas cooking stove and the washbasin. The afternoon had been unremarkable and pleasant.

"Why don't we get married?" he had asked suddenly.

When she looked at him she saw his warm smile but his eyes, studiously watching his thumb pressing on hers, didn't meet hers.

After a long pause, she asked, "Why?" Her voice was filled with wonder.

"Why not?"

Laughing, "No. I asked first. Why?" She was staring at him with a look of mixed confusion and surprise.

They fell silent for a moment, their hands still touching.

"Well, why not?" When she didn't answer, he insisted, "Why not, Aurelia?"

In answer, she took her hand back and gave him a look of disgust.

"Wait. We've got a kid. I mean, pretty soon, you know, we'll have a kid."

"So? Who needs to get married?"

"What's wrong with getting married?"

"I don't want to."

"Why not?"

She shrugged.

"Don't you love me?"

She stood up.

"I'm not going to talk about this anymore, Jason."

The door slammed behind her and, doing nothing to stop or follow her, he sat motionless as if waiting for her to reconsider.

Outside, a few steps from the kitchen, she stood for a moment. Guilt and sorrow and panic flooded her thoughts. She turned and went back into the kitchen, standing behind him helplessly.

"We don't need to do this, Jason."

"Yeah. I know."

After another long pause, she went to the stove, grasped the coffee pot, and turned back to the table. She knew it was what her grandmother expected of her, to marry a good man and have many children, a good life.

Pouring coffee into two purple cups, she said, "Why are you doing this? You know I don't want to get married."

Stirring sugar into the hot liquid, she thought, how can I explain to him that marriage, for me, is unthinkable. Doesn't he know that there is something in me that will never give in? Of all people, I expect him to understand this. Filled with love for him she looked at him, then closed her eyes and felt tears forcing their way out and knew that if he went away she would grieve forever. If she were to lose him now she would never care if the sun ever came up again.

"I've never misled you, Jason."

He said nothing.

"I've never said I would marry you."

"I've never asked you to." He looked at her without smiling.

"Well, yeah. I know."

"But now I am. I'm askin' you."

Tears welled in her eyes openly now, "Why are you doing this? Is it because you think you ought to? We're having a kid and you think . . . you think . . . "

"No. It's not just that. It's . . . I don't know. I want you to marry me."

She pushed her cup away and got up quickly from the table. Grabbing a coat from the pantry doorknob she said, "Don't do this, Jason. Don't do this." It sounded to him like some kind of warning.

She didn't look back as she ran out of the house and toward the barn. Heaving and grasping a bale of hay with both hands, she began to feed the horses.

When he found her later walking disconsolately around the yard, he reassured her that he wouldn't bring it up again. "I'm not angry with you," he told her.

She simply put her arms around him and said nothing.

The distant brick entrance of the Holy Rosary Mission School for Indian children yawned before her that night in her dreams, a century-old building with a wall where the names of hundreds of children, including her own, appeared, scratched into the stone with a distinctiveness that accounted for their own survival. It seemed so clear in her night dreams, unfaded by time and glittering in the sun.

She had stood on the shoulders of Billy Feather to put her name with the others on that brick wall. Red Skirt. Light Hill. Blue. Flute. Tatiyopa. Ehnamani. Big Pipe. A kind of wailing wall, Indian style. A place of grief and lamentation and joy and recovery. Nothing trivial or frivolous. Her small hand had held a pocket knife firmly as she carved and she weighed about eighty pounds and Billy held her ankles and her breath came heavily. The wind had moaned around her.

In that moment of dream time, she saw herself again, years later, in a different church some thirty miles away, that day when the death of Grandmother Two Heart was being ceremonialized, and she felt her breath come heavily again. Looking quickly at the frail and shrunken and yellow face of her grandmother whose pale, open-casketed presence greeted the relatives the minute they stepped inside the church door, Aurelia smelled liquor on the breath of her mother's youngest brother, James, as he found a place beside her. She saw tears fill his red eyes and she watched them stream down his face, showing that he was devastated by simple grief and regret. She felt herself angry and impenitent. Hard. Yet confused and afraid, for she had even then vaguely recognized that the death and burial of any elder, no matter how defunct and irrelevant, rendered the future unhindered by any known thing and immune to the restrictions and obligations brought about by the family's past.

She saw herself sitting stiffly, reluctantly handing her uncle a handkerchief which he put to his face as he began to sob openly. Wordlessly, amid the sounds of weeping, the relatives had waited for the service to begin and as they waited Aurelia closed her eyes.

She could not pray. Even then, she could not pray.

Sitting in the presence of the others in the dim religious room, with the wrinkled corpse of the old woman lying just steps away, she tried to rid herself of the memories, vague and distasteful, of her grandmother's life. It had been a life of subservience and denial, giving in all the time to the selfish old man. The old woman, Aurelia remembered, would have to ask two or three times before he would take her to town to buy beads or yarn. He was impatient because it took her a long time to shop for and buy yarn or beads. She used a certain yellow in her crafts, a greasy yellow color, she called it. She would go to one store and then the next to find just the right color. After her children left, she might have been expected to face up to her individual life. But she didn't. Or couldn't, for whatever reasons.

Aurelia saw her as she walked through weeds on the wagon trail along the creek, a habit of hers even when the weather wasn't pleasant. It was raining and the wind was blowing and Aurelia saw her bent over a cane and dressed in black. "He has women down from Greenwood and at Sisseton," the wind told the old woman, who simply walked on and refused to listen. All of her life, she had not listened to others. She never found fault with anyone even when they deserved reprimand, never criticized her children for their wayward lives, never gave anyone any good advice and, most of all, never told the old man what a fool he was. Aurelia felt her anger rise as, watching from the top of the hill, she saw a whirlwind gather up the old grandmother and carry her toward the creek.

7

Wisdom Comes in Bits and Pieces

The baby was expected in August. Now that spring was everywhere, Aurelia could not for the life of her explain why she stood alone at the kitchen table during these sun-filled days with tears streaming from her eyes. Especially since she felt a sense of anticipation. Lighthearted. Calm.

It was only in retrospect, she supposed, that anything ever made sense. After her Grandfather Blue's funeral the months had passed more quickly than she dreamed possible, and it was easy to remember the old man's presence, as though he were near enough to touch. She liked that.

As she poured herself a cup of coffee, sipped it carefully and held back unexplained tears only with the greatest difficulty, she knew that the best she could do was to simply wait out her present dilemma. All things will pass, Grampa Blue used to tell her.

There were times when she was unaccountably surly with her grandmother and arrogant with others, treating them as though she really didn't care for them. Then, immediately, she would feel contrite. She noticed this ambiguity in herself particularly as Jason was becoming more insistent, and she found that, instead of trying to make her own way, she had begun, rather grimly and resentfully, to accept the awkward position in which she found herself. She did not say it out loud, but she wondered if it was a sign that the notable arrogance, in which she had always had such confidence, was fading away into some kind of unwanted feminine lapse called impending motherhood. How disgusting, she thought. She had always had some pride in her obstinacy, her ability to shrug off any sentimental emotionalism. Yet now she was beginning to more fully understand the dilemmas of women everywhere and her critical judgment of the women she had known well seemed to be softening. Maybe I'm getting like them, she thought with faint self-hate.

The triumph of life and love supersedes everything, she had read in one of those magazines at the clinic during her last visit. She had read, too, that statistics show more suicides, more human depression, are evident in the spring than any other season.

"I'm a perfect example of some kind of failed specimen," she derided herself. She did not seem to thrive, as some women do, on her pregnancy, vomiting because of what was called by some "morning sickness" at seemingly irregular morning, noon, and night intervals. She was losing weight instead of gaining it. She stayed in bed mornings and sat up late nights in her grandmother's easy chair, unhappy over her failure to be transformed by the most sacred of all female functions.

Cousin Corrine's death in childbirth, the yellow dress bondage plagued her silent thoughts. She was becoming more confused. More lethargic. I'm turning into a fearful, pitiful, suffering crank, she thought, and there were moments of particular depression when she could think of no remedy.

Because Jason still lived at home with his family and she lived, as she always had, with her grandmother, it was easy to refrain from making decisions. There were many visitors to Grandmother Blue's home as the weather became more tolerable; though everyone expected that Aurelia might engage in some kind of explanation of herself, discuss some plans she had made for herself and the baby, she remained silent.

What has happened to me, she wondered. Almost nothing seemed to matter anymore. She often fell to weeping whenever Grandmother Blue tried to talk to her or make requests of her. She didn't seem to stand up for herself against the wishes of others, feeling that her friends and relatives were gossiping about the change in her ways, but she didn't really care enough to confront them, nor did she want to interfere. She was becoming secretive and afraid.

What troubled her the most was the vague feeling that her life was slipping away from her. That wasn't anyone's fault, certainly not Jason's nor her grandmother's, she knew. One must expect, she supposed, that to give life to another, one must sacrifice some of one's own. She had never wanted to be alone, not really, and now that she was to bear a child, she could avoid that tragedy. After all, Grandmother Blue would be gone someday soon, and then who would she have to love and care for? Who would love her?

Jason often tried a joking approach to Aurelia's surliness. "Hey," he would say, "it takes two to tango." Yeah, she thought, but, dammit, I never wanted to tango! What she really meant was that she did not consider herself a good bet as a wife and mother and she hated the thought of it.

"C'mon, 'relia," Jason would say as he forgot about his promise to never bring up the subject and urged marriage as a solution to the situation, "it's your last chance to be a June bride!"

"I don't want to be a June bride." Petulant. Cheerless.

"Yeah. You do!" he would argue, undaunted. "Every woman wants to be a June bride."

"What do you know?" she would respond, smiling in spite of herself. "What do you know about what women want?"

"Hey! You gotta ask? Lemme show you." And he would grab her, kissing her until she pulled away, laughing and delighted at his brashness.

At other times, during the evenings she spent alone at the setting of the sun especially, she would be more serious. She could go on and blame herself for getting herself into this situation, she supposed, but what's the point of that, she would ask. Blame and guilt were the two things, her grandmother often told her, that caused illnesses in otherwise healthy people.

Grandmother Blue, the constant companion throughout all the years of her life, who had grown to know Aurelia better than most and was also privy to much of the community gossip, knew that this time there would be no escape. This time, thought the old lady, as is often the case in matters of profound and sacred intent, it will be different. Her granddaughter, that independent, helpful, charming girl who had now grown to womanhood, would no longer be in charge as she had always claimed herself to be. If it was the girl's aim to will her life into some vibrant and wise happiness for the rest of her days, the old grandmother thought, she would soon have to get on some more sensible course. Knowing this, she waited and was silent.

8

To Place Sweetgrass on the Fire is the Legacy of Holy Persons

One day in May, Jason drove his car up into the front yard of the Blue place, mud flying everywhere. He was in a hurry as he always was. He strode to the front door and stood there several long minutes persuading Aurelia to come with him:

"We gotta go down there, to take my Uncle Lewis. He's got to go down there and meet with them dudes in the Clay County jail."

The newspapers all across the state were full of the news of the murder and rape. The radio, the television could talk of nothing else:

"City Jeweler Savagely Murdered,
Wife Raped by Indian College Student"

Leaper, a youthful relative of Big Pipe, was apparently apprehended after the police found him hiding under the bed of the white man who lay in his own purple blood, his head crushed and the room in violent disorder.

Lewis Grey Iron, one of the elder brothers of Harvey Big Pipe and therefore a father-uncle figure to Jason, a man considered by tribal people to be a religious leader and judicial advisor, was asked by the father and mother of the young accused murderer to go to the eastern part of the state and confer with lawyers and the police handling the young man's case. It was expected, of course, that he would minister to the spiritual needs of the young tribal man who had just destroyed so many lives, including his own.

Aurelia, reluctant to get mixed up in the whole affair, greeted Jason's invitation to accompany him with disbelief.

"I'm not going. Not there. Not for this!"

"You must come with me. This is important."

"Look, Jason. We're not even married. I don't need to get involved in your family's affairs."

"I need you to come with us, Aurelia."

"Why?"

"Because."

He stood, unmovable, unable or unwilling to put into words the idea that she was a part of him now, whether she accepted it or not, and he refused to acknowledge her reluctance. It was past the time when she could indulge her own sense of privacy, he thought.

"Go on. Go take care of your problems, Jason. I will take care of mine. You take care of yours. Just leave me out of it, huh?"

She was trying to set limits about privacy and family concerns, not realizing that such luxuries were no longer possible. At the moment, she simply didn't want to have anything to do with Big Pipe family matters. Nor did she think Jason should be concerned with her doings and she often told him so. Perhaps she had an unusual sense of separate space because of all the years she and her grandmother had simply gone their own private ways. She was unaware of how much this exclusiveness, this separateness, would have to give way now that she and Jason were trying to figure out what their relationship meant in terms of family and responsibility. It was becoming an issue between them because most of the time he just didn't pay much attention to her need for isolation.

"I just don't want to go with you," she protested lamely at last, hating herself for whining. "I'd just as soon stay far away from those people and that place! It gives me the creeps to even think about it!"

"I know, Aurelia. I know."

He stood holding the door. Asking. Needing her to understand. "I know. But somebody's got to drive him there."

"Why us?"

Exasperated now, Jason said, "I don't know why in the hell it's us. It just is! Get a coat, 'relia. You're gonna need one. It's windier'n hell."

"But he can drive! Why can't he take himself?"

She sounded like she was going to burst into tears and it scared Jason for just a moment.

He stepped inside the door and put his arms around her.

"Dammit, 'relia," he said softly. "His eyes is too bad! He can't see good enough to drive off the res. Down there. You know, in a lot of traffic!"

She said nothing but stood in his embrace stiffly.

Her grandmother sat quietly in the living room. Careful. Listening.

"I don't think he's got a license to drive. Off the reservation."

The final argument.

He turned and went outside, got into the car, and sat there waiting. He said a few words to old Grey Iron sitting next to him. And waited.

In a few minutes, Aurelia came out, threw a few things in the back seat, and then got in and slammed the door.

They drove away in silence.

Indeed, they drove almost the whole way without speaking, each one lost in his or her own thoughts, all three of them wrapped in the safety of silence, accustomed to handling one another's privacy after harsh words in this way, with great care. It was a preferred custom and no one thought it unusual.

At first they passed little villages and towns that looked like something out of the reknowned dust bowl: unpainted buildings, stores with brick facades showing off their *"built in 1889"* or *"since 1902"* logos, wrinkled old men hanging on to walking canes in the wind as they crossed the empty streets, a stray dog following a small boy toward the faded, dusty hardware store.

They saw overgrazed pastures and herds of livestock. Ravines filled with clusters of oaks and cottonwoods just starting to show a little greenery, cut banks the only other disturbances to the rolling hills. When they crossed the James River in the coolness of the afternoon, they noticed the square fields, passed the farmers on their tractors plowing up the black dirt.

They used no maps even though they were unfamiliar with the roads. Lewis Grey Iron had come this way one time in recent months, he told them, when he was invited by the Yanktons for a burial there. So, as they made their way, he commented briefly on which turnoffs to use, which roads to take, which towns he remembered going through.

When they got to Vermillion, the little midwestern college town on the Missouri River where the murder had occurred, it was late. They slept in the car and the next morning went directly to the jail.

"We are here to see Leaper."

"Who are you? Only relatives can see him, you know."

"Yes. We are relatives."

"Who are you? How are you related?" The inquisitor held a pen over the form to be filled out and signed.

"I am grandfather," said Lewis Grey Iron.

"Well, then, who are you?" the jailer asked, turning to look at Jason and Aurelia.

"Uh . . . well . . . ," Jason cleared his throat. "We can wait outside, here," he said, turning away.

Aurelia was immediately thankful that Jason was avoiding any face-to-face dealings with Leaper. It was one thing for her to be with Jason as he performed familial duties like driving the old man to his destination. In was quite another to accompany a sacred practitioner into the trauma of this kind of task. It was sure to be intrusive and highly emotional. She could not do it. It would have been inappropriate, in any case.

In Indian Jason talked to the old man, assuring him that they would wait for him in the lobby, and it did not matter how long it took. They would just be sitting here, Jason said, waiting for him.

Neither Jason nor Aurelia knew it then, but the killing of an aging white man, the rape of his old wife, and the terrorizing of the man's wife for many long hours, in this college town by the young Indian student high on dope and suffering from a long-neglected, untreated head injury, was to become a celebrated case in South Dakota, probably the most infamous crime committed since the Deadwood Wild West days.

Though Aurelia, in the beginning, had resisted accompanying Jason and his uncle on this trip, she was, as the next two days wore on, awakened to the issues involved in race relations in a state where many post-pioneer families were stricken with panic at the possibility of irrational behavior on the part of Indians. Many of these people had never seen an Indian up close. Listening to snatches of conversation in the hallways of the courthouse and jail, she heard people say, "Well, you know. These Indians are only a few decades removed from savagery." As though this act, this dreadful killing, was somehow a part of the historical traits of Indian-ness, attributable to their uncivilized nature. There was a lot of talk by defense strategists hanging about the offices, of "cultural conflict" for university students who came from "deprived" backgrounds, and a newspaper discarded in a wastebasket ran an entire inside section on the unhealthy influence of Indian reservation life on the young. It was probably meant to engender some kind of rationale concerning the sociological milieu in which violence by Indians occurs in white society; but to Aurelia, who read what she could and listened to what was going on around her, it attributed a racial motive to a drug-related crime that had begun as a burglary and went out of control. In the end, no jury was impaneled and the judge, unconvinced by any of the arguments, sentenced the young man to death. The general public was convinced that an appropriate mediation of the act had taken place.

While Jason and Aurelia sat on the hard wooden benches of the Clay County jailhouse that day, however, neither of them felt comfortable in the presence of the sheriffs, deputies, lawyers, and all the other people from the offices that served the justice system, some strolling unhurriedly and others rushing back and forth. Phones rang. Coffee and lunches sat untouched on official desks as people scurried to gather and sift evidence.

Some newspapermen, a couple from as far away as Minneapolis, stood in clusters talking in low voices: "Who found them?" "How much blood was there?" "Do you think they're gonna get him off on an insanity plea?"

The roomful of white men took charge, smoking cigarettes one after another, jotting things down on little notepads, all of them now and then staring at the two lone Indians in the waiting room, "like we have our two heads on," whispered Aurelia.

There was talk of punishment, there was talk of equality in the matter of Indian-on-white crime in South Dakota and the fact that the state pen was overloaded with Indians, some 70 percent of the inmates being natives. "Any society cannot tolerate rape and murder," Aurelia heard them say, "and Indians have to be treated just like anybody else." The middle-America folks who had the decision to make in this late-sixties murder case, therefore, sentenced the Indian perpetrator to the electric chair, the first such sentence rendered in the state in more than a hundred years. Some who may have felt consternation and dismay at the finality and severity of the sentence were, it was said, not surprised.

Aurelia watched Jason chain-smoke. She saw him lean his elbows on his knees trying to give the impression that he was unconcerned, but he was listening, too. Aurelia did not move during the hours that she sat in the presence of that public panic. Her body became cramped and stiff, and she could do nothing but wonder about the rendering of equal justice to Indian criminals in a situation such as this. Both she and Jason said later that they had felt the staid and compelling pioneer fear of Indians, which reinforced itself as the casual discussions of the case drifted throughout the hallways. It was a time and place and event which, unbeknownst to either of them, would become historical in the town lore and the libraries would keep in files every comment, every official response. Many decades later, witnesses, grey with age, could be heard to say, "Oh, yes. I seen him when they led him out of the place." Or, "He was a wild Indian, all right. I seen him."

The old grandfather, his pipe bag under his arm and some sage held close to his heart, had been led down the dark hallway where he sat in prayer with the youthful, remorseful, wild-eyed prisoner for most of the day. In the language which had been given to the people during sacred times, he prayed as though his heart would break, as though he couldn't stop. He wept throughout the ordeal.

Finally he came out, his face impassive. He walked, unseeing, past the curious bystanders. He said only, "*Hwo, Mitakojas.*"

The late afternoon sunlight blinded them as they left the dim hallways of justice, and they squinted into the sky. There are these places in the universe, thought Aurelia as she followed the men to the car, where the sunlight is most luminous, crystal clear and splendid, especially in the days just before the hot, muggy days of summer. Out of three hundred and sixty-five days of the year, she mused, more than three hundred of them bear such phosphorescence as this into the human soul and it is this fact of nature, they say, which accounts for the Lakota/ Dakotah way of life.

She wanted to talk about it. Like this: *Other peoples have called it Phoebus, Aurora, Helios, Venus, Ra. Names recognized as verbal custodians of great mythic sensibilities. Few know or care that the Sioux want to call it "grandfather," the important companion of Wi-win. Even fewer know that this is a profound recognition of the course of all life, and that this recognition makes the behavior and responsibility of old men like Lewis Grey Iron the more manifest.*

But, of course, she said nothing. Only the men and women who have connections to the spirit world have words in the ancient language to say these things to others. But Aurelia, herself a sensitive and thoughtful woman of some maturity, felt the profound nature of the moment.

Grey Iron wanted to camp at the river that night, for the next day he was supposed to talk to the lawyers. They stopped at a convenience store and bought a few groceries, then drove on a rutted road along the water's edge. They passed a very small but well-preserved log hut almost white with age, an historical place with a sign above the door, which was almost unreadable: "First Schoolhouse in Yankton Dakota Territory." It looked like 1856 or maybe 1838. They had turned off the paved road and found themselves on a dry road filled with great ruts, used, perhaps, by hunters or maybe the more intrepid fishermen who could maneuver small boats behind their pickup trucks.

They had not expected that they would be noticed, but just as they put out food and Pepsis on the blankets they spread out, a black-and-white City Patrol car drove up.

This was certainly out of the city limits, so they felt no apprehension.

"What'cha doin'?" a young smooth-faced cop asked.

Grey Iron did not look up but reached inside his jacket for a cigarette. As he did so, the young cop and his partner leapt from the patrol car, their hands on guns at their hips. Grey Iron, without looking at Jason, said in Dakotah, "Watch out for them. They have followed us."

"Have you got booze here?"

They looked at the bread, bologna, potato chips, and Pepsi spread out before them. Without waiting for an answer one of them stepped over to the car, looking inside, and as he stepped back toward the trunk he said, "You'd better open this up for me."

Jason took the keys from his pocket and unlocked the trunk for inspection.

When the young policeman found nothing, he asked, "Where is your identification?"

Jason produced his driver's license, which was scrutinized carefully. "Um . . . Fort Thompson, hunh?"

We could be from Mars for all he knows about Fort Thompson, thought Aurelia, who stood several steps away.

Handing back the license, he asked them how much money they had and they didn't answer him. He stood in front of them waiting. Tiredly, Grey Iron rose and fanned open his wallet showing three twenties.

In a tone of finality, the young policeman said, "Well, you can go ahead and eat your little lunch here, but after that, you'd better make yourselves scarce. Y'hear?"

The three of them stood still as the police car turned and pulled away. Aurelia put her arm around Jason and he held her close. This day had changed everything for both of them and all of the feelings engendered by the day's events—sorrow, joy, love, desire, despair, shame, rage, and pride—burned between them. Just now, at this point of seething anger and distortion, they seemed to sense the momentousness of the intrusion by the young policeman. Neither Jason nor Aurelia spoke their thoughts aloud. Jason knew that the quick, deep-seated anger that seethed beneath his calm exterior would be self-defeating in the long run, so he kept his silence. He forced himself to brush aside any thoughts of retaliation. Aurelia, her hand on his slim waist, noticed his deliberate, slow breathing and felt enormous pride in his self-possession. These fleeting contacts with whites, she thought, give me the impression that they are a people who can never show a true face. The games they play at every opportunity, the pretense. The arrogance. It was all so pointless. Vain. Worthless.

Grey Iron, nervous and distracted, pulled hard on his cigarette but he, too, said nothing. He started preparing for sleep. No one was hungry any longer, so after darkness fell, they unwrapped the food and put it out in the trees for the birds and small creatures. Trying to lighten their spirits, Aurelia playfully threw bits of meat and bread up into the trees. "Say, bird, how about a little junk food?" she said with a strained laugh. Even though the movement of the trees in the wind gave her a feeling of reverence for the place, she felt an intensity of distrust and agitation that she didn't know she was capable of feeling. She could hardly hold back the tears. She was no longer filled with anger, intemperance, selfishness, and resistance as she had been when they started the trip and she knew, now, that Jason had been right to insist that she accompany them. Her witnessing had changed everything between them.

Now, huddled under the trees with the man who wanted to be her husband and his aged uncle, she felt a closeness, a familiarity that had been missing until now. As they sipped Pepsi, they smiled and kissed and wondered what the future had in store for them.

The old man's voice was low as, in Dakotah language, he told stories far into the night. Aurelia, her head in Jason's lap, slept and listened fitfully.

"This was all Yankton Dakotah land," the old man said, and Aurelia felt him gesturing into the darkness. "The Ihanktowa(n), especially. But, also the Isianti, Hunkpati. Even the Minneconjous.

They all knew and we all knew these coteaus along the river as part of the greatest of the ranges for the wild buffalo east of the Missouri. We knew them like we knew our mother's face. It is said that Lewis and Clark killed their first buffalo here, between Elk Point and Vermillion in 1802. Catlin, the painter of Indians, thirty years later told the whites of the 'most immense herds' that he said 'darkened the whole plains.' We, of course, had known of this fact in our homelands and we had always taken great care to treat the buffalo and the elk sacredly but to the whites, it was great news. In fewer than forty years after that," he paused for a long time, almost as if he had forgotten, ". . . u-m . . . in the mere lifetime of a man . . . the buffalo were no more."

He got up with great effort and paced back and forth, long strides in the darkness, back and forth, then he took his jacket off and threw it down. He sat down again and continued.

"That is the legacy of the white man."

Aurelia struggled to stay awake but drifted in and out of alertness. The old man went on telling the stories, sometimes shouting, other times whispering, and Aurelia and Jason dozed, hearing only bits and pieces of it:

"The Indians of that time, you know, they spoke of the poverty around them at every meeting with the white men who came into our country for profit. Our people protested that the work of the soldiers drove the buffalo away and said that the thousands of hunters brought here by the railroads were murderers. That they exterminated the buffalo and the elk with their repeating rifles."

Jason moved his cramped legs and Aurelia sat up. She didn't open her sleep-filled eyes but listened to the quiet of the night all around, and the continuing story.

"Finally, the Indians said that routes for these soldiers and hunters should not be provided. Not by treaty. Not for any reason. They were, our relatives told everyone, the enemies of all living things and they would bring disaster into the world."

In a rhetorical mode, then, as if addressing a wider audience than just his nephew and Aurelia, the old man asked: For what reason do you think all those wars against the white man were fought?

He was silent for a long time, perhaps as long as an hour. Aurelia lay against Jason and the two of them, undisturbed, slept soundly. They were unaware that the old man, unable to sleep, had started talking again:

"When I was just about eleven years old, four buffalo were seen at Fort Thompson agency. Right there along the water. Everybody thought it was very strange for them to come right up to us, right in our midst. And we all knew that there was something wrong. Like when the coyote, a nocturnal animal, makes his daylight trips, or when a magpie flies into your tipi. We all knew that the world of humans was upside down. That something holy might be happening. It was like that. Right there along the water where my aunties lived, in the year 1902. I remember it because those buffalo were the last ones to be seen in the wild by our people. They were crippled, diseased. Pitiful. And they died shortly after that. People told for a long time afterwards that the old bull was shot with an arrow just before he died, and taken to Fort Sully where thousands of our relatives gathered for one of those kinds of ritualized offerings from the people. It is a well-known fact that his skull is kept even now and it is used as an altar by the relatives of those who danced at that time, those who lighted sage and sweetgrass."

"You know, *Mitakojas*," Jason and Aurelia were awake now, their eyes filled with the scratchy stuff of sleep. The faintest red had started in the eastern sky and a chill hung about the trees.

"You know, *Mitakojas*," Grey Iron said, "Leaper, the young university student from the reservation who has now become a murderer and rapist, is a relative with all of us and of all the tribes who have always lived here, along the river and out into the prairie and into the hills. Contrary to public opinion, our people have always been peaceful and industrious, and it is a terrible thing that the young man has done, and he must know that the great spirit weeps for him."

More asleep than awake, Aurelia looked toward where the old man sat humped over, rumpled and tired. She felt his warmth and compassion, his weary, absorbed castigation of the world as it had become, and she knew that she believed his every word.

"We have all undergone great change," he said, not looking up, "and our lives are intertwined with the *wasichus* until we hardly know what is happening to us, nor how we must respond to the terrible evil among us."

He paused.

"The young man will be dealt with by the *wasichu* now, and there is little we can do."

Aurelia and Jason looked at each other, startled. Grey Iron's voice had changed and the tenor of the story seemed, somehow, more adamant, dogged.

Jason put his arm around Aurelia's shoulders.

"We will be going home as soon as the sun rises," he whispered.

Aurelia finally understood that the journey into the white man's murder scene and jailhouse had ended. She understood that the old man was not going to see the white lawyers on this day, that he would leave it all to the providential spirits of the land.

Grey Iron moved as an old man moves and stood up. As though talking to himself now, persevering yet intense, he continued the story:

When the Harney Treaty of March, 1856, was made at Fort Pierre, my grandfather was there and he looked toward the redness, the yellow in the east just as I am looking now. And even though he refused to give his signature, because he opposed the general theft of the lands that the white man wanted, my grandfather told us later that it was an attempt by all Indians to uphold the Indian police principle. The sovereignty of the nation. The right to be ourselves. It was the only good thing that came out of talking to Harney because, everyone knew, he was an enemy of the people.

It was good because it upheld the notion that the tribes would always be self-governing, that the tribes would always have the last word on how to deal with our own people and our own land. If you don't know what the principle is, my grandfather told us, it is the idea that that we must handle our own legal, spiritual, and moral matters, an idea that has always

been, in spite of our treaty talk, rejected by the white man.
Until that principle is upheld, I say that talk is cheap.

Grey Iron put his hand on the front of his shirt as though acknowledging the presence of the dried sage which he kept buttoned up inside.

"It will get worse, my children. The general disorder is all around us. And very soon now there will be federal Marshals on our homelands. Again. Like they were when Sitting Bull was shot."

Aurelia stood up and stretched. She was troubled by the sudden reference to the public Indian protests now being explored in the media on a daily basis, the tacit association of the recently developed American Indian Movement with a history that she knew all too well. She was troubled by the old man's prediction.

She and Jason began to fold the blankets and put their things in the car.

"Come," the old man urged, "we will not pray this morning, not here, in this place. We must go home."

Then, just as suddenly, the old man stopped and lowered his head, his big hands rubbing together as though pain was felt in every joint, every muscle.

"Something . . . what is it . . . that has happened to us, then?" he asked, close to tears. It was a rhetorical question. Not one that he expected anyone to answer.

"What has made us, too, the 'wasters'? It is not a new question, you know."

They stood, waiting for the old man to be finished. Aurelia wished she could get him to stop. To stop talking about the things that she could not bring herself to think about . . . the overpowering oppressiveness of living like this . . . from one crisis to the next. Whenever she came close to naming the grief she felt now, the sorrow that was being expressed now at moments like this by Jason's uncle, she would become mystified, bemused, mute. She would hesitate and falter, unable to do anything, her thoughts diffuse and useless. She knew the old man had not run out of emotion yet, that he had not come to the end, and so she continued to listen. The story now seemed fragmented. Unconnected.

"One thing. That time that they told us about. When the people told about a party of five or six hundred Sioux Indians came on horseback across the river near here." He pointed vaguely.

Jason leaned against the car and lit another cigarette. He often gave the impression that he was not listening when people talked to him, but in the case of the old man Lewis, he always paid close attention.

"A long time ago," Lewis gestured with his hands, "they came with 1,400 buffalo tongues because the fur traders had cheated them out of the hides. And it is said that they traded the fresh buffalo tongues for whiskey."

Jason drew long and hard on his cigarette.

"When the medicine men found out about it, they were unable to punish them for their crime against the buffalo, a crime that was unheard of in the old days, but one which the Sioux knew to be heinous and obscene and unforgivable. The medicine men, you see, were under guard. They were held as criminals by the U.S. Government, and they were watched all the time so that they were not able to do good for the people."

Despair overcame the old man and he wept. "And we have been unable ever since to do anything about ourselves. Such crimes. They continue even today. And our people do not know what to do, how to behave. They do bad things."

It was the old man's explanation for a world that did not wish to be healed.

Jason put out his cigarette and reached for Aurelia and drew her into his arms. They held on to each other as they listened to the old man's quiet weeping. From that moment, they knew that they would no longer live apart, that their child would be born and, Jason whispered, "he will be *c'askke'na koskana wa nina n'ehi'napi*, that's the way the old ones say it. He will grow up and have four sons." Jason held Aurelia as he wiped her tears and he continued in a low voice, "He will go out and away from my lodge and wrap a fur about himself. In his lifetime he will see a white buffalo." The woman who would not pray and would not weep out loud could do nothing but believe in him and the story. She felt a chill run down her back and she pulled her wrap closer.

9

August 1969

Moving in with Jason, Aurelia was welcomed by his parents the very day they returned from the portentous journey with Grey Iron. Everyone talked enthusiastically of the future, pleased with the new arrangement. With one exception. Sheridan. The elder brother. Though he seldom visited the family any more, he came unexpectedly one day when no one was home and left a note on the table.

It read: "Who else is going to move in here?" His words were dismissed by Jason, who said there was nothing new about Sheridan's jealousy and meanness. Still, it made Aurelia feel uncomfortable and wary. There had been some gossip about the difference in ages between Aurelia and Jason, that she was robbing the cradle. She knew that this elder brother was a man who had the capacity to bring disgrace and disorder to the family. All she could do in this new family arrangement was keep her own counsel. And she avoided him.

Harvey brought into the house a large piece of uncut yellowed rawhide and helped his new daughter-in-law shape it for the outer shield of a new cradleboard. Jason and his male relatives hurriedly moved a trailerhouse to the Big Pipe place to accommodate Aurelia's grandmother, so that she could come and visit and return to her own home at will as was convenient for everyone. The days of expectation were remarkable, mindful days.

August came and with it the unbearably hot and fierce wind that turns the grass brown and brittle. On one of those late days of summer Aurelia, large with child, was walking toward the river and meditating and hoping that her time would be soon, when she collapsed in the wind and the sun, and was found alongside the road by her Auntie Mart. She was taken immediately to the clinic where her child, a son, was born.

"The wind," Aurelia said later, laughing about her collapse and the birth of her son, "it just blew me over!"

No one knew whether or not to believe her.

"The wind," she continued, feeling important now, feeling the change in status that comes with such momentous events in a woman's life, "the wind, you know, becomes, in late summer, like the relative of *Taku Skan-Skan*, like it has its own holiness. It gets contrary and wicked and it is almost unbearable. All I remember is that the wind was strong and it was pushing me around, that the white clouds disappeared into the pale blue of the sky, and the horizon moved. And the dry earth couldn't help me anymore and I couldn't walk."

After that, like all women who wish to find meaning in birth-giving, she told many stories of how Hokshina Blue Big Pipe (her *chunskay*, her firstborn son) had come into the world. The bare facts were these: Time: 11:16 P.M.; Wt: eight pounds and fourteen ounces; Lgth: twenty-three and one-half inches; Hair, black; Eyes, black; Race: American-Indian/Dakotah.

Ever after that Aurelia painted her maternal stories with broad strokes. Perhaps her persistence about these stories could be attributed to the fact that she was not, after all, a young mother. Perhaps because she was thought of by those in the community as past her prime, her stories were longer and more direct and regenerative.

When she told Blue about his birth, the stories oftentimes seemed out of place in these modern times, a bit foolish and self-indulgent, but she told them over and over again throughout the years, and he always listened attentively though no one could say whether or not he believed them.

"Who is that crying, I thought that just before I saw you.

"And here it was you! It was you! Crying! They put you in my arms and you blinked at me and, right away, I knew that you recognized me. You knew me!!"

She was always astonished at this revelation and, even as an old woman, years and years later, she did not lose her innocence about that filial recognition.

"The first thing I did," she would tell him, "I opened the blanket and counted your toes and fingers, like I thought you weren't going to be all there. You know, like there was going to be something missing."

She laughed, always, at such an absurdity.

"I turned you over and, sure enough, you had a dark streak on your backside. We are all like that, you know." Her voice would take on a tone of conspirituality.

"Hm-m-m, when I touched you, you drew up your legs, pulled them up to your fat round belly and you farted, and, you know . . . it was just like you stretched a mile or so. Your arms up over your head. You tried to open your eyes again but, instead, you opened your mouth and I fed you for the very first time."

She would smile in remembrance.

"I always think about what I was told then by Gramma," she would say more seriously, "that boys are hard to raise. But I talked to you like I had always known you and I was not afraid. 'Blue,' I would say, 'at last you are here. I been just waiting for you. You took a long, long time.' "

When there would be no response except an appreciative glance, she would go on:

"Gramma was in the room over by the window and she was saying over and over again:

Nawajin na hoyeya nawajob
I am standing here and praying

Her voice was full of tears.

" *'He cusni ye,'* (Don't), I told her. It will be all right. 'Don't sing like that anymore, Gramma,' I told her. 'Because it will only worry the baby.' So I started to sing some other songs to you. Songs that were happy.

"Your father, you know, he told me that I had done a sacred thing and tears came into his eyes. I remember, too, that he told me then that he knew you would *icimani* and become *takoja* to your own animal helpers. I was just lying there in the darkened hospital room when he told me that and it became so stuffy I could hardly breathe."

Aurelia's eyes would cloud over and she would be lost in her own thoughts. She would see Jason in her mind's eye as he walked toward her. He was always then, in those times, heedless of the fading blue sky.

She was able to believe, then, that Jason and his son would be among those Dakotahs who could run with magical speed and could see and hear across vast distances, that great disasters could be avoided, that the people would always be able to count their lives by the number of winters they survived.

Even then, though, she sensed surreptitious movements near.

Part 2

Tomorrow and Tomorrow

I lived in the shuffle of unborn motherlands, in colonies that still didn't know how to be born, with undrawn flags that would soon be bloodied. I lived by the campfire of badly wounded towns and devoured my own anguish like strange bread.

—Pablo Neruda (translation)

10

Creatures and Gods Laugh

The best campfires are always adjacent to the river, they say. The aroma of heavy smoke just across the river where the supernaturals sometimes stop the horses in their tracks, mid-stream, and the loud hawks in mid-air, is a reminder to the Dakotahs that water is their fate. The river seems shallow at first, but great tides rise at a moment's notice, especially when the sky turns grey and streaks of distant lightning flash, as though something is embodied there forcing the torrents along. The people and horses and buffalo, unafraid, stand still until it is over. The red-brown cliffs are covered up with foaming water and the people watch the whirlpools in fascination.

Dakotahs who have always lived along the rivers know that this kind of event often happens in August. Unaccountably, Aurelia thought she should keep a large hawk feather in the blankets of her child and she did so for many years and knew that he would eventually take the name Yellowhawk. Sometimes she would sit on a hill overlooking the river and she would speak to no one and, eventually, Jason would come and get her and take her to the house.

Although she had never seen them herself, Aurelia contemplated the meaning of the whirlpools. The two major events of her early marriage to Jason took possession of her. These happenings were three years apart and they probably foreshadowed how it was that she became a companion to Jason, her first husband, and how she was to become contented and happy as she had never been before. At least for that brief and faithful time.

The August of Blue's birth remained memorable and his childish presence brought the little family together. The not-unexpected death of Lewis Grey Iron in August almost three years later reminded Jason and Aurelia of the immense power and strength of certain old men, the Missouri River men, in shaping their destiny.

The morning of the old man's funeral had passed without incident and everyone, unhurried, met at the church.

"The thing I'll remember most," said Jason as he lit another cigarette, "is that he understood history and always gave us good advice."

"M-mm-m," agreed Aurelia. Undoing a scarf tied around her hair, she looked into Jason's face, the muscle in his jaw stiff and tense. For about an hour, silence his only reaction to the profound loss embodied in the death of his uncle, Lewis Grey Iron, Jason had said nothing. He and Aurelia sat in the pickup, its engine idling, just outside of the long meeting hall. Blue, already a toddler, was sober and grave in his mother's lap. They watched as the people, men mostly, gathered themselves for the procession to the family gravesite about two miles away, directed traffic away from the muddy parking lot, and gave directions to those who had come to honor the death of an elder.

Only when he saw his father step wearily into the saddle of one of the eight horses which would lead the processional did Jason pull on his gloves and get out of the rig slowly. As Aurelia slipped behind the wheel, he said, almost to himself, but with his head buried in Blue's chubby neck, "Hokshina, say 'Goodbye, grandfather. Goodbye to all the grandfathers.' " His eyes were dry and his face grim as he turned away.

Aurelia and the small child watched as he joined the others on horseback. They saw him take hold of a knotted rope and lead a young bay stallion, unsaddled and unbridled, at the end of the line. The elder brother, Sheridan Big Pipe, looking scruffy and unkempt, stood with a group of his cohorts at the front of the building, and when their sister Clarissa pulled up alongside

him in her car, motioning for him to get in beside her, he waved
her away wordlessly. Aurelia ignored Sheridan's dark looks as
she drove carefully out of the parking lot and onto the dirt road
behind the horse processional. He's such a fool, she thought to
herself.

Moving at a snail's pace, it seemed to Aurelia to be an endless
drive. At the grave, she heard the wheezing voice of Father Tom,
an asthmatic who was kept busy just *being* Father Tom for, when
it came to caring what happened to the people, he cared so much
he was very simply overwhelmed. Both physically and
emotionally. He was, to use a phrase of the people, "a bleeding
heart." Any real work of the church brought on uncontrollable
coughing spasms usually attended to by the women elders, who
then set about doing the work for which the ailing priest was
incapacitated. This day he was a little off-key but bearing up
reasonably well, intoning, "Bless us, O Lord. Bless the light and
the darkness . . . " and wiping his flowing eyes.

Jason was still silent when they returned to the hall for the
traditional gigantic meal and long speeches. He looked around
for Sheridan, who apparently had not stayed for the communal
gathering of food and talk. Aurelia and others tried to engage
Jason in conversation but it was no use.

"To lose our grandfather," many of the speakers said, "is not
unexpected. This is a natural thing for which the old man had
prepared. But what it means is that another generation of us
must step forward to possess the gifts of reason and harmony
that he has given us."

It seemed to Aurelia a pompous thing to say, for these were
serious times of upheaval the likes of which the people had not
seen in decades, and it would be only brief months before they
would all be engulfed in the era of change so exactingly predicted
by Grey Iron that it would seem uncanny, a time for which there
could be no substitute for the leadership of such elders. She had
the feeling as they buried the old man that day that things were
not about to get any better.

In the following year, the moment when the federal Marshals
came into the native homelands, just as Grey Iron had said they
would, no one, least of all the little Indian family settling down

beside the Crow Creek, could have prepared itself for the indisputable vicissitude, the shift, the about-face, the revolution that would confront American Indians.

It was a time of great expectations but few certainties and there were few who would keep the story straight. Aurelia was witness to it all. Her keeping of the stories, the people said years later, seemed directly linked to the powers that helped the people test the nature of the universe. In the larger narrative, there would be worldwide events which everyone would come to know. But in the tribal version, only a few undertook to explore the complexity of events and what they meant to their individual lives. Aurelia was, indeed, one of the few.

For years Aurelia had not wanted marriage. Neither did she want motherhood. Without fully comprehending how it all had really happened, she now had both. Her lifelong unwillingness to accept the inevitable role that grown-up Dakotah women since time immemorial have always learned to accept—that of bearer of children, feeder of the people, companion to men, and keeper of the stories—was finally done.

"It is foolish to think that that we can just live our lives without acknowledging our need for one another," was the way Aurelia's new father-in-law had put it.

So now she was in the midst of it.

Many things in Aurelia's life had changed, though her relationship with her grandmother, who embraced Jason as a traditional grandson by marriage, continued to be a major influence. Blue, unlike many children of the modern Indian world, was raised in his cradleboard and when he outgrew it, his mother did not take it apart, but instead hung it on the wall in a special place so it would be known as a revered object and part of the family history.

When her mother-in-law spoke to her, Aurelia quickly learned that she would speak only once. To say or ask more than once would make words between them, a son's mother and his wife, unreliable and meaningless.

Every now and then, though, Aurelia, always and innately suspicious, became afraid that there was some great cosmic joke to be played out. She felt like the woman who was struck by a lightning arrow when she least expected it, like that could happen at any moment and no one could say why. Maybe it was the natural fear in her brought about by knowing the stories about women that the Dakotahs tell themselves and each other. Those stories, the Missouri River tribal people say, tell you that the yellow woman is known to wither and die in a cyclical manner. It is a natural thing but frightening to those who bear the children.

The yellow woman asks the Oyate to cut her body up into small pieces, to wash them in the places where the water supernaturals live, and then plant them in the warm black earth along the river where the campfires smolder. These goings-on were acknowledged by Aurelia as the people's notions concerning the heroism in women, but she was neither convinced nor inspired by it. The tyranny of it as she carried the child in her arms along the river banks sometimes stopped her in her tracks.

Yet she felt within herself a happiness, a contentment, a personal space that allowed her to go about her life. The things that had at one time angered her almost beyond words now were accepted with mild approbation, and she had quickly taken up the matters of domesticity. One change, however, always necessitates another, they say; thus, a journey begun can only continue.

It was a time, it seemed to Aurelia, when many of the elders were going to the next world, when stress within the changing family put everyone on edge.

It was not only that Leaper, the drug-crazed killer of the old white man and his wife, was sentenced to die in the electric chair, becoming the first person to get such a sentence in the state of South Dakota in a century; or that every day in Aurelia's home brought about a new challenge, that people died and young ones were born.

This was the time, also, when there was much talk in America of "nuclear first strike," and everyone who watched television began to understand that the Soviets could issue a massive strike capable of destroying most cities in the United States within thirty minutes. Richard Nixon, newly elected, proposed a family assistance program with minimum standard income levels, but really didn't have the heart for it. No one had any way of knowing that within a few years, minimum standard income levels would be totally forgotten as Nixon engaged in a fight to save his own presidency.

It was a time, too, when stories from afar were incorporated into those home stories. Aurelia's cousin, Dale, on a two-week furlough from the Marines, was stabbed almost to death by a black man on Franklin Avenue in St. Paul while visiting his mother and sister on "relocation." Just a bit earlier, Eddie Benton Benai, George Mitchell, Dennis Banks, and Clyde Bellecourt changed the name of their fledgling organization, Concerned Indian Americans (because they didn't like the acronym), to the American Indian Movement, and began to get serious as urban guerillas.

In spite of these broader events of urban America, Aurelia's stories and Jason's and Blue's had quickly become part of the Big Pipe family life and memory on the Crow Creek Indian Reservation. They learned that if they wanted to be happy, they had to listen to the things they told each other about themselves. They confided in one another in those early years as they had never been able to before. Unskilled as they were with words of affection, they listened to one another and tried to show that they knew the future would be good to them.

One late night as sleep was coming on, with the winter moon, pale and white, streaming in the window, Jason said:

"Look, Aurelia, that is the moon that makes the leaves yellow."

She stared into the dark sky.

"It takes a long time for the moon to change. I wonder why they say the power is in the moon but not the water?"

"Who says that?"

"Somebody . . . "

"Huh-uh. What they say is that the power cannot stay in the water."

"Yeah?"

"That's what I've heard. Yeh . . . the waters can become something else, you see."

He said nothing.

"It continues to create . . . don't you see . . . "

"H—m—mmm . . . "

"What they mean to say is that it is one of the continuous creators, I think . . . "

"H-mmm-m."

She wondered if he was asleep.

After a pause, "Hey, you know, Aurelia, that first haying season when I was first home from 'Nam. Man, it was good. I saw myself, by some strange and random good luck, reprieved and alive. I sat shirtless against the swather and thought how damn good the sweat and the sun and the dryness of the slim Dakota breeze felt. Jeez." He shook his head in wonder.

He remembered how he had run water through his hair, splashed it on his face, and reached confidently toward the sky. The prairies of South Dakota, the hills of home, and the circles of sunlight could heal the spirit of any man, he had thought then. He remembered waving to Merton St. John and Mutchie Middle Tent and his dad, bent over the bailer. He could still see the old man holding up his jug of water, signalling for a break. Smiling.

"And then," his eyes were warm and inviting, "then I got you to look me over."

"I guess I did more than that, hunh?"

Her voice was low in her throat and she smiled and reached out to him. She felt his desire for her and, as her eyes fell shut, she thought, with you, Jason, I do not want anything except to wait for the time when you will want me again. She could not believe that this state of floating here in the middle of a despised domesticity was what had become her destiny. They had long since quit talking of marriage, but knew their devotion to each other to be better than any formal marriage of their acquaintance.

Jason Big Pipe shared what he had learned about the Vietnamese when he participated as their sworn enemy in one of the bloody Tet offensives of the war, and when he talked this way, Aurelia had little understanding of what it meant to her own life with him.

"The traditional Vietnamese said that the week of January eighteenth through the twenty-fifth sets the pattern for the entire new year," he told her, "and when they defended themselves against us then, during that time, they fought as hard as any of the Sioux warriors of our own history."

As she fell into a light and troubled sleep, she wondered if he was talking about the coming winter. Would it be hard for them? She dreamed of them making their way up through the hills in the dark, shoes slipping on the packed icy snow. In her dream, she saw many footprints and they were unaccountably dark.

A light snow fell as Aurelia stirred in her sleep.

Quickly, Jason sat up and as he did, Aurelia awoke, startled. She saw the fear in his eyes.

"Jeez," he said tiredly, after he got his bearings. "I'm getting as bad as Sheridan. These goddamn nighttime dreams . . . "

Elder brother, Sheridan, now so unconnected to the reality of tribal mores, had been a continuing source of concern even before Aurelia and he had begun their standoff. In fact, ever since he had come home to South Dakota from the war, he was a changed man. It was three years, almost to the day, since he had been wounded in the groin at Tay Ninh Province during the largest operation of the war up to that time and was sent home, forever maimed. He had been with the 173rd Airborne Brigade and was participating in the launch of a major offensive northeast of Saigon. He had been in jungle combat for one month short of two years.

From the day of Sheridan's return he had been unemployed, his wife and children on welfare, his parents and brothers and sisters isolated from his suffering simply because of his silence. He often sat alone in a darkened room listening to National Public Radio. He put his name on various mailing lists and went to the mailbox every day and read everything he could about the colonial war in which he had just participated. He rarely slept and had roaring nightmares when he did. Jason's reference to him made Aurelia tense and initiated an immediate denial.

"Don't say that!" said Aurelia gently and began to stroke Jason's neck. "You're not getting like Sheridan."

They both knew that Sheridan's behavior had been unpredictable and strange since he'd gotten back from Vietnam. They knew he drank himself into oblivion over and over again and fell into those deep, silent blackouts, often disappearing for days or doing things he couldn't remember afterward.

Sheridan's behavior and life were an uncomfortable subject and, though they tried to keep it secret in the family, everyone in the community knew and talked of the troubles the eldest son of Harvey Big Pipe was having. Some said that when he helped a white man in a reservation cattle theft a few years earlier and managed to avoid indictment by lying to everyone, including his parents, his behavior was directly related to his Vietnam War experiences, that he had come home with that "syndrome" everyone talked about. All of that, Aurelia was sure, was just an excuse.

Jason was reluctant to say much about Sheridan to Aurelia, because she knew that he, too, had lied during that same episode, to save his brother from indictment. It was a sore subject between them, something that had happened in the past that they wanted to forget.

"You know," he had told her, "the Vietnamese made a believer out of me."

"What do you mean?"

"They were right to fight off the Americans. The French first. Then the Americans. They were right. To fight to the death. To give everything."

"Oh."

She thought about all the Indian Wars her relatives had told her about. It was a consistent topic of conversation with people of her generation who grew up with the old ones.

They moved apart and began to talk seriously. Jason said, "Sheridan has been reading again."

"Yeah? What's he been reading?

"He told me he read about what Ho Chi Minh believed."

"What's that?"

" *Nothing is dearer than independence and liberty.* "

"Is that really true?"

"It is for me."

"Yes. I guess it is."

She felt they were being overly dramatic, foolish, for surely, it seemed so sacrificial. Nonetheless, when Jason told her that the Vietnamese had made a believer out of him even before the incidents at Crow Creek, and Pine Ridge, and all across Sioux Country in 1973 and January of 1974, she wondered what would be the result of ever afterward carrying in his heart the secret knowledge that the Vietnamese were right all along. Would he and Sheridan and even their younger brother, Virgil, be punished in some way? Would something awful happen because they had taken the idea of the Vietnamese resistance to heart, talking to each other about it, feeling that the word about the corrupt war the United States waged against the ancient Asian nation would spread and history would have to be rewritten? They talked openly of their disgust for the American/Asian war. The nation of their homelands they had so recently defended was, in their thoughts, now unreliable and grotesque.

"The war we participated in means something different to us as Indians, now," he told her.

She did not ask what that meaning was.

Outside, the snow swirled eastward toward the frozen river, the color of night. Powerfully, the wind swept across the prairie landscape, piling drifts against the frail houses and outbuildings and the trees bent into its fury.

Aurelia felt a great lonesomeness as he talked in a soft troubled voice into the night. She could not fail to see what was happening to them, that their hard lives would soon become unbearable to him because he was still young and unreflective. She knew him as a practical man. Those who are practical, she thought, bring about a personal disconsolateness that often leads to a diffuse and unattached despair. The more he talked, the more defenseless she felt. Sometimes when hidden souls are bared, there are only questions, no answers. Would he eventually leave her? And if he were to leave her, would there be anything that either of them could say that would make it right again?

"It is not true that upon their return from the battlefield Sioux warriors harbored the kind of doubts I have about this," he told her regretfully.

"Do you feel guilty?"

"No. Not guilty. But I feel that something terrible might come out of it."

"Something terrible? Like what?"

"I don't know."

"Nothing can happen to us now," she had said then, trying to make him see that she was confident. Serene.

Their baby had grown out of his infancy and life would go on. She tried to make Jason believe that his fears and hatreds were unfounded. Abruptly, she turned over and pretended to go back to sleep.

11

The Coming Storm

In spite of Aurelia's pretense that everything was all right, uncertain days seemed inevitable. When Blue had passed his third birthday and life seemed as good as she'd pretended it was, the Big Pipes watched helplessly at an approaching winter storm. As they listened to the howling, moaning wind one January night, it seemed a tacit reminder to Jason of the Asian prediction. Cliché or not, there was no other way to describe the voice of that wind, though people who haven't lived in the North Plains and heard it with their own ears are likely not to believe in it.

The freezing, penetrating wind swirled the snow into great drifts around the house and the sound was by turns vicious and pitiful, sometimes imitating the roar of an angry hurricane, other times whining a low lamentation of grief, like a man blowing his breath into a bottle. The stars were invisible and the coyotes, restless and excited, were quick to travel to their dens. The sky was full of swirling snow and when members of the family peered out of the windows they could see nothing but the whiteness of the storm.

Snow had been piling up for seven straight days and, "It's a good thing," everyone was saying. The hope was that it might turn out to be the break in the weather needed to end the drought cycle that had made a dust bed of the northern hayfields the past summers.

A couple of days earlier, just as the storm was beginning in earnest, Jason had felt its anger, and he found himself thinking again about the Vietnamese prediction as he walked back to the house carrying the mail. His jeans whipped about his legs in the biting wind as his fingers tried to shake open the letter from the Tribal Credit Committee. He saw that it was signed by the loan specialist, a guy named McQueen. He swore fearfully when he looked up into the whitened sky, the air even then filled with blowing snow, the kind that takes your breath away and smothers you in a matter of seconds, the kind recognized by humans thousands of years ago as that which made the universe a shrill and dangerous place.

Blue, trying hard to grow out of his clumsy three-year-old stage, had fallen from the couch and was crying bitterly, his face streaked with tears, as Jason pushed at the door, stepped inside, and slammed it shut against the wind. Jason picked up the little boy, dried his tears, and said, laughing, "Hey, Indians don't cry! Only them cowboys do the cryin', ennit?" He galloped around the tiny room, bouncing Blue into shrieks of laughter. "Hey, are you a Indian? Or are you a cowboy?"

"'relia," he called as he put the child down. "This guy needs a peanut butter sandwich."

Aurelia came to the kitchen door wiping her hands.

"He just ate, Jason."

"Yeah? What did he eat?"

"Pancakes. You want some?"

"Yeah."

"How many? Four?"

"Yeah. Four's okay." He was suddenly preoccupied.

He pulled off his bulky gloves, dropped some mail on the table, and flipped open the letter from the Department of Interior, Crow Creek Agency.

It read:

I have your statement from the Oahe Electric Coop in the amount of $135.81 which was past due for the months of October, November, and December, 1972 that you sent down here by the Extension Agent. Jason, when we made the settlement for the corn you sold, at the time you asked for money to pay your electric bill and get some fuel, which you got $200 for. The other day you wanted money to have your pickup repaired and I let you have $100. Why didn't you take care of this when you had the funds for this purpose? Some of these bills are from last year, you know, even from the year before.

"Son of a bitch," not yet finished reading, but angered, Jason threw the five-page letter on the cluttered table, sat down, and buttered a pancake, breaking off little pieces and handing them to Blue, who jabbered and smeared them across his mouth as he ate them. Blue lurched toward the couch in the living room just as Aurelia caught him to wipe his hands.

Harvey moved slowly through the living room to the kitchen. He poured a cup of coffee for himself, then another for his ailing wife. He carefully stirred three spoons of sugar into the hot liquid.

"Mama's not feeling too good," he said as he took the cup of coffee to their bedroom. They heard his attentive murmur as the old mother coughed quietly.

Slowly, Jason pulled his gloves back on, went out to the side of the house where there was a huge pile of wood covered with snow. He scraped away ten or twenty inches of snow from the top of the pile, picked up an armful of wood, and spent the next ten minutes hauling in stovewood, which he stacked carefully and deliberately in the large wooden box behind the heater. As he did so, Aurelia carried Blue into the kitchen and held him away from the cold air that swept across the floor.

The wood hauling was an obvious diversion for Jason, something psychologists like to call avoidance behavior. Both Jason and Aurelia knew that sooner or later he would have to go back to the humiliating letter from McQueen at the Department.

"What the hell am I going to do now?" Jason asked resentfully.

The question was rhetorical and, as Aurelia stood helplessly in the middle of the room, Jason trudged back and forth from the living room to the outdoor woodpile and back. She seldom saw her husband this anxious.

"You know, they could shut off the electricity any minute. Tomorrow, maybe."

Good thing Jason had stuck to his guns when the tribal housing people wanted to put electric heating equipment in his house, Aurelia thought. If he'd let them do so, they'd really be, to use one of Jason's favorite terms, up shit crick about now. Aurelia recalled what a hell of a time he'd had convincing them that he wanted to continue with a free-standing wood heater in his place. He had argued with them for months, refusing to move into the house until they had settled it in his favor.

Even his father had gone to the agency to tell them that certain kinds of heat caused illnesses in human beings. It was old Big Pipe's theory that winter heat, other than that from the cottonwood and ash and oak trees that grew along the river bank and the Crow Creek, wasn't good for his health. Not really convinced but worn down by the persistence of the argument, the agency officials let them have their own way even though it was not "within the bureau guidelines."

It was a good thing, Aurelia reflected, for right now she could name three of their neighbors who'd had to move in with relatives elsewhere because they couldn't pay their electric bills in their new tribal housing. People could get along without light but they couldn't get along without heat, she mused. Not in this weather. They could keep themselves, their child, and the old parents warm and fed at least, and she felt grateful for that.

Things looked bad, thought Aurelia, and she worried that Jason would lose heart. She had known little of his previous life, his enthusiasm upon his return from 'Nam for the new tribally funded economic scheme called the reservation "farm-ranch program" that his father had begun during his absence. She could not have known how happy he was that first August, home ahead of his brothers, finding his father aged and ill but waiting hopefully for his return and help. Jason had not yet passed his twentieth birthday, then, a Vietcong bullet still in his hip, and when he helped them cut hay that first August he knew he was a man who was happy to be looking into the Dakota sun again.

Nobody ought to live out their lives, he had thought then, without knowing about a place like this. He remembered looking up at the bluest sky and seeing a chicken hawk circling endlessly, searching for any hapless mouse exposed by the haycutters. Disappointed, the hawk had swung gracefully toward the river, falling below the horizon. As Jason watched he had vowed then to do the best he could to keep things going, even though hundreds of acres of his father's place had already been flooded by the hydropower dams.

Nine months from that day, his elder brother, Sheridan, a shy, strong young man when he left, came home wild-eyed, depressed, and addicted to whatever would make the nighmares go away. It was at that time that the family was awaiting word from young Virgil, a Marine jungle fighter in the Mekong Delta, a teenager whose name would eventually be carved into the black marble memorial to dead warriors in Washington, D.C.: *Virgil S. Big Pipe.* Though they hadn't known it then, Antony, the youngest, a Marine Lance Corporal, would fly to the coast from LeJeune on a military jet to accompany his dead brother's body back to the reservation for a military burial.

Jason's thoughts were now, several years later, caught up in the struggles of the moment. Sometimes he shared his fears with Aurelia, wondering aloud if that place in the sun was no longer that ceremonial place of his memory, if it was becoming a place of prostration and outrage. A place where people could only throw themselves down, physically and emotionally exhausted . . . a place of invented tragedy.

Aurelia, her face flushed from standing at the kitchen stove, a worried look on her face, flipping pancakes that her husband was too distracted to eat, was saying, "You know, we could use those kerosene lamps in the other room, don't you think, Jay?"

As far as she was concerned, the blackness of the night was no big problem, though having the child now complicated matters. She still remembered the years in her grandmother's little "government" house for the elderly down on the Crow Creek where there had been no electricity for the people since time immemorial. There never had been. Sensible people simply went to bed when it got dark and got up with the sun. Aurelia had grown accustomed to such a way of living as a child and, even when her Grandmother Blue purchased some kerosene lamps, and later the brighter, so-called Aladdin gas lamps, they were seldom used by anyone in the family. The bright new lamps were perched on top of the dressers and tables as ornaments, unnecessary and irrelevant to the way the old lady wanted to live her life.

But for Jason, the dark of winter would settle in early and he would find the long evenings unbearable. He was one of those who had quickly gotten used to the television programs, once the electric power was available on the reservation, and now he didn't know how to get along without them.

"Yeah," he responded with little enthusiasm.

He sat down, removed his gloves again, and picked up the letter to continue reading. The loan specialist who sent out these missives was a man who had been sent to the Crow Creek from the area office in Portland, Oregon, and he took his job seriously.

"Hey, 'relia. Listen to this." Jason sounded half amused as he read out loud:

This is the end-gate for check writing for personal things as the proceeds from the sale of corn is gone and the balance in your bank account is for the completion of the hog barn that is due to be moved in as soon as the weather clears up, and to pay for the electric wiring in the hog barn. It is doubtful if there is enough left to complete the work that is needed to be done and this is because of your flagrant spending.

"What does that mean, Jason?"

"Yeah. What the hell does it mean? Sounds like he thinks I have made off with some of the money or something. Flagrant spending, hell!

"Hell, I don't have no money. I didn't get nuthin' outta that corn. I got only five thousand bushels when they said I was supposed to get fourteen thousand! Fourteen thousand!? I don't know how in the hell they figured that!"

"Um-m . . . since it didn't rain practically all summer and not for two or three years."

"Damn!"

"And . . . they . . . you never did . . . "

"Yeah. We still haven't got all them irrigation pipes in. We was supposed to have them all going a year ago."

Jason clasped his hands behind his head and said, "Yeah, 'relia. Sounds like he thinks we been livin' it up, hunh?"

He gestured with wide, sweeping movements around the room at the shabby couch, scratched wooden tables, the easy chair held up at one end with a cement block, suggesting the meagerness of their surroundings, their lives.

Aurelia went back to the kitchen stove.

Jason sat for a few minutes more. How in the hell am I going to pay the electricity for the goddamned hog barn if I can't even pay the bills I got now, he wondered silently. What's the point of trying to save money for the pig barn if I can't even feed my wife and kid and keep my pickup going? What's going to happen to the old man and my mother?

He had had very little cash since a couple of months ago when his cousin, Vic Eagle, had come over asking for money and Jason had given Vic his last fifty bucks. Vic, who considered himself a political activist, was headed for Washington, D.C., for the so-called occupation of the Bureau of Indian Affairs offices in November, and needed just enough "coins to get by."

"A bunch of Indians from South Dakota are going," Vic assured him and, though Jason had too much on his mind to concern himself with such problems, he always wanted to help out his relatives. The political situation at Pine Ridge was worsening, they all knew, but what many of them didn't know was that the seventy-one-day siege at Wounded Knee, South Dakota, was about to begin. Federal Marshals and the FBI would arrive there on February 11, to take a stand against the American Indian Movement.

A few days before the storm, the old man had gotten his "old-age" check and with it they had purchased enough groceries to last during any lengthy blizzard. Just in time, thought Jason, as he went to the kitchen to pour himself a cup of coffee and wait until Aurelia put their supper of pancakes and beans on the table.

The dismal day wore on and as he looked out the window into the dim light of the evening, he said, "This is going to be a helluva storm, 'relia."

Winter was a time Jason feared. For Aurelia, more philosophical in her attitude toward the universe, it was a thrilling time because its threat reaffirmed their people's recognition that mere mortals were held in the naked power of the uncontrollable forces of the world and, for some reason, she embraced that truth. More than a rainstorm or drought, a blizzard was esurient, covetous, craving. It could greedily suck the breath from any living thing and often did out here in the North Country.

Still lying open and scattered on the table, the five pages of the letter from the Interior Department, Bureau of Indian Affairs, Fort Thompson Agency, seemed to stare accusingly at them when they got ready for bed. Aurelia, brushing her teeth, heard Jason's swearing as he crammed another huge chunk of wood into the long, oblong stove, banking it and turning down the draft. She heard him say goodnight to his parents in the other room and assure his father that they had done all they could. They got into bed, their toddler son asleep between them. They continued to listen tentatively to the sounds of the storm.

"I opened the gates to the haystacks down by the corrals," Jason said into the darkness. "Maybe the cattle will find their way in there so they won't get scattered and lost."

"Um-hum." Aurelia yawned.

"Damn dumb shitters."

"Too bad they're not buffalo. They at least know enough to push into the storm and sooner or later walk out of it."

"Yeah."

"I hope they aren't driven to the river."

"The ice won't hold 'em."

"Yeah. I know." The thought frightened her.

"At least not yet, anyway."

They lay staring into the darkness for several minutes.

"Jeez," he said softly. "Any goddam direction the wind blows, it drives them right along."

"Um-hum."

"I don't know about them fences. They could just go right down."

He flung his arm across the sleeping Blue, pulled himself toward the child and Aurelia, and curled around them, holding them tight. It seemed to Aurelia that he was particularly troubled these days. As they fell asleep their thoughts were filled with worries about the stupidity of domestic beef cattle, the treachery of the storm, their own money problems.

A few hours later they were awakened and Jason heard it first. Faint, distant sounds of moaning. Startled, he shook Aurelia's arm. She opened her eyes and they both lay in the dark listening, thinking that the cattle might be milling about the little house where they slept. As the sounds grew closer, they realized it was something else: a gasping, a lamentation, a human wailing. It sounded frightful.

It must be something or someone coming down the road into the yard, thought Aurelia.

Then, in disbelief, "Is that Clarissa?"

"It can't be."

His sister lived a quarter of a mile away, up on the rise toward the river. Too far on a night like this.

But it was Clarissa. It seemed that she had made her way across the banks of snow, breathless and fearful, fighting to stay upright in the heavy drifts, struggling blindly in the darkness to find her way. As she plunged across the road and down the little slope, the barking dogs ahead of her, she gasped and called for help, her low voice caught in her fear and the snow and the wind.

Aurelia flipped the light switch. Nothing happened. The electricity was off; whether it was deliberate or storm-caused really didn't matter at this point. Hurriedly, Aurelia lifted the glass chimney from the little kerosene table lamp and struck a match. The wick of the lamp flared, bathing the room in an eerie light. The frantic woman banged on the door, herself a tense, furious flare in the darkness, ready to explode.

Aurelia ran to the door and opened it and Clarissa fell upon her.

"*Ee-nah! Ee-nah!*" Clarissa blurted. When she saw it was Aurelia, she grabbed her arms, shook her, and cried, "Where's Mom? Jason?" Incoherent. Jagged.

Aurelia pulled back. She stared at her sister-in-law, who was shaking, her eyebrows and face masked in snow.

"Wha-a—?"

Jason came into the living room doorway in long underwear and bare feet, his hair rumpled, eyes squinting into the unaccustomed brightness.

Clarissa reached out toward him and shouted, "Hurry up. Hurry up. Get Dad. Something's happened at Gracie's place."

Before Jason could respond, Harvey Big Pipe, hearing the commotion, rose carefully from his bed in the back room, an old man, sick and tired, a man who had lived a long life filled with one crisis after another, one sorrow after the next, and shuffled into the living room. He was followed by his elderly wife.

They all stood and looked at each other, Clarissa wild-eyed, the rest of the family watching her as though she seemed far away and unreal.

"Sheridan," Clarissa began. Her face crumpled and she dug with stiffened gloves at the wet snow caked on her eyebrows.

"He . . . Dad . . . he . . . ," she began to choke on her sobs. Then, sagging with relief, her parka and heavy boots dropping clumps of snow to the floor, she stood shaking with great sobs and wept without restraint.

At the thought of Sheridan's way of life, Harvey grimaced. His eldest son lived in East Pierre on Myrtle Street with Frannie, a white woman to whom he had given the Big Pipe name. He had a bunch of unmanageable kids who ran the streets and came out to the reservation once in a while on the pretense that they could help work the cattle, put up hay, and brand, but in recent times mostly to borrow money from the old man or steal from him. Frannie's three brothers did nothing except play hard and acid rock on their stereos, smoke pot endlessly, and work only when they were forced into it. They usually lived with their sister and her husband of ten years until Sheridan would finally get fed up and kick them out. But, like vampires or bad pennies, they always came back. The old man thought it was a hell of a way to live and often told the family so.

Jason swore as he looked over toward his father.

Aurelia followed her husband's glance. Her fright left her at the sight of her father-in-law and all of a sudden she felt great anguish for the old man's pain. She looked at Harvey and thought, he doesn't need this, whatever the hell it is. She was fed up with Sheridan and his stupid, drunken ways. What a selfish prick. He never thinks about anybody but himself.

She looked into Harvey's face, impassive but puffy with sleep, his long thick greying hair tangled and unkempt. She saw him slump into a chair and pull heavy socks onto his vein-lined feet. His toothless jaws moved up and down but he said nothing.

Clarissa, suddenly spent, said anxiously, "We gotta get to Auntie's."

"Why? What's happened?" asked Aurelia, turning away from Harvey.

Before Clarissa could answer, Jason raised his voice, "We can't go noplace, Clarissa. Noplace!"

The housing center where their aunt, Harvey's younger sister, lived was on the main river road, but there had been no snowplows since late afternoon. And it was about six miles, a fearsome distance in this kind of weather.

"I don't know how you even got here from your house to ours." At that moment, Jason stood over his sister, angry but trying to be charitable. He began pacing.

Aurelia moved to the window and looked into the darkness. She saw nothing but streaks of snow driven across the night sky by a furious wind. She felt Jason's hand on her shoulder and heard him swear again.

"Shit!," he said, "that must be six foot deep out there." He turned toward his sister with a gesture of helplessness.

"I don't care!" cried Clarissa suddenly. "I don't care! We gotta go!"

She jumped up and began pacing. "Get your keys, Dad. Your four-wheel drive can . . . it can . . . "

"What the hell's the matter with you?" responded Jason angrily.

"Please!" she begged. She turned again toward her father.

"Something bad's happened. Something bad," she moaned in agony. "Sheridan . . . he . . . I . . . don't know . . . I . . . I . . . think he might have killed a guy."

The room fell suddenly silent and only the moan of the wind at the eaves filled the void.

Harvey lowered his head into his hands. His wife, knowing the torment of the life of their eldest son, turned toward the bedroom blindly.

Jason picked up his shirt from the chair next to the stove and immediately started putting on his winter clothing over his longjohns.

Minutes passed. Only Clarissa's weeping could be heard.

"Get your clothes on, Aurelia," Jason said into the quiet.

"Uh-h . . . no . . . uh . . . I don't think I'll . . . ," her voice was suddenly hoarse, thick with fear and shock.

"You must come. *(K)unchi* will be here with Blue."

When she hesitated again, he said, "They'll be okay."

She looked at him. His long fingers working the laces of his winter boots. The set of his full mouth. She felt her nostrils sting as she fought back tears. She stood in uncertainty, feeling like she always felt, like a tentative outsider when it came to matters of Big Pipe family activities. Or any family activities, for that matter. She'd had only her grandmother, after all, all those years. No recalcitrant brothers. No questions of responsibility to weeping sisters.

Hunched forward, he looked up at her, asking, knowing. His eyes would not leave hers. What did he possess, she wondered as she looked into his eyes, what does he want from me? What do I care about all this mess of life? Her profound remoteness had not left her, after all, she thought with some considerable misgiving. Then, without answers to her strange questions but suddenly composed and sure of herself, she turned away to get dressed so that she could accompany him into the storm.

A few minutes later Jason drove the four-wheel-drive pickup out of the yard, his wife, his frail old father, and his sister packed in beside one another, filled with dread, listening to their own silent fears. The headlights disappeared almost instantly into the heavy blowing snow, and Aurelia found herself peering out of the window into a white nothingness.

12

Dakotahs Believe

Many Dakotahs still believe there are monsters in this world and the only thing that can help them is their belief in the "living stone." They know that life was easier when Ish-na-e-cha-ge could talk to the animal people. But for now, life is hard.

During the frightening drive to the West Bend, while the wind moaned a warning in everybody's ears, *ma ye ksu ya yo, remember me,* the Big Pipe family members rode in silence, listening, worrying, each thinking his or her own dreadful thoughts.

Whenever Jason drew into this kind of quiet silence, Aurelia knew that he was taking on, again, the *chu(n)skay* kind of responsibility that should have been his brother Sheridan's. It always isolated him from her, this need to be the son, the brother, the father of them all, the one on whom everyone could depend. There would be no question now that he would rise to the occasion, take quiet charge, make decisions, find excuses to get Sheridan out of trouble. Again. It was Jason who managed the ranch, fed the cattle, did the day-to-day work that needed to be done, gave advice to his sisters, brothers, even his parents sometimes.

It was no wonder, thought Aurelia, that he tried from the beginning to tell me what to do. It's surprising, too, she mused, how much he gets away with it with me. Here I am, after all, here I am. In spite of his boyish looks, his seeming impetuousness, his youthful ways, his good looks, in spite of his naïveté, his what-you-see-is-what-you-get attitude, he is always the one, thought Aurelia resentfully, on whose shoulders it falls to do whatever nobody else in the family will do.

It left very little time for her, his new woman, and his child, she thought selfishly. Amidst these angry thoughts, she was filled with concern and pity and, suddenly, he seemed very dear to her. Tears sprang into her eyes and she felt for a moment she might burst into sobs. She blinked furiously and thought, what he possesses is a family and his family is now mine. We reside in one another and I suppose this is love. She turned to Jason's father and took one of his gloved hands in hers and held onto it tightly. It was a moment of rare intimacy, an act of a daughter-in-law that would in ordinary moments be thought to be impolite, arrogant, invasive.

Harvey did not look at her but held her hand tightly. She knew he approved of her for he always treated her as an equal. Though he never voiced his opinion about her one way or the other, she knew that she had brought a sense of stability to the family that Harvey appreciated. She had the feeling that Harvey would not have been more pleased with her life with Jason had it been one of those arranged marriages, like those of the past, in which the people had grown to have great confidence.

Aurelia looked over at Clarissa, whose face was pinched, suddenly old beyond her years, almost unrecognizable. Though Clarissa, the mother of a large family herself, depended upon Jason, the uncle of her children, to do the right thing, she seemed at times faintly jealous of Jason's relationship with Aurelia and what it had done to elevate his standing in the family. She was sharp with Aurelia, often ignoring her. They could be in the same room but not speak. Aurelia, in her effort to help out like a good in-law, often felt rebuffed by Clarissa's coldness. In spite of that, Aurelia, at this moment, felt heartsick when she saw the grief on the woman's face. She was the one who had gotten the bad news firsthand. Her fears were palpable.

Aurelia was jolted out of this trance when, suddenly, the pickup slipped and skidded across the snow-clogged road, coming to a stop in the deepest drift at the low embankment. It happened in a split second and she yelled, "Watch out!"

"Son of a bitch!" Jason swore at almost the same moment. He got out and began shoveling while the others sat bundled up against the frigid wind. The yellow headlights made the drifting snow look ghastly, like an enveloping, smothering fury. After a few minutes, Aurelia, behind the wheel while the others pushed, was told to "Gun it! Gun it!" As she did so, the pickup surged forth and one of the snowchains snapped. It took Jason another half hour to repair it before they could continue their fearful journey.

When Jason, Aurelia, Clarissa, and the old man pulled into the housing center at the West Bend, they saw a police van, an Agency police car, and an ambulance shrouded in heavy snowfall, the red lights flashing into all the dingy, dark corners of the neighborhood. Snow was flying everywhere and Aurelia wondered selfishly if, in spite of that hindrance, other folks were standing at the windows peering curiously into their pitiful lives. She found herself hating this shameful invasion of their family privacy, all of a sudden defensive and protective. But she said nothing. They went inside, boots and all, crowding into the shabby little room already filled with people, and stood awkwardly in the doorway.

This was a house on J Street, one of the many tacky, white-man imposed semi-urban paths built for Indians by the federal government as part of a 1940s housing project. A low-rent housing project. An Indian ghetto, some said. It wasn't called cluster housing yet, but it was a forerunner to that bureaucratic concept which rose out of the stereotypes white people held about how the Sioux lived.

"They all lived together, you know," said the Washington D.C. paper-pushers, "the tribal way." Thus, what people like Aurelia called low-cost Indian ghettos were built on reservations all over the west. "People living in each other's laps," said Harvey Big Pipe and other cattlemen who lived out on their own lands. Many people became vocal critics of the plans. It was Harvey's prediction that the people would be reluctant to live in such a way, sitting around in scrubby backyards only a few feet from their neighbors' with little to occupy themselves.

As Aurelia pushed her parka from her head and tried to catch her breath, she wondered what Harvey was thinking about this place. It was dismal and close, and though it was filled with Auntie Grace's cooking aromas, it struck Aurelia as dark and ominous and sad. The house was situated in a neighborhood that was ordinarily filled with trash, old cars, broken furniture, children's toys, and sagging fences. Harvey's face showed no emotion as he nodded his greeting to his widowed sister who, for decades, had lived amongst neglected, blunted people, unmovable in their poverty and perverse in their hatred, legitimized by their own silence and hostility to the outside world. In spite of it all she had remained hopeful.

Auntie Grace continued talking, uninterrupted by the newcomers, almost in a frenzy. A young Indian man in uniform, his hat on his knee, knelt beside her with a notebook, scribbling and asking questions.

"Jerry, that Jerry fella there," she looked across the room at the disheveled white man whose hair jutted stiffly over his shirt collar. "Beecham I think they call him . . . him and his brother's girlfriend, Babe, that one," she pointed with her chin to the skinny brown-haired girl in jeans slumped on the sofa, "they wuz all here."

She took a deep breath and made a conscious effort to slow her speech. She drew a handkerchief from her apron and dabbed at her wrinkled face. During the unexpected lull, Aurelia went to the sink, filled a glass with water, and took it over to the old aunt. Aurelia knelt beside her and held her hand for just a moment as she drank thirstily. Grace, now past sixty and in poor health, had lived in her little trailerhouse off and on for thirty years, and she harbored few illusions about life. She had always felt sorry for Sheridan and his miserable wife and his *eyeska* children and because of that she often put up with their wild and violent behavior when no one else in the family would do so. Trying to be hospitable, she would cook big meals for them, allow them to bring in their friends and their booze, tolerating their wild and undisciplined children who ran about the house hollering at one another, hitting and slapping, fighting and crying.

Aurelia stole a glance at her husband, who was standing beside his brother seated at the kitchen table. Jason was offering him a cigarette.

"How long had they been here?"

"What?"

The old aunt looked over at Sheridan. He sat with his eyes closed.

I don't believe I hit him that hard, thought Sheridan when he saw the body of his wife's brother, Nick, lying in the snow in front of him, still and limp. He stared up at Jerry, another of his wife's brothers, who stood above the body with his arms askew and a broken table leg dangling from one heavy fist. He noticed that Jerry's long, blond hair stood away from the collar of his light shirt in a kind of horse-tail stiffness. There were no lamps on the makeshift streets at the edge of the housing center but somehow, perhaps in a refracted shine or gleam from the whiteness of the storm, Sheridan could just barely make out the shabby houses, some with broken windows and no doors, backyards filled with old beat-up cars humped in the snow, several silent, shaggy dogs too old or too beaten to do anything but stand with their heads hanging. There were shacks of every age and description now frozen into a frightening vision of agelessness. It was the winter landscape of reservation poverty, a whiteout from the edge of oblivion, and Sheridan was all too familiar with the scene. "You shithead!" he mumbled into the wind. Anyone looking at him could not help but believe that an indifferent god, motionless and detached, presided over this man's cruel destiny. The look of detachment on his face showed how little he cared about the consequences of human acts or fate.

He clasped his hands together and felt the knuckles on his right hand, and they were swollen, cut wide open and bleeding. He saw a large woman who looked vaguely familiar to him, her face red and contorted. She was screaming hysterically from the doorway even though the men stood in perfect stillness and the fight was finished.

"Jerry! Sheridan! Stop! Oh . . . please stop!" Sheridan thought he saw a couple of neighbor women on the broad street in front of him about ten or twenty paces away, standing eerily, silently in the widely drifting snow. They didn't come any closer, afraid perhaps, if not of the

wild-eyed men and vicious storm swirling around them, then surely of the frightened woman who was screaming her fear and grief into the freezing wind. Sheridan felt only numbness.

"I called the cops," shouted the hysterical woman and, as Sheridan looked over at her, it was as though he was seeing her for the first time, far in the distance, a million miles away. She was a soft, plumpish woman, saggy in the middle, with great, round thighs bursting the seams of her pale dress.

As if in slow motion, she lumbered toward him and he watched her advance upon him, in a moment of sudden terror, her dress changing color into a kind of khaki green with brown, bloody, purple splotches. He shrank from her as her round, bare legs, splashing, disappeared into the brown-greenish water along the marshy banks of the Asian river. She grabbed him and started pounding his shoulder and chest.

"Tron thoat!! . . . tron thoat . . . khoi ong ta kia!" "Get away! Get away from him!"

She pushed him with such force that he fell backward onto the hood of a parked vehicle, and he bent over to shield himself, suddenly so weak and exhausted he could barely stand.

She grabbed his hair and pulled his face into hers. "Grace called Clarissa," she hissed, her contorted mouth suddenly dry from all the yelling. "And, you . . . you . . . better cover your goddamned ass!" Her face twisted and she emitted a great cry of anguish and beat on him.

He watched in fascination as the heavy woman, clad first in khaki, then in pale orange light, turned from him and knelt at the side of the young man whose skull was cracked, blood oozing from his nostrils into the heavy snow. "Shit!" she screamed hoarsely into the wind. "Shit! Shit! Shit!" In a moment, Sheridan saw her great strength as she lifted the young man's thin shoulders and shook him, doll-like, crying loudly, "Nick! Please, Nick!"

Then, as if in despair, she let the lifeless body plop comically back into the snowbank. "He's dead," she began to moan and flail her large white arms into the snow around her, mindless of the bitter cold. After a few moments, she got up and looked at Sheridan with blazing eyes. "You're gonna pay for this, Sheridan. You're gonna pay!"

Indistinguishable, after years of useless marital discord, drunkenness, poverty, her hatred for her own life and his burned on between them and Sheridan could do nothing. The heavyset woman *who had been his wife for nearly ten years turned away from him and took her younger brother, Jerry, by the arm. As she did so, Jerry, white with shock and fear, dropped the broken table leg into the snowbank. No one noticed the blood on its broad, jagged tip, and the weapon was hidden minutes later by the brush of the snow in the uncompromising wind. Weeping in anguish, Frannie and Jerry led one another back into the house where Nick's skinny girlfriend, Babe, leaned against the door, shivering. I don't believe I hit him that hard, thought Sheridan Big Pipe, as he stood in the freezing, blowing snow, haunted, cowering, alone.*

"How long had they been here?" the uniformed Indian was asking Grace for the second time.

"Before, you mean?"

"Yes. How long had they been here before it happened?"

"All day. They wuz here all day. They come over here kind of early, about noon, with Sheridan and his wife, just about the time it start to snow real heavy again."

Grace put her bony fingers to her forehead and rubbed the skin just above the eyebrows, as if she had a headache. Aurelia offered her two aspirin, but when the old aunt shook her head, Aurelia went to the kitchen and took them herself. Then she stood beside Jason, lit a cigarette, and listened to what the old woman could tell about the event. Her chest ached and she wondered how much more Auntie could go on.

"Well, then, ma'am. What happened then?"

"Uh . . . I didn't really know who they wuz. They come over here for dinner and to visit, I guess. With my nephew, Sheridan. Here."

She looked around briefly and gestured toward Sheridan, sitting, head down and hands clasped, at the kitchen table.

"Had you seen them before?"

"Oh, yeah. I seen 'em cuz they run around with Sheridan. But I don't really know them."

Grace started to cry and the young policeman waited for just a minute until she composed herself again.

"What happened then?"

"They wuz drinkin' around. Then Nick, he come over. He could hardly make it down the road, there, the snow was so bad by then. And when they seen him drive up, Jerry and Babe, they run into the bedroom. There," she pointed to the room off the dark hallway.

"Oh," said the policeman, surprised. "Nick wasn't here with them, then?"

"No. No. He come over later."

"And then what?"

"To hide from him. You know. They run into the bedroom to hide from him." She paused.

"I guess," she said, shrugging her thin shoulders. "And he was real mad, lookin' for Babe, he said. He was real drunk. Couldn't hardly stand up. Called her all kinds of names. Said she was slut."

"Um-humh."

"Guess he was right about that, anyway," she threw a mean look in Babe's direction. Babe didn't bother to look up.

"What time was that?"

"Uh, it was late. Maybe about ten?" Her voice rose, questioning, as though someone else in the room might be more precise.

"So. This went on, more or less, all day, then?"

"Oh, yeah! They wuz around here all day and then he come."

"And then what?"

"Well, uh . . . ever'body was real drunk, you know . . . 'cept me. I don't drink, you know. I'm an old woman, you know."

"Yes, ma'am."

"And he set here and wuz drinkin' some with Sheridan and his wife. For about a hour, I'd say. Maybe more. And finally he heard 'em in the bedroom. He run in there and the fight start. It end up out here," she pointed toward the outside door.

"Do you know who started it?"

"What?"

"The fight. You know who started it?"

"No."

"How did they all get outside, if the fight started inside?"

"Nick come out of the bedroom and start cussin' at Sheridan and Frances. 'You dumb shits,' he says. 'You knew all the time! Didn't you?' he says. Accusing them. 'Didn't you,' he says. 'You knew!' he says to them. Real mad! Mean-like, you know."

"And then what?"

"He knock Sheridan down and then the fight start again and they all run out."

"Is that it?"

"Yes. That's all I know."

In the silence that followed while the young policeman wrote furiously in his notebook, Harvey Big Pipe went over to his aged sister. He knelt beside her, put his hand on her shoulder, and said, *"Tokto eyas tanyan awaniglaka yo."* (You had better take care of yourself.)

She did not lift her head or open her eyes. She barely whispered: "I'm okay. *Yoksice sni ye."* (Don't worry.)

Before they could say anything more, Jerry got to his feet and shuffled over to them menacingly.

"Hey, goddamit! Talk English! Talk so the rest of us here," he gestured wildly about the room, "know what the hell you're sayin'." He leaned down toward the woman who had just given the whole story and said, "I'm not takin' the blame for any of this! Sheridan did it, you know. You know it! An' he's not gonna get out of it!"

One of the young policemen moved closer to him, took him by the arm, and said, "Say, now, you calm down."

"Well, I'm not takin' no fuckin' shit from nobody!"

"Why don't you get in the patrol car and we'll take you to the Fort and you can tell us your story down there."

"Hey, just a goddamn minute! I ain't goin' down there!"

His sister, Frannie, stepped up beside him.

"You go, Jerry," she said. "You just go on ahead, Jerry. An' don't tell them nuthin'. I'll be there as soon as I can. An' I'm gettin' a lawyer, too. You just go on ahead."

At the same time, another policeman moved to put the handcuffs on a subdued, red-eyed Sheridan Big Pipe, who shuffled to the door without a word to his relatives.

His Auntie Grace, surrounded by her brother's family, watched him go. She felt drained. The day of the blizzard, which had started as she sprayed the mirrors and windows, making the rag squeak her enthusiasm for cleanliness and expected company, had gone on for several desolate hours as she'd helplessly watched her nephew and what she called his "white trash" in-laws get drunk and quarrelsome. It had ended with the murder of the white man in the blowing snow. Now, traumatized and weary, she simply put her head back and watched the whole thing flash before her eyes.

On the telephone to Clarissa she had said, "A man is dead just outside my door. He's bleeding into the frozen snow. You must get your brother, Jason, and come quickly." She thought she seemed very calm, and later, when she talked to Harvey, she said, "It was like somebody else inhabited my body."

Staring now out of the open door, she saw her nephew stand for a moment braced against the wind, then disappear into the patrol car. She saw Jason and Aurelia stand with their arms around each other, as the police car labored through the snowdrift and out of sight.

The next morning when Aurelia awoke she felt disoriented, couldn't think for a moment where she was. She didn't remember Auntie Grace's look of despair, nor Jason's quiet fury. She couldn't remember how she had left Grace's house last night, defeated, and could not say anything with any clarity about what had passed for explanation between the family members.

They would all be making excuses for him, she knew. As far as she was concerned, Sheridan was a selfish man and a fool. *Waci-t'usni!* (Brainless one!) Where did he get his conceit from, anyway? What made him think the family could rally round his mistakes over and over? She couldn't remember, but she hoped she had kept her silence last night.

She rolled over and felt the empty place next to her. Then, finally awakening more fully, she smelled the burning of sage and knew that Jason was up early, smudging himself and worrying about the ordeals to come. These seemed to be the worst of times.

She lay back, blinded momentarily by the glare of the winter sun on the white walls of the bedroom. When her eyes adjusted, she saw little black marks and streaks on the wall beside the bed, marks made by Blue's shoes, probably, or his dirty hands. Faint, hair-like cracks in the plaster were everywhere and she followed them with her eyes, tracing the lines, twists, and turns. They seemed so unpredictable, like there was no pattern, no reason, no way to link one angle with the next. Though the sun was shining, Aurelia felt no uplift of the heart and though her husband's prayers were sacred, she had no way to share their presence. Nor had she even wanted to. She threw the sheet over her head and, in a moment of abandon said to herself, Now no one will know I'm here, no one will come near me.

She felt Jason sit on the corner of the bed, silent for just a moment.

Then, "Hey, what are you, invisible?"

"I wish."

He pulled the sheet away but he wasn't laughing.

She would have given anything to hear him say he loved her but he only took her in his arms without a word. They held on to each other, breathing hard and jaggedly, holding back the words of desire. Instead, they made love without touching each other, with no caresses of the hair, no warmth. The need they felt was bittersweet and unsatisfying. Aurelia held back her tears. After a while, Jason composed himself and lay beside her saying nothing. Finally, Aurelia got up and went to the kitchen to prepare breakfast.

The dreaded letter from the Department still lay on the table, abandoned the night before in haste and panic. She looked at the sheets of paper strewn around carelessly and thought how distant yesterday seemed. They had moved into another dimension in just a few hours. Their dilemma now seemed much more grave.

It couldn't have come at a worse time, the letter from the BIA loan specialist for the tribe. During the most vicious snowstorm of the season, when they were worried that the cattle might perish in the blizzard, when they had to rush off in the middle of the night to see about Sheridan who was implicated in the murder of a white man on reservation trust land. In some kind of drunken brawl. When their electricity was cut off.

Aurelia was never one to complain, but she was beginning to feel that there was some kind of conspiracy against them. On this morning and for the rest of the winter they would use the wood stove in the living room for heating and cooking.

Jason came into the living room and together they read the letter from the BIA loan specialist again:

> You can't say that you haven't had assistance in your operation, Jason. Just think of the Government employees who have spent countless hours with the construction of your hog barn by doing what physical labor the weather would permit, by helping to pour the concrete floors last fall as well as other construction work. This was done to save you money and to lay out the plans of the building the way it should be done. There was a bit of drinking going on among you and your wife when the new hog barn first started under construction. This is one of the quickest ways to become a failure.

The letter made Jason furious and he looked about the room at their poverty, the crummy furniture, the cracked linoleum covering the worn wooden floor. He flung the letter down again. Later that day, the rescuing of more kerosene lamps from Grandmother Blue's old house brought them some amusement, if only momentarily. They lifted the glass chimneys to light oil-soaked wicks with long matches, saying, "It's back to the good old days."

Some, of course, actually remembered the good old days; Harvey, for one, smiling at his old wife.

"What do you think of this?" he said, more serious than he wanted. "We give up thousands of acres of treaty-protected land for hydro power and we're still in the dark, ennit?"

He knew better than anyone present that the federal agency called the Bureau of Reclamation, responsible for the Missouri River Basin Hydropower Project, had singlehandedly caused more damage to Indian lands than any other public works project in America. But for now, in the face of his son's murder charge and a bad winter ahead of them, he didn't say more.

It was only later, when the logs had been put in the stove and everyone had gone to bed, when Aurelia sat at the kitchen table with Harvey, unable to sleep, she heard him say: "For years I listened to the tribal council men say that Indian land was chosen over non-Indian lands for such public works, that it was another way to remove the people from their treaty lands."

Yes, she thought, I believe you heard that, old man. Price out Indians and ship them off to live in the Twin Cities, the ghettos of L.A., on some federal subsistence grant money.

"Federal water agencies made money," Harvey told her. "Who else profited is anyone's guess. They been talking about 'just compensation,' but there's nothing 'just' about it."

Aurelia moved from the table, bundled herself up in an easy chair, and warmed herself by the potbellied stove.

"You remember, Aurelia, when we got word that Virgil was shot to death in Vietnam?"

"Yeah. I remember, Harvey."

"It was that same time that I read in the paper that San Franciso-based firms purchased the right from the federal agencies to divert yearly water from the Oahe project to the nation's largest coal slurry pipeline."

She didn't say anything.

"You know what that means?"

"No. Not exactly."

"It means that while my son, Private First Class Virgil Big Pipe, gave his life in Vietnam, the water that had belonged to his people, the Sioux Nation, for hundreds and hundreds of years, was being sold off. By thieves."

They lapsed into a convivial silence.

Oftentimes, thought Aurelia, it is only after the fact that a victim knows what he or she should have done, what he or she might have done. Surely, in the case of all of the wars fought by all of mankind, the negotiating table proved more treacherous than the battlefield. Twenty years after our own war for the river, she thought, we Sioux are looking with a mixture of sorrow and envy at our neighbors the Crees, victims of a similar damming of their native lands of northern Quebec near James Bay.

She got up and went to the shelves in the corner.

"Here, Harvey, read this."

He took the paper and squinted. Handing it back, he said, "You read it to me."

As old Harvey rolled a thin paper around his finger and

poured Bull Durham from a sack, tamping it carefully into the handmade cigarette, she read out loud:

> *the ongoing fight by the army of engineers and lawyers to defeat the Crees looks like one of those honorable battles of courage that will be hard fought. The Crees, not given to mincing words, have put up a burial monument called a sepulcher, a real yet mythological vault which they take to be a receptacle for their sacred thoughts, and on the epitaph are these words:*
>
> *"This monument is erected in memory of our Cree Ancestors who, having lived off this land for thousands of years, now rest under the waters of the reservoirs of the LaGrande Complexe. I know that my redeemer liveth, and that he shall stand at the latter day upon the earth. Job 19:25."*

Aurelia held the paper in her lap. "Isn't that sad, Harvey?"

"Yeah." He sat smoking, meditating.

Finally, "It's a continuing fight, Aurelia. To preserve what's ours, what is Indian. It just goes on and on."

She sat quietly, in thoughtful agreement with the old man.

As Jason Big Pipe and his woman, Aurelia, went about their lives that winter of the early 1970s, bundled up against the cold, they would haul a few dead trees lying along the shore of the ravaged river into their yard, chop them into chunks of firewood, and carry them into the house, stacking them carefully.

Sometimes, when a spider would emerge from the bark into the warm room, himself surprised at his own survival, Blue would get down on his hands and knees and follow it until it crept into the woodwork. And then he would ask his mother about its destination: "Where does the spider go, Ina?"

She never answered right away, but if he asked again, she would make up a story. "Swiftly, innocently, the primordial spider weaves her way into the cracks of ceiling logs, a moment ahead of the wasp," Aurelia would say in Indian.

Interjecting an air of mystery, Jason would sometimes join in, talking in a low voice, "You must stack the fireplace wood and resolve to be more . . . cunning."

"The woman who lived here before me," Aurelia would

continue, "now silent, traceless as the wind, she knew how to keep a fire. She walked these steep hills in winter, scouting for firewood, past the grease brush, beyond a loosened fence, and when her children grew, she refused to send them to school . . . "

Blue, stretched out on the warm linoleum in front of the fire, would begin to yawn.

"Alone, the woman who lived here before me cried for fire. Her grandfathers went part of the way with her, and when lightning struck a tree she dried the meat they had provided. At nightfall they pushed her around in the dark and let her go.

"Her relatives danced upon her grief."

When Blue's eyes fell shut, Aurelia would continue the story for her child's father, an adult version of the prophecy, and her eyes would be smiling. "Like the primordial spider, she webbed her way into ceiling logs managing to look back at the space of human order, her old, yet innocent eyes assuming that hidden gods would rescue her."

"Please. Please," Jason would say, joking and exaggerating, and reaching for her. "More. More."

"Yu-u-u-u."

"How come your gods know so damn much, Aurelia?"

"Well," smiling, "spiders are like that!"

They didn't have two nickels in their pockets and, without an occasional meandering jackrabbit brought in with Jason's .22, the commodity handouts of cheese and butter, and their white neighbors' occasional purchase of a cash load of hay, they wouldn't have had food for the table, nor money to buy the things needed for their growing child.

Sometimes, on their outdoor forays for firewood, the old man, Harvey, would go along, even though his health and his ordinarily strong faith in the idea that things would "work out" were failing, and his brief comments becoming more cynical.

He and his son would look at the long cement slab, laid out there last summer for the proposed hog barn, perfectly outlined in the white snow. In an attempt to assess the situation, Harvey would say, "Looks like the hogs will live better than we do."

Jason, often depressed and silent, would laugh derisively, "Not if they're going to depend on us payin' their electric bill!"

Within a few weeks, by the end of February, the weather had cleared up a little, much of the snow was gone, and what was left of it was dirt-streaked and crusted on top of the windblown frozen ground. The days of endless February grayness penetrated the human soul and there was nothing to look forward to except more grey days, more of the icy gloom. It was the time on the ranch of endless feeding of cattle, endless waiting for the sun to shine. Jason and his father had been among the lucky ones, though, for unlike their neighbors they had lost no livestock during the blizzard. They had attended a couple of unsatisfying committee meetings at the Agency during which they were told that they were in serious financial trouble.

After the weather cleared up, another letter arrived and Jason finally went to confront the loan specialist, McQueen.

"Hey, look," he said, pacing the floor in the Agency office, "you may think I'm just some kind of dumb Indian. But, listen! Even I know this much. If I have no money to pay the bills I got right now, I'm not going through with that goddamned pig barn and then have more bills I can't pay. Think of the electricity that thing is going to take!"

McQueen, who had grown up in a well-to-do neighborhood of one of the boroughs in New York, was a recent graduate of the business school at Boston University. He had always considered himself a liberal Democrat, before it had become a bad word, and had always wanted to "do something" for the poor. It was the way he was raised, to give back. Working here on the reservation, though, he was fast becoming disillusioned.

"These people!!" he would think to himself at times when things would go wrong, "I just can't understand why they can't do things!"

Naturally, he rarely voiced these thoughts publicly—certainly not to any of his colleagues here at the office.

"The deal is struck, Jason, and you can't back out now. Not now!" he advised his distraught client. He sat back into the leather chair and struck a match, holding his pipe close, puffing.

McQueen, who had gotten most of his information about farming and ranching in South Dakota from the County Extension Agent, felt it was his job at this point to take a positive and supportive role, to offset the language of accusation he had used in his recent letter, which he had in front of him:

> In management, you should be interested enough in your corn harvest to know where the corn went if it should have produced 14,000 bushels, since you did not come up with this number of bushels that it was supposed to have. If you had come up with the 14,000 bushels of corn then you shouldn't be in financial trouble. Management is to keep a record to see why your returns aren't as great as they are supposed to be. It is estimated there is about 15 bu. per acre field loss, for one thing, caused by ears of corn dropping off before harvest, plus the many down rows made by your kind of old corn picker that was never touched. As was suggested, you should have taken your family and your child and your folks and picked up this corn as there was an estimated 2,000 bu. on the ground and on these down rows. You should have made every effort to harvest all that has been produced and not be wasteful.

Looking at it again, he had to admit that the letter did sound as though he thought Jason was neglectful. But the facts were the facts and as he scanned the file papers quickly, he decided this might be a good time to discuss this more fully with the client. He had been wanting to . . . just at that moment, his thoughts were interrupted.

"The hell I can't quit," Jason was saying, shaking his head. "I'm not going through with the pig barn and that's that. I'm not doin' it! I don't know nuthin' about pigs anyway and what I do know I don't like! Cattle, okay. But pigs? Hell, we don't even hardly have a good word for them buggers in our language!"

Jason, not really knowing if he should laugh or cry, looked about the room as though seeking an escape.

"I don't know how in the hell I got into this mess, and if you want to know the truth of it, I'm real sorry I did!"

"Look," began McQueen. "You did a wonderful job of irrigating your corn last summer, even when we didn't have all the irrigation pipes in place. According to the plant population and the size of the corn ears . . . "

"There you go again," Jason interrupted, "with all that mumbo-jumbo! Jesus, what are you, some kind of asshole?"

The ordinarily polite and soft-spoken Jason Big Pipe was fed up. From that time on, McQueen, acquiring a new name in Jason's mind, was referred to as Asshole.

"Hell," Jason continued, "don't you know it didn't hardly rain all summer? And the summer before that? Don't you know we didn't have no irrigation pipes on half that corn? Don't you know that they even lowered the river round the end of July just when we needed it most? Shit! Where you been, Asshole?"

Refusing to be insulted but with his tolerance being strained, McQueen tightened his jaw, looked down at the papers in front of him, and continued: "according to the plant population and the size of corn ears, the yield should have been a max of 125 bushels per acre."

"Should have been! Should have been! What the hell is this? Some kind of wishful thinking? I didn't make nuthin' on that corn. You think pickin' up two thousand bushels is gonna make my day? You think it's gonna make a difference? Listen, the hole I'm in is too damn much, too damn deep! It's sure as hell deeper'n two thousand goddamn bushels, let me tell you that! I can't do it anymore."

Jason continued pacing. He felt desperate.

He began again, leaning across the desk and looking into the mild, calm Asshole eyes.

"What I'm telling you, Asshole is, wake up, man! I'm goin' broke and my kid is eatin' commodity cheese and pancakes and you're tellin' me to get that pig barn up, get all the electricity hooked up this spring? What I'm tellin' you is that I cannot pay my electricity bill *now*. They've cut off my lights for weeks now. What I'm tellin' you is . . . "

"Wait. Now, listen, Jason . . . "

"No. You listen, white guy! Why don't all you assholes out here on the reservation go back to Vermont or Maine or wherever the hell you come from? You don't know nuthin' about Indian

Country out here. This ain't corn country for profit! How many times I gotta tell you?"

The silence that followed was painful for both of them, but once accusations start, they often pour out like lava from an erupting mountain, and Jason couldn't stop himself.

"How come you're so smart? If it's so goddammed easy, why don't you take your goddamn MBA and do it yourself? You white guys like to run things!"

"Now listen, Jason. I'm not running things here. White men aren't running things here. Indians are running this deal. Even the Tribal Credit Committee and the tribal council have got you on their list as failing to live up to the expectations of the program."

Aurelia was not privy to much of this confrontation. As a rule, she did not attend the meetings, and because she was not what the government employees would call "legally" married to Jason, she was asked to participate only when it was to their advantage.

For days prior to this exchange, though, Jason had been telling Aurelia he was going to have it out with them at the Agency. That they had to make arrangements to extend his loan and cancel the pig barn development. "That's all I'm asking, Aurelia. That's not too much to ask."

"They're just going to put the blame on you instead of the system, Jason," she advised.

"I know," he said.

"And I don't want to be pessimistic, but they're not going to extend your loan. They're just gonna let you go down."

"I don't know. They might come around."

"I hope so."

"Maybe I can convince them," he said. Then, as if giving in to a reality check, he said, "I have yet to meet a white man who did not know what's best for Indians. Who doesn't think his abuse should pass for compassion."

"Why bother, then?"

"For my own sake."

"Well, there's something to be said for that. On paper, you know, Jason, it sounds like life can go on. As though destroying a river and its people can be remedied by 'good management.' By picking up corn on the down rows, bringing up uncomplaining children on commodity cheese. It sounds good on paper, I guess. Sounds like it really could happen, yes?"

They both knew that the philosophy underlying much of the ancient and modern legislation affecting the Native Americans, and certainly much of the history of Indian policy as it affects the indigenes, whether or not they have signed treaties with the occupiers of their lands, assumes that the lives of people of apparent good will can get better with hard work and determination; that the bootstrap-pulling of one's self from down under is merely a matter of will. The two of them had been around enough to know this thinking of empire builders and they often spoke of it with Harvey.

"Whatever you think of it," Aurelia had told Harvey recently during one of the frequent talks, "the Big Pipes are going broke and the empire builders aren't looking back." She sometimes thought she hated America and what it had meant to her.

"It is very discouraging," Harvey agreed.

McQueen, child of nation builders, was certainly one of those hopeful philosophers and he was doing the best he could for people less fortunate.

He let himself get angry in his rugged meetings with Jason. His face would redden as he faced up to Jason's accusations, which he considered eminently unfair.

"Don't tell me. Don't tell me Indians aren't running things," he would shout finally. "I meet with those committees every day."

He clenched his fists. "And let me tell you, they are Indians. Indians from right here on this reservation."

His hands opened and he struck the surface of his desk with his flat palms.

"Indians?" Jason shot back. "Get real, Asshole! Those guys on the credit committee, they do what the BIA tells them to do. You know that. They go by regulations and procedures. You know what BIA means, don't you?" Without waiting for an answer, he yelled, "Boss Indians Around."

Asshole stood up.

Before he could speak, Jason, on a roll now, said, "And listen, they don't know nuthin', either. They ain't out there trying to feed fifty cows and cuttin' hay when there ain't none to cut. They're not trying to grow some goddamn corn in the middle of a goddamn drought. And let me tell you this. They sure don't know nuthin' if they are tellin' me to keep on with this shit I got myself into."

After this shouting episode, the room seemed extraordinarily quiet. Asshole stood his ground, looking grim-faced and flustered.

Jason noticed office workers down the hall peering around doorways, curious yet trying to maintain a professional distance.

He lowered his voice and said, "Hell, those goddamned so-called Indians you got on those committees, they never even paid a phone bill, let alone . . . "

Suddenly, he had run out of anger. Exhausted, disappointed, and near defeat, he sat down. "I don't know what I'm gonna do," he said and he was momentarily filled with self-hatred.

As Jason put his hands to the sides of his head in a gesture of frustration, Asshole, an innately compassionate and caring man, began in a newly reasonable, helpful, and businesslike tone.

"Well, now, Jason," he sat down and cleared his throat. "Ah, I'll tell you. Everyone here is behind you. We want you to succeed."

Jason looked him without emotion.

"Now, your loan is in the amount of $38,000 and for you to succeed you must simply comply with the regulations and procedures of the Farm and Ranch program and cooperate with all who are assisting you." If he had some notion of how repetitious he sounded, he didn't reveal it.

Later, when Jason told Aurelia about this episode, he seemed to feel a tiredness she'd not seen in him before, a kind of mild disgust born of a new recognition.

"You know, Aurelia," he said, "I watched his eyes and he went on talking so goddamn confident. And, his eyes, you know? They were pale. Empty of anything except a . . . a kind of . . . kind of . . . innocence."

"Innocence?"

"Yeah," Jason said, lighting another cigarette. "I just don't get it. I don't get a guy like him. And all of them. They're all alike."

"Who?"

"Oh, you know. All those white guys that think they're god." He paused.

"You try to tell them something, and . . . " he shrugged.

"And so, I just kind of gave up, you know? I just thought 'what a goddamn waste of time!' I just thought I might as well listen to him and not say anything."

Jason watched Aurelia and repeated, in a voice filled with wonder, "You know?"

She waited to see if there was more he wanted to say. In her own confusion, she recognized Jason's description of the incident as his own despair.

"And he was telling me, 'You must, Jason, you simply must learn the value of things. You are in a very tough spot right now for hog supplement and expenses for next year's operations.' "

He lit another cigarette, "It was like the man heard nothing."

Gesturing, his voice changed, he mimicked Asshole: "Also, you are unable to make your loan repayment, not even the interest. So, you should come into the office and make a request for a modification of your loan for action to be taken by the Tribal Credit Committee, Tribal Council, and the Superintendent. You should bring your father, Harvey, in also, because he is an original signatory to this agreement."

Jason had been standing rolling down his sleeves, getting ready to put on his jacket, when Asshole had said this. Really shocked at this new but old and redundant suggestion, the outright falsity of the words themselves, he had thought indignantly, What the hell is this? Some kind of double-talk? Didn't he know that they had already talked about modification? And they'd said no! The image of his father, his toothless, cold-puckered face lost in the mist of his own frosty breath, grunting and heaving two-hundred-pound hay bales to the frozen prairie ground from atop the pickup truck every morning and evening since Jason could remember had wavered before his eyes, and he had thought: What does the old man have to show for a lifetime of hard work? Who is it that says a sick and frail old man, seventy, eighty years old, must continue to work until he drops just to keep himself warm and fed? Is there no reward for a long, good life?

Jason had said nothing in response to Asshole's directives but, he thought wearily, I've already talked to the Tribal Credit Committee and I know what their answer is.

He'd stuffed his hands in his pockets and breathed heavily. Asshole knows what their answer is, too, he'd thought cynically, closing his eyes momentarily. This is one of them "chin up" talks, hunh? Well, from the safety of the shore, Asshole, it's okay for you to tell a drowning man "chin up."

Without another word, he had stood up and walked away. He had gone to the jail and talked quietly with his brother, Sheridan. What they talked about was as unfathomable to outsiders as any talk is between warriors.

He hated to mention this jail visit to Aurelia, for, of course, she would recognize it as the moment she had feared, as that moment when he would be lost to her. In some distant recesses of his own thoughts he knew that all of this had been crucial to the two of them, a divisive place from which neither of them could be redeemed.

Late that same evening, Jason, with liquor on his breath, found Aurelia sitting at the bedside of his mother, spooning large spoonfuls of corn soup into the old woman's reluctant mouth. The old mother's cough had worsened and now she was refusing to get out of bed.

"I talked to Sheridan today."

"What did he say?"

"He says he's probably never going to see the light of day again."

"What do you think?"

"I think he's right. It's pretty goddamn hopeless."

He went into the kitchen and forgot what he was going to do there; then, remembering that he was hungry, he poured soup into a large cup and drank it down.

Aurelia returned to the kitchen with the nearly empty bowl.

"Well, your mom ate a quite a bit." Her voice sounded hopeful.

Jason, his eyes dull, his hunger sated for the moment, had already drifted into the other room and as Aurelia rinsed off the dishes, she knew that his drifting away was both real and emotional. A result of a recognized failure to find solutions to the problems of their lives, as well as a response to her stubborn and rigid domesticity, to which she was becoming unaccountably drawn in spite of herself.

Wiping her hands, she walked over to the chair where he had flung himself down. She stood facing him. Her thoughts rambled. Who was it who said "a table and a chair, that's all you need"? Some fool. Jason turned his face, his too-beautiful face, toward her and she felt a terrible pain. For a moment more she thought there was the beginning of an affirmation around his eyes, but it was quickly gone.

"To hell with them," she said. "To hell with all of them."

His eyes did not change.

He's one of those dark men, she thought, who will not live without justice. He no longer sees me. She couldn't look back at him. She turned and began tidying up, lifting books and magazines, emptying ashtrays.

The days and weeks passed. More letters arrived in the mail, but they lay unopened on window sills.

One day, Jason and his father left for the Agency immediately after breakfast. Their mission on this day was to go to the jail to see Sheridan again. They were not talkative nor were they optimistic. Yet they seemed driven by their endless and not very productive negotiations with the police, the lawyers, and the courts concerning Sheridan's long-delayed release and the matters of bond for his release. They can't hold him forever without indictment, they thought. They have to let him go.

"Don't ask," Aurelia said to Jason as she finished one cup of coffee and poured another. She held up her hands. "I really can't go again."

"It's okay," he said.

"There's nothing anyone can do," she said agonizingly, rubbing her fingers together as though they hurt.

The thought of Jason's brother's cheerless cell and her and Blue's pathetic visits would depress her for days afterward. She did not speak the words, but her thoughts were that she could do nothing to help anyone but herself. She wanted to go to the river, not spend the day driving and sitting in a cramped jail visiting room. And she wanted Jason to go with her to the river, though she dared not say it out loud.

"Maybe it would be important for him to see you, though." Jason sounded hopeful and somehow contrite. As though they'd had a quarrel and he was trying to appease her.

"No. What's important is that Blue shouldn't go there to the jail . . . to that jail . . . anymore . . . to see his relatives. We are not criminals. He shouldn't think his uncles are criminals. And he shouldn't go there anymore. And neither should I!"

She was adamant.

Jason and his father left and Aurelia smoked several cigarettes before she decided to bundle Blue up and take him with her and walk out toward the little pasture dam. She wondered if the ice had broken up yet; if the water was clear and the horses getting ready to foal.

The wind was still bitter, strong and insistent, but spring was in the air and she refused to worry that she was late this month. Three weeks late. Or was it four? With her mother-in-law lying in bed, unable to shake off a persistent cough, the windows could not be opened and the rooms were unbearably stuffy. It would do her good, she decided, to get outdoors and Blue was always ready for an adventure.

Stopping at the trailerhouse before she left, Aurelia spoke to her grandmother.

"How you doin', Gramma?"

"Good," said Gramma Blue, her voice low and hoarse. She was sitting at the table cutting quilt squares. It was a familiar scene.

At somewhere near ninety-five, the old woman was still up early in the morning, still eager to see the sun and hear the song birds of the prairie in the spring.

Grandmother Blue was part of a Santee family of rice gatherers, a woman who had spent her early years at a place called Prairie Island where she had learned the ways of drying, parching, husking, and winnowing the rice that they gathered traditionally from the eastern lake country in times past. Often she had been the one in the family who parched the rice, then spread it on a canvas net and husked it by pounding. It was a chore for the young and healthy, for it took much stamina and skill. Rice, in those days, was an exceedingly important part of the Dakotahs' economic base and they called it *psin-ska*. Few now, except this old woman, had any memory of those times.

Walking over to the table littered with cloth designs of every shape and color, Aurelia exclaimed, "Grandmother! Are you making another quilt?"

"Looks like it."

"You must have made a thousand quilts by now!"

"Well," said the old woman with a pretense of grumpiness, "I gotta do something, don't I? I can still see, you know!" She pointed a gnarled finger toward her eyes.

Aurelia smiled and kissed her grandmother on the forehead, something she wouldn't have thought of doing during most of the years they lived together. It was a reflection of an intimacy brought about, ironically, by their living now in separate houses.

"I can't stay long. I just thought . . . "

"Say, granddaughter," began the old woman with as much enthusiasm as she could muster. "Did you listen to the radio this morning?"

"No. We don't get anything on our old radio except KGFX and they're no good. Besides, I think our batteries are dead. Why?"

"They said this is the sixteenth day over there at Pine Ridge that the U.S. Marshals and state troopers are there."

"Oh?"

Aurelia, largely informed by the media since the February "occupation" of Pine Ridge Reservation, but also told by friends and old classmates, knew of the demonstrations that were being held everywhere around the country. She'd been told about Denver, Colorado, as far away as Gallup, New Mexico, the struggle against oppression in Indian Country was going on. It was a time of activism, marches, killings, racial incidents of all kinds. Some said there was a cordon around the whole state of South Dakota.

"They are calling it a 'siege' and they said . . . and . . . "

Aurelia interrupted her grandmother. "Don't listen to that stuff, Gramma."

The old lady, rebuked, fell silent.

Immediately, Aurelia felt sorry for her hurried comment. "What I mean is, we really don't know what's going on over there, and they're just probably telling a lot of lies on the radio."

"It's supposed to be on TV, too, they said," Gramma Blue continued.

"Um-hum. I know."

"I'd like to watch some of it."

"Yeah. With no electricity, it's hard to keep up with the news."

"Aurelia," Gramma persisted. "It looks serious."

She sounded more concerned than Aurelia had ever heard her in recent times. Aurelia wondered what the old woman knew. She wondered about the relatives the old woman had at Pine Ridge. Had she heard from them? Aurelia didn't think so.

"Well . . . "

Aurelia thought tiredly, what isn't serious? It's serious that Jason and his father can't pay on their cattle loan. It's serious that Sheridan is still held in the jail without a lawyer . . . what is it now . . . two? . . . three months? With nothing happening except the taking of depositions from his crazy in-laws. It's serious that cattle prices are down and there's still no irrigation pipes in place. And, we can't pay our electric bill . . . and . . .

She leaned over, hands in her jeans pockets, and gazed out of the window. She saw the pale sky and the brown hills and the water in the distance. It's serious what they've done to the river, she thought, for it will never be the same. The river is gone forever and the trees are gone and there is nothing more serious. Those cottonwoods whose rings show that for centuries, hundreds of years, there has been a consistent pattern of life. Now there is no future.

Trying to distract the old woman from talking about the siege at Pine Ridge, she said, "Do you remember, Gramma, when we stood out there at the dam site and Kennedy spoke to the people?

Do you remember what he said?"

"No." Gramma smoothed the corners of a cut square and placed it carefully on top of another.

"He said 'this dam provides a striking illustration of how a free society can make the most of its God-given resources.' Do you remember that, Gramma?"

When the old lady said nothing, Aurelia said, "I remember the exact words . . . 'that which God gave us' . . . " Her sentence drifted away.

The old woman turned and looked at Aurelia like she was talking nonsense.

"Wh . . . what are you talking about?"

"Oh, nothing, Gramma. Nothing. I know. I know. It is serious, Gramma, over there at Pine Ridge, but you just shouldn't worry about such things. I wish . . . I wish . . . "

Aurelia had intended to leave quickly, stopping for only a moment, but when she saw the concern in her grandmother's eyes, she sat down and pulled her chair close to the table. She could not ignore the old woman's memories, nor her own, for she knew they were all connected.

"What's the matter, Gramma? Why are you thinking about this?"

"One time," the old woman put down her cut squares of fabric and took a handkerchief from her pocket and wiped her hands and face. "One time," she went on slowly, talking in the old language, "I asked my mother why my stepfather, a man from White Clay, walked with a limp and she said that at Wounded Knee he received three bullets, one in the left ankle, one just above his right knee, and another that passed through his scalp."

"You never told me that before. Not in all these years."

"I know."

"How come?"

"I don't know. I heard about those people when I was growing up, when more than three hundred unarmed Lakotas were shot to death at Wounded Knee."

"I know. But I didn't know about your stepfather."

"Yes. He was a very good man. He treated me good."

"Grandmother, please don't think about these things right now. Things will be all right. I just know they will."

They wept together for only a moment.

"Isn't that where Vic went?" asked Gramma Blue, wiping her eyes.

"Where?"

"Down there, to Pine Ridge."

"I guess so. That's what we heard, anyway."

Vic was a favored nephew of Harvey Big Pipe. One of his favorite sister's sons. He had been away in college, had been in the Army before that.

"We heard he was in Rapid City for a while, almost as soon as he got back from that 'takeover' in Washington, D.C. And then later we heard he was in Calico."

This was a reference to the political gatherings of what the media were calling "militant Indians."

"Is he all right?"

Aurelia shrugged.

"You can't help but wonder what is happening, granddaughter."

"Yes. What I heard is that down there at Pine Ridge they're trying to impeach the government, the councilmen, the chairman."

"What does that mean?"

"They are trying to get them out of office. To get rid of them."

"Why are they doing that?"

"I don't know, Gramma."

But Aurelia knew a lot she wasn't sharing with her grandmother. She knew much about the serious problems on the reservation in the state: no money, no jobs, no financing, bureaucratic incompetence, waste, flooding, relocation and termination, inadequate housing, especially the so-called cluster housing that many people had accepted under duress.

They were building ghettos, everyone said. The people there, like the Lakotas and Dakotahs everywhere on the homelands, were used to living in family groups, along certain coteaus and creeks in certain kinds of cultural groups to which they claimed allegiance. Not just around everybody, anybody, in such close quarters.

Aurelia cut the conversation short but later, when she gave it more thought, she knew that this talk with her grandmother had been crucial.

When she stood up to go, she said, "Gramma, can you come over for supper tonight? We won't have too much, but I made a raisin pie. Can you make it down the steps okay?"

"Yes, Grandchild. I'll be there."

Aurelia waved goodbye then, saying, "We're goin' walking, you know. Me and Blue. This is the first decent day in a long time."

Her grandmother smiled and nodded.

Blue had already staggered out toward the gate, loaded down with so many clothes he could hardly walk, and Aurelia ran to catch up with him. She knew, as did her grandmother, that what turned out to be the seventy-one-day siege at Wounded Knee was not unrelated to the daily lives they lived, and the surveillance of the feds was everywhere, even at the Fort and in the more rural West Bend. Though the old grandmother didn't know it, two FBI men, one a white man and the other an Indian from one of the Northwest tribes, had questioned poor Sheridan in jail, trying to find out something about his cousin, Vic Eagle, even suggesting that Sheridan himself was part of an AIM conspiracy of some vague sort, and if he could tell them something, they might let him off easy.

"Shit," Sheridan told his brother Jason during one of his visits, "If I was AIM I'd do something more sensible than get drunk with my stupid *wasichu* brother-in-law!!"

Grandmother, ninety-five years old. Talking about siege, asking if Aurelia thought Vic was at Pine Ridge. Remembering stories far back. What was that all about, she wondered, as she walked toward the river with Blue. This asking and telling between the two of them, she knew from long years of experience, never happened in just a haphazard way. It always meant something. In the name of her own personal sanity, she didn't want to worry about what was troubling her grandmother on this beautiful day, but she couldn't shake a lingering foreboding from her thoughts.

The old stories always carried with them meaning for the new and had little to do with coincidence or chance. Aurelia had grown in her confidence that her own memory and her grandmother's never failed them, that this is what they had always thought made the stories themselves dependable. But figuring out what they meant was where things often went wrong. The reasons for that were simple enough.

In the past, when changes in people's lives occurred for their own sake, of their own accord, in the process of the natural world going about its business, patterns of knowledge could be known and useful, and traditional storytellers could affirm the meaning of people's lives. Now, Aurelia mused, in these modern times, when outsiders and nontribal interests influenced everything, the people who might have become the tellers of tribal stories could only witness. They could only stand by the stories, know them, and remember them.

It was a philosophical idea, but out of it came the frightening possibility that from now on many of the real stories would remain untold, and the stories that were told would be unreliable and without meaning. Perhaps the people themselves would fall silent, though their lives would be lived in panic. Unfulfilling and even irrelevant.

Her thoughts were suddenly interrupted by Blue's jabbering. Aurelia stuffed her gloved hands into the wide slash pockets of her coat and gave in momentarily to the exhilaration of the cold air. She felt like throwing her arms toward the sky and shouting the names of the birds and small animals who had once lived here but now, because of the destruction of their habitat, had moved on or died. To call them back and tell them it was all right. Instead, she wrapped her arms round her thin body, shut her eyes, and lifted her face to feel the chilly sun.

"You can't help but wonder what is happening." Isn't that what Grandmother had said?

That morning Jason had left early to see, again, about bail money for his older brother. Either bail money or what they called collateral. The lawyers he wanted to defend his brother against the murder accusation were asking him and his father, Harvey, to sign over some land.

"But our land is trust lands," they objected. "We can't do that."

On the contrary, the lawyers told them. There are ways to get this done, and, being lawyers, they could develop appropriate strategies. For two months they had been arguing over this matter of bail. So it was that the family began to feel that their resistance had kept Sheridan incarcerated on the murder change that they were convinced was unfounded.

It was a crucial matter for Harvey, for he had refused all his life to take his lands out of trust for any of the reasons thought up by Agency officials, reminding them that the tribe's treaty status with the federal government was supposed to protect not only his life but also his resources. Unlike many, he had read those treaties. He had been told about them by old Benno, and Bowed Head, and Grey Plume. They had told him what they meant. Trust lands were held separate, the old ancestors had told him, from all civil and criminal and legal activities. If Indian tribes didn't hang onto their lands, Harvey told everyone who would listen, they would have nothing.

In the beginning, he said to his children, it was his own unconscious impulse to redirect his own personal destiny away from the unfortunate modern fate of many American Indians, that drift toward landlessness, anomie, assimilation. Later, he said, it just could best be described as a matter of life and death.

In spite of his reasoning, he was told that the courts that were now in charge of his son's destiny couldn't let a murder suspect out on anything less than his land bond. The courts were obligated to be sure that Sheridan would show up for trial, he was told, and what else did the Big Pipes have but their land?

It had already been weeks, no, months since the police had taken Sheridan off in the patrol car in the middle of a blinding blizzard, and his isolation was profound. Jason had been his only constant visitor. His mother had never gone, not even once, to see him. The court-appointed lawyer lived way down at Gregory and had to drive four hours each way every time they had a conference about the case.

The family was in turmoil about the situation. "You'd think the whole thing was some kind of fishing rights case, for Christ's sake, 'relia," Jason had raged, referring to the current litigation concerning the Yakima and Umatilla tribes of the Northwest, the Chippewa and Wisconsin tribes. "Or some goddamned treaty negotiations!"

"What're we gonna do?"

"Something."

"What?"

"All we want right now is him out on bail. That doesn't seem like too much to ask."

"Of course not. It's not like he is some kind of criminal. Some kind of dangerous person!"

"I don't know many white guys, though, lawyers or cops, especially, who aren't, in back of all their bluster, scared of Indians. Especially guys like Sheridan."

"Yeah."

"He's not even guilty of that murder, Aurelia. He didn't do it."

"I know."

"He's not guilty of murder," Jason repeated.

"Stupidity, maybe, hunh?" She said it in a kidding way, looking apprehensively at her husband, who could always be depended upon to defend his brother in any case.

Surprisingly, he pursed his lips and nodded his head in agreement, "Or just plain being a drunk."

He wasn't defensive. Jason knew, more than the others, that this brother had long been a recalcitrant, difficult person, one who seemed drawn to doing the wrong thing even as a boy. The two of them had had many fights "to the death," as male siblings sometimes will. Sheridan, it was said then, was the one who beat the dogs, bullied his little sisters, lied to his parents; and it was almost a relief when he had gone off and married a girl no one knew, a Frances Beecham from one of the little off-reservation towns. No one in the family had the slightest idea who she was or knew anything about her, and she was quiet as a bird whenever she showed up with Sheridan. He had stayed out of the Army for a while because of his marriage and children, but eventually, when he couldn't find work and when his father no longer wanted him on the ranch, he had enlisted.

"They did a shitty job of investigating," Jason said angrily. "They say that guy was killed by some jagged object but even if they knew what it was, they can't find the murder weapon. Sheridan sure didn't have nuthin' on him!"

"For all we know," Aurelia had said then, grasping at straws, "he might be being framed by his wife and the other brother. What's his name? But what can we do about it if we can't even get him out of jail and a decent lawyer?"

"Yeah. The lawyer we've been talkin' to wants him to plead guilty."

"Uh-huh. And do what, eight to fifteen?"

"Who knows? The kind of juries Indians get around here, he could get life."

"Or death," she murmured.

They'd sat commiserating with one another when Aurelia, always trying to be helpful, heard herself saying, "Maybe we could get some of those AIM lawyers. Those big shots from New York? They're all over these reservations these days."

"Shit!" Jason had responded derisively, the undisguised contempt heavy in his voice. "All they are is civil rights lawyers. Too damn busy doing the important stuff that will make a name for themselves. Them civil rights people are useless to Indians. Where the hell's them treaty rights lawyers?" he had finished bitterly.

Jason's angry voice had filled their cluttered little house in the past weeks; he'd started drinking, his frustration hurting them all. Aurelia, who had lived all her life with her subdued Dakotah grandmother, was accustomed to a quiet, subtle response, or none at all, when aggravations occurred. Now she had to deal with a husband whose voice filled the rooms and whose open hostility was sometimes frightening.

"The Dakotahs recognize aggression as an important human trait," her grandparents had always told her. "Both good and bad. Good because the Dakotahs have always known how to go to war in defense of themselves. Bad, because it is something that makes humans capable of beating their wives and children. Thus, we know that aggression in personal lives must never be met with aggression. It is the reason that we raise children the way we do, never raising a hand to them. It is the reason that we take great care to deal with one another in accordance with the *tiospaye* [extended family] knowledge and ritual."

Jason's aggression, his passionate outbursts, his abrasive behavior often intimidated her into a cocoon of silence. It was difficult to face up to him and tell him when his behavior was unacceptable. Maybe I was never supposed to marry a man with such passion, she thought. Maybe I'm not the kind of person who can handle open hostility that comes from ordinary family frustrations.

With those fears and trepidations in the back of her mind, she looked toward the small pond nearby and was disappointed to see that the water still had a glassy thin layer of ice on it. She felt chilled.

Sometimes in midsummer, she thought wistfully as she hugged herself to get warm, if you get here very, very early in the morning, even before *Anpao Wichahpi* has left the sky, and stand alone close enough to see the river in the distance, half of the east sky gets pink and yellow-orange and gold and you think the world is on fire. It scares you! You think it is the day the earth first began. Or, if you are a Christian, it's like you've been forgiven your sins. Or maybe it's like the great spirit has reached toward you to present the powers of the universe. It is overwhelming.

Especially the morning after a summer evening's rain, she thought, then even the dead can speak to you. And the things they tell you, you don't want to hear.

Then, suddenly, the sun breaks over the hills and it turns out to be just another ordinary day. The same as any other. And there you are, pitiful and familiar. It always reminded Aurelia of when she was a child and her grandmother would find her off somewhere in the evening when the sun went down. Alone. Weeping into the pink and orange sky for no reason at all. Grandmother told her even then, giving her advice for when she would be older: *Life is hard, wicincina. That's because women, in the beginning, belonged to the sun, and it's only when he lets her free that she can have her life.*

On this occasion, the sun had been up in the sky for hours. Aurelia stood quietly while Blue crouched down on his haunches, picking at the little rocks along the frozen shore and throwing them with his unsteady hand at nothing in particular.

For some unexplained reason, she recalled with anguish Jason's urgency, his passion for her in the beginning. She knew, at that moment, that what he had felt for her was not unlike that pre-sunrise flare of her imagination. Why had she not been afraid then? Why had she chosen not to resist him, a young man who appeared at her grandmother's parked car that day long ago to say, "I have come for you." She knew then that he was a man too much her junior with too little studied resolve and too much selfish intent, who behaved as though every moment were the last futile moment of life. Always in a hurry, sometimes as impatient as Blue. Even now, years later, she didn't know about the rightness of her submission or even whether it mattered if she went back to the house she shared with him or kept on walking into the distance. Toward that place of that fiery surprise, toward the place she thought of as the *circle of dancers* where the spirits gather and the dangers of the universe diminish.

Suddenly, shaking off serious thoughts about Jason and the misgivings of her grandmother's early morning conversation, she grabbed Blue in her arms, swung him around and around, laughing giddily, making him shriek with joy and fright.

Breathless, she turned and, still laughing, she started walking back toward the house with Blue in her arms.

13

Dissent and Disappointment

> ... in the old days when the people were making plans
> for survival, the women would say, "Bring us skins and
> meat and we will do the women's work ... "

Unfortunately for Aurelia, who had maintained hope in the face
of hopelessness, the days from then on did not improve. Reason
simply seemed to vanish from their lives and, much as she tried
not to let it happen, Jason moved for the most part away from
her and into his own new and strange space.

It was in May of 1973 when Jason, who had finally signed
the illegal document that put up three hundred and eighty acres
of Big Pipe land as collateral toward the lawyer's fee and bail
bond, came down with pneumonia, and his brother, who had
by now spent more than three months in several jails, grasped
freedom not as a penitent but with a secret vow that he would
never again love nor care for anything or anyone.

The brothers were done with their many desultory
conversations with one another, but the echo of them
resounded:

"I think they can't get you to sign over trust lands for my
bail," Sheridan had said over and over again.

"Yeah, but what are we gonna do to get you out of here?"

" I don't know, but if it's illegal, don't let them lawyers make
you do it."

"You can't," Aurelia said about the land. "You mustn't. Maybe we should talk to the judge or somebody like that."

"Who says the judges are honest?"

Their cynicism knew no bounds.

Sheridan had occupied tiny damp-floored cells for months, sometimes sharing his space with crickets and spiders. He had grown a cactus plant in a coffee can which Aurelia and Blue had brought him one sunny day before the police took him out of the tribal jail. He had become very nearly an intimate of the grey-haired library volunteers who wheeled the book wagon to his cell, left books for him to read, and chastised him for chain-smoking.

Just a week or so before Sheridan's release on bond, Jason had sat on a stool before him, talking between violent coughing spasms about what he saw as the realities of the case: "The only reason they're holding you is because you're Indian." It had come to only Indian/white racism for them now.

"Yeah."

"That and the fact that they can't arrest the Indians who have holed up at Pine Ridge and make it stick."

"Oh, but they're gonna get them, too."

"Yeah. I'm sure they will."

After a moment of silence, Jason ventured, "I don't think they can go on with the charges against you, brother. They got no murder weapon. They're gonna have to drop the charges and I think they know it. Eventually, they'll have to drop 'em."

"Yeah?" Doubtfully.

"All they got is your wife's statements against you and they can't use that! Can they?"

After he had heard that Frances had given depositions in the case against him, in an effort to save her brother Jerry, Sheridan had never once asked about his wife or his children.

"Well, they still got Jerry."

"Who knows what his story will be?"

"It sure isn't going to do me any good."

Jason sat tiredly, his head down. A sick man, he sat with his eyes closed, his right hand combing through his long hair. He didn't know how to tell his brother that their mother would probably not last the night, that her sickness and imminent death had more to do with grief than with any specific physical ailment.

As he left the building he made a long-distance telephone call to the lawyer in Gregory and said he would have to get his brother's release papers soon so that they could attend either the last day's death vigil or the funeral of their mother, whichever came first.

"Did you sign the land collateral papers?" the lawyer asked.

"Yes."

He went home then to bed, where he stayed nearly a week. During his collapse Aurelia took his mother to the clinic, where the old woman clung tenaciously to life for several more days.

The wife of Harvey Big Pipe, mother of four sons, died before the arrangements for Sheridan's release could be made. Though Sheridan could not, therefore, go to her four-day wake, he was shackled and accompanied by two armed guards and allowed to attend her funeral.

Aurelia cut her long hair as a profound expression of solemn desolation. The old mother had been a quiet presence and they had shared every day since Aurelia's marriage, and it was a loss not felt since the death of old Grandfather Blue.

Jason and Harvey accepted the death of the old mother as they had accepted her life. But for Sheridan, made more skeptical because of recent isolation, there was no solace. He hung his head and wept bitterly during the burial ceremony.

The lawyers and police were accused by the family of being inefficient and uncaring but, more to the point, the fear that Sheridan would escape was palpable in every conversation the family held with the authorities.

"Why would he escape?" asked Harvey, outraged at seeing his son bound during the funeral. "He is innocent."

"Where would he go?" asked the other members of his family. "This is his home."

It was well known by everyone that Sheridan Big Pipe had spent much of his early life giving precious little thought to long-standing historical conflicts concerning the rights of people like himself in such a democracy as America. They knew, too, that he had cared little for the family's good name. Even after his

Vietnam politicization and his return to the fold, he had remained a passive critic of American policy and a family member upon whom no one could depend.

But what people didn't know was that the pain and isolation of incarceration had changed him. With the exception of Aurelia, who had always known of this possibility and feared this man's influence on Jason, they would have been surprised, too, to learn just how it had changed him: his behavior now was a matter of intention, no longer of chance.

He, not unlike thousands of prisoners before him, had found reading an enjoyable and useful pastime and had begun a long-delayed, if brief, self-education. He had often asked for specific library holdings, even state historical volumes and law papers and documents. Though never before much concerned about his appearance, he became meticulous, even vain, shaving every morning and washing his long hair daily. More significantly, he finally realized that the murder of a white man on reserved, tribal, trust lands carried with it all of the troubling overtones of a race-related crime. Especially now, in the heat of the so-called uprising or occupation at Pine Ridge by Indians from all over the country. U.S. Marshals were still all over South Dakota negotiating and interviewing; funerals were being held at Wounded Knee. The courts were scheduling arraignments in Rapid City of those Indians who had participated in the astonishing revolutionary event.

Sheridan's reading showed him that tribal courts, inefficient and weak, depended upon the federal system for justice and directive; that state courts simply wanted to defend their anti-Indian interests; that the feds would always waffle when faced with ethical and legal conflicts; that most lawyers, when they dealt with Indian legal matters, mostly just wanted to get it over with and collect whatever fees they could, however they could.

All of this new perception, though hardly noticed by anyone in his family except the woman who hardly ever spoke with him or looked at him, made possible his secret vow to deliver himself in his own selfish way. Suspicion called forth suspicion and he wondered what his sister-in-law knew about his unspoken thoughts. For sure, she was listening for signals from him, but he would not reveal himself.

Watchful and uncertain, Aurelia knew Sheridan was looking for a loophole of some kind. Any kind. Put up the land. Lie. Flee. He was a man filled with deceit. I'm just a spectator in all of this, she mused. But I know people like Sheridan who choose to save only themselves. And I know my country as well as anyone. I know what it means to us all.

No one, not even Sheridan, could have said then what his uneven promise to himself meant, the vow that he would love no one. Nothing. Ever again. Aurelia's suspicion of this vow by her brother-in-law, though she told no one, put in her heart the fear that she and Jason and the little family they loved would suffer the grief advancing toward them, knowing that it had nowhere else to go.

Within a very short time, Sheridan's secret vow to pull out made his delayed but eventual release from jail a certain miscalculation.

Sioux Country is at its best in the spring when the air is clear and time, though ethereal and soundless, seems momentary. No one expects that anything will stay the same from one moment to the next.

In spite of that, the change in the house of the Big Pipes was unbearable. Harvey said nothing for days at a time and slept little. His wife's clothing and kept things were given away in accordance with her sisters' wishes. Sheridan, who put up a bed in the closed porch and slept there fitfully through brief cool nights, could be seen walking in the bare yard after dark and before the sun rose. His past haunted him:

The sun was warm. He was home from Saigon and the spring rains were about to begin. Alone, not by choice but because he didn't know how to ask anyone for help, he had gone straight from the bus depot to the hills, up to the highest peak in the Paha Sapa for some kind of spiritual commemoration of his deliverance from a warrior's death. Even before he went home to his wife and children. He didn't know whether to be glad or sad, but, in spite of his recent wounds, he climbed for two days just to see if he could do it.

The first day he slept and then, ritually, he walked the daylight hours, hour after hour, in each path of the four directions, always returning to the sacred circle. He did this for four days but he saw nothing, not even a re-creation of his battlefield experiences. He heard nothing, not even the firing of guns. It seemed to him there was nothing, no one to speak to him; nor was there anything to excite or confuse him. The animals and birds did not come to him.

He did not know the words to the remarkable ceremonies which, they say, used to show the Sioux conception of the perfect, ideal life of a warrior, though he knew he had relatives who participated in the ceremonies regularly. He tried to remember the songs, the warrior songs of courage, but he could not. He ate nothing and because he could remember none of the songs he sat in the darkness until sleep came mercifully on the last night.

He wept: Hoh, i's e'kta (Oh, what's the use).

A few weeks after the old mother's death, Aurelia experienced an event for which she might have been unconsciously waiting in uncalculated dread. The night was quiet and Jason had not come home yet. As darkness fell she had gotten up from her reading chair to open the door and let the cat out, when she saw in the shadows men silently bringing long crates into Sheridan's porch bedroom. She drew back into the living room, walked stealthily into Harvey's room to find him standing in perfect stillness peering out of a window. She stood with him holding her breath. As they watched, Harvey silent in his grief and she stricken with terror, Sheridan and his cohorts brought in plywood crates. They were long, slim crates, the kind used by the military to move long weapons.

"*Tuktel* Jason *he?*" whispered Harvey hoarsely.

Aurelia shrugged. She had not seen Jason since early that afternoon. She wondered why Harvey had asked. Did he think Jason was involved in this? Or did he expect that Jason would come and confront these intruders? Was this isolated tribal farm home to become a hiding place for weapons now that the confrontation at Pine Ridge was ebbing to a close? What were the plans of these secretive men? How long could all of this go on?

There seemed to be no accounting for the significant change they had both seen in Jason. He no longer had long chats with his father in the evenings, with Blue sitting at their knees; neither of them laughed or told stories; rather, they sat in silence and Jason seemed impatient with the little boy. Often he stayed outside and didn't eat meals with the family, claiming some late chores. When he came home late Aurelia sometimes smelled liquor on his breath and at those times he turned away from her in bed.

Aurelia and her father-in-law watched breathlessly as the men finished their task and slipped away into the darkness. The next morning, following the astonishing night ritual by shadowy men, the whole thing seemed unreal and Aurelia kept her silence.

Just after lunch the four of them—Jason, Aurelia, Harvey, and Blue—walked up the steps to the BIA building at the Agency. They opened a heavy door and entered a hallway where there were several empty stalls. A telephone rang at the other end of the hall, and they walked up four steps to a small alcove where they sat down and looked into the face of a man they had known all their lives.

"We'd like to extend your loan, Jason," Titus said sympathetically, "but the real truth is that the funds for this program have been put on hold."

Titus sat behind the grey metal desk, cupping his knees in his hands, rubbing the arthritis pain he always felt this time of the afternoon. The Big Pipes sat in a row in front of the desk looking like hard-to-manage children being punished at recess: sullen, burdened, guilty.

They thought Titus looked uneasy and he avoided eye contact as he said, his voice low and strained, "They . . . uh . . . they declared a moratorium on the federal monies that come into the program."

"What?" Jason sounded disbelieving.

"They've declared a moratorium."

Titus had been dreading this meeting ever since the loan specialist had told him that the Big Pipes would be in to see him. Anybody'd have a hell of a time trying to explain this one, he thought. How do you explain that your "trustee," the federal government, which has just coincidentally flooded half of your ranchlands, has as a kind of compensatory damage fee loaned you $38,000 for a new house to live in, a new pickup, Hereford breeding stock, and outbuildings and equipment—and then suddenly wants its money back? That because cattle prices had dropped three years in a row, the hayfields had not produced, and the congressional interest in the policy had undergone drastic revision, it not only wants its money back, it wants it *now*.

This was supposed to be a long-term, lifetime deal here, Titus thought silently, and now these people are having the rug pulled out from under them. They would have to sell their livestock to pay back the government. Some of the more insensitive bureaucrats he knew were even suggesting that their lands be taken out of trust and sold so that the loans could be paid. There were times when Titus wished he were still breaking broncs and riding the rodeo circuit.

"What the hell is a moratorium?"

"It's a way . . . a way . . . uh . . . a moratorium is . . . "

At Titus's hesitancy, Jason said, "A way to stop the funds, hunh?"

"Well, yes."

"Why not just say it, Titus?"

"Well . . . " Titus spread his hands and looked embarrassed.

"Um . . . m . . . who?" Jason asked. "Who done it?"

"The feds."

"Oh."

Titus tried to sound businesslike. "They've been taking a second look at the . . . at the . . . uh . . . effectiveness of the reservation cattle and hog program. You know, the one you're on." His gesture included all of them. "And, I guess, I guess they just decided that it's too tough to make it."

"Too tough, hunh?"

"And so they've put a moratorium on the program for now. Put a cap on the monies, you know."

Aurelia was stunned. She thought Titus seemed genuinely concerned and sad, but she had the feeling that he was just making excuses. She watched him rub his aching knees and shake his head.

"There's not much, you know, that the tribe can do. It's a . . . it's an unfortunate decision . . . but . . . " He gestured helplessly.

We've known this man for years, she thought. Here he is now, nearly sixty and at the end of a long and troubled career as an Indian politician and bureaucrat, and he's learned how to handle the system and put aside its consequences. Though she may have had those thoughts because of her fear and anger, it wasn't so. Had she been able to know his true thoughts, she would have known that as he looked at the young man who sat at the desk in front of him, the old man Harvey, and herself and the child, he knew he was watching three generations of people whose hard work, good intentions, and dreams and promises were going down the tubes. He didn't feel good about it and he wished he didn't have to be the bearer of this kind of unpleasant news, though he'd been doing a lot of it lately.

What will happen to them, he was wondering. Maybe they'd have to be "relocated," he thought, grasping at straws. After all, Jason was still a young man and he could learn a trade. Perhaps he should tell them about the trade schools in Minneapolis or Oakland.

"It's pretty much out of our hands, Jason."

Aurelia looked at her husband and could see the struggle in his face. The circumstances here, which made him beg, were unacceptable, but he did it anyway. A last and final gesture.

"Well, you know, if I could just get enough money to make it the next coupl'a three months. Maybe we could ride it through. And, if they'd just back off'a that loan payment."

"If we could do it, you know we would, Jason. We'd like to help but we just can't. There's nothing we can do."

Well, thought Aurelia. It was done.

Neither Aurelia nor Jason and certainly not Harvey believed the story that they were being told. They didn't believe that there was anyone here who wanted to help them.

Titus may not be a bad person, thought Aurelia defensively, but he sure is a good liar. Maybe he had even talked to McQueen, whose tongue-lashing of Jason had been overheard by a lot of people. Jason, she knew, felt he'd been bawled out pretty good by that loan specialist; that the guy considered him a deadbeat; and that the program had, more or less, washed its hands of him.

"When did all this happen, Titus?" asked Jason. "It's kinda sudden, isn't it?"

"Yeah. I suppose."

"Well, uh . . . "

"Actually, Superintendent Boe just got the word last Wednesday. And we haven't got the letters out yet. But we've been kind of expecting it, you know."

"Expecting it? I didn't know nuthin' about it."

"Yeah. We were talking to them up at Cheyenne River and even in North Dakota now for a couple of months. About how the program is being shut off, there is no money, and people are having a tough time."

"Oh, yeah?" If that was the case, thought Jason, why was Asshole trying to get me to go ahead with the hog barn?

"I know you've been having it tough, Jason."

Titus looked at Harvey for confirmation, but the old man sat without moving a muscle, his eyes averted.

"We never figured on the drought, you know. We never figured on the falling cattle prices. The price of corn is down, too. You know. We just never figured on all this."

"Never figured on it, hunh?"

"No. You can't always tell, you know. How these things are going to go."

Jason said nothing. He shifted his weight. He felt sick, like someone had just punched him a good one in the stomach.

After a few silent moments, he said, "Well, un . . . what do you think, then, about . . . "

He had no idea what his next question was and surely didn't expect that Titus had any answer for it should it somehow be put forth.

Titus cleared his throat but said nothing.

Finally: "Well, what the hell am I gonna do, then . . . there's no way I can make my payments. And even if I sell the calves and make anything on them, I'm probably gonna have to buy hay again to make it through next year."

"Well, now, Jason." Titus sounded suddenly businesslike, brisk, like he had a solution. "I don't know just what will happen for sure. But I think you had better get an appointment with the BIA superintendent and talk to him about your options . . . "

"My options?"

"Yeah. What this means is that we, the tribe, we don't have no money to continue this program and you have just been put on hold. And I don't know exactly what they'll do about it."

Jason wondered who "they" were but before he could ask, Titus got up and gestured as though to shake hands, indicating that the meeting was finished satisfactorily.

"Maybe we'll have to set up another meeting with the Tribal Credit Committee. You'd better go down the hall, Jason, and set that up."

Aurelia took Blue by the hand. Harvey stood up and reached for his cane. When Titus offered a handshake, the old man ignored the gesture. Jason turned and felt himself and his family being ushered out into the hallway.

"*Doksh'a*," said Titus with a stiff smile. "When you hear from them, you let me know."

Titus turned back to his desk and Jason touched his shirt pocket, looking for his cigarettes. He glanced at Aurelia, then at his father. Their faces were masks of desolation. So here we are, he thought. How many shitty meetings with the Tribal Credit Committee had he already had in the past? Enough. he didn't think they knew much anyway. When he'd met with them ten days ago they had said nothing about the so-called moratorium, whatever the hell that was. If they knew so dammed much they might have at least warned him.

Aurelia looked about the BIA building, walked slowly followed by other members of her family toward the exit, looking into the two or three doorways where people sat at their desks, or stood at chin-high file cabinets thumbing through files and mountains of papers on desks. Some lounged in their chairs or stretched, telephones to their ears, coffee cups nearby. She lifted Blue into her arms and left the building accompanied by those she loved and a swiftly mounting feeling of dread.

☙

The next morning Aurelia sat at the dining room table considering her own options. It was something she had not been in the habit of doing in recent times, but she remembered how it was when she first discovered her unexpected pregnancy with Blue and how she hadn't been able to bring herself to make decisions. It seemed like a hundred years ago but lately, because of the family turmoil, she had much the same grave sense of uncertainty.

Her quarrel with Jason that morning, listened to by Jason's father and brother, had been provoked by her uncertainty and did little to clarify things. But at least some of their troubles were now in the open.

"I'm getting sick of you just thinking about the damned loan. And Sheridan's situation," she had started. "And your own problems. And . . . and . . . every . . . everybody else's," she ended lamely.

It had startled him.

He might have expected that she would feel what he viewed as a woman's selfishness from time to time, but to express such outrage about it in front of his father and brother was a breach of good taste that was quite unlike her. It was not the way of a good Dakotah woman and they both knew it.

"What are you talking about?"

"I'm sick of your being so cranky, Jason, and taking it out on me."

"I'm not taking it out on you."

She noticed he didn't deny that he was a crank and felt momentarily vindicated, so she went on with it.

"I'm sick of the way you're acting. You're never home. You never say anything. I can't talk to you. You're being unhappy, tired all the time! And Sheridan. And those guys he always brings around here. What's happening? What's going on?"

He wouldn't look at her.

"There's a family here, you know," she gestured widely, knowing what they both knew, that it was a pitiful excuse for a family. Everyone isolated from everyone else's thoughts. Secrets. Unresolved grief. But, for the sake of Blue, she had to pretend. "You never laugh anymore. You . . . you . . . hate me, I think. And I don't know why."

She was referring to the secret that had been troubling them both, that their lovemaking, when it happened at all, had become an expression of silent, joyless need, no longer a delicious, exciting affirmation of their love and respect for each other filled with the reverberation of laughter. They both knew what she wasn't saying, that many times lately he had turned away at her touch. Distant. Unreachable.

"No, 'relia. It has nothing to do with you."

She wanted to believe that and perhaps in her heart she did. Yet she couldn't stop herself.

"Yes. It does! You act like you hate me! Why?"

He didn't answer.

"I feel like . . . like . . . "

"Well? What?" She knew he didn't like her accusatory tone and his voice took on an angry edge. "What do you expect me to do about it?"

That was a good question. And he was probably right. Much of what was going on between them these days had to do with troubles, expectations, uncertainties that neither of them could control. Still, she thought, that was no reason to take it out on her.

"Do?" her voice rose.

"Yeah. Do!" he said sarcastically.

"Nothing! Goddamit! Nothing!" She twisted the knob on the gas stove so hard it fell into her hands. "Shit, Jason. I don't expect you to do nothing about it!"

She turned and threw the knob across the room as hard as she could. It hit the wall, bounced back, and lay at his feet.

He didn't move.

"And you know what?"

He looked up.

"I'm *never* disappointed!" She fairly spat out the words.

"What the hell does that mean?" he asked, picking up the knob and turning it in his fingers.

"Figure it out!"

The back door of the kitchen entrance swung open and Blue, innocent and unaware that he was treading toward his parents' battleground, came in. He was puffing, carrying two good-sized rocks. He put them under the wash table.

"Take those outside," his mother said without thinking, wanting him to simply get out of the way so she could finish what she had started.

"I'm gonna . . . "

"You're gonna take those outside," she said, her voice rising into a threat.

He picked up the rocks and went outside with them. The door slammed and the silence hung heavily in the air.

"'Jeez," Jason said accusingly. Then he got up, placed the knob on the windowsill with great care, and followed Blue outside.

That had been the end of it.

What about options, Aurelia thought now, sitting at the table whiling away the morning hours. God, she wished for the stabilizing influence of Jason's mother. She knew she would never have yelled around and accused her husband in the way she had if his mother had been in the room. Aurelia had never shared an intimacy with her mother-in-law, but her mere presence was always one that brought about a kind of maturity of behavior so much needed by the younger woman.

It was getting late. Another cup of coffee later, she still sat motionless.

What's the point of this, she mused. Me sitting around here. Jason never talking. She wondered if Sheridan's release from jail had something to do with it. No, she guessed that what was wrong was probably wrong before that, but his being here and his sneaky behavior just made it possible for Jason to pretend that things were all right.

The harassment from the people at the Agency office had become unbearable in the last few weeks and that was at the root of the trouble. No solutions to that came to mind. No answers.

She got up and went to the stove aimlessly and looked out the window. She turned, went outside, and walked disconsolately to the corral. Blue came from the back of the house and, in a gesture that revealed his childish understanding that something was wrong, he followed her to the corral, saying nothing.

Without thinking, she whistled for her horse. Once. Then again. She saw him jerk his head up. Then he trotted toward her, looking expectant. Her hand reached under his neck, catching hold of his mane, and she led him into the stall. She threw a blanket across his back, then saddled him slowly and deliberately and pulled the cinch tight. She put her foot in the stirrup and mounted him with the grace and confidence she had always felt with horses. She grabbed Blue's outstretched arm and swung him up behind her.

"Hang on!" she yelled at her son and kicked the gelding a good one in the flank, recklessly. She heard Blue's startled, delighted laugh, and she felt his fingers dig into her waist as they were both jerked sideways when the animal took off. She drove the horse up a west slope, and then they galloped flat out toward the river a mile away, her elbows flying.

"Hang on, Blue!"

There was no sound but the wind in her ears as they galloped on toward the long grass, the circle of live trees at the base of the draw, the sloping curve of the fluvial landscape. And they galloped on. The sky was so blue it brought tears to her eyes and she squeezed them shut. Her nostrils hurt as she held her head poised sideways into the wind.

The dammed river was in the distance and its surface shone like crushed diamonds, but Aurelia knew its gleam to be hiding a terrible ruin. She looked at it through squinting, watering eyes filled with the sharp wind, and wondered if she would ever be rid of her grief.

Every time she saw it now, she would say, this used to be a river. A great river! The muddy Missouri. The *Mni sosa* they used to call it. Yeah, that's what they called it. A goddamn muddy river. Fecund. Brutal. Teeming.

Meandering, like rivers do, like the Platte and the Cheyenne. Kind of going first this way, then that way, with a mind of its own.

Used to be a great river, she'd say over and over. She wondered about what was told by some, that the muddier the river, the sooner a dam will silt up, topographies erode, and fishstocks be damaged. What, she wondered, did all that mean to the future?

She remembered the time Harvey's brother went to the Agency to tell the government people that they should not construct the huge dams.

"The river," he told them, "is like the blood flowing through your arm. It cannot be stopped up. Even for a short period of time. Because an infection of some kind will set in. It should not be done." He even predicted that the dam would "slip" for years and years and would finally let itself go, get itself free. Tribal politicians, geologists, and engineers smiled indulgently as they listened to the old man's fears and predictions.

Well, Aurelia thought, as she rode on relentlessly, what the hell isn't infected? Ruined? Her thoughts went back to Jason, to her accusations that morning, and she felt a sudden, terrible regret. She wanted to unsay what had been said, to make amends, to find refuge again in his desire for her.

Even in the flare of her regret, though, she never thought for a moment then that he would really leave.

Finally she heard Blue's faint, "Stop. Stop. Ina . . . please stop," and she pulled in the reins. She felt a wrench in her stomach as the animal's choppy gait brought them to a quick halt. Blue was screaming, half-crying, half-laughing.

She slipped out of the saddle, let the reins fall to the ground, and grabbed her son, hugging him so tight his breath came in grunts.

"Blue. Blue," she murmured between her own sobs. "Don't be scared. Don't be scared."

His breath caught. "I'm not scared, Mom." Tears filled his eyes.

She knelt on the ground, holding him. They both cried together, comforting each other, the little boy because he was frightened by the wild ride, his mother for reasons that she could not say. In this vast landscape that was so much a part of her full heart and that stretched across the horizon, she had the awful feeling that they were being separated from the past.

A few days after the surprising, uneven argument with Jason, Aurelia stood at the kitchen window watching an approaching car in the distance and, all of a sudden, she knew why her grandmother had asked her worried questions that day. She knew for sure now why Jason turned from her touch. It was because the old woman knew that the warriors would be gathering.

Now Aurelia knew it too.

The sun was high in the parched sky as the Oldsmobile came round the bend in the river and up the graveled road, then down a sloping hill to the Big Pipe place, bringing with it Vic Eagle and the news of an American Indian Movement rally in the capital city, Pierre, South Dakota. Aurelia saw Jason, still glum because of the harsh words between the two of them, refuse to look up, but she noticed that Sheridan grinned broadly and greeted his cousin with enthusiasm.

She could not hear their words but knew what they might be. She held her face in her hands for only a moment before she turned away and knew that when she looked back, the yard would be empty.

For nearly two months, not until the late summer, Aurelia would not know the whereabouts of her child's father, nor would she know of his activities. She, of all people, knew about journeys, though, and she knew about the brothers and their need to make a path at the edge of the world where the stars are close. An inevitable thing. From the beginning, when the holy one took water and made the spirit folk (stars), the journey of the Sioux would be a journey of reciprocity. It would always happen, it was said, in every generation. Even knowing that, though, did not stop her from wishing, as all humans do when they find the universe filled with cold and suffering, that they could be happy, that life could be easy. That the rivers could continue as they always had. Even knowing all of that did not stop her woman's tears.

14

A Warrior's Torch

Had Aurelia been within hearing distance of the men who stood beside the Oldsmobile that sunny day, this is what she would have heard:

"I'm headed to that rally up there at Pierre, and from there I'm going to Mobridge," said Vic.

"Yeah? What's going on up there?" asked Sheridan.

"They're having an International Indian Treaty Council meeting."

"Um-m."

He didn't want to show his ignorance so he didn't ask what that was. He couldn't imagine that nearly four thousand Indians from ninety-seven first nations across the United States would gather there on the Standing Rock Indian Reservation at Fort Yates, to talk about tribal self-government as the only hope for their future survival, the only hope to stop the desecration and theft of their lands. He'd had no plan that he would be among them, that he would be witness to the complex coming together of Indians from all over the continent. He hadn't known, either, that when he left this time, he would never come home again, and that if he did not, a warrior's perfect death in the traditional way would be irretrievable. Even had he known it, he lacked the courage and integrity at this moment to care, one way or another.

Within minutes of Vic's arrival, the three young men were on their way to the political gathering, driving hurriedly into the glare of the sun. Warm and unburdened, Sheridan fell asleep in the back seat and woke only when he smelled the sweetness of the joint Vic was smoking. He could feel the reluctant presence of his younger brother, Jason. His tension. Anger. He reached up from the back seat and took the cigarette from Vic, put it to his lips and sucked hard, holding it near and precious.

It was a long but pleasant drive along the coteaus of the river into town, the motion of the car slipping through the hills, easy and relaxing. In their sights for nearly the whole fifty miles were the dead brittle trunks of trees that had once lived along the water, and they were shining silver against the river's grey banks. The endless gradations of grey, white, dark brown, and eventually yellow-green streaks across the hills, bathed in the sunlight like paintings under glass, clean and fresh-looking, gave evidence that death need not look frightful.

There was a lot of history along the water's edge, but the young men, with the exception of Jason, knew little of it. Nor did they give it much thought. They could not know that over at Brulee, beyond the hills, out of their sight and invisible to them both physically and spiritually, a traditional tribal man was wiping himself with new sage in preparation for prayers with the people gathered on the homelands for ceremonial purposes as ageless as the wind.

Such communal ritualizations explained the holy presence at that place of the people who were all blood relatives, and they served as occasions for the recounting of family histories. The oldest stories would take on substance and everyone would ask how to be a responsible Lakota/Dakotah person. They would form a center for themselves within the four directions and place the landmarks in the appropriate places they had always known.

These motivations, some have said, would stand in sharp contrast to the reasons for the political gathering of AIM at Pierre, where there would be little or no interest in the reciprocity so important to the *tiospaye*.

Smoking *pesi* in the warmth of Vic's rumbling car and in the sweaty presence of one another, the young men were quiet, thoughtless, vaguely aware but unwilling to admit to one another that going their way as they were now, as so-called militants, was far removed from the kind of spiritual life common to many of their relatives, the famous medicine men, the traditionals, their fathers. They wanted to cling to the idea that they were warriors in the old way—but unlike the warriors of the past, they were only skeptics. They knew nothing of what the future would hold for them.

Vic was driving and talking loudly and obnoxiously. Sheridan, half-dozing, half-awake, kept his silence. Only Jason, refusing to listen or pay much attention to the polemics of Vic's one-sided conversation, watched the river with interest, surprised at thinking, ruefully, about the times when rivers all over the country were places of destination for tribal people. He was reminded of the time he and Aurelia had taken his old uncle to see their relative, the murderer Leaper, and how they had camped along the river and how the old man had told them about the intrusive ways of the white man. In his heart he knew it was then that Aurelia had decided to love him, and his unexpected thoughts about her were both bracing and upsetting.

He felt the pleasure of her little story about *hit u kala place*, Little Mouse Place, and her ideas concerning that mythical connection of the river to the land and the people; how much she wanted the names, the connections to continue, how much she wanted to believe that rivers could be mythical connections to the universal spirits, not mere pathways to commerce nor instruments of profit.

He could not stop thinking about her. He longed for her approval and hated himself for needing it. He should have told her he was leaving and should have made her believe that his leaving had nothing to do with her. In the foreground he noticed stalks of ironweed, tall swamp grass and, in the distance, as far as the eye could see, the dark and fussy sky.

At that same moment Aurelia was cooking eggs and brewing coffee for Harvey's supper, and making peanut buttered toast for Blue. As she placed a glass of milk on the table for the little boy, she thought: He should have told me he was leaving, should have made me believe that his leaving had nothing to do with me.

The young men had not expected to be stopped as they pulled into the dusty, cowboy town where the rally was to be held, but just beyond a small bridge lying across some backwaters, a policeman wearing the badge of the capital city, showing a yellow dome on a white background, waved them down. He was tall, a strapping man with blond hair, a thin mustache, and crystal blue eyes.

"We're stopping everybody to ask if you got guns and ammo."

"Nope."

"We're lookin' to stop anything before it gets started here," he told them. "You got any firearms?"

"Hell, no. We're here to listen to some speeches."

"Oh, yeah?" His John Wayne voice sounded as though he was about to get tantalized into something he might regret.

Jason smiled. This is the kind of guy, he thought, that says "a man's gotta do what a man's gotta do" and puts his hand on the gun at his hip.

"Yeah," said Vic, undaunted, in-your-face cheerful. "You ever heard of freedom of speech?"

Sheridan, slumped in the back seat trying not to be noticed, said quietly to Vic that he'd better shut up before his big mouth got them into trouble.

Then Vic laughed his just-kidding laugh, showed the cop a valid driver's license while he jumped out, and, to show how accommodating he could be, opened the trunk, revealing only the most fragile of spare tires, a couple of unmatched gloves, and an empty beer can. The cop waved them on without another word.

"Jesus Christ, Vic," said Sheridan, whose color was only now returning to his face, "don't you know I'm out on bond?"

"Oh, yeah," his cousin responded, laughing. "Jesus, I forgot! A fuckin' murder charge, no less. Oh, shit!"

They drove slowly and turned onto one of the residential streets behind the state capitol building. They parked and headed for the rally, the crowd already charged up, tormented, waiting for the new storytellers, the modern, pop ritualists who would replace the familiar:

Sacred and religious in form, a man with red-wrapped braids offering the secrets of self-sacrifice and regeneration appeared in front of the crowd and began acting out the divine play. He carried a torch of fire in one hand and red, black, green, and yellow streamers in the other; he strode dramatically to one side of the stage and handed them away.

His beauty was dazzling. He wore a beaded vest, blue jeans, and a brilliant colored shirt of satin with ribbons at the shoulders. It was like he came down from a rainbow, the people said afterward, unaware that they were being taunted.

His dance with an old mother from the crowd who had no speaking part was meant to symbolize his bindings to the Earth and his relationship with the Buffalo Nation. Yet, in his arrogance, he told them he would be the one to produce new rituals and mythic stories to respond to the ecological, social, and economic changes and disasters. Not caring about the power of the whirlwind to which the old mother was related, he held an eagle wing above his own head in a show-off way, and they stepped solemnly to the beat of the drum.

Other figures wearing a variety of costumes, with offerings corresponding to rites and invocations no one had ever heard of before, stood still on the concrete steps and told the oldest and newest stories, changed known and unfamiliar hymns, suggested the possibility of their own sacrifices. Some stories were known by everyone:

I was not hostile to the white man. We had buffalo for food and their hides for our clothing, and we preferred the chase to a life of idleness and the bickerings and jealousies, as well as the frequent periods of starvation, at the Agencies.

But the Grey Fox came out in the snow and bitter cold and destroyed my village. All of us would have perished of exposure and hunger had we not recaptured our ponies.

Then Long Hair came in the same way. They say we massacred him, but he would have massacred us had we not defended ourselves and fought to the death.

Some songs had always been sung:

> The Sun, the light of the world,
> I hear him coming,
> I see his face as he comes.
> He makes the beings on earth happy
> and they rejoice.
> O Wakan-Tanka, I offer you this world
> of light.

More of those who were said to be representing the creators had learned their parts perfectly and told the others in the most convincing way that they would collaborate with the sun, that they would listen to the songs and prayers of the four grandmothers.

The domed building loomed in the background as a symbol of colonialism and offered a realistic background for the long speeches by the man in the beaded vest and another who joined him from the crowd.

The dialogue told of the valor of the two speakers, informed the others of veiled intentions from evil ones, exhorted the people to "clear the way in a sacred manner," and promised two things: We shall be pierced by holy men. And, We shall be told the stories.

Meanwhile, the brothers Big Pipe, Sheridan and Jason, along with their cousin Vic Eagle, nearly faint from exhaustion and mental excitement, became a part of the choir. They sang:

> Who is the ghost over there?
> *He tu we che ya e e*
> Who is the ghost over there?
> *He tu we che ya e e*

Even while the hymns, the songs of deep significance, were still being composed and sung by the people, their voices and the dances continued, the young male witnesses decided on the setting out.

They would go east in the manner of all young heroes in all myth. They would follow the barren river to the place of the black and red colors, to the famous circle of dancers. The people would crowd about them again and the song would bring back to life the sacred trees. Their purpose would be to keep alive what everyone knew about tradition in a place made sacred again by their very presence. It would be a journey of lamentation as well as pleasure on the road from oblivion to recovery, a human quest to give back the story.

One of the largest uprisings ever against the federal government of the United States culminated on Sioux Indian lands in 1973 at Wounded Knee, many miles away from the mist and fog of the Missouri River, further away from the flickering mainstream of America. Hundreds of Indians holed up there and the dust rose like clouds so that no one could see the faces of the dancers. It was almost like a whirlwind, yet no one faced the east and no one called for the Corn Wife; without the acknowledgment of traditional ritual and the role played out by Yellow Woman, the drama would close. The uprising so embedded in the Sioux evolutionary heritage could not become the essential link between the physical needs and the spiritual imagination of the people and the land. But, as a healing seance, it was inevitable. It sucked the pain from the people and it was powerful and it was highly respected. Two of the Big Pipe brothers, Jason and Sheridan, were among those who now believed that this stand on Indian land for Indian rights was an inevitable process of history. Yet even they knew little of mythology and reason.

Dozens of Indians lay wounded during those hard days. Many were killed. Oddly, the Corn Wife, who was known as a co-tenant in every myth and ritual of the past, played almost no role in the significant tribal drama. She was, for some inexplicable reason, a mere witness.

In 1974 and subsequent years, U.S. court actions were brought against as many Indians as were massacred at the place that was the origin of grief in 1890.

15

The Return

He seemed changed, not only in his looks but in the way he walked toward her when she first caught sight of him against the pink and orange-yellow sky. She kept on digging the posthole at the corral as he came toward her and then she stood up and he stopped a few feet away. They simply stood and looked at one another.

He seemed unknowable, harder, chimerical, like a man who had never seen himself as a potential leader of men and now was amused at the thought of it. She was cautious as he stepped toward her and flung his arms around her wordlessly. She tried to remind herself of the hope that their own recognizable history as lovers could repeat itself, that because of what they cared about, they might be able to survive and go on together. Instantly that reminder failed her and she knew there were things between them—political things, family things, distances, long-standing grievances of loss and death—of which neither of them would ever speak. It would be these things that would come between them forever. She was the mother of his son, a tribal heir who could rise to tribal power in the contemporary world. Sadly, she knew that world would lack the charm of the previous one, which had had as its essential beauty the recognition of the Corn Mother's power.

Aurelia's worrisome thoughts were brought on by a selfish one that perhaps she had given herself over to witness and record the narrative so completely that there was nothing left, nothing of her own intentions for her own life. By the act of making witness, she had at long last understood many things, not the least of which was her own intention to be an ordinary woman of imagination. No more tragic destiny. No more distractions. No more indecision. She would move on and be happy.

It was no one's fault unless it was hers for expecting too much. She wavered briefly, as he stood over her and held his breath against her own. Ah, Jason, she almost said aloud, but she found she had no words at all for him. The tribal police would be here soon, she knew, the FBI, the others, asking about the whereabouts of this one and that one. The prosecutors would be looking for Jason's comrades, political activists on trial.

She wondered, standing close and hearing his breath, if their love for one another was completely changed now, as everything else was changed. The excruciating recasting of love made necessary in this kind of struggle, both political and personal, was something she knew something about, for it had happened, hadn't it, with the old man, Tatekeya. Jason and Aurelia, standing alone against the vast horizon, could say little about their future.

"Where's Blue?" he asked after several long minutes.

She turned and motioned with her chin toward the watering trough down at the other side of the small horse pasture, half-hidden by the rows of trees.

"You okay?"

She nodded and wondered why he had asked. Then she gestured toward the west. "Your dad is cutting hay over there."

Jason looked in that direction and heard the low sound of the machine his old father had somehow got started. The grass must be awful brittle by now, he thought, and he knew that the old man had been waiting for him to get back.

"How is he?"

"He's okay."

It was the best they could do, talking like this, saying nothing. All the nights she had lain in bed alone wondering where he was had used up her tears, her anger and fear.

He sat on an old hayrack and could say nothing more. He watched her tamp the dirt around the post as the sky in the west turned crimson and gold.

Finally, "Sheridan's gone."

She stopped, sat back on her heels, and looked at him blankly.

"I think he took off for L.A."

"Why L.A.?"

"I don't know."

"What about . . . about . . . he's supposed to stay here for the trial, isn't he?"

"Yeah."

"What about the land, Jason?"

He shrugged and let his eyes drift toward the glow in the west. He seemed to have no answers, he seemed unconnected to the expectations that were in her heart. To be here at this moment with him, she thought, seemed to suggest that they could go ahead with life, actions, days and years of living without consequences.

She removed her gloves and sat still. She was stunned, not knowing what to say, what to think.

The old man and Jason had put up the land, hadn't they?

A familiar reluctance came over her as she peered into the flare of the setting sun, noticing the uncommon shine on the distant horizon.

"Uh . . . " he seemed uncertain as he looked around at the house, the buildings, the hills. "Uh . . . was anybody here looking for him?"

"I don't know," she said, puzzled that he was only fearful, not philosophic, or knowledgeable, or real.

"I don't think so. I know that the lawyer wrote a letter but I don't know what it said. You'll have to ask your father about it."

Then he changed the subject.

"How's Gramma?" he smiled.

"Good." She smiled back.

Together they stood up and walked, arms around each other, toward the watering trough where Blue, his jeans sopping wet and his hair grey with mud, turned toward them and held up his dirty hands, smiling, too.

It was only later, after a thunderstorm had passed overhead in the night, after they had made love and lain in each other's arms, that she knew she would leave him because she did not want to wither and die.

The abrupt and unexplained absence, the dulling domesticity, the bitter failure to save the land, the death of the old mother and the disappearance of the wayward uncle in whom the father and brother had vested their trust had seemed too unforgiving, too grave, much too grave. Besides, she thought as she looked at his quiet face, he is too young. Too treasured. Too surprising and at the same time too predictable. Too much like the spring wind blowing around the dust left over from the winter's piles of snow. It had been such a long journey.

I can't stay here, she thought with more clarity than she'd ever felt before. I'll fall from my horse, drown in the muddy river, get run over by a car. I'll put on a yellow taffeta dress and bear its edges until I can't bear them any more. And then I will have no more expectations. For the first time she knew that such a fate was no longer acceptable to her.

She thought these things as she lay in stillness beside him, unable to sleep but recognizing his sound breathing in the total darkness that engulfed them. A sound that had the same rhythm as her own soft breath. Unforgettable. Exquisite in its meaning and pain.

She turned away from the sound of his breathing, warm and soft. She pulled the sheets toward her heart and listened, her eyes wide open. She knew the sound had great meaning, an audible spirit of something that was receding, like the thin yellow sky at the edge of the world, just before the sun rises. It was a sound she would carry in her heart forever. Aurelia closed her eyes and held in her breath, held it in for a long time, but knew that such a resistance could last only a short time. Finally, she released it like a long sigh and slept.

Épilogue–1988

hin han ke ("the end comes this way")
it is true that when you are no longer
a part of the tribal story
it is cause for
great sorrow

Though classicists have always believed in endings, the real Dakotah storytellers like Aurelia do not. You see, she thinks of the story only if it goes on and on into the next story and the next and beyond. She doesn't believe in exile and redemption, either. For Aurelia, there are some things you cannot pay for or mortgage or pawn or repurchase. Salvation and sin are unthought of, exile a magical fantasy. She says that for the Dakotapi, there is the "going out," and they will tell the "going-out stories," but only if they are connected to the return and to the knowledge of the Corn Woman.

In the case of the brother Sheridan Big Pipe, he became lost, unknown, and after a while they told no more stories about him. He was without comment, without remembrance. Whatever the reason, Sheridan disappeared and no one in the Big Pipe family ever heard of him after he was bailed out of jail illegally on the strength of their land collateral. Nor did they ever again, in all their lives, or in the lives of the offspring, know of his whereabouts.

For them he was a paradox, a puzzle, and he no longer entered into the continuum of their stories. *Dignus vendice nodus.* No longer prime or fathomable in the heart of the tribe. No longer in that place where everything tribal belongs, *Dak o ta hoc 'oka*, where everything is known, enclosed in the sacred location of the first ancestor, no longer prolonging the possibility for knowledge of the people.

No one among them, not even those of the next generation like the young Blue, would have believed for a moment that he could have ended up in Houston, Texas, for they knew no stories like that.

Indecipherable, then, Sheridan Big Pipe lived out his days in some furnished rooms on Market Street in south Houston, oddly surrounding himself in a bookish, library-like atmosphere with historical papers and manuscripts and reading materials of every sort. Much as he did during his brief incarceration, he read a lot on Indians, treaties and law, texts on the U.S. Constitution and the history of the world, biographies of the Nez Perce and Vietnamese headmen, Joseph (*Hin-mah-too-yah-lat-kekht*) and Ho Chi Minh (*Nguyen Sinh Cung*), along with chronicles of war. He thought it something more than coincidence that Ho Chi Minh was born in the year of the Wounded Knee Massacre—1890. He thought it something more than mere chance that Chief Joseph of the Nez Perce had known in his heart of the murderous intent of the soldiers of the Seventh Cavalry years before they slaughtered the women and children of the Lakota Minneconjou; that the Wallowa chief's flight to join Sitting Bull in Canada, largely forgotten by even his own people, spoke with passion and courage to everyone who valued freedom. Sheridan Big Pipe wept, alone and disgraced, as he read that in 1879, eleven years before Wounded Knee, Joseph's future was sealed.

He sat often in a huge brown chair, thumbing through pile after pile of papers, newspapers, pamphlets, magazines, folders, clippings. He would move one pile to make room for another, search through the third stack and place it carefully on top of still a fourth.

Throughout the years he had never discarded a single paper. He had saved, literally, hundreds of copies of magazines that he had salvaged from trash bins throughout the city, and books on every subject. If, on occasion, he couldn't remember a particular text's significance, he would stop his shuffling to reread it, for perhaps the dozenth time, study it with great care, and, slowly, put it in its proper place. Orderly. Purposeful.

Throughout the nights, long after this alien city neighborhood had locked its doors and turned its lights down, he continued to turn from one stack of papers to the next, shifting in the old brown chair, moving in a half-circle like a broken, mechanized thing seeking just the right programmed place. On his shirt lapel he wore two bronze stars, an oak leaf cluster, and his sharpshooter's medal.

Sometimes, when the morning light streamed through the side cracks of the heavy shades that covered the windows, he would sink into the chair, arms lax, his head with its mane of thick grey hair thrown back, and he would lie in this grotesque oblivion that he called sleep for several hours.

Thus, Sheridan Big Pipe lived in the modern, nontribal world. Desolate and alone, he had moved to these rooms more than a decade earlier, right after he had left the black woman, herself an exile from South Africa, a political activist interested in Indian causes, who had lived with him as his wife; and some time after he had walked away from a murder charge in 1973, perhaps, or perhaps not, with the intent to disappear into urban America.

He was presently ill and very afraid. He had been a janitor in a seedy hotel in downtown Houston ever since his arrival in this sprawling southern city where no one really knew him, who he was, or where he had come from. Some spoke to him in Spanish but when he did not answer no one cared. He had worked weekends and, just recently, had been forced to quit because of ill health. He was now past fifty years old.

Houston was a city in which Big Pipe could wander, conceal his identity, and busy himself with inconsequential matters; a city that went its own way and didn't notice him; a place that spawned Neiman-Marcus shopping sprees for the rich in a glittering downtown where American Indians like himself, refugees from all over their own country, could walk the streets watching their images reflected in the shiny windows of the black limousines that lined city block after city block, sleek symbols of American affluence lying in wait for the evening showings to be finished.

Big Pipe had never gotten accustomed to the hot, dry climate, nor the constant air conditioning of the downtown buildings, and now that he was frail and ill he seldom left his room, rarely socialized with anyone; even quit, cold turkey, his evening bottle of Tokay.

The persistent, dutiful black woman who had for a brief period declared her love for him continued to be a caretaker. She telephoned him every week and came over now and then with a pot of stew or hot, baked fish wrapped in aluminum foil. She tried but never really understood the deep silence in which he lived his life.

He seemed to be an anomaly in the modern world: born and raised in the West Bend of the Missouri River Country of the Sioux to be a good and kindred soul, he knew himself as a disgrace to the Isianti, the Hunkpati, and the others of the North Plains tribes who had once ruled their own lives, the people who had become remarkable centaurians, proud and relentless warriors during what the white man called early prehistoric times. People who eventually settled, after the rise of the white man's way of life, into cutting hay, raising a few beef cattle, and defending their own political and legal sovereign rights on a daily basis. People who continued to know the deities who had created the world. Sheridan, the firstborn son of a large Dakotah family, wept every day now that he was very much alone and had come to know that his loss was eternal.

One remarkable night when Sheridan opened his eyes into the darkness of his room, he could neither move his legs nor lift his torso from his bed. The muscles in his back and upper body were limp and useless. He could only flail his arms at the elbows across his chest in a gesture of futility.

He gave a low cry of sheer fright, as if he expected that someone would come to his assistance. But no one heard him. He lay in panic for three days without water, without food, his own dried urine and feces caked about his thighs. Finally, he rolled from the bed to the floor where he was found by the black woman on the fourth day.

Mumbling.

Incoherent.

In the Presence of River Gods

Contents

Preface

This is a work of fiction. It is also the third story in the Crow Creek Trilogy. (The first is *From the River's Edge*. The second is *Circle of Dancers*.)

Names, characters, and events are the product of the author's imagination. The story, started in 1960, continues to be told through this section, called *In the Presence of River Gods*. This portion begins just after the Supreme Court of the United States announced a decision that redefined the federal government's "taking" of the traditional sacred lands of the Sioux as a "theft." The matter of the crime of theft was in the courts of the land for more than sixty years and the perpetrators never confessed. Through all of this, the women and men of this tribe move on in their lives together, communal, mindful, caring deeply about the history they share.

In the same year, 1980, an Indian woman was murdered in Walworth County, South Dakota. Like many crimes, this one too went unsolved for many years. Finally, in 1995, seventeen years after the murder, the perpetrators of this crime, two white men, were named and they were taken to court and convicted.

Portions of transcripts from both trials are referred to here.

This story of fiction, like all the stories of the Crow Creek Trilogy, suggests that the notion of crime and punishment in Indian Country is often simply a matter of whim, an odd or capricious idea.

keyapi

The Hindus of India and Bangladesh still immerse themselves in the Ganges River, in spite of the fact that it is filled with toxins, human remains, and garbage. They do so five times a day because the gods require it of them.

The Dakotapi of North Plains still believe in the *Mni Sosa* spirit who lives with them in their river country, even though the river and the land have been destroyed by hydropower dam development and technology.

They know that to lose contact with the river gods is to lose everything. It is to these peoples that this trilogy is inscribed. It means that there is a future for all peoples of the world if they continue to have communion with the spirits.

1

End of July, 1980
A Drive Toward the North

Jason and Aurelia drove most of the way to Eagle Butte along the river without speaking to one another; she because of a vague dissatisfaction, he because he knew now that he was no longer the extraordinary person with whom she had much in common. After being together for the better part of a decade, it was a hard thing for either of them to admit.

This silence had been going on between them for months. Though it was almost acceptable and even expected, it was as tedious as the land and the sky and the endless highway. Two hundred miles, across flat lands that curved in a great circle away from the river and then eventually returned to fluvial hills and draws and ravines that indicated a nearness to the huge, violent, caged river and the flimsy dams upstream. The two silent travelers who had once meant so much to each other now nursed a blameless hurt that they carried with them in an aura of solemn composure as endless as the endless hills. They stared at the road ahead from the dusty car windows.

The ten-year-old Chevy van had no air conditioning and the hot August prairie wind was unbearable. The smell of dried grass and weeds, the once-living vegetation that had now succumbed to the relentless sun, clogged the air. All along the road tall sunflowers bent toward the heat, forming a thick line of shrubbery that made the two-lane highway seem narrower than it was. At least it seemed to slow down the sparse traffic, so accidents on this highway were a rare thing. The tall weeds almost obscured the man walking down the right side of the road.

Without speaking Jason pulled to the side of the road and motioned for the young Indian they'd had in their sights for the last half mile to get in the back seat of the van on the passenger's side.

"Move over, Blue," Jason said. The young boy, looking disgruntled and sleepy, moved to the window.

"Hey, I'm glad to see you . . . how about it, Blue?" Philip was out of breath, sweating, his white shirt open at the collar and streaked with dirt, sleeves pushed up past the elbows.

He tried to punch his nephew in the ribs, but Blue was not in the mood for it and shrugged him off.

"Jesus, what're you doin' walkin' way out here?" asked Jason as they pulled back onto the road. Before Philip could answer, Jason said in wonderment, "Jeez, you're the last person I expected to see way out here."

"Yeah." They laughed, happy as they always were to see each other. Their bond was not based on anything except simple familial expectations and devotion.

"In the middle of nowhere, hunh? Yeah, I'm staying up here with Uncle Antony. Out in that little trailerhouse, you know? It's out on June's place. And she said we could put the trailerhouse where there's water and a septic tank."

"Oh."

Aurelia, in the front seat looking down into the sleeping face of five-year-old Sarah, said nothing. She had often found Philip too secretive about his doings. And Antony, Jason's younger brother, even more so. It was a family trait that on the one hand she admired and on the other, in a family of independent men, she found exasperating. Ever since Antony had got back from the Marines he had gone his own way, confiding in no one. Both Philip and his Uncle Tony were affable enough, always joking and enjoying life, but Aurelia found them, when they were together, reticent and distant. Besides, Tony was a drinker known for his unpredictable behavior and everybody was concerned about his influence on the young nephew, Philip.

354

Ever since he had accompanied the casket of his brother, Virgil, home from Vietnam Tony's attitude had been brash and reckless.

"Hey, you're not doin' her, are you?" asked Jason.

"Who? Junie?"

"Yeah."

"Shit, no." Philip said this in a voice heavy with disgust.

Aurelia was not interested in this conversation, thought it tactless. She gave Jason a hard look. Jason shrugged as if to say, well, you gotta ask if you want to know anything.

She felt like some comment was expected of her.

"Where you headed?"

"Home. Back up there to Tony's."

"Where you been?"

"The last couple of weeks, you know, they been having some meetings down there at Kyle, and I was called to come down there and see what could be done to get ready for whatever decision the Supreme Court made about the Black Hills case."

"Oh." Both Aurelia and Jason nodded approvingly.

They all knew that in June of that year, 1980, the Supreme Court of the United States had ruled on an old case concerning whether the Black Hills had been taken illegally from the Dakotah/Lakota people. The people had waited for the courts to give an answer to the question that started in 1920: was the land taken illegally? Eventually the court had said yes to their question and added, "and therefore, we will pay you millions." This matter had been at the center of a vigorous debate throughout tribal circles for decades now, and it had certainly been at the causal center of the uprising of 1974 on the Pine Ridge Reservation. At this moment, on this hot day in late July, though, everyone knew the payoff was unacceptable to the Sioux. No one knew what to expect, what the next move should be.

"Sovereignty was the only reason for the Wounded Knee AIM, you know," Philip said, filling them in with information they already knew. "That's the way I see it. Whatever the cost of it was, and I don't mean hard cash or settlement or nothing like that, it was worth it. You can't go on being beaten down and oppressed forever."

"Yeah," Jason agreed.

"We're not gonna let the feds off. This is a big deal, here. It means everything, you know?"

"Yeah," agreed Jason. He recalled the so-called takeover at Wounded Knee six years before; the loss of an elder brother, Sheridan, to the movement; the loss of old friends who were never the same again.

How best to handle this matter was on every tongue, because several generations had grown up with the story of this struggle, and now that they had come this far they were inclined to believe that they could talk of land reform, sovereignty, and survival as a people into the next century.

The wind streamed into the windows as the relatives chatted comfortably about inconsequential things and some things not so inconsequential: "Did you know we brought Gramma Blue to the hospital at Eagle Butte?"

"Hey, yeah," Philip said, concern in his voice. "I heard she fell down the steps."

"Uh-huh. You know, she's pretty heavy. Broke her hip."

"Maybe I'll get up there to see her and I'll look in on her."

"Yes." said Aurelia. "Please come and see her. She would really like that."

They dropped Philip off at Antony's and as they drove away, Aurelia and Jason began to talk of serious things, something they seldom did anymore.

"Everytime I see Philip I get into a different kind of feeling," said Jason. "He reminds me all the time of the long-standing situation here, that white South Dakotans have always found our people and the Sioux Nation objectionable, that their white immigrant heritage is the basis for their objection to us, and that our lives, even our everyday lives, bear that burden. Sometimes I don't think about it but he always reminds me."

"I know."

"He's right, you know. And he's a young man who can carry on the struggle for the return of lands stolen."

"Yeah. It's hard, the way he lives. But to him it's a life. It's a life. He was born in a back room at Clarissa's place, he told me once, when she didn't even have running water and enough to eat."

"*O-hanh*. Clarissa really had a hard time. I remember when he was born. I was just a kid then and proud to be an uncle."

"And seems like he's learned how to stand between those who care and those who don't." She wondered how long it would be before he, too, like so many others, would become disillusioned with his efforts.

The whites in the area had looked down on the Sioux and had harbored a resentment of the Lakota/Dakotah ownership of land for two hundred years. There were still unsettled conditions in Indian Country, and the recent lower court decision saying that the white immigrant ancestors were thieves of Indian land sent them into a kind of collective white rage. From schoolchildren to those on the farms to the politicians in the state house, there was resentment at the idea that their immigrant ancestors had participated in an historical theft that might now have to be publicly acknowledged.

"Who the hell do these Indians think they are?" the whites often said to one another. "They never owned this land. They don't know how to own land and farm it. They're just a bunch of drunks, anyway."

Attempts to dissolve tribal governments had always caused confusion and criminal acts to be perpetuated against Indians as the federal courts assumed jurisdiction. When the federal courts couldn't do it, they conspired with the state courts to make the process go their way.

"Who is responsible for the theft of the Black Hills, anyway?" they would ask. "I didn't do it. That stuff that you talk about happened so long ago, you can't ask me to be responsible."

Scholars and historians and people of note were even more certain that the Sioux tribes were to be discounted in any ongoing story about the region.

"They weren't even here early on," many of the historians of the area said about the Sioux. "We don't know exactly when they came here but probably not until about 1775 or so. The first tribes were the Brules and the Oglalas. They migrated up the White River and the Oglalas along the Bad River. Maybe the Santees were in Minnesota at that time."

"But maybe not," others rejoined. "Could be that they came

up from the Carolinas. Some place like that, you know."

"The eastern Indians were forest-dwelling hunters and gatherers. They were in Wisconsin, too, don't you know."

The possibility of acknowledging the theft of 1.3 million acres from such meanderers across the prairie lands as the Sioux Indians was a denial so baffling and unfathomable to whites as to be cataclysmic. No one could speak of it in sensible terms.

Aurelia knew these stories and others like them by heart. She had heard them all her life. There was always talk about lazy Indians and half-breeds. Once when she had gone to a clinic in a white town when she was pregnant with Sarah, the white nurse had said, "Do you mind if I ask you a question?"

"No."

"Are you Indian?"

"Yes."

"How much Indian are you?"

"How much?"

"Yes. Are you . . . uh . . . are you . . . a breed?"

"I'm an Indian," Aurelia had said, exasperated.

"Well, that's all right, you know. There's nuthin' wrong in being Indian, you know. We are all alike. Some of the best people I know are . . . "

Jason had laughed out loud when she told him of the encounter. Now she sank back in the seat of the old van and thought about how dangerous these questions and these assumptions were. She looked back at Blue, her *chaunskay* (firstborn son), his eyes closed, his smooth face so perfect. What would be his legacy? Would they still be asking him forty years from now, "How much Indian are you?" Would he have to answer again and again, "I'm an Indian"? And would they still say, "They weren't even here, you know. They came from Wisconsin, or Carolina, or the Bering Strait or someplace else in the imagination"?

She remembered old Tatekeya, the old Santee man who had loved her so long ago. Before Jason. Before she had her children. He used to say in his ironic way, "Well, you know. The trouble with us Sioux is we're not immigrants. We didn't come here from someplace else so they can't figure out who we are."

As she was remembering, a look passed between her and Jason and the present was upon them. What about them? How had they drifted apart?

Already she is getting ready to leave me, he thinks to himself, and there is little I can do. This weekend trip back to the place at Crow Creek was just her way of putting it off, avoiding it for the moment. His look drifts toward the prairie and dusty field and a dead, hollow tree illuminated by the fading sunlight. He says nothing.

Aurelia watches him stare briefly at the summer landscape. How typical, she muses, that neither of us will speak of our most personal thoughts. But, then, what is there to say?

2

August 5, 1980
A Girl Is Missing

A few days later, when Aurelia was pushing her grandmother's wheelchair slowly and deliberately on the sidewalk in front of the Mary and Joseph Care Center at Eagle Butte, she felt relaxed, full of compassion. It would be a good day, she thought. Grandmother seemed immune to the hot wind, her thick brown arms lax, her wrinkled hands outspread on the long blue flowered dress covering her puffy knees.

"Is the sun too hot on you, Gramma?"

"Nope," the old lady wheezed.

The flat brick care center building, an extension of the Public Health Hospital constructed in 1960 after the dam up north was built, looked to Aurelia like it was crouching surreptitiously, hiding itself behind the untended bushes that had survived the regular summer hailstorms and winter sleet that often covered the landscape of this Agency town to the north of where she called home. There was something almost sinister about it.

"I ain't had a good night's sleep since I come here," the old woman complained. "It's good to get outside. Maybe I'll sleep tonight."

"Yeah."

Aurelia and her kids, Blue and Sarah, were staying temporarily with her old school chum, Connie, who had never married and who was known for taking in people who needed assistance. She had worked as a clerk-typist for the BIA since she was eighteen years old.

In January, when Grandmother fell and broke her hip, Aurelia and Jason Big Pipe had brought the old woman here for doctor's care and were told that the old woman would have to stay for a rather lengthy healing period.

"Jeez," Jason had said then, after sitting in the waiting room for most of the day, "what're we gonna do now?" He was discouraged at being away from his place at Crow Creek for even a few days but was trying to be supportive of Aurelia, this woman he'd now lived with for more than ten years. He had walked away from the swather in the middle of the afternoon when she called, left his hay down in the field. That always invited rain. Delays. He was worried. Moldy hay he didn't need. It wouldn't be long before he'd have to start feeding cattle and he sure as hell wasn't ready for that winter chore.

"Well," said Aurelia with an air of finality. "I'll just have to stay here with her. I can do that for a while. And you can go on home and take care of things."

She put a tone of resignation in her voice even though she was happy at the thought of getting away. She needed to get away. She hadn't known for months how she was going to tell Jason she wanted to leave him. Maybe he already knew. She could hardly say "I want a divorce," as they had never been formally married. But it had been like a marriage and now she felt that it was over.

No one knew how long the period of Grandmother's recuperation would take. The old woman was probably over a hundred years old and her bones were as brittle and light as dried leaves. She was very frail in spite of the fact that she was huge and still overweight, as she had been for most of her adult life. It was doubtful, the doctors told Aurelia and Jason, that she would ever walk by herself again.

Slowly, with the sun in their eyes, Aurelia and her grandmother made their way with the wheelchair through the cracked and rough and difficult walkway to the store. There was always a lot of traffic at the end of the day, people picking up groceries for dinner, kids on bicycles dashing in for a cola or chips. Young mothers carrying a baby in one arm, a six-pack of beer in the other. Older people with plastic bags filled with something to cook for dinner. As Aurelia and her grandmother picked through the aisles looking for toothpaste and cigarettes, Aurelia felt that there was a strangeness in the way people looked at one another, a kind of mutual consideration of something in the community she knew nothing of.

As if in answer to her unstated thoughts, the woman at the checkout stand said, "Did you hear about that girl?"

"No, what girl?"

"Oh, that one. I didn't really know her. They said her family finally reported her missing to the police, but they said she's been gone for three or four days."

"No. I never heard. Hm-m-m. Who was it?"

"I don't know. Last time they saw her was last Tuesday and she was standing in front of the liquor store, they said."

The checkout girl threw three packs of cigarettes from the rack behind her into the brown sack, then added the toothpaste and stood waiting for Aurelia to find the right change.

"Hm . . . m . . . "

Aurelia thought of the pretty girl in jeans she had seen the other day standing in that same spot. The border town just off the reservation.

As she counted out change, she said, "Was she about twenty or so?"

"Yeah. Yeah . . . she was out of high school, they said. Yeah. They think something happened to her."

She turned toward the register and rang up the cash.

"What?"

"Hunh?"

"What do they think happened to her?"

" . . . Uh . . . I guess they think somebody got her . . . took her . . . you know . . . "

Aurelia turned and pushed the wheelchair out of the store. They went back to the care center without talking. They said goodnight and Aurelia walked back to Connie's place, an eerie feeling hanging in the darkness and the trees. It turned out to be not such a good day after all, she thought.

She remembered seeing the pretty girl. She had reached the connecting highway, had turned sharply to the right, and had driven through town as she usually did where the streets were almost always empty after ten o'clock. She had noticed the pretty Indian girl standing on the sidewalk in front of the liquor store, alone, her arms folded. The girl looked dressed up even though she was wearing faded jeans, looked as though she were ready for a party, her hair smooth, earrings shining. Aurelia had crossed the little bridge and in her rear-view mirror had seen in the late summer light a pickup pull in, stop in a cloud of dust, and spill out several white teenagers, their boyish smiles and laughter distanced by the last light in the sky. As Aurelia was to find out later, no one after that evening had seen the girl again. She had failed to come home. She had vanished.

As Aurelia walked to work the next day she watched a flight of geese in the air and felt chilled. This was the kind of day that threatens one of those grey autumn rains that makes the trees go yellow and damp, she knew. Soon summer would be gone. Already it seemed like autumn was in the air. She started work by making coffee for the public meeting and went about her usual work in the tribal kitchens with a feeling of detachment.

"The land left unused will waste away," the state Republican congressman was saying to the grey-haired audience made up of white ranchers and farmers. He was ministering to the choir and he knew it.

"Well, I agree with that," said the tall, stooped man wearing a huge, white cowboy hat and dirty boots, "but we need more water to irrigate the land. If that is what you mean, I agree. We cannot waste the land like you said. I really think we're on the same side. I think we are agreeing instead of disagreeing. But I want to ask you this: why should we," he gestured around the room to include his fellow farmers, "why should we get only 7,000 acre-feet of water a year to service 19 towns in western South Dakota and Wyoming when they're gonna give the feds rights to put us out of business and give 20,000 acre-feet to be used for industrial coal slurry? Twenty thousand to seven thousand. That's not a very equitable ratio."

Aurelia threw the coffee grounds in the wastebasket and got a new filter from the box. Carefully she measured out the coffee and the water and plugged the extra coffee maker into its outlet. She uncovered the layered cakes and cut them into squares.

When she finished, she motioned to Connie and sat down on one of the benches at the back of the room, picking up her lighter and cigarettes. As she smoked and listened to the coffee maker burble, she heard the scraping of chairs, the grumbling of voices in heated exchange. She heard Connie blowing her nose and coughing. She looked around and wondered what she was doing there. It was a roomful of white men arguing about "unbridled federal bureaucracy" in a conference room on an Indian reservation. They had invited some of the tribal council elected officials to attend, but not one member of the twenty-man Indian council had showed up.

"You wanna know why the Sagebrush folks have got so much clout?" the old farmer went on heatedly now. "It's because they know that local control over federal lands is the way to go. It is the only way to go. We must have a multiple use program if we are to get anywhere because there's one thing I know. Us farmers gotta have more water."

When the river was first assaulted by the engineers who were going about building dams for what they said was farm electricity and local use, there was no reaction at all. No complaints from the local populace. Whatever Indian politicians said fell on deaf ears, like "pissing in the wind," Jason's old father had said. Years and years of silence. When there is no reaction, it gets easier to assault again. It's like taking a knife and stabbing someone. The first time it is done, it is an enormous, shocking criminal act full of rage and blood and broken vessels and bones. Then the next stab wound seems easier. And the next is even easier. Until the stabbing becomes just a motion . . . nothing more, nothing less.

Now, twenty years after the dams were built in the river, there was plenty of reaction. A little late probably, but reaction nonetheless. Some said the only reason for the reaction now was the threat of recent political action that had resulted in the Indian defense of the land, the efforts of the American Indian

Movement, the Supreme Court calling the "taking" of the Black Hills a "theft," the destruction of the myths whites had told themselves for a hundred years. "A rank case of theft," the Supreme Court in its belated wisdom had said. There was talk of a West River Aqueduct, a river pipeline between Cheyenne River and Bad River. These white folks would have to get the Indians on their side if that was ever going to become a reality and that's why they met at Eagle Butte.

There was no mention of absent Indians. Neither was there any mention that this proposed pipeline would be a replica of the old trail from Cheyenne River Reservation to the Rosebud. Probably no one at the meeting knew of it, as many of them or their precursors had moved in from elsewhere. It was in the memory of most Indians, though, or their grandparents who had never lived anywhere else, that a hundred years ago this trail was well known to the people and had been used for a very long time; those horseback riders, those drivers of the long strings of wagons with lots of extra horses, dogs, kids, ponies that followed the commerce, making journeys throughout their own country for one reason or another.

Some said that the wagon ruts were started in the late 1800s when both Chief Hump and Sitting Bull travelled these trails going to the other reservations in the south; some said there was a telegraph station on these roads, the Deadwood Stage where they changed horses; some said these were the trails made by Indians travelling to the Pierre Indian School or the Rapid City Indian School. Whatever the truth was, these were roads well known to the people.

Trails like these followed the rivers and they were famous among the people, like the old Route 66 or the Jersey Turnpike or Interstate 5 to Vancouver, heavily travelled joining the north and the south Indian villages. Now it was to be called South 63 to the freeway and now it was to be a river pipeline to dozens of little towns that deserved to die their own natural deaths. A way for white men to postpone the inevitable.

"Now, I know," said another man from the audience, heavyset and poorly dressed, his rough face red above a chinful of whiskers, "that they're saying that to swing around the Black

Hills with that water in a pipeline . . . it's gonna cost nearly four hundred million dollars.

"Where is that going to come from? *Your* pocket?" He looked directly back at the speaker in the white hat.

He sneered and chewed on his pipe. As an afterthought, he went on, "Those Sagebrushers, yeah . . . they want to control . . . yeah . . . but where they gonna get any money? From *your* pocket?"

There was only silence in the room. And fear. And anger. What were they afraid of, Aurelia wondered as she went about her tasks. Each other? The government? Indians?

The speaker shook his head. "I got enough people in my pocket. I know that, for sure." His eyes were bright as he searched the faces around him.

The Indian women coffee servers stood in the anteroom behind the counters in silence. Arms folded. Waiting.

Aurelia switched on her pocket radio and tuned it as low as she could and held it up to her ear. A prairie fire was burning a hundred acres of grasslands forty miles down the road. Near the little immigrant town, Dupree, named after a Frenchman fur trader in 1760. The Sioux Forest Fighters from Rapid City, called the Black Hats, had started to arrive to assist the locals in putting out the fire. The only thing that would help them, the radio announcer was saying, was the greyness of the sky and the misting in the air and the possibility that it would rain. Mercifully, he said, there was no wind to speak of.

"Hello, country bumpkin," whispered the radio into Aurelia's ear. Strains of music from the western country station mourned its brand of lamentable loss and grief, guitars plinking and harmonicas humming the thoughts these singers had in their heads that never let them go.

She thought of the white storyteller on TV last night. The educational channel she and Connie watched when they were bored with shooting and mayhem and detective stories. "The wind, tearing across the prairie at a hundred miles, taught me that the universe has no obligation to you at all," the white storyteller had said last night.

Today, sitting in the roomful of farmers arguing with one another, she had time to reconsider what the old scholar had said. Oh, old man, you're quite wrong about what you learned concerning the universe, she thought silently; on the contrary, the universe is obliged. It knows us and has known us since the beginning and whatever spirits are here, they care about us, the Dakotahs. Don't ever say the spirits don't care about us, that the universe is indifferent.

She felt an enormous sadness listening to the cowboy song, listening to the white farmers talk about irrigation. They were so pitiful. There was no consolation here, she thought, as she continued to listen to the radio and smoke one cigarette after another. The radio had no news about the missing Indian girl whom no one had seen since August 3.

"There is just no evidence," the sheriff had said and that seemed to be the end of it. His one and only public statement. It was as though she had simply vanished, as though she had never been on this earth, a mere figment of the imagination.

3

September 5, 1980
A Green Pickup

It was a few days after this meeting, when Aurelia was driving home from town alone, that she noticed the headlights of a car following her. At first it was slow but then it came close, persistently following.

She was driving Connie's car, travelling fairly fast, and they followed for twenty minutes. Suddenly, they passed her, a green pickup full of young men, two dogs in the vehicle's bed. They passed her, she would tell her family later, "like I was standing still." Then they slowed down and she did too. She noticed that the license plate started with the number two, a Pennington County plate. Rapid City. The Black Hills. As the road twisted higher, the hills around her seemed very black, indistinguishable from the surface of the road, and the starless sky, by contrast, was a light blur. She followed at a safe distance for a couple of miles but when they slowed even more, she flipped her lights and started to pass them. As she did so, they accelerated their speed to match hers. As she drove faster to pass, they did, too. As she went slower, so did the green pickup.

Frightened, she gripped the steering wheel and looked into the cab of the pickup. Though she couldn't see them clearly, they were white men. Young men. The driver laughed and his lips stretched over his long, perfect, white teeth. The young man next to him put his hand to his puckered lips and patted them, making the racist gesture of pretended Indian chanting, a stereotype familiar to most everybody around here.

Aurelia tried to decelerate so that she could get out of the passing lane, but the pickup slowed again. She stepped on the gas and her car shot ahead and she thought for a moment she would escape. The pickup, though, followed closely behind, inches from her bumper and started blinking its lights, high and dim. High and dim. Bitter saliva filled her mouth and her heart raced. They drove on like this for several miles, Aurelia breathless and gasping. She looked ahead and saw the lights of the Agency. Desperate, she turned into a driveway, careening wildly, taking down three fenceposts. The green pickup swept on.

Aurelia ran to the door of the little farmhouse, asked to use the telephone and called the police. She remembered the license plate number and reported the entire episode.

She thought: Who are these creeps? Like many other questions, it was a question that would go unanswered. If an investigation followed her report, she never heard of it.

The so-called militia movement was on the rise in this part of the country and a few young white farmers, who felt they represented people in rural areas in the west, had begun secret ways to express their anger at minorities, at the government and politicians. Long a silent cause for white supremacy in the West, such a movement had many origins, and now men were silently organizing, secretly sending ammo in the mail to other groups, buying and selling weapons, terrorizing people in isolated and individual instances, expressing their long-standing and fevered hatred of Indians, the government, anyone with whom they disagreed.

What renewed these militias on the rural scene was open to debate, but they might have started in the prairie country as innocently as the imitation of what began as the gaudy medicine shows traveling in wagons across the land, hoping to sell tonics and salves, hoping to take advantage of people. Profit and greed were the motives for most things in this part of the world and these two motivations often resulted in violence and intimidation.

The medicine shows of the old West often exploited Indian names, like the Kickapoo Medicine Company. When things went bad, as they often did, the pitchmen headed for pool halls, saloons, and lodge meetings. There they met disgruntled farmers, racist and fearful immigrants, and there they freely attacked the government, the free press, and the Indians, all of whom were blamed for their shared misery and failure.

This was 1980 in the Great Plains, when various people who worried that they were losing the American Dream were talking angrily about the Sioux Nation, which was seeking restoration of lands, land reform in the Black Hills, billions of dollars in damages. The tribes were refusing the federal government's offer to pay them for land stolen. They were asking Congress to halt the illegal payoff on the Black Hills case, ever since the Supreme Court's decision defined the "taking" as a "theft." Indians wanted their land back and the local whites were afraid that they might get what they had been asking for.

Besides, everything was changing. Young men in the West were no longer being drafted, because the draft had been dismantled following the trauma of the Vietnam War. Many of them were at loose ends. They were not working. Their farms had been plagued by drought for several years. So they began to join the self-serving organizations of their fathers to defend the land. They feared Indian landlords just as their fathers and grandfathers had feared them, and they felt their own ways of life were at risk.

All Aurelia knew was that she had been frightened and harassed by a pickup full of white guys and that she would not again drive alone on the isolated roads of her homelands at night if she could avoid it. Without thoroughly examining the harassment, she had the feeling that the frightening episode was part and parcel of the racist climate in which the people lived, that it was not unconnected to the white farmers' meeting in the tribal hall, that it had everything to do with the disappearance of the pretty girl, that there was risk and danger everywhere.

4

October 4, 1980
"We're Alone"

The night Aurelia had seen the girl was clear in her mind and it became clearer after the green pickup incident.

She had taken the kids for a last fishing trip on one of those autumn days, the red and yellow leaves falling all around them, and then afterward they went to get some groceries. It was just a couple of weeks into the school year and she was late getting home. As she drove Connie's car home that day, the sun was giving up its last flare, pink and orange in the western sky and she suddenly felt terrible loneliness. She remembered herself, again, a little skinny child sitting on the hayrack crying into the wind. Again, crying. Always crying at sunset.

She shook this old ghost of an incomprehensible childish past from her memory and looked over at Blue, a big boy now sitting in studious concentration in the front seat shuffling kings and queens on his knees from a new deck of cards. Sarah, asleep in the back seat, was stretched out like any guileless five-year-old, her knees apart, her face streaked with dirt and sweat.

It was a beautiful drive and Aurelia never failed to notice the beauty of the place. The car slipped easily through the dusty hills and passed over the bridge on the tree-lined Little Moreau River, tributary to the Mni Sosa. People and horses, the main crops here on this Indian reservation, were nowhere in sight. It was the kind of place where if you stood away from the river and the cottonwoods you could see a hundred miles without encountering any human presence. The kind of place Aurelia had always counted on. She felt good.

This place was designed and drawn, redesigned and redrawn by treaty makers of the old days, over and over again as U.S. Government surveyors responded to the greed and need of burgeoning America. Still, as the twentieth century waned, this was one of the largest Indian homelands in the country. Cheyenne River, they called it, though the Hohwoju people here had other descriptions they used to recall the ancient times.

The Corps of Engineers had spent decades here, reinventing the world and the river in an image unrecognizable to the spirits whose home this had been for millennia. Native communication with the river and the land from then on had been disturbed and disorganized by the artificial intrusion of damming the river, an act of modern progress signed into law by several federal and state administrations but finally by the great war hero Eisenhower in 1954, a man of great hubris who didn't flicker an eyelash as he reorganized any universe, on the battlefield or off.

Aurelia appreciated the perfume of hundreds of wildflowers and berry bushes, most of them finished with blooming now, the faint scent drifting in and out of the window, open just a crack to screen out the massive swarms of mosquitoes that rose from the weeds this time of the late afternoon.

She knew, also, that she had probably moved on forever from her life with Jason Big Pipe. Mostly by chance, she had made her way for the better part of a decade with Jason and had borne his children and had wept with him in the sad times and laughed when times were good. Now a silence had fallen between them. The old means by which they had come together had been used up and it was up to her now, as it is always up to women, to leave the shelter of a warm and safe place grown unaccountably bleak and cold.

Quietly, her son Blue looked up. Their eyes met and they listened together to the quiet hum of the engine.

"We're here . . . " he paused, " . . . *alone*, aren't we, Mom?"

"Yeah," she responded quickly.

Hey, this kid has got it right, she thought. This kid knows this kind of place. It's like he has always known it, like he has lived it. And he's only eleven years old. She felt an exhilaration that seemed sudden and shocking. He knows that!! I can't believe he knows that. God, it takes some people all their lives to know these things! She wondered if he could read her mind.

She gave him a bright smile and he squinted into the sun and saw it leave the horizon. He smiled back.

"The sun's gone, now, too. Ennit, Mom?"

"Yeah." She wondered if she was misreading what he was trying to talk to her about. If she was, she didn't want to hear about it.

His relatives and hers, who believed themselves primary and alone in the universe and morally attached to it for thousands of years, had been ancient survivors of the attacks on their way of life by invaders of every sort and now were compelled in a reservation system where they were no longer innocent, no longer warriors; instead, players of endless games with their enemies. Yet they would always know this place of their origins, it seemed.

"Each of us, Blue, carries that knowledge about this place. That we are alone. The spirits that surround us are alone, too. We must all get accustomed to alone-ness because that tells us, finally, that nothing lasts except the earth, that no sensation can really matter any more."

He had gone back to the kings and queens and she knew he was no longer listening. But there were times when she couldn't stop herself and this was one of them.

"It's a moral idea about the people and the land, not just loneliness. It's when you connect to the alone-ness of the place, acknowledge it, it's like growing up, you see. And it is the most important thing to know. Because it assures you that human beings are responsible to do the right thing."

She lapsed into silence, then said aloud, "I'm so glad you know it, Blue."

The philosophical nature of the Sioux acknowledgment of the universe and its relationship to the people was always a hard thing to know. Especially nowadays, confronted with the Bambi mentality of America's moviegoers. And it was no different now for Aurelia and her firstborn son. It's not just the land and the rivers and the little animals, the people would say. It's the sky and the whole universe, the sun and all of it. It is the Sioux belief that the universe has known them since even before they were the Star People, maybe even when they were made from water. And the Sioux people, in turn, have known every place in the universe. This is what they have told themselves, anyway.

Aurelia opened the window and stretched her arm out, letting the bugs skim over her ever so lightly. This is Sitting Bull Country, she thought, and she scanned the sky; the clouds were huge and white, the edges covered in silver as the sun went down, the air getting heavier every moment.

As she drove into Eagle Butte, there was a man running casually down the road in the opposite direction. It was Hermist Grey Bull, Connie's brother. He was the widowed father of Greg and Chazz and lived out in the boonies away from the villages and the traffic. He wore a blue headband and black pants and a light blue sleeveless shirt. He seemed indifferent to cars and traffic and livestock in the fields. He ran in concentration of the moment and place, a familiar figure in the community who could be seen running for miles at the close of any day. She drove past and watched him in her rear-view mirror, his arms and shoulders moving in a rhythm that was slow and deliberate. It was a beautiful thing, she thought, a man running in complete absorption of the moment.

It was near dark now and Sarah had awakened. She was sitting up, whining.

"We're almost home, babe," Aurelia said in an effort to console her.

Connie met them at the door, Blue and Aurelia struggling to carry in the grocery bags, the two women talking to each other about how late it was. Sarah's whining grew louder and she was quickly blaring her unhappiness in a huge, low voice that seemed frightening, at odds somehow with how small she was. As her mother watched curiously, she lurched toward the door and stopped long enough to throw up on the wooden steps.

Connie, in a rush of tenderness, grabbed her up and dashed off with her into the kitchen bathroom.

God, what a day, Aurelia had thought at the time. She knew they shouldn't have had that last ice cream. She hoped she'd have time to go to the ball diamond or the park to walk and stretch and sweat it all out. Or maybe the gym. She needed exercise. Now that she lived in town she missed the horseback riding that had been a part of her routine nearly all her life.

Connie's nephews came out and stood around watching while she hosed off the vomit and carried in what was left of the groceries. All the Grey Bulls looked alike. They had a neatness about them, even the teenaged Greg and Chazz, though they were taller than anybody their ages. Aurelia looked at them and saw in them the beautiful nose and cheekbones of great-great grandfather Charles Grey Bull, his portrait from his days of Christian ministering at Sisseton hanging on the wall in the living room. They said nothing but followed Blue to the back bedroom, where he pulled candy bars from his pockets, threw them on the bed, and began reshuffling the deck of cards.

The only light in the house was the flare of the television screen in the living room. As Aurelia put groceries on shelves and in the refrigerator, she heard Cronkite's voice punctuating the news of the day. He was saying : *"It's been for 180 days that 53 hostages have been held in Teheran and today at a time when people were saying that things couldn't be worse, they suddenly got worse. Three Arab-Iranians took over the embassy located in the fashionable district of Hyde Park in London. They demand that 91 Arabs imprisoned in Iran be released."*

It was a night just like this one, perhaps, as the respected newsman informed America of its present global interests, on which the girl, in an obscure Agency town on an obscure Indian reservation, had disappeared. It was that night of going about doing whatever trivial things people do that the pretty girl vanished. It is so odd, Aurelia thought years later. It is so odd that the miracle of life, the sheer doing of such ordinary things— standing alone on a street corner, or driving down a road, or looking at how the sun sets, or listening to the evening news— these normal acts become the extraordinary ones that you can't forget. You run them through your mind like some old-time newsreel. The finality of every moment is something human beings don't pay attention to until it is too late. But, surely, those ordinary things that occupy ordinary human beings are what you come, eventually, to look hard at. She closed her eyes and saw again a brief glimpse of the slim girl as she had driven home, the sparkling earrings, the folded arms.

It was an interesting time for America. A time when both ordinary and extraordinary things were the focus of a kind of collective audience participation. Overseas, confusion reigned. Iranian embassy people blamed it all on Iraq. Khomeini called for the overthrow of Iraq. Prime Minister Margaret Thatcher said it was a problem between "Persian Iran and Arab Iran."

The Carter policy at home in the United States was said to be inconsistent and incompetent.

The Cambridge diet was all the rage.

Gasahol plants were started in western South Dakota, and Cuban refugees lived in Tent City in southern Florida.

It was an interesting time in Sioux Country because the Sioux claim for the Black Hills, after sixty years, came to decision in the Supreme Court of the land and their claim that the Sacred Place was stolen from them was confirmed. To the white folks of South Dakota, it was an astonishing legal decision, outrageous and wrong. For the Sioux, it was the answer to their prayers. Now they would go forward as a nation of people lucky enough to regain the loss of an unlucky past.

And then there was the missing Indian girl.

Later, after the news, Aurelia was sitting on the porch smoking a cigarette in the quiet darkness. Hermist appeared out of nowhere. He startled her and she jumped up.

"Hey, I'm sorry," he said.

"Oh . . . it's you."

"Yeah . . . did I scare you?"

"Oh . . . not really . . . it's okay." She sat back down. "I'm just jumpy, I guess."

She didn't know if she should tell him about the green pickup, so she said nothing.

"I'm here to get Greg and Chazz and get on home."

"Oh."

He stood for just a moment more and then, impulsively, sat down on the steps beside her.

She offered him a cigarette and he shook his head.

She shrugged and they sat in awkward silence. What does he want, she wondered, as he sat next to her, suspicion and near paranoia always a part of her cynical thought process.

"What do you want?" she asked, not looking at him.

"Nuthin'. Why? You think I want something?"

"Yeah. I just want to know what it is."

He laughed. Softly.

"So you can be ready, hunh?"

"Yeah."

Connie came out, slammed the door and sat down beside her brother.

"Whatcha doin', Hermist?"

"Nuthin'. I just come over to get the kids."

"Why don't you let 'em stay overnight?

"Hm . . . m."

"They're not hurtin' anything and they're playing good with Blue."

"Oh . . . Okay . . . it's okay with me . . . I just thought they'd been here long enough. And I don't like 'em to be gone too long."

"Yeah, I know."

"They got things to do around home, you know."

"Yeah. I know."

They sat in silence. Aurelia couldn't remember when she'd seen so many dark clouds in the night sky. They were black and huge, making eerie, jagged streaks across the heavens. The moon was just a sliver and everything seemed foreboding and the wind seemed to be rising. She wondered if it was going to turn cold, turn into a hard driving rain.

Suddenly Hermist stood up and, not looking at either of them, said, "Well, I'll see you. Probably tomorrow." And he disappeared down the road as quickly as he had come.

After a moment Connie stood up. "Gee . . . it's dark," she said to no one in particular. "Guess I'll be going to bed." Abruptly she left Aurelia on the steps.

Aurelia sat alone for several long minutes. The day had inflamed her eyes and they hurt and she thought about how good it would feel to take a warm shower. She threw her cigarette to the ground and stomped it out and, shoving her hands in her jeans pockets, she looked past the trees to the silent view. There was a curious dark silhouette against the slip of the moon in the starless sky.

She felt she was getting settled here at Connie's place, at least for the time being. She wondered what she would do when her grandmother got well enough to leave the rest home. She went inside and prepared for bed.

5

October 20, 1980
The River's Edge

Everything that Aurelia had known about Jason was known at their first meeting. It was remarkable that they had been together now all these years. It was remarkable that she had loved him so, that she had cared for him, that she had waited and longed for his touch. Remarkable, too, that it was over.

Jason rarely explained himself and she, too, was noted for her failure to share her thoughts with others. He'd had young lovers, school girlfriends, before he took up with Aurelia, partners who had shared his bed and his body and his brief life in the Army, before Vietnam. As for herself, she'd loved an old man about whom she seldom spoke and she'd had no young lovers until Jason. Once Jason had decided on her, though, there was no one else for him. He may have been distracted by many events or passions, but other women was not one of them.

Now, after the birth of two children and years of a hardscrabble life, it seemed to Aurelia that she was actually moving on, taking steps toward someplace unknown; yet she recognized that she was not a doer, that she was a person who witnessed events and waited for things to happen. She was waiting for life after Jason just as she had waited for life before Jason, she was waiting for Grandmother to die or get well, she was waiting for children to grow up. She was waiting for the Black Hills claim to be settled in an ethical way. She was waiting to hear what had happened to the pretty Indian girl standing on the street with folded arms. It was 1980 and she was nearly fifty years old. She didn't know what her real life was. She had begun to lapse deeper into her old ways of silence and cynicism. Yet she knew things were changing in the ways that they always changed in her world, slowly and inexorably.

The community where she stayed now with friend Connie seemed to be a place newly carved out of a vast, flat prairieland. In fact, it was just that. This Agency town, like others up and down the Missouri River, had been what they called "relocated" when huge hydropower dams were built upstream and downstream. The wind roared through its streets in the winter; horribly battered men, some of them quite young, hung about the street corners and the cafe in good weather and bad. Beer cans and wine bottles were thrown into the weeds along the walks. In the recently designated park in the center of the town, men would be found lying as if dead, the telltale white rim about the mouth. Huffers with dead eyes and agonized grimaces.

It was Friday, nearly time for Blue to be home from school. She had sat out in the sun for much of the morning. She knew there would be an afterschool game and that Blue would play and that she would have to go and watch. Maybe she could get Philip to go. Maybe Uncle Tony. Maybe Jason would come for the weekend but, somehow, she doubted it all.

She had seen the posters of the latest evangelist and knew that Connie would want to go and would ask her to go, too, after the four-o'clock game.

In the fall of the year after the kids went back to school, the Christians on Indian reservations always started what they called "family meetings." There was a place, the circular place just beyond the tribal hall, that seemed most convenient for large gatherings, and as Aurelia, the kids, Connie, and Philip went there that Friday, they walked past a deep curve in the ground. They looked around and noticed the wide expanse of the bound river. Treeless, the river seemed like a gigantic misplaced waterscape on a level with the brown prairie grasses now turning brittle. Huge bright blue and white waves. The colorless prairie. No one spoke and the kids seemed unnaturally quiet as they walked together.

At the turn of the century this ground was used as a racetrack where Indians from all over the north plains came to race their horses, bred for long legs and speed. Those horses had been something to see. Even Aurelia remembered those far-back spectacular days. Sometimes sulkey races, buggy races of all kinds took place here, too. Three or four old Indian men, still wearing long braids and moccasins, well known among the people, owned the horses and the buggies and were in serious competition with the horses and equipment of those white men who dominated the county fairs. Aurelia had relatives who had been in the racing business, so she knew this place well. Many of the younger men had been rodeo riders. It was a time that was almost gone, now. Nowadays Sioux Indian kids grew up and lived their entire lives without ever riding a horse.

There were concrete steps left from those early days but no buildings. Steps like some kind of rock formation led them into the circle. The curved land like a dry river channel was still clearly marked. Now it was like a band shell for shouting Baptists or stately Catholic priests carrying golden goblets filled with the body and blood, or even Indian ministers from the various churches in the area talking about God and Jesus and the promised land. These ceremonies didn't occur often, but they still took place much like the old convocations the Christians had used for conversion purposes back in the late 1800s, back when they converted everyone in sight, even the unwilling.

Aurelia, Blue, Sarah, Connie, and Philip walked past the mostly old folks who sat in rows of chairs or on blankets thrown carelessly on the ground. With people who knew them well, there was much handshaking and nodding and smiling. Connie greeted her nephews and found a place to sit. Blue and Sarah flung themselves down on the ground, half resigned to be there but happy, too, to play with the other kids.

Never much interested in the community gatherings devoted to what she considered a forced religiosity, Aurelia touched Connie's arm. "I've gotta get out of here," she said.

"Okay."

Aurelia took Philip by the arm and they left.

As they walked away they heard the minister saying, "I'm here to give you consolation . . . may God bless you . . . "

As they walked along the river, Aurelia reminisced.

"When I was little, we came here one time for something, some kind of gathering that had to do with people coming back from the military. The returning warrior thing, you know. Might have been just after the war . . . not Vietnam. The War, you know? I was just a kid."

"The *big* war, huhn?"

They laughed and she was reminded of how much older she was.

"Yeah. We came from Big Bend and we stayed for a couple of days. If you look that direction," she pointed west, "and if you go over those hills and over there a ways, every time I come here . . . I remember . . . I always thought that is where the Hoga-Ta(n)ka lives. *Yuka hoga waka ki heya ke.*"

She looked up at him to see if he was believing what she was saying.

"Even now," she went on, "I think that he lives there. Really. Have you ever heard that story?"

They were walking slowly toward nothing, just looking toward the expanse of the treeless river banks, the shoreline dark and damp, and, to the right, the rolling beautiful hills.

"Um-m-m . . . No, I don't think so."

"Well, I don't know if he lives there, because, you know, he also lives in the water." She was saying this in her calm, reflective way, and Philip was leaning away from the breeze, lighting a cigarette.

She sat down on the root of a dead tree, her hand carefully caressing the whitened skin of it where the bark had worn away.

"Yeah. I always wondered about that. If spirits can't live forever in the water, I guess that's what makes that story important. They are restless, you know. The spirits."

He thought she wasn't making much sense, but he waited and was silent.

"They say that he came up partly out of the water and he was getting acquainted with the Dakotahs and they liked him and they, kind of, you know, took him in. And they fed him so good that he just got bigger and bigger," she gestured.

"And pretty soon he just engulfed them and then he laid down on them and he put his arms out and made his body flat and wide and he became, like, kind of, *zuzuecha*," she made a zigzagging motion with her right hand, "crawled like that . . . away from the water. *Heche-ya* . . . "

She pointed toward the hills, "And, over there, there is a butte and it has a kind of mesa-like top on it and that's where he is. Today, he is still there. I've seen that place because my grandfather took me over there, once."

"Sometimes," Philip said, "when stories like that are told, they say 'well, I've never seen it, you know, but' . . . I don't know why that is."

"Yeah. I don't know either. But my grandfather, he really knew!"

"This story is really about the Bad River, over there," she lifted her chin toward the western hills. "And it is a river which is a tributary to this one here, just like everything is connected . . . the Cheyenne and the Moreau, so everything is related, every place, every story is connected to the next one."

"Um-huh." He smiled and said jokingly, "I can believe it. I can dig it!"

"You're a believer, huh?" Lightly.

"Yup. I'm a believer."

"Could happen." Her voice rose as if she'd asked a question and she smiled. It was a kind of joking way to end the conversation. But there was no question in Aurelia's own mind about what she believed. For sure, she believed in the spirits of the river.

In the moments of silence that followed, Aurelia looked closely at the waves on the river, how it seemed rough, sudden and swift like a breakneck thing out of control.

"Jeez," Philip said as though reading her thoughts, "I remember when I was a kid and I thought the river was wild, on its own, when they never wanted me to go swimming, my mom and my gramma. Remember? They were always talking about how dangerous it was."

"Yes. I remember, too."

"'member how my mom was? She nearly had a fit when I went swimming. 'Be careful,' she'd be yelling at me 'til I got out of sight."

Aurelia smiled and nodded.

"They always talked about the undertow . . . the dropoffs." They both looked toward the Christian gathering in the distance. The old women sitting on the ground, the minister gesturing and holding an open book. They noticed that many of the chairs were empty and that the children were running between them. They said nothing but walked on.

There was no sound but the lapping of the water and, occasionally, a loon-like sounding of a bird on the beach. Pretty soon they heard human voices, singing. The sound rose and fell with the wind. It was bad singing, off-key, slow and dirge-like.

Philip looked toward the singing. He furrowed his brow and said slowly, in a voice filled with wonder, "That sounds like hell, don't it?"

She laughed out loud and couldn't stop laughing.

He shook his head and they walked on, admiring the vastness of the place that surrounded them. Philip, this young nephew of Jason's, had become a quiet presence in her life and in the lives of her children. He visited once in a while now that they were both away from home, a way to keep in touch though he seemed in many ways to be drifting aimlessly.

"I don't plan to stay here too long," he had told her once.

6

October 22, 1980
A Game of Skill

When Aurelia walked into the unusually silent house one Saturday after work, she found Hermist and Blue playing chess, quietly and in earnest.

"Hey, Blue . . . I didn't know you could play chess." She felt like she was intruding into a private place.

"He's teaching me," he lifted his chin toward Hermist.

"I thought you were supposed to be babysitting." She looked around for Sarah.

"I am."

As though she wasn't there, Hermist was saying, "Most of the time the game is over before all your pawns even get into action, so don't think it's like checkers. It isn't. The whole thing here," he spread his hands over the board, "it changes real slow, very gradual. And you have to watch everything."

"Only the center pawns," he gestured, "here . . . are entitled to advance . . . in this case . . . here . . . and they should advance very cautiously . . . "

Blue sat with his hand cupping his chin. His fingers were tapping his cheek.

"You know what cautious means?"

They smiled at each other, a private appreciation between student and mentor, and Aurelia stood watching them, the door ajar and her car keys making a distracting noise.

"This is a white-man's game," Hermist told the youthful Blue. "It's not like Indian games where what you see is what you get and you know that people are out to get you in whatever ways they can. Just right out there."

"Yeah?"

"Yeah. This is tricky. It's devious. You gotta think devious if you want to win at white-men's games."

"Yeah?"

"Yeah."

He smiled.

"You know what devious means?"

At that moment, Sarah fell off the counter in the kitchen and set up an enormous howl.

Hermist threw up his hands as Blue dashed into the next room to rescue his sister from her latest mishap. She was crying loudly, saying something between sobs about peanut butter.

Hermist got up and pushed back his chair.

"Hey, Blue," he called, "I'll be back later. Tonight. Okay?"

He went to the door and Aurelia followed him out. "I gotta go and pick up my boys at—"

"Did you hear about that girl?" she asked, interrupting.

"Oh, yeah," he said. "Everybody's out looking, I guess."

"They're saying she was out drinking."

"Yeah? That's what they always say. That's real Indian, don't you think?" Sarcasm filled his voice.

"You can't even disappear anymore, but what they say you were drunk!"

"I bet it was those white guys they say pulled in where she was last seen."

"I think it was."

"They're supposed to be questioning some of them. Rounding them up, I guess."

"Who is questioning them?"

"I don't know for sure, but I heard the city police and the county sheriff and even the Bureau police are supposed to be working together on this."

"But they don't know where she is?"

"Not yet, anyway."

"They don't know where she is, even. How awful!"

"Yeah."

He walked toward his car, she beside him. Hermist was one of the first men Aurelia had gotten friendly with after she came to live with his sister. They often passed one another but had never spoken at length. She hadn't known him in school because he was a couple of years ahead of her, but she had known two of his sisters, Connie and Marie. Hermist didn't pretend, as many Indian men did in public situations, that women were off limits. He was reserved and courteous with women but had a tendency toward a friendly, joking way with them.

She felt at ease with him, like she'd known him before.

"What do you think is going to happen?" She lifted her arms and drew her heavy, long hair to the side in front of her shoulder. She started to braid it slowly and absentmindedly.

"What?"

"About the girl. What do you think is going to happen?"

"I think they're going to screw it up. What do you think?"

"I think some white guy is into this and they're not going to find him."

They looked at each other, unsmiling.

"I think they don't want to find out. Maybe they already know who is involved. And they don't want to know any more cuz it's one of them."

"Yeah."

"I don't know . . . " He was standing still, watching her.

"What are you looking at?" Before he could answer she said, "Don't look at me like that."

He was going to say "like what?" but stopped himself because he suddenly found himself fascinated by the nearness of her.

As Aurelia stood still braiding her hair, she watched him drive away. She wondered if he was with anybody. She wondered what he meant when he said they would "screw it up." Who was "they"? Did he mean intentionally or because they were incompetent? Who knows about *cautious*, *devious*, she wondered.

Hermist enjoyed a good reputation. Didn't drink and carouse much. He had been happily married and a good father to his two boys, Greg and Chazz. His wife had died when the boys were in diapers and he had raised them since then with the help of his sister, Connie, and his mother's sister, a blood grandmother to the boys, and they tried to raise them in the Sioux way.

7

November 1, 1980
Selective Prosecution

"I been going to that sun dance down there at Pine Ridge, you know. I been there a coupla times now. Alls I want," the white guy with long hair was saying, "is to pray with them, with the eagle feathers and the blue feathers. You know, like you Indians do. I been having a lot of trouble lately and I need to straighten out my life."

Philip felt sorry for the white guy, whose thin white t-shirt was dirty and who looked strung out. Two of his buddies stood beside him and they looked pretty bad, too.

"I really think the Indian religion is where it's at," one of them said, nodding his head. "It's a real spiritual connection to the land. And the animals. I think I'm beginning to understand the coyote. And the bear."

To Philip this talk sounded pretentious and absurd. Who the hell understands the bear or the coyote, he thought with just a hint of contempt. These white guys are pretty strange, he thought. In spite of his immediate reaction he kept his silence.

They walked together over to Tony's car. Philip took his keys from his back pocket and opened up the trunk.

"I really want a spiritual life," the white man was saying. "I need it."

"Yeah. Well, I been using these," Philip fingered the longest perfect goldens with the red tips, "so they are in the sacred way.

But some of these here are extras." He opened a blanket that held an enormous number of feathers, plumes, both wings. He picked up a severed eagle head, saying, "A guy from Fort Thompson wants this for his traditional dance outfit. They sometimes use them for right in the center of the bustle."

He held it with great care for just a moment. Then put it back nestled in the plumes. He took, one by one, several tail feathers and one large fluffy plume and held them in his left hand.

"Here, I could give you these . . . "

"No, man . . . you don't need to give 'em . . . I got money."

"Here," Philip said again, as he held them out with one hand, put his right hand on the trunk lid, and slammed it shut.

"I got money." The white guy held out a hand full of several twenties. "Here . . . I been saving up. Here's two hundred."

Philip took the bills, folded them in half, and stuck them in his back pocket.

"You want some of this?" The white guy handed over a small plastic packet of marijuana, mostly stems. "Here's some weed."

Philip shook his head and moved away.

"I got more stuff . . . " Philip shook his head again.

As the white guy put the plastic bag back in his shirt pocket, he said, "Well, anyway, thanks. Thanks for the feathers. Thanks a lot. I really appreciate this . . . you know . . . "

As the trio of white men drifted into the darkness of tall grass and parked cars, Philip walked back toward the dance arena where Jason and Aurelia and Connie, his uncle Antony, and the kids were sitting in the chilly night breeze. He felt apprehensive for some reason he couldn't quite put his finger on, but at the same time he felt relieved. Now at least he could get some propane for the stove in the trailerhouse he shared with his uncle.

Philip wouldn't see the white guy and his friends again until two weeks later, in a courtroom in Sioux Falls when he was being arraigned on charges of selling eagle feathers. By then the guy had cut his hair in a neat style and was wearing a suit and was said to be an undercover agent from Salt Lake City, Utah.

"It's his word against mine," was Philip's rather lame defense when he talked to his family about his predicament.

"That's not too encouraging," said Aurelia. "Fact is, you poor Indian, nobody's going to believe you. You don't stand a chance."

But, more to the point, Philip said, "The sacrifice of the eagle and the religious use of feathers is all we have left. Them eagles was from my grampa's place down there on the Crow Creek. On the river. Harvey Big Pipe's place. On the treaty side, you can say that Indians are hunters and, therefore, we can hunt the eagle; on the Religious Freedom Act side, you can say that we have a right to believe and practice our old ways and help others to a way of spirituality."

He said that the charge didn't apply to Indians who are protected by treaty.

In court, the judge said, "The First Amendment is designed to protect religious beliefs but practices may be regulated by the state."

"So much for religious rights," was Aurelia's cynical response as she heard the judge's decision: Philip got a year's probation after the all-white jury found him guilty on all charges. And they fined him five thousand dollars, a sum that might as well have been five million, considering his meagre prospects.

It all happened so fast. When he got back to his grandfather's place, to the place of Harvey Big Pipe, he went out away from the river to an isolated place where he fasted for four days. He knew what he did was done because he needed a little cash money. And the need for money was not a good rationale for ethical behavior. He had succumbed to that need and was filled with regret. The sting that had apparently been in motion for several months had swept him up at the last minute.

He and other Indians who took a good look at the case knew that the publicity generated from this obscure little case was good for James Watt, a bureaucrat from one of the western states who flew hurriedly into Sioux Falls that month by private jet to announce the indictments to the people of America and South Dakota, who needed to know that he was protecting them and the eagles from Indians. Too, Watt needed to get the Sierra Club people, the environmentalists, off his back. To suggest that he was protecting the eagle was key to charging up the emotions of people who followed such cases in the newspapers and on television.

"But you *were* selling eagle feathers," said Aurelia, outraged and angry.

"Yeah. I know."

"You *were* indicted on eight charges of selling eagle feathers and six charges of selling migratory bird feathers."

"Yeah, I know."

"What kind of Dakotah Indian is that?"

"Yeah. But I didn't sell the migratory . . . "

"I know it was a sting. We all know that. Every Indian in the Country knows that! And we know they got you . . . But does any of this make you proud?"

Philip knew the question was rhetorical. He knew that she had come to the courthouse every day and had sat there in support of him. He knew she was saying these things for her own good, not his.

"That fellow, what was his name? Uh, Watt, Secretary of Interior, James Watt, he came into Sioux Falls, South Dakota, for your trial, just especially to let us know that a crime has been committed by Indians and that criminals like you will be prosecuted to the full extent of the law!"

Philip had been quickly convicted in a jury trial with not a single Indian on the jury of his "peers." His defense continued to the very end to be that he possessed eagle feathers lawfully, that the eagles were from his grandfather's place on the river, that these charges didn't apply to the Dakotah Sioux who are protected by treaties. As it turned out, Philip was one of nine Indians in South Dakota and four in Wyoming who had been rounded up in the sting operation. It was well planned and well executed and was rushed through the courts without much adversary opinion.

After this ordeal, Philip was ready to do something drastic— to leave, maybe. Leave this place behind. He went to his uncle's trailerhouse to start packing up his things and think about what to do. Maybe somebody would see him doing this drastic thing, packing up to leave. Maybe somebody would stop him.

"Yes. I'm getting out." Philip said to Aurelia when she saw what he was up to. "Every Indian homelands is the same. There is just too much slow, water-torture-like stuff here. I don't mean like police torture or like government incarceration or like banning or burning books or burning down churches or Ku Klux Klan crosses burning in the yard, no real things like that. Nothing so obvious or violent or in the open. If it was in the open, if they were burning books or churches, you could fight it. Indian life in America isn't like it is for the intellectuals in Africa or the political enemies in Iran where people are put to death. Places full of agents ready to kill you. It's not like that.

"Here in Indian Country you just waste away. You can talk to no one. Or you can talk to everyone. Talk yourself blue in the face. Yet, you can do nothing about the endless trials, the poverty, the abuse, the drinking, the joblessness. The laws they pass to steal your lands or take your kids away from you or prevent your religious and spiritual life. There is no one to even have a decent thoughtful conversation with because they say . . . what are you . . . just another whining Indian, hunh?"

"So, you're getting out . . . are you?"

"Yeah. Might as well. I guess I'll go back to Rapid City. Or Minneapolis, maybe. And I'll get a job. The Twin Cities. Yeah. That's a nice place to be. I went there once when I was on leave from the Army, you know, and I could find work there. I can always find work, doing something, you know. I can drive a truck or load or something."

He looked at her. Her hair, tinted grey now, fell about her face and down her back, straight and smooth until it turned under at the ends. Her eyes were slits, her mouth full. Her eyebrows were perfectly arched and her high cheekbones gave a beautiful symmetry to her dark face. She was always reading these days or had some sewing in her lap or, sometimes, she was sanding diamond willows into canes, her only claim to artistic tendencies now that she and her grandmother no longer collaborated. She had quit beading or making quilts. Sometimes he came upon her with Sarah in her lap reading or just resting, rocking the child with a look of contentment on her face. She was getting older and he knew she would never go back to his uncle, Jason, and he felt incredibly sad. She had been a good auntie ever since he could remember, a dependable, hard-working person, and he always knew that he could turn to her when no one else would listen. He looked away.

"I feel like I'm choking here."

"Well, you are choking here, Philip. I know you cannot stay here and live. I can see that you must leave. It's bad for me, too. But I have no wish to go to Minneapolis and wouldn't even if there was some chance of it."

She put her arms around him, leaned her head on his shoulder. He was a good relative and she'd known him since his childhood.

"You were making gestures all the time, Philip. You wanted to start a political conversation with those in power, find solutions, you wanted to help people. That's your mistake. You can't expect that kind of thing, you know, just have to deal with every day as though it alone mattered. Just the day itself. Because it does, you know. And you have to watch out for yourself because nobody else will. But the police. Now. They're after you now. And you'll never have any peace. I know you'll have to go. At least for a while."

"Yeah. It'll be okay. The problems aren't going to be solved in Washington, D.C., with the Senate Select Committee on Indian Affairs. I know that. I know how Washington is. I've been there, after all." He thought about the AIM days when demonstrations on the steps of the Capitol were attended by everybody, grandmas, kids, and all.

"Do they still just go out for a drink?"

"Sure. That's what they do. You know how it is. They all go to those meetings and gatherings then they leave and they have a cousin who works in Interior and they go visit her. And an uncle who pushes paper at the BIA. And they go out to his place for a meal. And then they have another drink. And then they take a taxi back to the airport.

"Things're not going to be solved here at home, either. Or at the state capitol. How to keep the governor off the Missouri River is on a par with how to get a dialogue going with politicians and their cohorts about anything at all. Public silence is a tool used very effectively by those politicians in Pierre, or in any county government meeting, or at the federal level. There is no dialogue about the return of stolen lands or the bettering of education for our children or the 80 percent joblessness that is all around us. Truth is, there is never going to be a dialogue. Especially about the land that they stole. And they are still stealing it even now, as we speak."

It's like the disappearance of the girl, thought Aurelia, remembering that August night, remembering the slim girl standing with her arms folded as if waiting for something or somebody. She had disappeared and no one except her relatives had said anything. The family came to town every day and went to the sheriff's office to see if any police were out trying to find her. They sat in the county offices, in the tribal offices, even at the Bureau offices in Aberdeen, and smoked cigarettes and then they went downtown and had coffee at a local greasy spoon and then they went home to bed and a sleepless night. And there was no dialogue, nothing done, no arrests, no one found guilty, no crime of record. Just a disappearance and a family grieving and the everlasting river lapping at its shore.

A day at the end of the month had been set aside to honor the veterans and at the same time all of the tribes of the Sioux Nation had organized a gathering that had a political agenda. This political meeting of the tribes was several weeks in the planning and all of the leaders were to be there.

For a while there had been very little talk concerning the Supreme Court ruling: "In 1980 the United States Supreme Court affirmed the findings of the Court of Claims, citing its conclusion that *'[a more ripe and rank] case of dishonorable dealings will never, in all probability, be found in our history.'* "

Newspapers and television stations across the country carried the news far and wide:

> *Sioux Nation*
> *Awarded Largest*
> *Land Settlement*
> *17. 3 Million*

Then the huge November meeting of the tribes of the Sioux Nation took place in the capital city of the state of South Dakota, at the arbor located on the grounds of the federal boarding school.

"It is now clear that a political solution must be found to settle the Black Hills claim," it was reported in the letter sent out from Pine Ridge. "Unlike other Indian Nations, bands and tribes, the people of the Sioux Nation have continuously and vigorously pressed their claim for the Black Hills from 1877 to the present time."

Every group was represented by a traditional speaker and they took turns saying what was on their minds. It was a charged-up, incredibly vital public expression of tribal sentiment. Some talked in English and some in the elegant language of the tribe. But all of them said, in one way or another, "The settlement must involve the restoration of federal lands in the Black Hills to the Oyate."

In spite of that, an Indian man, a Seneca Nation man, from the Bureau of Indian Affairs in Washington, D.C., announced that each tribal group (Oglala, Santee, Minneconjou, Yankton, Sihasapa, Hunkpapa, Crow Creek, and Sicangu) that had sent a representative was required to submit a plan for the distribution of funds, the payout authorized by the U.S. courts and Congress. He spent considerable time shuffling papers and talking about deadlines.

One by one, the native speakers got up to say that they had no plan for distribution of funds because they represented tribal people who refused to accept the money. The seventeen million was just money, after all, they said to one another and to the authorities of the United States Government and its collaborators the representatives of the Bureau of Indian Affairs, in contrast to the 1,300,000 acres of land which could restore them.

When the news of this meeting got out in the next few days there were even bigger headlines:

> *Sioux Refuse*
> *To Accept Payment*
> *For Black Hills*

All of the national television networks soon converged on the places where South Dakota Indians lived and worked, to get statements concerning this astonishing turn of events.

Philip, known by everyone there as the grandson of Harvey Big Pipe, stood in the arbor beside his uncles, Antony and Jason, that memorable day. He was very young and as a young man, he was worrying selfishly about his own personal predicament.

"I was questioned by the police. The sheriff. The FBI . . . " he told his uncles as speaker after speaker rose to reject the settlement. "I told them everything."

"But you *were* selling eagle feathers," Jason said irritably, trying to listen to the speakers at the same time he was listening to his nephew.

"I know. I can't say I wasn't. I told them everything. Very simple. Straight."

"What do you think they care about your reasons?"

Philip fell silent.

"This is a violation of Sioux ways, too, you know. Selling eagle feathers is unheard of!"

Philip sat through the rest of the meeting and felt quietly chastised. Still, he was encouraged by the men who talked on behalf of them all, the men now past mid-life who knew all the stories of the land, the old men who could look into the eyes of the government officials, show them the papers on which the treaty signatures appeared, the possessors of the rights that allowed them to continue as sovereign tribal people.

"We have fled from no one," one old and gentle man from Brule said in a soft speaking voice. Leaning on the arm of a young girl who appeared to be his granddaughter, he said, "We are most humble and we are proud and we have stood our ground and we do not accept your money."

Philip looked around and wondered if any of them, any of these men, had the shell medicines in their bodies that he'd heard about. He wondered if any of that notion about medicine had ever been true, or if it was just some kind of superstition. His grandfather, in the sweatlodge used to talk about the "shell in the throat" medicine, and the throwing it up and how it was given only to certain people. He wasn't even certain about how the words were said . . . *wamunha?* Something like that. Maybe it was peyote but he didn't think so; some of his relatives, and his paternal grandmother in particular, seemed to oppose that church and its dependency on a medicine that did not grow in their tribal places.

It was easy to believe in the traditional sundance of the people, because it was just all there. Everything about it could be verified in the land and in the tribal language. But there were other rituals that weren't so easily comprehended. He wanted to know of these matters and felt bereft when no one ever talked beyond just making a quick reference about these things, not even old Harvey.

Philip wondered about that white man who had been so sincere, who had needed the feathers. Who was he? Why would he pretend? Philip understood the feds and their need to be rid of the Sioux. But the white guy who had told Philip of his need for a spiritual way to live his life had seemed so sincere. So sincere. How could anyone believe anyone or anything? He felt like such a fool.

Philip wondered what he would do. He felt a terrible anguish about his own behavior and was hardly able to interest himself in the speeches. His uncles had a right to expect better of him.

The speeches went on and the sun sank from the sky and the people walked away from the round circle of the arena. The dancers and the singers with their drums would be here soon to replace the seriousness of the spokespersons. Aurelia and her children would be here and people would smile and dance until their exhaustion took them over. Aurelia would dance for the first time without her grandmother, who now lay gravely ill, unable to get well, unable to walk.

She would confide in Philip later that there was very little rational explanation for anything in this world. Whether you lived or died, whether you disappeared or not, whether the supreme court of the land was virtue or devil. Whether . . .

"It's like a flip of the coin, or the dealing of a card, or the turn of a wheel," she said, gesturing and smiling.

"No," said Philip with emotion. Angry now. "I won't buy that, Auntie! There has to be some rationale for this world!"

8

Looking Ahead

There was a flurry of political meetings attended by tribal people and organizations in the next several months and Philip decided, on the spur of the moment, to be a player. Maybe it was his Auntie Aurelia's uncommon and sassy comments about his behavior. Maybe it was his despair. Whatever it was, he put to the test his belief in the concept of nationhood for the people. He believed in tradition and talent, that to be poor and downtrodden and exploited and stupid was not the Dakotah way of life; that if, as he told Aurelia, "you use even half your brain you can be yourself! an Indian! and you can help in gathering all of the forces of a traditional people because we have the right to a decent future.

"Anybody who doesn't believe that," he said in anger, "can go to hell."

He didn't say it in an insulting way and he certainly didn't mean to insult her. Neither did she interpret his words that way. In fact, she found his anger encouraging.

The first meeting he went to set the agenda for his new political behavior. It was at the tribal hall. He walked in, a cigarette in his hand, his black pants pressed with a sharp crease, his white shirt open at the collar. It was the old boarding school uniform and he knew he looked good.

His sleek soft hair, pony-tailed, shone in the artificial light and he put out his cigarette at the door. Acknowledging greetings, he walked to the drum where his Uncle Tony nodded and he shook hands with the others. They knew what to do and so Tony started with a very slow beat as the people in the room fell silent, listening only to long minutes of the heartbeat of the drum. Philip, his voice high and strained, began the song of coming together and he was joined by the others.

They all knew, in spite of their hopefulness, that they lived in a country filled with a new people who did not know the old songs they sang or what the songs meant. They realized that theirs was now a country where *Apocalypse Now*, and *Grease*, and *Coal Miner's Daughter* played in rural theaters. Where Indians and whites were told in television commercials that they'd better use a certain kind of deodorant if they didn't want to lose a girlfriend or an imagined sex life. A country damned by tourist development that lured government officials into shameful money-making schemes based largely on greed and exploitation.

Reclining Bear, the old treaty man from Crown Buttes, spoke: *Nape che-u-za-pi.* "I want to shake hands with everyone here."

He spoke of the good times when children were fed and when they all knew what it meant to be Dakotahs.

He said this time would come again when their land was returned to them, that the thieves had now admitted their theft and that things all over the world would improve.

People listened politely and then they shuffled chairs toward the three tables at the side of the room.

"Hey," Philip said as he seated himself at the table with those who, like himself, imagined themselves to be politicos. "Hey, we need to come together and write down the legislation we want to promote. That's what we're here for."

The chubby Indian lawyer from Boulder seated next to him started handing out papers. "Here's a draft," the lawyer said as he went around the room, his fat hands deftly shuffling papers.

"You want your land back, you gotta do the work."

"The Bear Butte matter," said Philip, "could be settled by the state. They could just decide to return it. They could, you know, return it to the people they stole it from."

That got a few knowing smiles from around the tables.

"But," he went on, "for sure, the other, the Black Hills . . . that's something else. They want us to take the money. We won't. So you must come up with further arguments. We've come a long way on this . . . we've still got a long way to go."

He lit another cigarette.

"It's just that us Indians, us Siouxs, we think the world is inevitable. You know? Well, it's not. Not anymore. You gotta make your world if you're gonna live with the white man. Make it whatever the hell you want it to be.

"Right now," Philip went on . . . and then he seemed to change his mind, seemed to have an afterthought of sorts. "By the way, have you went by Bear Butte lately?"

He looked around the room and all eyes were on him.

"It's shit, man. Tacky little sheds and coops everywhere, abandoned cars and run-down trailerhouses. An American flag flies from a fencepost. You can see it from the road. Abandoned missile sites all along there! 'Adopt-a-highway' signs. What the hell is that? Adopt a goddamned highway! New Dawn Center. 'Rugs for Sale,' like some kind of Arabs at the market."

He waved his arms. "You cross the Belle Fourche River there, and there's a sign. Did you ever stop to read it? You know what it says?"

His fingers punched the air and his voice was filled with outrage. "It says: 'Bismarck-Deadwood 1876 Trail.' "

They stared at him from around the room.

"It says: 'Indians watched with envy the passing of their lands to the whites.' "

He stood up and said with a voice filled with anguish: "What the hell kind of history is that . . . the passing of their lands . . . *the passing of their lands?*"

His voice rose: "Envy? Envy? What the hell do they think thirty years of *war* was about? It's no goddamn accident that Fort Meade and Bear Butte are within seeing distance of each other. You get it? Does anybody *get it?*"

His exasperation was palpable and people in the room didn't know if he was mad at history, or whites, or them.

"So now," he said as he calmed down, "the broken-down bodies of Indians and veterans can be treated by the public health at Fort Meade and you can go to the top of Bear Butte and see the world. And you can talk about the 'passing of their land' like it was some kind of natural phenomenon, like the passing of spring into summer or summer into winter."

He paced. "And litter control is the message of the day, right? Adopt-a-goddamned highway," he said in an exaggerated tone.

"Shit," scorn was heavy in his voice.

The meeting lasted into the evening. Aurelia picked him up in Connie's car as the wind died down and darkness fell. He dashed toward her headlights, the wind whipping his pants, and he wiped his face as he got in and slammed the door.

"Let's go."

"Shall I drop you off at Tony's?"

"Yeah."

He examined her face in the faint light from the dashboard. A fine profile, her grey hair drawn away from a smooth, pale, oval-shaped face.

"Why didn't you ride with Tony?"

"Aw . . . hell . . . he's going into town."

They both knew what that meant.

At the meeting Philip had said, "The Sioux must find our origins by looking ahead, not behind us. We know who our mothers and our fathers are. We're not like some who claim not to know who their fathers are. Like them colonists who are looking at England. Europe. Or Spain. For their fathers."

To some it may have seemed like an odd paradox, since his mother, Clarissa, had rid herself of his father years ago and he, Philip, was one of the many who grew up with uncles and grandfathers instead of a father. Besides, he had been nurtured in a household run by a couple of women who were strong and influential: Aurelia, for one; his mother, Clarissa, for another. And his grandmother Big Pipe, as well. It was no paradox to him, though. He knew the men in his family as intimately as he knew any familial relationship, and he held that knowledge in great regard.

It seemed to him legitimate to say: "We know who our fathers are," even though he'd not spoken a word since childhood to the man who was his biological father. It was a philosophical matter accepted by him without question.

He had said then at the meeting: "To know your father in the native world, in today's plastic world, this New-Age world of earth goddesses and grandmother Moon, is to know you are not an immigrant. Not a colonist. Us Siouxs know that we are not just some obscure tribe in the wilderness, fatherless seekers of a colonist's definition in the New World. We never surrendered to those who came lately to this riverside and this prairie."

He had been talking to his fellow tribesmen about the nature of the Sioux world and its connection to the fathers of the Sioux universe.

"We know our fathers," he said over and over. "We do not seek them like these immigrants do and like their descendants do. Our fathers are all around us."

Heads in the audience nodded in agreement.

"We know our lands! And the rivers! And the Fathers all around us. They are all around us."

Sometimes he talked in English.

Sometimes in the old language.

He waved his arms.

It was the kind of oration that had always been essential to the people. It was the kind of meeting that white folks, if they had somehow stumbled into it or overheard its shrill voice, would have called foolish. Historians, when they overheard this kind of oratory, tended to call the Sioux the windbags of the Plains, not understanding the function of such convocations.

But Philip, a fatherless Indian who had grown up with uncles and grandfathers and the land all around, was adamant about his history. He was a young man who tried to do the right thing. A young man who knew failure but was filled with anticipation.

He was a young man who had been with the people and on the land all his life. He was curious and intelligent and making an effort to find his way. Only a few days before, he had sat at the back of the room during a meeting called by the state's Attorney General Meier. He was the only Indian to attend the white politician's community discussion of what was called "the adjudication of water rights" concerning the Missouri River. It had seemed to Philip then that the white politician was outlining a model that would allow white thieves to shape and articulate their right to steal the Missouri River water from the tribes.

Philip was very suspicious of their motives. It was nothing new, he believed. It had been going on since the beginning.

Later, the old treaty man, Reclining Bear, had been asked by Meier to address this group, as a way of "coming together." The old man began by recalling the time when the land and the river still meant what the myths of the Sioux people said they meant.

"After that time," he told the white folks at the gathering, "foreign soldiers roamed the plains. They killed, burned, looted.

"Afterwards, all our valuable things were put in museums in New York, Philadelphia. Our children were sent away from their homes to learn an alien language. Even the river itself has had to learn new ways of being."

The whites at the meeting were silent and everyone got in their cars and drove home.

"It doesn't matter what Reclining Bear says," Philip told Aurelia as they drove into the night. "Those people don't know what he means. They haven't got a clue!"

"I know," she replied. "It's like he has to be nice . . . civil . . . to his intellectual inferiors." She gripped the steering wheel and said, "It's so sad."

"Sad, yeah. But it makes me mad. Like . . . he has to suck up to people who'll never see the world as he sees it."

Silence filled the car as they thought about the lives of men like Reclining Bear, who tried to articulate a history and a way of life not so much different from other histories and other ways of life throughout the world, but ways unappreciated in a new world bent upon destroying them.

"And then," continued Philip, "you know what he told me? He said, 'Well, you can't complain . . . you are still living on your land. And the old time is forever lost. And what happened a century ago,' he said, 'it happened. It happened.' "

"Hmm . . . m." She didn't know how to respond.

"What's the answer, Auntie?"

She was quiet for a long time. She felt the urgency of his question.

Then, finally, she said, "I don't know, kid. I really don't know. But there is one thing I do know and you should remember: no one has the right to steal our land, the land that has been known by the Oyate since the beginning. No one owns the rivers where the spirits live."

His face was unreadable.

She felt her voice tremble. "They had no right . . . it's not right . . . no one has the right to kill the river . . . because . . . because . . . "

She couldn't finish.

"I don't believe in miracles, Auntie."

She didn't even ask what miracles he referred to . . . the return of stolen land . . . the survival of the river spirits . . . the . . .

"No. Neither do I." She turned to look at him carefully. "No," she repeated. "The age of miracles . . . the *ohunkaka* times, they are over with. That's what Reclining Bear was telling you. We must be realistic about that."

"But . . . but . . . " he struggled " . . . that doesn't mean that justice isn't possible . . . does it?"

"Yes. No. I mean, maybe that is the answer, kid."

"What? Justice?"

"Yeah. Just because a moral world is no longer possible, we must not assume that a just world cannot prevail."

He was silent.

"Yes?" she asked.

"Yeah," he said slowly. He nodded his head as though he was just beginning to understand. "They claim to be a just people. They claim to be a democracy that astonishes the world . . . like no other . . . ever!"

"Yeah . . . don't they?" She said it with assurance in a voice that suggested potential.

"I'll believe it when they return the Black Hills land that they have stolen . . . when it is ours again. By title. I'll believe it then."

He was serious. His statement was not rhetorical. It was not an accusation. It was a prediction.

He remembered what the old treaty man had said, that the old days have happened and they are gone forever.

Aurelia and Philip sat together in silence, her eyes looking toward the window from which she could see the fluvial hills. She saw in the distance the Missouri Breaks diminish and the dark hills begin to rise.

They drove the rest of the way to Tony's trailerhouse in silence, their thoughts careening wildly, beyond words, beyond solution.

9

December, 1980
The Diamond Willow

Aurelia gathered the kids, Hermist, and Connie together for an excursion out along the river and the creeks to seek out what she called "some decent willows," the kind she used for shaping and whittling into various kinds of crafts. It was early December and everyone was trying to look forward to the holidays when there would be a lot of cooking, visiting, and the children home from boarding schools. It seemed quiet, a waiting time. They noticed little winter birds in the trees, some light flurry of snow as they drove through town looking at the Christmas decorations.

Hermist, known in the family as a reluctant Christmas participant, was making snide comments in the back seat. As Aurelia and Connie ooh-ed and aah-ed about the Christmas lights, he was saying, "Hey, look at that! It's Las Vegas!" He encouraged the boys to make fun: "Look . . . there's more lights than a casino!!" They laughed and had fun and for the rest of the day Aurelia referred to him as "Bah-Humbug."

It had been months since Jason had driven Aurelia into Eagle Butte to stay with her grandmother during the recuperation period. The kids were doing well in school and Aurelia had been living on her grandmother's old-age check while the public health care center tried unsuccessfully to use various therapy methods to strengthen the old woman's legs enough for her to stand on her own and walk by herself. Aurelia had found a part-time job cooking at the tribal center and she walked by the river often and at length. She realized that Jason, too, knew that their lives had changed. She was busy away from the Crow Creek, for the first time trying to absorb a world outside of herself.

For a while the air coming off the river seemed to be warmed by the sun and it seemed like they could have the afternoon and nothing would interfere. Of course, anyone who knew them knew that part of the joy of this kind of trek along the creek was the joy of speaking freely. They found that they liked to talk as they walked and Hermist had taken to accompanying her on her walks, making time for that even as he kept to his own daily running habit.

They would talk about recent events; about the politics confronting the tribes; about the coming Christmas, her first in several years away from Jason; his sixth Christmas without a mother for his family since his wife died in 1974; the community planning for winter events, including the many activities that involved their children.

Because of the chill in the air, maybe this wasn't the best time, as Connie had complained, to go out looking for the willows that Aurelia said she needed for the making of diamond willow canes, but they finally agreed to go because the leaves were all gone and you didn't sink into the soft ground along the backwaters. And the snow had crusted so that you could move easily among the trees. Blue, Greg, and Chazz had dashed off as soon as the car stopped and were off exploring somewhere across the little bridge. They could be heard through the trees talking and shouting at one another. Sarah, trying to keep up, could be heard half-laughing, half-crying, "wait, . . . wait for me," as her brother and the others hurried down the creek, skating on thin ice in their huge Army surplus boots.

It was an arduous task and the grownups immediately fell to tramping among the bushes trying to find just the right kind of willows. After only a couple of hours, Aurelia felt like giving up. She was tired and was thinking that she needed to go back to Connie's to rest and fix a decent supper. As they walked, she asked Hermist, "Do you think that meeting of the tribes a few weeks ago will be a turning point?"

"I don't know," Hermist said. "I used to think that kind of thing would be useful, but now I don't know. You know, last summer that Judge Brown, that judge that presided over the AIM trials, you remember? He resigned."

"Why?"

"Just age, I guess."

"What's that got to do with anything?"

"Well, I mean . . . it just means that things have changed, you know. So it seems like there is no place for us to go, now, to get a hearing. The cases are over with, the newspaper guys have quit coming around. There's been a clampdown on the federal decision concerning the Black Hills case and the people are just expected to take the money and that's that. There's just nothing going on. Seems like we are all discouraged and silent."

"No," she said. "They're having meetings all the time."

"Oh, well . . . "

"I feel rather hopeful. You know, Philip . . . you know . . . my nephew? . . . he is going to meetings and keeping things going."

"Yeah. I heard."

"But what about those other claims? You know, about the stuff that went on at Pine Ridge way back in those days they now call 'militant' days . . . yes?"

"Yeah. And that's a big mistake."

"What?"

"Well, it's a mistake to clog the courts with all that crap and it's mostly the white people who live on the reservations and it sure won't do Indians any good."

"Yeah . . . the whole thing is so tacky."

"I think so."

"They want in excess of two million dollars for the damage that came out of the 1973 occupation?" Her voice rose as though she had asked a question.

"Already, they're calling the AIM guys terrorists." He laughed derisively. "Shit," he said in disgust. "Terrorists!"

"Can you believe that?"

He knelt to look at the skinny aspen, dead for a couple of

years and already soft and rotten. He straightened up. "A reject, here, I guess." She came over to inspect it and nodded her head and they walked on slowly.

It was true that churches and homes of whites were burned during that period of upheaval. Now, in securing justice for all, the principal plaintiffs were the white people, the Wounded Knee Arts and Crafts owners, victims who had lived on the reservation for decades; adding to the confusion, sometimes they were as penniless and helpless as Indians. These whites, who lived on Indian reservation lands as though they belonged there, had hired a Washington, D.C., law firm and were after compensation for their losses. No one asked how it was that whites had now become the victims at Wounded Knee.

"I read in the paper that there were one hundred and twenty-two innocent victims of the Wounded Knee uprising of 1974, one hundred and twenty-two plaintiffs that need to have money to make them feel better."

"One hundred and twenty-two innocent victims! Yeah. Mostly white people who don't belong there anyway." His voice was heavy with sarcasm.

"It's so absurd."

"That started last summer, didn't it?"

"I think so. I haven't heard how it all came out, but I'll bet you anything those people get their money. And the discussion about the return of stolen land, the reality that all kinds of people don't have decent housing, the education problems . . . all that will be forgotten."

To Aurelia, talk about political matters had always been a part of her interest and until she got to know Hermist, Philip had been her only confidant. Jason had quit discussing much of this kind of thing with her years ago. And her grandmother, so frail and in so much pain, had not held an insightful conversation with anyone for weeks or months about anything, let alone the political complexities of justice for Indians. Connie was just plain not interested.

The place in the community that Hermist had made for himself made him privy to a lot of news and that was one of the reasons Aurelia liked to talk with him. He worked in realty for the Bureau of Indian Affairs, went to school meetings with his children, attended the parents' meetings as well as the sports gatherings. He had proven himself a sort of reluctant role model as a single father for years. People respected him because he had not just given up his two boys to his female relatives to raise. Every kid on the reservation could say "my gramma raised me," but few could say, like Greg and Chazz, "my dad raised me." It was a distinction, all right, in this day of threatened family life.

Sunlight was fading in the lateness of the day and the wind came up, penetrating their wool clothing, but no one, as they tramped along the line of trees, complained. Aurelia carried three long, dry, dead willows, all with the appropriate "bumps," as she called them, toward the car. Neither Connie nor Hermist had found any.

Hermist reached for them and carried them for her, inspecting them closely. "Hey, these are pretty good, don't you think?

She didn't answer as she removed her gloves to light a cigarette, just looked at him, raising her eyebrows. She and he both knew that he knew next to nothing about what a good diamond willow looked like.

It was nearly the end of this Sunday and everyone was tired when they got in the car and drove back to Connie's place for a late supper. As Aurelia said goodnight to Hermist later, in one of her rare moments of expressing her true feelings, she said, "Thanks, Hermist. This was really a great day. I really appreciate your help."

"Even if I don't know what I'm looking for, hunh?"

She smiled.

"Really, it's good for Blue to have someone like you and your boys. We're really pretty isolated, you know."

He grasped the hand she held out and felt her warmth. He said, suddenly shy as a schoolboy, "Yeah. Yeah."

10

January, 1981
Was the Land Taken Illegally?

Christmas that year was a skimpy affair. Aurelia and the kids spent most of the day at the care center with Grandmother Blue and the rest of the Christmas vacation playing the games they'd received as gifts. She noticed the deterioration of her grandmother: the old-woman smell that pervaded her room at the care center and her body, the gaping, dry mouth and the vacant eyes.

If others were sad about the breakup of Jason and Aurelia, she was, too. She went about integrating herself in the new community, but half-listening, half-hearing what people were discussing, a newcomer to the Agency, a transient almost with nowhere to live permanently, a visitor while her grandmother was being treated at the tribal hospital. The voices she heard in the store, down the street, voices of people she didn't know or recognize, often seemed distant and disconnected.

One day in the store she overheard, "Does it strike you as ironic? or interesting? or strange? or worth noting at least that in the same year that the U.S. celebrates its centennial, the Sioux Nation defeats the U.S. Army at the Little Big Horn? That those two dates are one and the same?"

Two well-dressed Indians stood at the door, each holding sacks of groceries and pulling on gloves and raising their overcoat collars. They might have been nonresidents, home for the holidays visiting with relatives.

"Well, I don't know. Is that right? I never really thought about it."

"What do you think it means?"

"Damned if I know."

"Could it mean that revolutions aren't really anything at all except what people say they are? That soldiers and armies milling about and scaring the shit out of everybody, that they are just massacring and sacking, nothing heroic or patriotic? And after they're done they hang up the crucifix and begin orating and out of it all they describe a sacred revolution or an image of one and that's all it is, an image?"

"Hmm-mm."

"And then they write books and convince others and for a hundred years it goes on and, finally, they convince the world that what really happened was not a deliberate genocide but a way to make a nation?"

"Well, all that helps, don't it?" The man with a plaid scarf laughed sarcastically.

"It works, you know. Don't it?

"Then the revolutionary police turn into colonial police and it all starts all over again and someone else, some other people or nation, becomes the revolutionary?"

"Yup. Jeez, look at that sky. Son of a bitch. It's going to storm like hell tonight. Hope I'm not going to get stuck here in one of those notorious snowstorms."

The voices drifted away.

She looked up and saw Harvey standing next to the grapefruit counter. He saw her at the same time she saw him and they stood stock still looking at each other. He seemed thinner, greyer. Older. Much older than she remembered. He was unkempt and he had lost some more front teeth. Yet in important ways, he seemed the same, the same green overcoat with the fur hood, the same square cap with the flaps over his ears that he used in winter to take the place of his wide-brimmed Stetson.

But she noticed how he stood, stooped. He looked like he was tilting to one side, one shoulder higher than the other, and she knew that he was having a bad time of it. His back was bad again, as it had been off and on for years. Immediately, she felt guilty. Who is cooking for him now that she had left Jason? Was Jason cooking? Was he cooking for himself? Was Clarissa helping out? Probably not. She was a selfish neighbor and an even more selfish daughter.

His left hand touched the grapefruit and he said, "Looks good, don't it?" As though he had seen her just last week instead of months ago. He put several grapefruits in a brown bag, paid for them, and left the store. She went with him and held his arm as they stepped carefully down the walkway. She couldn't start any conversation because she had nothing to say.

Finally, after he settled himself in the pickup, he spoke, but in his nonintrusive way. He wouldn't speak about her absence, whether she would come home, whether she and Jason would . . . could . . . he didn't even ask about his grandson, Blue, or his granddaughter.

"We're here to talk about restoration of Black Hills land." He shifted uncomfortably, looked up the street and didn't meet her eyes.

"Yeah. I heard they were having a meeting. The Oglalas and the Minneconjous, isn't it?"

"Jason's here somewhere," he looked up the empty street. She wondered if he wanted her to look for Jason, but she didn't ask.

She simply stood with her hands in her pockets and he said nothing more.

After a few minutes, she put her hand on his shoulder and then turned and walked blindly down the street, forgetting about the things she needed at the store. Neither with hope nor hopelessly, she knew that Harvey missed her and that her life as his daughter-in-law was over, that their lives had changed enormously in the last few months. His wife had been dead now since 1974 and their eldest son, Sheridan, had disappeared years ago, and the youngest boy, Virgil, had been killed in Vietnam and it wasn't as though the old man didn't know loneliness or grief. Both Aurelia and Harvey knew life had to go on. Harvey was a man of great strength, fearless and dependable. She had appreciated both of those attributes. She missed him, too, but knew she would never go back to the Big Pipe home even after

Grandmother got well and even if the kids wanted to go home, and she didn't know why. All she knew was that she had stayed there as long as she could. She couldn't say exactly why, in the same way that one could not say why the girl had disappeared, or why silence permeated the Black Hills land issue, or why Grandmother could not get well. Some things, it seemed, simply had to be accepted or tolerated.

As she walked home staring into the grey sky, Marie Grey Bull's white husband, his car slowing down in the street, called out to her from the window.

"You want a ride?"

"Okay." Grateful for an interruption of her troubled thoughts, she got in and settled in the back seat. She and Marie smiled at each other, masking their natural suspicions of one another.

"How're you liking things here?" he asked.

"It's okay."

"How is your grandmother?"

"She's not any better. Her bones aren't healing."

"Yeah. That's the way it is with old people."

"Uh-huh."

Marie, with her usual air of superiority, turned and started taking stock of Aurelia's political views. She thought in her usual vapid way that Aurelia's connection to the Big Pipe family in recent years had made her an AIM sympathizer. A political person who might be unreliable or dangerous.

"Are you going to the treaty meeting?"

"I don't know. I just now heard about it."

"I'd go but they always treat James like some kind of pariah." She gestured toward her white husband.

"Um-mm." Aurelia wanted to stay noncommittal. Indian women marrying white guys was an issue with a lot of people, especially the old men who ran the treaty organizations. Maybe it was historical.

Marie raised her eyebrows.

"Jim, here, you know," she put her hand possessively on his arm and he turned and smiled, "ever since he came up here to teach the language, you know, they just can't quite accept it."

Aurelia said nothing.

"You know what I mean . . . that a white man can teach their language."

"I know."

"You heard?"

"Well . . ."

"What have you heard?"

Aurelia shrugged and hesitated. She thought, well, I didn't hear anything except the echo of old Tatekeya, that old man who had so much influence on my early life. He told me what Old Benno said, way back at the turn of the century, a prediction: "Just wait," he had said, "the white man will come back here and teach you your own language."

It was one of the many ironies commented on by the old ones. After all the years of punishing children for speaking their native tongue, getting them to forget it. After they have forgotten, the white man comes back and teaches them a version of the language that has no real cultural value anymore.

Aurelia felt uncomfortable. Marie Grey Bull was one of those ridiculous women, she thought. A petty woman. One who would fail to understand the bonds of culture and blood. Connectedness and shared values seemed just another of life's barriers, not something that could destroy tribal legacy. And the white-man husband. He was a nothing, a zero in Aurelia's eyes, though Marie had always taken great pride in marrying him.

Aurelia glanced over at him. Why on earth would the school have hired this man, she wondered silently, when there were a dozen people just down any road that could teach the language? He wore his hair long, had on faded jeans and an expensive suede jacket with beaded medallions attached to every pocket.

She gazed out of the window and commented on the coming snow and managed to escape any further discussion, thanking them profusely when they reached Connie's place.

"Marie and what's-his-name gave me a ride home this afternoon," Aurelia said to Connie as they prepared supper that evening.

"James."

"Hunh?"

"His name is James."

"Oh. Okay. Marie and James gave me a ride home."

Connie pursed her lips and shrugged.

"I don't want to start anything," Aurelia began, "but . . . "

"Yeah. Yeah. I know. He was a former VISTA worker, you know, who came to this reservation a couple of decades ago. Prior to that he had studied anthropology, then theology and even considered the priesthood."

"No kidding?"

"Yup. Then he met my enchanting sister, Marie. The stunning Indian beauty. Gave up everything to live on an Indian reservation with his Indian wife."

"What motivates people like that?"

"Who the hell knows!" After a little while, she said with a smirk, "Lo-o-o-ve???"

Hermist, standing at the door in his sweats chewing a fruit bar, joined in, "Well, why not?"

"Because," snorted Connie.

"It's something more weird than that. It's weird! Weird, I tell you." She was on a roll now, as she mashed the potatoes with a hand masher and talked, mashing and talking with equal vigor.

"I think he thinks Indians are ex-o-o-o-tic. Or, we're diff-er-ent. Or we're path-e-tic and we need him to help us."

"He's arrogant," said Aurelia. "That's what I don't like about him."

"And he doesn't have any men friends," said Connie. "Just hangs around with Indian women, you know."

"Oh, yeah? Look at me," said Hermist. "I'm hanging around Indian women."

They ignored him.

"Have you noticed that, Aurelia? He just hangs around women."

"Yeah," and she began to laugh. "He even talks like us, and he doesn't even know how hilarious he sounds."

Hermist wouldn't give up. He moved close to Aurelia, leaned an elbow on the counter where she was cleaning radishes, and looked sideways at her.

"I don't know," he said with pretended seriousness. "I like hanging around women."

He picked up a radish and chomped it down noisily. "Nothin' wrong with hanging around Indian women," he repeated.

They knew the potential for their conversation was over with, that he wasn't going to let them get into some serious gossip.

"Hey, brother," said Connie, "go call the kids. Supper's ready."

He straightened up.

"Get 'em over here at the table. Do you want coffee?"

"Nope," he said. "I got a meeting to go to." He took his watch from the zipper pocket on his shirt and slid it on his wrist. "No thanks, ladies, can't be here for supper. Looks good, though. I'm a little late already. I'll be back at nine to get the boys."

He left and the family gathered at the supper table.

11

February, 1981
River Gods

The day was breaking and the brightness of the sun reflected through heavy clouds. The day wanted to be warm but there was a persistent morning chill in the air. It was one of those days that seemed a contradiction or a dilemma to those who were looking for clear signals.

Aurelia's daily visits to the rest home now became increasingly dreary, and this day was no different. These days could only be a prelude to what she would consider the worst of times and a personal calamity that would be unbearable. Even though the grandmother suffered from spells of dizziness that kept her in bed, and palpitations of the heart and an exhaustion that would have made anyone else impossibly irritable, she did not talk of her physical ailments. In fact, she talked of secrets and the past in a private calm that seemed almost eerie. She talked softly, as though to herself, yet with the implication that what she said might be interesting to a public audience out there somewhere. Maybe it was like the animals outside her window were listening, as she had often claimed. It was a belief of hers that forces in the world listened in to the conversations humans had with one another. She often told Aurelia to be careful about summer outdoor conversations because the snakes, the primordial creatures that preceded even the birds, wanted to possess human knowledge. "It's good that it's February, she said, "the moon of . . . " and her thoughts drifted away.

As Aurelia watched her grandmother wither away, saw for a fact that the old woman's legs were refusing to get their strength back, she listened in despair to Grandma's favorite current subject: semi-lucid recitations of the Santee way of death, what to do, how to confront the foremost challenge of life.

"It is what we always did when someone died. It's what I want you to do for me when I die," the old woman said. "I will have only one request. I want you to go to the river to get the cottonwood trees that they use to make burial scaffolds. You will have to find someone who knows how to do this. Because hardly anybody remembers. Hardly anybody knows anymore that when the *unktechis* made the spirits they were made in water and of water. River water. Rain water. Water older than the dirt we walk on. The stars were made this way, you know. And that's how come it is up to the cottonwoods to tell the story and help the Dakotahs."

She was referring to myth. She was telling about the connections, the way all things are related to all other things.

For the old lady to suggest that she could be buried in the old way was simply outrageous and it troubled Aurelia. The old ways of burial had been outlawed by the federal government for a hundred years. The old woman was fantasizing. She was out of her mind. The very thought that her grandmother might no longer be reliable as a storyteller frightened Aurelia, who had always considered her grandmother the most sane and realistic of anyone. She knew, too, that storytelling was at the heart of historical teaching and that to get the story wrong was to lose history. But then, only so much can be expected of the old ones. Maybe it was time for Grandmother to say anything she wanted, to fantasize and to make up her own stories, to transcend whatever earthly understandings had confined her.

"Everybody used to know but hardly anyone knows anymore," the grandmother was saying, "that the first search made by the *unktechis* away from their place of origin was the search for dry land and the search for *wi yo hi ya n pi,* which refers to the coming toward them of the sun from the east. And they would say *wi yo h pe yata,* which refers to where the sun goes down. Everything would come from the east so fast and go toward the west so fast that it sounded to the people like a waterfall."

She paused and her breath came hard.

"And the cottonwoods would grow there. Along the river. They would grow there and eventually, either when you die or when you come upon them in your dreams, *they will reveal themselves as human beings* that live and thrive along the river. I have seen the trees so I know it is true. And I have seen them as humans in my dreams, too. So I know it is all true."

She was toothless and the edges of her eyes seemed crusty, dry yet weepy. Her large nose seemed even larger in a shrunken face discolored from years in the sun and a failing body. Her blistered lips shone.

"We have been a water people," she said. "Dakotahs. Yes. Yes. We are Dakotapi. They used to call us *hoganasinsinotonwan.*"

It was a word Aurelia hardly knew the meaning of, hadn't heard for years, but she knew that it connected the Sissetons to the fish, suggesting shiny fish-like scales, a word almost lost in the distant past.

The old woman was rambling. Talking to herself. And her voice seemed far away.

"Before you cut the tree you must sing the song that belongs to them. She began a high crooning, sometimes in English, sometimes in Dakotah:

> *He created it for me enclosed in red down*
> *He created it for me enclosed in red down*
> *White ash covers the buffalo skull*
> *It is true*
> *It is true*
> *He created it for me enclosed in red down*
> *He created it for me enclosed in red down*

It was a soft sound that filled the room with both melancholy and pleasure.

"Next time you come, Granddaughter, you must bring new sage."

Even though it was not possible this time of year, Aurelia answered, "Yes."

Together, they sang:

Takan he miye do
ma wakan he miye do
(I am so mysterious)

They clasped each other's hands and were amazed, and though they didn't see one another clearly, they smiled and felt restful.

These kinds of talks were almost nightly recitations now. The old grandmother could talk of nothing else now except death. At last Aurelia felt all right about why she wanted to weep every time she saw the dead trees still and white, the dams and the swift water and the seething foam made at the spillways. The vast emptiness caused by the destruction of the river. It was because she felt empty-handed as she looked into the future, and as she looked into her grandmother's pale, watery eyes. She knew how weak and helpless they all were. It was explainable now and it had to be faced up to, so why not weep? Yes. Why not weep?

"If you sacrifice *shunka*," the old grandmother said relentlessly, "you must paint him blue before the sacrifice. It is the right thing. The kettle is mysteriously placed in the center of the west tipi and there is a dance and you must paint yourself. You must sing: *'dewakana kinuktge de wakan do. yo o ha e ho ho ho,'* and if you sing it long enough and with your heart, the mystery will appear. And it will be a good thing."

Eventually, before the old woman died, she quit talking in English altogether as she told of Sissetowan myths of life as she knew it here on this earth:

"Sunka kin he, tokaheyapi he ehan," her eyes closed, her mouth slack, *"tokaheyapi he ehan, wowic'adapi kin he. Oyatepi ob ic'imani Makata-wic'oni tec'a hed hdipi."*

The dog, a primordial figure, it is believed, accompanied the people on their journeys in the present world.

She looked like she was asleep, like she was never going to wake, like she had just given it all up. So easily. Without pain and without regret. Her words were slow and clear and precise.

Aurelia held her grandmother's hand and felt warm and rested. Her head was tipped forward, nearly touching the old lady's legs, wasted and bony under the blankets. Would the world survive this old woman's absence, she wondered. She didn't think so, and because she didn't think so she listened to the well-worn, familiar story and knew that it was a way for Grandmother to prepare herself for what was to come.

Throughout the afternoon, the story unfolded and Grandmother's recitation of the figurative lives of the Sissetons filled the room:

Sunka toked taku unspe kin he TOKAHE, wic'as'ta tokakeya he, WAGAG'A, hec'a MAKATA-wic'onipi he ehan, etanhan ic'u.

He got his instructions from Tokahe the first man, a creator, during the primordial period. He protects, guards, follows. He is a carrier and is obedient.

Anakiks'in, awanyanka, ihakam u.

He is a carrier and is obedient.

Watoks'u q'a waanag'optan.

It is said that he carried Tokahe out of the primordial world so that no one in the present world except the Sacred Dog knows of Tokahe's whereabouts and no human being has seen Tokahe since that time.

Dec'ed oyakapi, Sunka he, TOKAHE yuha ahdi, ic'imani Makata-wic'onipi he ehan, hec'ed tuwena nakahah'ac'n Makata-wic'onipi, es'ta, Wakandapi-Sunka is 'nana tokiya un kin he sdoye kte, tuka, Oyate wic'as'ta unpi he tohnina TOKAHE wayakapis'ni anpetue dehanya, hec'etue nuwe, Mitakiya.

Grandmother Blue got worse on the fourth night, but Aurelia would not allow them to give her morphine. She sat for two more days until finally Blue came into the room and said in a very formal voice, "Mother, you must come home."

Aurelia shook her head. "Come over here," she said.

Together they listened for the old grandmother's breathing. "She doesn't know who I am," said Blue.

Grandmother's eyes, though they were clouded and sightless, widened when she heard his voice.

"*Taku? Taku? Mahpiya?*"

She felt for his hand and held it for the longest time. She held tight to his strong, boyish hand and then relaxed. Held tight and then relaxed, as if she were touching his young life and savoring it. Finally, she let it go and said in English, "You must never let the river go without me."

She lay back and closed her eyes.

At the Catholic funeral a few days later, Blue asked his mother what his great-grandmother had meant about the river.

"I don't know," she had to admit. "It's just that the river is a lifeway, a place where the spirits reside, a place of origin."

"But, Mom, you can never stop the river," he said in a puzzled voice.

"Yes. You are right. You can never stop the river."

Two days after the old woman's funeral at Crow Creek, a not-unexpected event attended by everyone in the community, Aurelia was in her grandmother's mobile home near the Big Pipe place, cleaning and packing up the belongings of a long life now ended. This was the thing to do when a long and satisfying life came to a close and it was not altogether unpleasant for Aurelia to handle with care the things that had been saved, the things that her grandmother had collected and cherished. It was a task that was undertaken alone. These were the things that would be part of the giveaway feast a year from now.

Unexpectedly, Jason appeared at the door.

"What will you do now?" he asked.

"I don't know," she answered.

He stood in the doorway as she drove away.

12

April, 1981
Talking and Dancing Is No Small Thing

Connie's house became Aurelia's refuge after the death of her beloved grandmother. She went nowhere for months. She wore the same thing every day, her shiny black jacket and jeans and scuffed cowboy boots. She seemed beyond time, beyond grief.

Blue spent his days and nights, more time than he spent at Connie's, with Hermist and his boys, staying at their place for weeks. Sometimes he didn't see or talk with his mother for several days at a time. Sarah and Connie stayed out of Aurelia's way and Jason did not come to see them after the funeral. In the busy lives of the community, the slight dark woman was hardly noticed. The days went on this way in the winter of 1981 and it was the longest winter of her life.

One spring evening she used her inability to forget about the loneliness as an excuse to drive into town and go to the Silver Spur. She passed Hermist running and this time he looked up and waved, but she drove on as if she hadn't seen him. She went to one of the few places in town where you could sit at the bar and "drown your sorrows." In fact, on the mirror above the counter a sign displaying that motto in huge red letters hung in the shadows of the dimly lit saloon. As an accompaniment to the slogan, a group photo of likely candidates holding up a huge, slick, and watery glass of foamy beer surrounded a scantily clad blonde with a big smile.

This was a place that often started gathering in the lonely as well as the sociable about four o'clock in the afternoon, but Aurelia had never before come here and as she looked around she began to realize how noisy and inappropriate it was. It was hardly the place to go if one wanted to contemplate a genuine and late stage of grief but, feeling desperate, she ordered a beer and listened to the mournful cowboy music and took the time to indulge her heartbreak.

She sat alone in the little country bar full of white people, men mostly, strong-armed, thick-legged men who never looked anyone in the eye. These were people who liked to stay by themselves in specific groups who knew their place. There were certain cliques of the hard-working people who could tell stories of when their granddaddies first came here, who settled where first, what the past looked like to the pioneer children of immigrants. Aurelia did not look up, nor did she see the stare from the watery blue eyes of a young white man, tall and curly haired, his hands folded in front of him, his face expressionless, a kind of baby face, round and smooth.

Just as she ordered her second beer she looked around the room and saw Hermist at the door.

He stopped at the cola dispenser in the corner and put in several coins. Then he sat down on the stool next to her, a can of 7-Up in his hand.

"What're you doing?"

"Oh, nothing."

They were quiet for several minutes.

"You know," she began as she looked into his face, "she never did say 'I want to die.' She didn't want to die, you know. She didn't."

Hermist sat close to her. Too close, his knees almost touching hers. She moved away a bit. "She was going to . . . going to . . . "

But what was the old woman going to do? Was this just more of Aurelia's fantasy, that her grandmother had had something yet to do on this earth? Something undone?

Her eyes were moist and they looked to Hermist like the eyes of a wise but deeply troubled woman.

"How 'bout a dance?"

She felt momentarily uncomfortable but wiped the sweat from her hands on her jeans and got up from her chair. She walked with the walk of a confident and composed woman to the side of the tiny dance floor. They stood for several minutes making selections at the jukebox.

"I didn't know you knew the old boarding school stomp," she said as they began to dance, doing something old, some shuffling from the fifties that required them to actually touch each other occasionally—nothing like the new dances being done by those around them, the can-of-worms kind of dances where you just squirm and wriggle like all the other worms. Their dance was rhythmic, almost sensual, careful and slow.

As he deftly took one hand and turned her around a couple of times, he said with a smile, "Thought I was too old for that, huh?" His hands were warm.

"I didn't know you ever came here."

"There's a lot of things you don't know."

"For sure."

"I'm a great dancer," he said, smiling and showing off, shoulders and feet in perfect time. "Didn't know that, did you?"

"Nope. Didn't know that!"

They danced until she could smell his sweaty body, like they were driven, like they knew a story between them that couldn't be put into words. Neither of them spoke another word as they danced. She let him hold her close for some moments and wished that she could tell him something, anything, everything, like it used to be with the old man, with Tatekeya, the old man whose name was translated as "wind-belongs-to-him," the old man who had been her first love.

Later, seated at the table, she began to tell him some of the things she had on her mind. Things she would never have shared with anyone because they were words of despair, anger, self-pity, whining words that would have humiliated her had her tongue not been loosened by alcohol and grief. She ordered another beer and then another. And another. She wept and talked, and it went on and on until finally she was slurring her words, incoherent and loud and uncaring. She stumbled to the door. It was midnight and they had been there eight hours. Hermist followed her out to her car and helped her inside. Then he drove her back to Connie's place, stunned at what he had witnessed and ashamed that she was now silent, sitting with her head hanging in a drunken stupor. He was embarrassed for her and for himself.

Neither of them had noticed, as they pulled away from the dingy bar, the young white man with watery blue eyes and curly hair and a smooth baby face who made his way in the shadows to a green pickup streaked with mud and dirt.

13

April, 1981

Aurelia, a woman isolated from much of what was happening around her, knew as she turned the pages of the calendar and as April came along that this was a month that claimed to be like no other. She knew that everyone said so: poets, songwriters, politicians. She knew she was simply living this spring from one day to the next, her life as dry as the dry wind that swirled around her. Indeed, during this Dakota April, the month of promises failed to bring the badly needed spring rain, and instead delivered only the relentless wind and dust.

The State B wrestling champions were honored in a spring festival and parade on a downtown main street and Aurelia with her children and Hermist with his boys stood in the wind, the chilled, yellow air permeating their limbs and bones.

Carcasses of winter storm-killed livestock were hauled off to be burned so that the farmers could start their spring plowing. It was the worst winter cattle loss in fifty years.

The body of a fourteen-year-old girl was found in a cornfield and everyone at first thought it was the pretty girl missing since May, but it wasn't. It was a different girl. She wore nothing but a flimsy shirt and heavy socks and her body was covered with dust. Men from the neighborhood were questioned. All denied any involvement and the girl was buried with no further comment, no further investigation.

The drought was noticed first by the prairie dogs. Near

Mahto the little creatures moved into new places, relocating to build their little towns in new ground, hoping to survive even as others crowded in on them. They darted in and out of their prairie holes and barked at one another in anguish and fear.

Usually the farmers just ignored them, but when the grass got scarce and there was no water to help the corn grow, the little creatures became more noticeable as pests. With no irrigation in sight, someone had to take the blame, and the prairie dogs were as culpable as any scapegoat.

"Yah . . . we can use poison," said the farmer, puffing toward the paintless barn where he kept his equipment.

"Yah . . . I've used zinc phosphate before. It's real good. Ninety-eight percent kill in the infected areas."

"Boy, it's real dry out here." Every step was followed by a cloud of dust.

"Yah. And these sons-a-bitches only get worse when it's dry. Seems like they start to multiply even faster."

"They start eating each other, you know. A female will go eat the offspring of another female."

"Well, I don't know if they eat them. But they sure as hell kill each other's offspring."

"If they're gonna do that when it's dry, why not just let them kill each other off as the drought gets worse?"

"Nah! That's too damn slow and you can't never tell."

They walked on with the sprayers in hand.

"Look at that . . . "

They saw a prayer circle, a formation of rocks that looked as old as the land itself.

"Looks like one of them Indian prayer things."

"Yah . . . I s'pose they used the dogs, too, in their goings-on. They're still real superstitious, you know. About the dogs."

"The cattle losses were real bad last year and now this spring there's no water. Seems like everything's against us. I'm waitin' to git into my fields. I don't know exactly what to do."

"Maybe we'll have to do like them marijuana growers, hunh?"

Their laughter was loud and derisive.

A plane loaded with 25,000 pounds of marijuana had gone

down in a field beside the Missouri River and the white men involved were found to be from bordering states.

"Move to Nevada or Minnesota, hunh?"

"Well, I guess so. At least they got enough water to grow marijuana!" They laughed again, together in their misery.

Seriously, one younger farmer said, "That takes a lot of water, don't it?"

The others took it to be a rhetorical question and said nothing.

The Attorney General of the state had called another meeting to discuss the water situation for white farmers who lived near the Bad River, the Cheyenne River, and the White River. He was concerned about the groundwater rights of the western two-thirds of the state and the Black Hills, now that the Supreme Court had said that certain lands in that area had been "illegally taken" from the Indian tribes.

The meeting was called a "drought meeting," but in reality it was a meeting to adjudicate water rights, and it was serious business to the state officials who needed, again, to defend themselves against the Indians. It seemed to some to be the very function of the landscape as the whites saw it now, the vision for themselves as land barons.

Nevertheless, no one wanted to talk about the "Winters Doctrine," as they didn't want to talk about any troubling thing. This was a turn-of-the-century legislative pronouncement first enunciated in the Upper Missouri River Basin, which again termed the tribes sovereigns who, after the wars, agreed to go upon reservations and in the process retained for themselves rights to the use of the water and power to administer, control, and exercise those rights independent from outside control or interference.

The girl was only fourteen.

She hung out her thumb and grinned when the pickup slowed down.

"Where you going?"

"Into town. Can I get a ride?"

"Sure."

She sat between them and was quiet. She held her head

*down and looked at the flat-heeled black work boots, worn and
greasy.*

They rode in silence for several miles.

The truck stopped.

"Get out."

"What?"

"Get out. Here. NOW!"

His voice was harsh.

"And, you little whore, you better run for it!"

*She stumbled down the ditch and crossed the barbed-wire
fence. Looking back over her shoulder, she saw them coming.*

"Run, goddammit."

She turned and ran. Heard heavy footsteps behind her.

*Tackling, he grabbed her ankle and she felt a blow on her
right temple as her head struck a rock. She knew nothing more
after that.*

At the very moment the girl ran for her life, and the prairie
dogs were being annihilated on the South Dakota prairie, an old
water rights lawyer from Washington, D.C., was meeting with
the tribes in Rapid City, South Dakota. His grey suit hung on his
frail frame and his fingernails were broken and yellow. He was
a white man who was considered by his colleagues to be a man
of estimable intellect and integrity. At the newly built Holiday
Inn, festive in its Easter regalia, he was saying: "It is an ongoing
practice to devastate the Indian Tribes today. The Secretary has
said that under the McCarran Amendment the Tribes are
subjected to state court jurisdiction in regard to their rights to
the use of the water. He is wrong and we all know it. The Indians
are right now in irreconcilable conflict with politically powerful
water users who are claiming rights under state law."

The wind streaked across the eaves of the hotel building,
situated on a knoll that could look directly at the blackness of
the far sacred hills a few miles in the distance. The old man's
wavering voice was heard throughout the carpeted room: "You
tribal people must expose the deadly consequences of being
subjected to state court jurisdiction. There must likewise be
exposed the devastating consequences of federal officials

practicing deceit upon the Native American tribes under the guise of 'settling' conflicts among the Tribes and non-Indian claimants. These matters are often the direct result of the Secretary of the Interior's violations of the tribes' vested and reserved rights for the benefit of Federal Reclamation Projects or similar projects."

Harvey Big Pipe, leaning heavily on a cane, and his son Jason, pushing the blind Santee spokesperson John Tatekeya in a wheelchair, made their way slowly toward the podium where the old lawyer stood talking with audience members.

They shook his hand and thanked him and went away.

14

April, 1981
Heavy with Silence

Philip was selected to go with several others to a private meeting in Washington, D.C., arranged to take place without fanfare in the Senate Office Building.

On the morning he was to leave from Bismarck, he slept late, a persistent cough bothering him enough to interrupt a good night's sleep.

"Nephew," said Tony, handing him a bottle of whiskey, "here, take this. It'll cut that cough in no time."

"Sore throat," croaked Philip as he pulled on his best boots, fingering the crisp collar on his shirt, ignoring his uncle's offer.

Tony, hung over and remorseful, sat on his rumpled bed with his elbows on his knees, his hands dangling.

"In 1881, you know," Tony began, in the voice of someone just sobered up, "in the spring, in April, just like this," he looked vacantly out the window, "fur traders and Indian chiefs met on the banks of the Moreau. Crazy Horse. Sitting Bull. The LaVerenderyes. Red Cloud, Struck-by-the-Ree."

He fell silent.

Trying to show some respect even though he was a bit disgusted with his uncle's recent behavior, Philip joined in. "Yeah? Hunkpatis and Oglalas and Ihanktowan, hunh?"

"Yeah."

"So?"

Philip brushed his hair and slapped some oil on his palms and ran his fingers through his hair over his temples. Quickly, he wrapped his pony tail in an elastic band.

"1881," mused Tony. "They were meeting, making speeches. Committing the crime of subverting the public order."

He spoke the last words as though he had just read them from the dictionary.

"Oh, yeah?" Philip turned and looked hard at his uncle and smiled. "What are you saying?"

"Oh, nuthin'." He looked up and his eyes were dark and unreadable. "Nuthin', really . . . except it's dangerous when you're considered a menace to the public order."

Philip said nothing.

"I oughtta know. I just about got throwed in last night." He laughed, muttering, "public order . . . public order."

Philip turned to leave, coughing, blowing his nose.

He decided to ignore this veiled, mysterious talk, yet the irony did not escape him. He just didn't have time for it this morning.

"Man! I'm gettin' one hell of a head cold."

"Here," said Tony again, following him out of the bedroom, still offering the bottle of whiskey.

"Nah! I'll get something at the drugstore." Philip swallowed two aspirin while standing at the sink in the kitchen.

"Here's my ride, Uncle." He peered out the window.

"What they say is 'promises, promises.' " Tony's voice droned on as Philip saw his ride stop in front of the little trailerhouse.

"I'll see ya."

"Yeah. I'll see ya."

15

May 4, 1981
Along the Banks of the Missouri River

The old white farmer would have missed it entirely had it not been for the sun. He was out in his pickup looking for some three or four steers, driving slow, jerking across the new furrows, careful to stay toward the edges of the field near the fence line. It was early, the sky was clear. Where the fence was down he drove carefully, hanging one arm out of the window and looking for tracks along the soft, mushy shoreline, a cigarette hanging from his lips, long grey hairs on his neck covering his greasy collar. The sun shone on something white, something long and white. Something long and white. He stared. Something . . . something . . . long and white.

For just a moment, he felt deeply frightened. When he could move, he put his foot on the brake, got out, and hung on the door for a few moments more. Then he walked toward the object. Slowly. He was filled with dread. Now he could see that it was the skeletal remains of a human.

The skull was devoid of flesh but it still had long black hair, matted and dirty, covering its hollowed-out face. His eyes narrowed and he knew instinctively that he should get away and get the police.

It was nine months after she had been shot five times and left for the fishes that the old rancher found what the coroner called "skeletal remains" covered in what her relatives and an old grandfather called *mini wi to ye,* frog spittle or the green that collects on stagnant water.

They all knew who it was. They all knew it was the missing Indian girl, missing all winter, since last May. Now they saw that the body had endured one season of the frozen river and then washed up in the thaw of the hottest spring months they'd had in years, exposed to the sun and the wind. And exposed to the unrelenting glare of the reality of violence in a country where Indians and whites meet, where crimes of hate and stupidity are rarely solved. In a way, it represented the kind of crime well known to Indian people all across America: the thefts of land that are never acknowledged nor settled, the claims that fall into deep silence for decades, the failures in attempting to find answers to the simplest questions, the lack of appropriate solutions. Mysterious deaths and silences were nothing new here.

Fluctuating reservoir waters had been rising and falling for more than two decades along this river and they often left slick muddy beaches or soft, devastating pollution in alluvial soils. For eight hundred miles, from Fort Peck in Montana to the Yankton reservoir near the Nebraska, South Dakota, Iowa borders, along the entire length of the Missouri River Power Project, aquatic vegetation and huge timber stands had been destroyed by the monster dams and reservoirs. Bacteria attacked whatever the water held for any period of time and quick destruction of the natural world was noticeable. Life and death in this environment seemed unaccountable.

North of town and along the shoreline where the body was found, the waters had grown thick with fallen cottonwoods, and farm and ranch dogs lapping along the shore often limped home only to drop dead with swift and unaccountable infections. The unsuspected bacteria of unknowable tidal traffic, which had held the precious body of the murder victim for almost a year, now had taken its measure.

Fallen cottonwoods, all manner of driftwood and tree roots littered the shore for hundreds of miles, looking for all the world like the war carnage left after a massive battle. Stiff skeletons of trees still stood as surviving clumps up and down the river even twenty years after their roots were drowned. These fallen remnants had been amongst the live trees often sacrificed by the Sioux people to build the scaffolds that would hold in a sacred manner the remains of deceased human beings on their spirit journeys into the next world.

Now the sacrifice of the fallen trees seemed a useless waste. They had not held the body of the young girl in a sacred way, safe from marauders. No songs had been sung for these fallen remnants. No prayers had accompanied their demise. They, like she, were swamped and decayed, victims of those destroyers who knew nothing of the consequences of a lifeless river.

The discoverer of this horror stood helplessly, his wrinkled face a mask of tragedy, as the sheriff and his deputies dragged a board toward the spot, lifted the remains with shovels and placed them in random order on the carrier. They also picked up five slugs.

"*Mini wa ti co ga*" (the scum on stagnant water, water moss) wept the victim's male cousin, who had come in one of the sheriff's cars.

He covered his mouth with a cloth and refused to go near. "What shall I tell her mother?"

He looked across the expanse of the inlet and imagined the miraculous beings rising up, their desires to smell the sweetgrass driving them toward the surface away from the mythic round lodges so far, so deep in the water. It was late afternoon and he wondered if they would all be destroyed.

The officers covered the bones with a tarp and carried the skeleton to the ambulance and shoved it inside. They drove to the coroner's office at the Kurtz Funeral Home, housed in one of the fine brick buildings in this northern plains white-man's town, population 5,940.

No one would know for nearly twenty years who was responsible for this outrage, what had happened to the young girl; that she had been brutally beaten, raped, and killed and then disposed of in the choppy river like so much refuse. In retrospect, it is possible to speculate that it must have been done by those who possessed a deeply felt hatred, a racial hatred of

Indian womanhood, their faces hot, their large white hands grasping and cruel, their feet and legs flailing in the coarse dirt, the smell of exploding gunshots choking their lungs.

No one except Indians connected the atrocity to the matters of racism, to the long simmering hatred of one race toward another, to the matters of destination and ambition and journey's end. Aurelia, as she would come to think about the atrocity years later, remembered Tatekeya's grief concerning the changing of the river, his notion that this despoiling of the river was one of the vain and foolish and terrible things that humans are capable of if they have no history. Tatekeya had often told her of the people's suffering.

"We are interviewing people," said the sheriff, his thin bearded face in the shadows, "we have no suspects."

16

News

Hermist left the Bureau office as soon as he heard the news that the body of the missing girl had been recovered from the river and he began to run, unhurried, to his sister's house. He fell into the familiar jogging rhythm that years and years of habit had made prosaic. He was unnoticed. Alone.

It was eleven in the morning, and a warm rain was falling, soaking everything; a long overdue and welcome rain beginning a new season. A new time. A time of hope. It would encourage the dirt farmers of the region, who would think that their luck, at last, had turned.

Hermist smelled the sweetness of the first spring rain and felt a surge of adrenaline as he went on running down the street. He jogged past the rural electric offices, down the alley and along a row of flimsy, pale houses once painted in bright blue or gold colors, a builder's attempt to disguise their tackiness, an attempt that only made them look cheaper as they faded in the harsh weather of the area. Typical substandard housing. The empty fairgrounds where summer dances were held looked trashy, unkempt, not yet cleaned up from the severe winter snow, ice, wind.

He listened to the pounding of his feet and hoped he'd get there before Connie and Aurelia and the kids heard about the grisly find.

Aurelia, home alone, was startled when he opened the door

without knocking and called out. As he came toward her she asked, "What's wrong?"

He put his arms around her and said, "They found that girl that has been missing all winter."

She first thought of the fourteen-year-old but then quickly remembered. She wondered how many more were out there.

"They found her? Where?" She didn't know if she felt fear or relief as she stood in his embrace. "Where?"

"In the river. Just outside of town. Off the Reservation. Near the church . . . out there. North. It's pretty bad and her family is there."

"In the river! All winter!"

"Yup. Shot multiple times."

"Jesus!"

"Yeah."

"Who did it?"

"I don't know. They don't know."

Immediately, they thought of the white men who hung around Indian reservations, the drinkers, the drifters. It's degradation, thought Aurelia. It's a problem of racism and how they think about Indian women. We're just treated like worthless crap, she thought. It's historical. It's always been like this . . . It's a way of despoiling the dignity of Indian communities, to treat the women like they are worthless.

They stood in silence for several moments.

"No one is going to see this as an atrocity connected to the racism in this community," Hermist was saying, his face dark and serious. "They'll just say it is a woman out drinking and whoring around."

Aurelia remembered Tatekeya's grief concerning the destruction of the river and she felt that the white man's treatment of the earth, always suspect to herself and others, was one of the terrible things that reverberated throughout all of the human relationships surrounding them. Now, for Aurelia, at least, the actions toward both the earth and humans were no longer shrouded in ambiguity. The destruction was all around. And it was there for everyone to see.

"Well," she said, "whoever did it, they're still out there.

They're still here . . . amongst us."

"Yes."

Aurelia, who had little contact with those outside of her family and community, and therefore little firsthand knowledge of the ways of others, depended on the stereotypes, the biases brought about by her observation of the behavior of those drunks her mother used to hang around with after she abandoned the family. Aurelia remembered the men. The drinking. The violence. There was no doubt in her mind that whites held long-standing historical contempt for Indian womanhood and that such contempt and racial hatred were at the center of this community's present agony.

As though reading her thoughts, Hermist said, "This is a race crime. I don't want you and Connie and the kids to be here alone."

"Where can we go?"

"I want you to come out to my place."

"But that's way out there in the boonies."

"Yeah. But it's safe there. Nobody ever comes around."

When she said nothing he asked, "Do you want to do that?"

"Yeah," she said uncertainly. "We could do that. For a while, at least. I'll tell Connie and we'll get the kids ready."

Before he left he put his arms around her and held her for a long moment. It was an embrace that indicated the tenacious presence of their concern for one another. They knew, though they did not speak of it, that what they felt at that moment could become a tender and enduring love.

As the news of the missing Indian girl swept through the community, the people were grateful that at least part of the horrific story was now known to them. It gave them a sense of clarity concerning the dilemma of their lives. The pretty victim, shot five times, had been dragged to the river and dumped like so much waste or refuse, and she had lain there undiscovered for the better part of a year.

What it meant to many of Aurelia's friends was that a terrible evil existed in the white communities and small towns that surrounded Indian villages in the area.

What it meant to Aurelia was that the violent murder of an innocent human being had been shrouded in a deliberate denial and sustained silence for too long. When she read in the local newspaper that the sheriff had said "we have no suspects," she knew it was a cover-up. She talked to those close to her about the deliberate lies concerning Indian deaths, the running-down of native pedestrians on isolated roads, the thefts, the incidents of harassment, the mysterious stabbings and unexplained accidents. She took this killing to be further evidence of racial hatred.

As Hermist had predicted, the gossip that came from the white community was slanderous. Blaming the victim, they said: "You know, she was hanging around the men at the liquor store for sex. She probably got what she asked for."

17

1981
Telling of Dreams as Time Flies

No one was arrested. There were no suspects.

There were moments and days during this time when Aurelia repeated to herself, over and over again, that things would work out and if she could just tolerate one bad day, surely the next one would be better. Truth was, she believed she had probably lived through the worst of the bad days and the future, whatever it held, would be brighter.

The water itself, the Missouri River sounds and songs and stories that had engulfed the human occupants of this place for as long as anyone could remember, seemed to Aurelia now to be untranslated and unknown. No one knew what to expect, whom to trust. The silence of the people indicated that the ability to move within the languages of the universe no longer echoed in the lives of the human beings who occupied the place. The earth and the river held their secrets in spite of the reality that humans behave badly. As people were to find out, rivers hold no fingerprints, only memories.

As Aurelia took stock of the shocking discovery of the remains of the murder victim, and as the days and weeks passed, she told her son, Blue, not to worry about where the young woman had been, what had happened, and who was responsible; that the young woman was simply unlucky, that things happen, that bad people do bad, horrific things. She told him these simplistic things because the merciless crime was unfathomable to her, and she was not sure how to tell him that the whites in the community were responsible, that their hatred for Dakotah women was a sickness in them, and that she and the family would have to go on living amongst them.

To comfort her son, she told him with certainty that Dakotahs were not implicated in such crimes of the world because they had always believed that water was a place of origin; that fish were their distant ancestors; that they would never violate the river; that dogs could speak to them because they, too, were relatives; that the dances and songs and gestures of the river were ways of language; that the stars had always known the beginnings of human journeys into the wind. She told him one story after another in an effort to help herself, stories that could not be verified and that he probably could not understand fully but that he nonetheless listened to attentively. Blue stayed close to his mother for several days and kept his little sister with him constantly.

"*Mah!* That's what we always call *wic'a' ak'i'yuha(n)pi.*" Aurelia whispered and pointed to the gathering of stars in their familiar formations. "I guess he is supposed to be related to *wichapi sunkaku* . . . an older brother, kind of . . . "

The three of them, each child in the curve of the arms of their mother, stared into the heavens as they spent evenings stretched out in the yard at Hermist's place. With no street lights, the darkness was all around them.

"It's a constellation. That's what they call it in science classes. See?" She raised her arm and pointed as Sarah sat up and put her head back and stared, "it has four stars situated at the four points of what they call the Big Dipper . . . "

"I can't see it," ventured Sarah, frowning.

"There . . . right next to that long string of stars. See?"

A long silence followed as they searched the skies and thought their own private thoughts.

"Sometimes they call it in English *"man being carried,"* because one time when a Dakotah was lost, they put him inside their blanket, their four points, carriers, and they helped him to get across the sky to where he lived, to where the Dakotahs live."

Sarah swung her arms in a wide circle to show the vastness of the sky.

"It was a lo-o-o-n-g ways, I bet."

"Yes, *wi-nona*, it was a long way . . . that's what the people are thinking about when they do the blanket dance at the powwow. Did you know that? The blanket dance . . . when they ask that you donate money. And they always say, 'this is for the singers who have come a long way' . . . remember? It is a kind of journey re-creation. And, yes, it took thousands and thousands of years . . . and the Dakotahs have never forgotten the assistance they got from their relatives. Sometimes they even carried us when we were too afraid or too tired to go any further and even, they say, gave us their own sacred rituals so that we could know important things. You know, like the sundance and stuff like that."

"Mom. Do you think . . . ?

"What?

"Do you think Dad knows this story?"

"Sure. He knows it. And so does Grampa. And so did your *k-unchi*. In fact, your gramma once told me that the Dakotahs believe that what is in the stars is here on earth and what is on earth is in the stars."

"Mom. Do you think . . . ?

"Wha-a-at? . . . Gee, you ask too many questions." She put her fingers in his ribs and he started to laugh.

"No, Mom . . . Mom . . . do you think Dad is going to come here and get us?"

Almost instantly they were all serious. Sarah tried to make herself small next to her mother's body, knowing this was a subject her mother avoided.

Aurelia thought about all the things she could say in answer to the question, all the lies she could tell, all the unhurtful evasions.

She put her arms around Blue and Sarah and said softly, in answer to her son's level-headed, sober question, "No." She paused, "No, Blue. Your Dad is not going to come and get us."

"We are not going back," she said, and they sat together and looked into the boundless sky.

Someday, when he is older, she thought, and when I can acknowledge it myself, I will tell him about the ambiguity between what you want and what you can expect from mere human beings.

18

September, 1981
A Walk in the Autumn

After a few days, after the shock of the discovery of the body, the neighborhoods seemed to relax. Connie and Aurelia went back to the Agency and were, after that, careful to lock their doors, careful to be off the streets at night. They kept a closer watch on the children.

The summer passed and the finding of the girl's body was no longer on the tongue of everyone in the community. There were no more questions about the investigation, and the fear dissipated.

In the heat of one autumn afternoon, Aurelia and her nephew by marriage, Philip, walked together within seeing distance of the river, along a sidewalk smeared with grey and white bird droppings and covered with leaves already exhausted and dried by the fierce summer wind; along a trail where, the night before, tourists had trampled the ground, had driven their RVs and trucks pulling boats along the banks and parked and cleaned their smelly fish, throwing the entrails along the banks; to the newly designed Indian Museum/Community Center, at present bustling with untidy and noisy children on a field trip from school. Yellow buses filled the tiny parking lot, their drivers either smoking cigarettes while cleaning fingernails with pocket knives or leaning on steering wheels gazing absentmindedly toward the brown hills barely noticeable from a distance.

Thoughts of the young murder victim accompanied them and Aurelia recognized then, though she kept her silence, that she could never again look at the water in innocence.

The woman and the young man walked, taking long and matching strides.

"Are you gonna marry him?"

"I don't know. Probably."

"Has he asked you?"

"Yes."

He put his hands in his pockets. "Gonna get middle class, huh?"

"What do you mean by that?"

"Well, he works at Realty, doesn't he?"

"Uh-huh."

They fell silent, she because she felt insulted and unduly criticized. He because he was afraid he had gone too far.

"Nothing wrong with that, Auntie. Nothing wrong with being middle class. They been telling us at some of these meetings I've been going to that the middle class is the backbone of any democracy." He said the last part of that sentence with mock sincerity.

She looked at him and shrugged. And they both silently wondered what good it would do to be middle class if the land was not returned, if treaties were not honored, if the practice of religion was not free, if women were not respected and protected . . . if the children . . . if . . . if . . .

"What are you going to do?" she asked him, as if to change the subject.

"I'm headed for Minneapolis."

Her eyes focussed on the chipped sidewalk at her feet.

"Yeah," he said, "I'm leaving at seven in the morning."

She nodded. "You could go anywhere and do anything," she told him.

"Yeah . . . well . . . Auntie . . . that's what I'm going to do. Go anywhere. Do anything."

"No. I mean it! You are smart, you know things. You have the right attitude. You think like a Dakotah . . . you . . . "

"Yeah. I can go anywhere. I can do what I can do to get the land back, to make it safe for the people. To protect the people. You know?"

She smiled as he opened the sliding glass door for her. Pictures of the Sioux chiefs lined the walls. They went directly to the shelves of books behind glass doors.

"The treaties are all here. I mean, copies of them are here," she told him. "All the papers, reports; lawyers come here all the time, I'm told, because there has been a lot of donations and reclaiming of our records and everything. Museums have returned things to us, you know. There's been a lot of donations."

"Yeah. Good."

"You can get some copies of things before you leave."

Aurelia looked toward the glass door and saw her former father-in-law, Harvey Big Pipe, drive into the parking lot.

"Look. There's your grampa."

They turned and watched him come toward them.

He told them in solemn words, without tears, without anger, that Tony, his son who had survived Vietnam and had come home from his warrior's life, had shot himself to death and that they were to come with him to the death scene immediately.

19

September, 1981
To Make a Getaway

They found Clarissa huddled over her brother's body, weeping quietly, and had no idea how long she had been there.

A terrible sobbing shook Aurelia as she knelt beside her relatives and she wept with sorrow and rage and with a yearning to go on and on weeping.

She felt a hand touch her hair.

Jason said, "Don't cry, Aurelia. He just said 'to hell with it' and he bailed out and he had every right."

Though he was comforting her, Jason was stricken at the loss of another brother. There had been four of them. Now he was the only one left. He sat heavily in a chair and closed his eyes. *"It's all right. It's all right,"* he whispered as if to himself. He thought of Vietnam and said out loud, as if in the face of disaster, *"E-vac . . . E-vac . . . E-vac . . . "* It was as though he heard his buddies yelling warnings to save yourself in the face of enemy gunfire . . . *"incoming . . . incoming"* . . . as though he were trying to run and could only shuffle and could not get out of danger. It wasn't the same thing but it felt just as bad.

The floor of the tiny mobile home was strewn with beer cans and wine bottles and the blood of Uncle Tony, whose head was cradled in Clarissa's lap, a sister who wept into the long and formidable night, at last surrendering the young inert body to those who would prepare it for burial. Another burial, though this time so unexpected and unaccountable.

The morning began in the sunless chill and Aurelia stood motionless in the kitchen that was so familiar to her, the place where she had loved and where she had raised her children and where she had been a good relative.

She shook her head and tried to gather her wits. She hung on to the silence and felt that everything was frozen and suspended in the distance. Then she began to cook. It was always the thing, perhaps, that kept women from going over the edge in grief.

She and Jason had taken beef ribs and other cuts and without a word between them they began to cook. Together, as they always had, they prepared for another communal grieving, this one with a finality that neither of them could bear. She would boil the meat and the bones until they were soft and he would grind them and feel the greasy parts and they would put some of it into soup but some of it would be saved to make the dried cakes and all of it would be considered a rich, exquisitely fine choice food that would honor the relatives in their grief. A hundred years ago this was done with the flesh and bones of the sacred buffalo. And the chokecherries and the corn.

Long lines of men and women, some old, some young, children of all ages, stood for the second burial in such a brief time, and the wind stung their eyes and the young warrior was laid to rest with all the proper songs sung over him. There was some comfort for those who had raised him in the traditional ways.

Epilogue

Now it is a time when the ancestors of *Ikce* eat from tables whenever and wherever they can, like scavengers. It is the time now when the people who have lived beside the waters for a very long time fall into arguments with the turtles who, for any old reasons, are driving the fish away.

It is a hard life, but everyone knows that the powerful spirits of the land will defend the sunlight that shines on the river.

1995
A Hearing in a County Courthouse

It is a day in November. Cold. A skiff of snow blowing across the parking lot is a harbinger of the days to come.

The grey-haired woman's eyes seem crusty and wet at the edges A film seems to grow over the pupils.

She had not known the girl who had been shot and raped and dragged to the river almost twenty years ago, had only caught a memorable glimpse of her years and years ago . . . but she is here at the request of her relatives to listen to the explanation of the crime.

The grey-haired woman is Aurelia Blue and she has lived all her life in the presence of the water spirits of the Sissetons. Over the years, she has asked herself the silent question: Is there some point in time when you get over the rage?

This has not been a story about murderers and rapists. Nor is it a story about a specific crime. It is not even about a particular victim. It is a story that gives a frame of reference for those interested in how it is that a memory-laden people live their lives; a context, if you will. It is a story about myth, a story that Aurelia Blue has told to others and that has become the stuff of history, an ingredient of the oral narrative poetry transmitted by word of mouth from one singer, one teller of tales, to another.

Aurelia is a woman neither old nor young, her hair held in a long, heavy braid that reaches to her waist. She makes her way down the streets of the silent town and enters a huge brick building. Immaculately dressed, stylish in a black coat and black low-heeled cowboy boots, she lets the heavy door swing shut and walks toward the stairs, her heels clicking, across the marble black-and-white floor. Her face is a mask, her slitted black eyes show no emotion.

She glances at the old clock on the wall. It has stopped at 10:08. No one knows in what year it stopped ticking. Like everything in the building, it is old and grey in disuse.

"No cameras, tape recorders, no food, no drink, no guns," reads the sign at the second-floor landing. "By the order of JS, Sheriff."

She finds a seat in the back of the crowded courtroom and sits uncomfortably on a hardwood bench made of stressed mahogany. The courtroom is dead quiet, two fans turning slowly and silently in the whitened ceiling. Long windows and long bookcases line each side of the yellow-walled room. The smell of years and years of decay stills the air.

She thinks about the two young men who raped and murdered the pretty Sioux Indian girl and dragged her behind the pickup to the river and threw her in as though they believed the curse of their own histories would protect them. It did, of course. They lived *as innocents* in their own communities for nearly twenty years after that horrible crime. Had it not been for a disgruntled wife in a divorce matter, these murderers might have remained innocent. Unknown. Undiscovered.

As she clutched her coat about her, Aurelia found herself wondering who they really were, how they lived their lives. She sat quietly. She let her mind wander: they were probably descendants of middle Europeans, twentieth-century descendants of the first white men to reach the land of the Dakotahs. Their relatives may have been from some place like rural Germany just outside of Stuttgart, or Westphalia, or places in the Netherlands along the Baltic Sea, or from places with unpronounceable names in Bosnia, or even from Kilkenny or Donegal who came into the Dakotah Nation homelands more than a hundred years ago.

They very likely came up the James River, the Missouri River, the Red River, and, like immigrants everywhere, like their needy and hopeful children, they brought with them their religion. In this case, these murderers had had Christianity in their blood for two thousand years.

Their ancestors probably plowed up the land in dirt-stiffened overalls and threw wheat and rye seeds into the furrows with their filthy hairy hands and lived lives of desperation through the worst of times, hostile Indians, wars, drought, depressions.

What drove them on? No one knows for sure. Fear, perhaps. And necessity.

And, yes, hope.

Eventually, after several generations, many of these folks were to become the cattle and wheat barons in the new land. But for a long time they were mere peasants and they dug up the dirt because that was all they knew. For sure, they knew nothing of the history of the Mni Sosa Country, which existed for centuries before their arrival, the crowned buttes, the stunning beauty of a stark prairie place where the natural grass was as high as the knee, where a native people composed grass-dance songs and gathered to worship the stars and the sun, and to speak to the river spirits. These peasants settled down in a land that belonged to an ancient tribal people called the Sioux and began to call it their own.

Patriotism and loyalty to America were not big things in those early days. These Germans, along with their fellow immigrant European displaced persons, the Czechs, the Irish or Brits, the Romanians, Serbs, Norwegians, and Swedes, thought only of making money and making children, many of whom died in infancy, and so they determined that it was better not to get too attached to their children. It was better, they resolved, to love the money. This determination became a value system of profound significance.

Ordinarily, they steered clear of the Indians who had known and possessed this place for thousands of years; called them dirty savages and drunks. They stole the land whenever they could and required their emerging governing bodies to limit Indian participation on the basis of birthright in one of the great democracies of modern times.

As a consequence, there have never been any banks or financial institutions on Indian reservations. Even today, there is almost no commerce, no employment, and Indians were forced to go to the so-called "border towns" for their jobs, ultimately setting up bingo palaces for their other needs. It was almost as though the whites wanted to keep their Indian neighbors at the stage of horse stealing if they couldn't make them disappear altogether. In spite of that, Indian homelands had begun to flourish at the time of the girl's murder, hospitals and schools and government offices and churches the main centers of interest. It all happened through sheer force of will. And, finally, Indian people began to have money to spend in off-reservation towns like the one where the murder occurred. And that's what the unfortunate girl was doing that evening when she disappeared, spending a little money and enjoying herself in a town run by wheat barons and tenant farmers, auto mechanics and clerks and hoers of beets.

In the 1940s, just after the Good War, the offspring of these early immigrants, along with their federal government, took control of an encouraging world by damming up the Missouri River to keep it at bay. Half a century later, they could do nothing about the dogged Red River's intention to get its revenge for all the rivers in the world when it devoured the carefully nurtured towns in the worst flood ever recorded. By that time, the relatives of the early dirt farmers were everywhere in North and South Dakota, scattered like the wheat seeds, bearing witness to hard times.

Racism was rampant on both sides, but as long as Indians went to reservations to live, as long as business and farming held up, the whites could claim it was their own right to occupy the land. Their sons had gone off to all the wars, most particularly in 1846 when the United States declared war on Mexico and the West became in the imagination their own, their new homelands.

Their sons' sons voted for Teddy Roosevelt when the rape of the West was in full swing. And they never looked back. A hundred years later, Roosevelt was chosen to occupy a place of honor on a western mountain carving called Mount Rushmore, a tourist mecca for the world located in the heart of Indian homelands.

Whites continued to improvise history in their classrooms and textbooks and it was only after a nationwide uprising in the 1960s that a storm of protesters began to debunk these well-entrenched and delusional stories. Some of their own children were the major critics of what they had told themselves and others about how they deserved a glorious past even if they had to invent it.

The West, of course—the prairies and the Missouri River Country—had never belonged to these immigrants. Nor to their children. Furthermore, none of their fertile generations had ever understood its fragile nature. Always, the restless Indians who travelled the dusty roads and grasped the flimsy future in whatever ways they could said that it was not to the whites that the land belonged, because they harbored too much fear and doubt in their dealings with it. They said it was the Dakotapi, who were recognized by the land and the rivers as relatives in a primordial and unforgettable journey, that told them who they were.

Aurelia roused herself from these thoughts and watched the fans slowly turn the stale air. Two houseplants caught her attention. They, like everything in the room, looked old and neglected. She took eyeglasses from her coat pocket and wiped them carefully.

She would never claim this odd tale for herself. It was, after all, a story that belonged to all of them. But she was a woman of circumstance who lived in these times and who was witness to the clouds gathering in to bring the rain, and she believed that she was witness to things that could only be explained as stories about old gods and outrage. She imagined the mist rising from the earth and the river and she sat still, her hands in her lap. She closed her eyes again as the hearing began.

Q. Was he . . . at that point in time was he talking about killing her or anything like that?

A. I don't know, sir.

Q. So he tells you to go rape her and you did?

A. [Nods affirmatively.]

Q. Correct?

A. Yes, sir.

Q. And you penetrated her and you ejaculated, right?

A. I believe so; yes, sir.

Q. After you got done raping her, you returned back to the pickup?

A. Towards that . . . yeah, walked away, yes.

Q. And then he raped her again?

A. [Nods affirmatively.]

Q. Is that right?

A. Yes, sir.

Q. Then when he got done, he walked back to where you were by the pickup; is that right?

A. No, sir. He was laying on top of her.

Q. When he got done raping her the second time?

A. Yes, sir.

Q. He laid on top of her, okay. And then what did he do?

A. Then he hollered at me to get the gun.

Q. As he is laying on top of her, he yells at you to get the gun?

A. Yes, sir.

Q. And you . . . did you say no or did you just stand there?

A. I said no. I was scared. No, I quit. I don't know why. I was scared.

Q. You were back by the pickup that time?

A. I was away from him, closer to the pickup, yes. Where exactly I don't know if I was right next to the pickup.

Q. But you are 40 to 50 feet away from him?

A. Yes.

Q. So he had to yell for you to hear him?

A. Yes.

Q. And so he gets up and goes over to the pickup himself?

A. No. He . . . when I refused to get the gun, he said . . . he said . . . to get my butt over there and hold her down.

Q. So did you go over there then?

A. Yes, I did.

Q. All right. And then he walked away at that point in time?

A. Yes.

Q. Then he goes and gets the gun, walks right up to her, and shoots her.

A. Yes, sir.

Q. All right. You then chain her up to the back of the pickup and you drag her down by the river?

A. Yes, sir.

Q. And you were approaching speeds of 25 to 30 miles per hour when this was done?

A. I guessed that because they said how far did you drive. I said I had no idea how far we drove. I just said I'm assuming it was a distance because I know we sped up when we got to a quicker speed, and I said probably 20 miles an hour.

Q. I think you said 25 to 30 mph?

A. Well, yeah. I was guessing. A complete guess. I have no idea how fast we were going. He made me ride in the back of the truck.

Q. You rode in the back of the truck?

A. Yes. He told me . . . and that's in the statement, too, told me to stay there and make sure the body didn't fall off.

A telephone rings in the distance and as a clerk hurries to answer it, Aurelia gets up and leaves the room. Her eyes seem crusty and wet at the edges. A film seems to grow over the pupils. She finds her way through the streets to her car. She feels that someone is watching her.

At certain places just beyond the river, brown trees have dropped all their leaves and light brown buttes shine as they turn purple when the sun goes down. Lakes and ponds of water are caked with snow.

In some places the hills are as yellow as the sun and the endlessness of them is interrupted only by the ancient breaks in the prairie's surface causing ravines and gulches. This is the land roamed by what the white-man's science has named the t-rex, the tyrannosaurus and the dinosaur, the creature oddly predicated in a vast Dakotah mythology as having power during the *o-hun-ka-ka* times, the sacred era prior to humanity's presence, and they are referred to by the indigenous peoples of the land by various names, sometimes *iya* or *unkcegila* or *unktehi*. These figures are well known and related, both honored and feared by the people whose courtesy toward their history has always been ceremonialized.

Here in this place in early November, before the snow piles high, the huge white moon, faint, dim, can be seen in the late afternoon even before the sun goes down, barely visible above dark blue clouds on the horizon. Whitened, it hangs above the colored earth like a foreshadowing of the evening, the clear, cold nighttime when the creatures on the land can sleep or roam as is their pleasure.

Aurelia drives away from the white-man's town into the vastness of the hills and she sees the prairie town as a small jewel, a bright, white-lighted place. She turns on the road to the river and the jewel disappears from her view.

The car radio plays some jazz and stops for the local news at ten o'clock: "The winterkill of cattle has been as severe as any time since the turn of the century," "The 4-H students from Brainard will visit the Selby School District next month," "The Cozy Cup Cafe is closed for remodeling."